If We We

Adam Karni Cohen

To each one goes their own delusion
  – Catullus

Table of Contents

Vulcan Betrayed

1969

"Why is Mama yelling?"

"It's nothing, Lissa, just Papa. Go to sleep. Buonanotte."

"Dio? Will you tell me a story?"

"Go to sleep and you can dream your own stories."

"Please!"

"All right. Once there was a god."

"Was he a powerful god?"

"Yes."

"Did he have a beard?"

Distant yelling.

"Go on! I'll be quiet, I promise!"

"He was a god called Vulcan and he was the craftiest craftsman in the universe. He could make a necklace out of stars, or a warship from seaweed. He could craft a little girl's smile, without even having to tickle her."

"Hee hee!"

"He had a massive workshop, where he kept all his hammers and metals, and servants called the cyclopses. They each had one eye and were always angry and kept bumping into each other. And, yes, he had a beard."

"Gods always have beards."

"One day, Vulcan saw the most beautiful goddess in the universe. Her name was Venus. He fell in love and begged the king of the gods to let him marry Venus. The king needed Vulcan's skill, and so he said yes, and they were married."

"But what did Venus think about that?"

"She didn't like it. So whenever Vulcan turned his back on his new wife, to make her a necklace or a bracelet, she would go have fun with Vulcan's friend, Mars. Mars was the god of war. He was big and scary, and he loved the ladies."

"Hee hee! I bet Vulcan found out."

"He heard about it from the sun, who sees everything. Vulcan got very angry, and he made a plan. The next time Venus and Mars were in bed

7

together, he pulled a net down on top of them. Then he called all the gods to come and see the trapped lovers. And that was how he got his revenge."

"But, Dio, wasn't that bad for him too? Didn't everyone laugh at him?"

"Laugh at Vulcan? I guess they did."

"Poor Vulcan."

"But he was a god!"

"It's still not a happy ending. There are never any happy ending in these stories."

"Ok, Lissa. It's quiet now. Time for sleep."

"Dio? Does no one live happily ever after?"

A kiss. "You will."

"Will you always look after me?"

"Always."

"Will you always love me?"

"Always."

Quiet voice. "What about Mama and Papa?"

"Close your eyes. Go to sleep."

"Ok. But I love you."

"I know. Buonanotte, sorellina."

"Buona...notte..."

And in the house, silence.

Verona, one evening

One evening in August, 1999: that heat which turns Italian cities into furnaces. Through the half-empty streets of Verona raced an ambulance.

Inside it, Jennifer wiped her brow and gripped the metal frame of the bed. She glanced at the Italian woman sitting beside her, trying to remember her name, M-something, and then back to the girl on the bed, the still face, the short black hair, eyes shut, breaths shallow: her daughter.

"Anna," she said, "Annie, you'll be all right. Ok? Anna?" She squeezed a hand.

The ambulance stopped, the doors flew open, and Jennifer hurried out after her companion as the waiting orderlies lowered the bed onto a trolley. They rushed in, through corridors of dazzling white, Anna's head rolling whenever the trolley turned. At a set of double doors, the orderlies continued through as a young doctor with red eyes stopped them and addressed her in Italian.

"I don't understand," Jennifer said.

"He asks what happened," said the Italian woman.

"But I wasn't there," Jennifer said.

"I will explain it in English?" The doctor nodded and the Italian woman continued, "So, we have the lunch and after, Anna stands up. She is getting angry. Then she is..." The woman took heavy, shuddering breaths, hands circling in front of her as if she was struggling to breathe. "Like this. And she is shouting. She says her chest hurts. She takes a step, and she falls."

Jennifer shook her head, trying to erase the image of her daughter collapsing. "There are obvious procedures we need to take," she said to the doctor. "First I'd like to see the cardiologist."

The orderlies returned with the trolley before he could reply. Jennifer saw that one of Anna's hands had moved up to her face; her eyes remained closed but the lids were fluttering.

"Annie, can you hear me? It's Mummy."

Now the doctor was reviewing the scans. His cheeks were smooth: he seemed too young to Jennifer, and she tried to look over his shoulder, but he closed the file and gestured at the bed. "Now we must go to monitor," he said.

He led them to a ward that was close to empty. Jennifer stood behind one of the nurses, who began tapping on Anna's arm. "Try the other one," she said, but the nurse ignored her, and kept tapping on the forearm. Now she withdrew a needle, eyeing the tanned skin, though Jennifer could see no vein. "Wait!" she said, but the needle broke Anna's skin and the blood rose into a plastic tube, and she heard the beating of an electronic pulse.

Jennifer exhaled slowly and sat down. She was surprised to find herself still wearing a t-shirt from that morning.

"We look after your daughter now," the doctor said. He gave a small bow, a gesture that touched her, and left them.

She laid her palm against Anna's forehead. It was smooth; there was no angry frown tonight. "I'm here, Annie. You'll be ok. We've got more churches to see. Right? What was that statue you wanted us to look at? The Jesus one." Beyond, she saw the blood pressure readings:

...99/65, 99/64...

They were low, but stable. She began to run through possibilities: give it forty-eight hours, maybe seventy-two, they could transport Anna back to London for testing, and she knew who she'd get to handle the case; but if Anna didn't recover quickly enough... Or if...

Her thoughts were interrupted by a sigh from the foot of the bed. She had forgotten about the Italian woman, who was still standing, fingers playing, face anxious.

"Sit," Jennifer said, regretting her tone. She recalled the woman's name. "Please, Melissa, sit here."

Melissa sat down as if afraid to disturb the machines around the patient.

"Thank you for your help," Jennifer said.

Melissa's lips twisted, not quite a smile nor a frown. "Anna says you are a doctor."

"Yes." Jennifer studied the stranger's face: the half-isosceles of her nose, the hard chin and sharp cheekbones. One of Melissa's eyebrows went up, questioning, and Jennifer said, "It's just that you remind me of your brother, of Claudio." But she couldn't talk about that now, she had to concentrate. She looked about her at the ward. "I'm impressed by this hospital," she said.

Melissa smiled sadly. "My brother and I were born here. It is the best hospital in Verona: all the students learn here. Also, my father came, three months ago. Before he died." Melissa grabbed her hand. "Will Anna be well?"

Jennifer leaned back, alarmed by this sudden movement and the hot breath on her face. "Yes," she said, "she's stable, and you're right, this is a good hospital. They'll find out what's wrong. Anna will be fine. Of course, she will."

She felt afraid of her own voice: it was not that of a calm doctor, but the tone she had heard so often among her patients' parents, of one fearful person reassuring another. Her eyes felt sore and her head felt light as she turned back to the electronic pulses and the blood pressure display, hiding her face, letting their quiet rhythm calm her. The minutes passed with slow breaths.

...97/63, 98/64...

The call of her name made her look to the entrance. A figure approached rapidly, bulky in a sweat-stained t-shirt, slightly stooped below his massive head: it was her husband. He went straight to the bed, kissed Anna's forehead, and checked the paperwork and machines.

"Was an MI," he said with a deep rumble, the Leeds accent sounding strange in this place. Jennifer nodded. His voice wavered. "Why?"

"We don't know yet, Chris."

"Where's the staff?"

"They come every fifteen minutes." He started to walk away. "Chris, don't," but he marched out.

She saw that her son had come in behind and was standing at the foot of the bed, his head jerking around the room, eyes continually darting back to Anna. His tanned face was flecked with traces of acne. He was still wearing his backpack. "Sam, come and sit." He did not move. "Sammy." She sighed.

...96/63, 97/65...

Chris returned with their doctor and another medic. "The cardiologist," he announced. He folded his arms while the Italians moved across the body, speaking quietly to each other.

The young doctor turned to Jennifer. "We continue to monitor her."

She nodded.

"Could take her in for a TOE," Chris said.

"It is early," the cardiologist said.

"Best way to be conclusive."

Jennifer felt the calm inside her slipping. "Chris –"

"In the UK –"

"You're not helping –"

"At this point –"

"JUST SHUT UP!" The men froze. "You don't know what's happened! I've been here half an hour and I'm COMFORTABLE. We have to wait. Not second-guess. Ok? Ok."

The doctors hurried out while Chris hovered above the bed, frowning. Finally, he sat down on the opposite side, checking behind him to see where the doctors had gone. Jennifer moved her chair closer and began stroking Anna's hair. Her eyes drifted back to the blood pressure display.

...94/63, 95/64...

Jennifer fell into a trance, conscious of the movement around her, but never letting drop her watch over the body of Anna and the electronic numbers. The room was quiet and when they were all sitting, only the pulse spoke as Anna's heart worked on. Jennifer had only this to do now, to keep watch on her daughter.

...94/62, 91/60...

A minute passed.

...84/57...

She sat up.

...76/51...

She cried, "Get the doctor. Chris. *Signora*. NOW!"

The machines started beeping.

...69/49...

They rushed in as the beeps began to stutter. The doctors leaned over Anna.

"She goes for surgery!" the doctor said.

The orderlies unhooked the bed. They ran towards the exit. Anna's hand fell off the side of the bed.

"Annie!"

The doctor led them out. Each lamp above her was blinding. The corridors were dark with hostile shadows. Chris was muttering, "Stupid, stupid, stupid." They hurried into an empty white corridor.

"Here is the operating room," the doctor said. "I will report with more information."

Chris jabbed a finger at him. "What's the surgeon's experience?"

"Chris, please."

"Sir," the doctor said, "you must permit us to look after your daughter."

Jennifer watched Chris sit down opposite the door, leaning forwards as if to rush at it. He spoke about the different possibilities, the valves of the heart, the tiny muscles, his voice droning on and on.

"Please," Jennifer said.

His thick breaths filled the silent corridor. He stomped his feet. "What if they –"

"WE CAN'T HELP HER, CHRIS," and she pressed her hands hard against her eyes; but she could still picture the blank door opposite, her daughter inside, and the brutal work being done to save her.

*

Inside the operating room, the surgeon and his team moved across the body of Anna Morris. The anaesthetist covered her mouth with a mask. One nurse sterilised her chest, another thrust a tube down her throat. The surgeon finished scrubbing and studied the scans. The patient had come into hospital unconscious but stable. In the past hour, a valve had ruptured in her heart, now blood was filling the lungs and starving the body of oxygen. She would die if he did not repair it.

He began to work. He sawed open the chest and cut through the tissue, exposing the heart. Every touch against his gloves was slick with wet blood. The gentle hum of the heart-lung machine began.

"Blood pressure?"

"Stable. Low."

The grey picture flickered up, and now he could see the rupture. "There," he called. He leaned in with his assistant to study the picture.

He swore.

"What is it?" the anaesthetist asked.

The surgeon was young, and this tiny corner of the heart was damaged beyond his ability. "Page the senior," he said. A nurse hurried out.

"Oxygen sats falling," the anaesthetist reported.

"More fluids. Clamp."

The nurse returned. "Paged him."

The surgeon stared down. The blood was relentless. He estimated they could wait twenty minutes, after which he would have to proceed. But he knew his own abilities. Alone, he could not save this patient. She was going to die.

*

In the corridor outside, time grew thick and Sam felt restless. He knew that he mustn't cry. It was his fault that Anna was in there, but he had to

13

keep his thoughts in order, because only by staying strong could he save his sister. He forced himself to look away from the blank door, and pulled a blue notebook out of his backpack. On the cover was written *Anna Morris*, and above it, *Vulcanalia*. He'd spotted it after the ambulance had left, on the dining table of Melissa's home, and grabbed it before his dad had brought him here.

Sam leafed through until he came to the back of the book, where Anna had written, at the start of the summer:

By the time I get here, my plan should have worked: Mum and Dad are back together, Sam and Su have solved their cases, and I have found True Love. Er, world peace, too.

Now Sam saw that she had added new words, and he frowned as he read.

Well, here we are! At the end of – what to call it? An adventure? Think not! Summer of love turned shit turned hopefully sort of love.

I should tell Sam what he did, that I'm proud of him. Claudio's stories were what the doctors needed. Thank you, signor.

What do these gods have to do with anything? Who cares about Vulcan, or Venus – or even Mars? Well, they brought us here, didn't they? They're part of Mum and Dad's history, aren't they?

I get it, now, though I didn't at the beginning. Claudio's myths aren't ancient. They're about now. They're about people, not gods. People who yearn and lie and never get what they want. Maybe that's what the first myths were about too: just people; confused, angry, hurt, hurting each other, hiding behind masks. The moral of the story is this: never believe that people have their shit together.

Another moral: don't trust parents with anything as serious as love.

Ok! So! What's left? Pack a bag. Grab the train. Uni! Infinite possibility!

Enough. This has served its purpose. Thank you again: stranger, Claudio. You certainly made this an interesting summer.

Close the book, Anna, and start to live.

The door opened as Sam began to cry.

I – The Museum of Myth

What if a single ladder of flame
Rushing up through the elements
Reduced heaven to an afterglow?
– Ted Hughes, *Tales from Ovid*

Melissa: Dawn

July, six weeks earlier, and a low purring throb drifted up from the atrium. It came in through the half-open window, snaked along the marble floor, and crept onto the bed to rest beside the ear of Melissa Collina. Her eyes opened as she recognised the coos of the turtle doves. Her room had filled with a soft beige light; it gave her the sense that she was not yet awake, that this was the continuation of a dream that might transport her to a lake.

Then she heard a flapping of wings and a scratch on her window. A loud coo. Another. *Get up, Melissa*! sang the turtle dove, *Get up*! It was no dream: she was home, in Verona, and whatever a turtle dove considered reality to be, Melissa was now sharing it.

This thought was followed by another, and she sat up. Today was Saturday: the day she would tell Ernesto her decision.

She lifted her necklace off the small bedside table and picked her way through her own private labyrinth: the stacks of books and museum brochures, the bag of tennis gear meant for charity, and between them all, on tables and floor and leaning against the oak cupboard, scores of objects loaned from the museum: vases, statuettes, marble heads, Mercury, Caesar, engraved tablets, fragments of tombstones, and her favourite, a display case of ancient jewellery, gilded bronze plants, plates of engraved rock-crystal, embossed gold bands with purple garnets. Her room was chaos beyond mere tidying. Only she could bring order to it, for which she needed time, which brought her back to her first thought: today she would tell Ernesto that she was resigning.

She pulled out a black dress, took a deep breath, and then placed it back in the cupboard. No, today would be different.

*

Melissa had lived in this house all her life. It was in the old town, just south of the river. Her father had bought it as a run-down block of apartments. "It cost me everything," he told them as kids, pasta shells falling out of his mouth as their mother looked on with disgust. "A huge risk. You understand, Claudio? But I never make a stupid risk. What did they say in the magazine, Susanna? *The most valuable private residence in Verona*. A risk worth taking, I think. Haha!" Their mother scowled, but the children smiled, because Papa's laugh was infectious, and much preferred to his anger.

He had gutted the building to create an atrium with a swimming pool and garden, a refuge for the turtle doves. The living quarters sprawled around it, across two high-ceilinged floors built with concrete, glass and marble. Since every room overlooked the atrium, noise from one carried to all the others.

It had never been a happy home, but now it was a silent one.

The dining room too was quiet, but for Melissa's fork against the bowl of fruit salad, and the faint pleasant drone of Violetta's radio in the kitchen. Melissa had not noticed before the thin triangle of sunlight reflecting onto the glass of the dining table: it came from the window behind her father's empty place. She glanced at the newspaper and saw a note: *Signor Battillo called at 7:25.* She wondered if he was at the museum. She could try him there, but her heart began to race as she considered what she might say. She sat back and sipped her espresso, trying to savour the steam against her eyes.

A soft tread announced Violetta. The housekeeper's large figure was draped in its customary black. "*Buongiorno, signora.* That is a lovely green dress. Do you want anything else? I can make you eggs."

"No, thank you my dear – this is perfect, and delicious." Melissa smiled at the ageing housekeeper. She must consider Violetta's retirement: there would be a pension, and the housekeeper and Roberto would be welcome to stay in the house. But how could Melissa persuade Violetta to live here and not work?

She was mulling on this when Violetta slapped her hands against her hips. "Fruit salad is a breakfast for birds. Your mother ate eggs every morning."

Melissa scowled. "I am not my mother."

"No, *signora*, you're not, but –" Violetta hovered by the entrance, shaking her head at the fruit. "On a weekend, you should eat more."

"Enough discussion," Melissa said sharply. To appease Violetta, she added, "You know, a funny thing happened to me yesterday. There was a class of schoolchildren at the museum. They were doing one of those summer courses, you know the kind: they study for two weeks in summer because they failed their exams. I spoke to them for half an hour, and do you know what? One of them looked just like Claudio."

Violetta's mouth twitched downwards. "How so, *signora*?"

17

"His eyes, the way he moved. I was telling them the story of Jupiter and Semele. Once upon a time, the king of the gods fell in love with a beautiful woman, Semele, and they lay together. But his wife was jealous. She came down from Olympus and tricked Semele, and the woman died in Jupiter's arms. This boy raised his hand and said, 'Excuse me, miss, how does a god fuck a woman?'"

"He said what?" Violetta cried.

Melissa chuckled. "The teacher was furious. 'You will apologise to Signora Collina immediately!' But the boy looked so much like Claudio." Her voice drifted. "That's how he used to tell myths. What did he say? Something like *shitty, cacata*. Was it Hercules?"

"I'm not sure, *signora*."

"Well, he didn't speak to you about such things, I suppose."

Violetta pulled a cloth out of her apron and wiped her eyes. "You know best, *signora*, but I don't believe such stories are good for children. About death. And – and – sex."

"Don't be so prudish. First, these were teenagers. Second, my mother told me these stories when I was little – my mother, who ate so many eggs. And third, that was why we built the museum." Melissa took an angry bite of an apricot. Why must Violetta be the one to get so distressed about this story? It was just a funny story about Claudio, nothing sentimental in it at all. "Anyway," Melissa continued, "this boy was just like him. When I finished the story, I asked the children what it was about. The same boy raised his hand and said, 'It's about how sex is dangerous.' The children all laughed. But I thought, that's exactly right, what Claudio might have said! Wavy dark hair, Violetta, and dark, staring eyes. Hey? Maybe if I ate eggs I wouldn't see such things?"

Violetta's shoulders slumped. She drew a long breath and exhaled with a puff. "We-e-ell," she said, "it's not the first time, *signora*. I think any boy might remind you of him, at the moment, since your father – he passed away."

"Don't be ridiculous. Why any boy? You weren't there. This one looked just like him!"

"We forget what people look like, *signora*."

"Fine, let's forget about it. Thank you for breakfast."

The housekeeper bowed her head and backed into the kitchen. Melissa scowled; she had won the argument but lost her composure. Violetta's constant refrain of *signora* was no accident, designed to remind Melissa that she was still unmarried at thirty-six, still living in her father's home, she should get a move on. It was how others viewed her too, those beaming women at the museum's gala parties: *Melissa the strange, too old and odd to marry, too rich for her own good, so aloof, so ready to be an old spinster, alone in her big house.* She was an orphan, brother-less, a *signora* by default, a maiden too old to be a maiden.

"But today," she said. Today she would act for her happiness. Her eyes fell again on the note; Ernesto had called an hour ago. Today she would tell him that she was resigning as President of the Museum of Myth. She had chosen freedom. She had so many ideas, not tallied up like the museum's budget.

She had a duty to make an orderly handover. For this, she needed Ernesto. She grew anxious again as she imagined his dry voice growling questions. *What about the fundraising? Who will oversee the education programme? Who will I report to?* And worst of all, *What would your father have said?*

She must be prepared. She must be able to explain herself.

*

It was years since Melissa had reflected on the origins of the museum, but now she found her thoughts spiralling like a bird from the sky, back to the beginning, one that only she knew, a secret knowledge of how it started: one summer day, when the family was driving to their lakeside home in Garda.

It was all of them, the way Papa liked it, him at the wheel, Roberto trailing in the other car in case Papa must leave them as he often did. Mama sat beside him, while Claudio and Melissa were in the rear. Melissa was six – or so she now believed, for there was no one in the world to contradict her, and she must choose the version to recall. If she was six, the year was 1969, and Claudio was twelve, and his leg was just long enough to reach out and kick her so that she cried out, "Ow! Move away!"

"There's no space!" Claudio said.

"No space!" Papa thundered. "In a Mercedes? Spoiled brat."

The children fell silent. Claudio glared at her but sat still.

"When I was your age –" Papa said.

"Shut up," Mama said.

"– I slept in one room with my brother and three sisters, and our mother and father. One room! The other room was for everything else. Eating, living, studying. My little sister, Melissa, that's who you're named after ("I know, Papa"), she would practise dancing in there too. Everything else – washing dishes, going to the toilet – that was outside, where there's plenty of space. You too," his voice went dangerously quiet, "can go outside, if you keep looking at your sister that way."

"No, Papa," Claudio said and pretended to smile.

"Tell me," Mama said, returning to an earlier argument, "was that hovel as clogged up with shit statues?"

"I was too poor for statues, even of shit. Haha! Now I'm rich. I can afford anything. Wine, sports cars, flashy suits. What do I buy instead?"

"*Cacata charta,*" Mama said, quoting the poet Catullus. The Latin phrase meant *shitty sheets*. Melissa would understand this reference only as a teenager, when she was helping Mama with her commentary. *Shitty sheets*, meaning *for sex*, implying *with whores*.

"I spend my money," Papa continued, "on my family. Even you, dearest. My only luxury is this car. Who do I buy these statues for, if not my wife? Brilliant classicist. So good at Latin." He spoke the last words with a sneer.

"For me?" Mama gave a girlish laugh and tossed her head so that her silver hair spilled back over her seat. "Such a genius businessman, poor man, married to an idiot academic. I'm so stupid, children, that I need three statues of Venus. Your father has three copies of Venus that are exactly the same, all for me. One in his study. One in the bedroom. One in storage. Now why would he buy three statues that are exactly the same? Shall we ask him?"

"Why, Papa?" Melissa asked, anxious to please them both.

"She wants to know, Federico. Why do you have three copies? Come on, kids, Papa isn't answering. Why, Papa? Why, Papa?"

Melissa repeated it once, but she saw Papa's fingers turning white on the black steering wheel, and she began to tremble and fell silent. But Claudio kept going, "Why, Papa? Why?" though Melissa tried to nudge him.

Then Mama asked once more, "Why, Papa?" and with a jerk of the wheel, Papa swung the car to the side of the road. Melissa tumbled into Claudio's lap. She looked up and saw dust swirling outside the window. Mama's head lolled sideways.

"Are you insane?" she yelled.

Papa slapped her.

"Oh, Why, Papa?" she started to sob. "A statue for every whore. No, there aren't enough! One for every whore every night. Every slut, everywhere. *What crueller things than this do enemies do when a city falls?"*

Papa slapped Mama again. Through her tears, Melissa observed the precision of Papa's movements, like the machines in his factories: draw back, propel, strike.

Mama said, "Or is it that bitch? The one who shot herself! Because of you. Peasant! Murderer!"

Papa exploded. "DON'T EVER," and he raised his hand again, but Claudio shouted, "Papa! Mama! I want to make a museum for the statues!"

Their parents froze, silent, panting, leaning towards each other, blood in their cheeks. Suddenly both spun back.

"SHUT UP!" Papa yelled.

"DON'T SPEAK, YOU IDIOT!" Mama screamed.

Claudio sank back into the leather seat, head on his chest, and began to cry. Melissa moved over and took his hand and squeezed it when he didn't reply. Melissa urged herself to be strong, as Claudio would have told her, were he not crying and their parents not in earshot. For soon they would be far away from here, alone by the water where freedom was endless, playing games, reliving myths of reckless heroes and dastardly gods, such myths that were alive but truer than life. For Melissa understood that there were no happy endings, and so what could be better than a world where each time a hero died or a god acted cruelly, there were no consequences, and the tale could be reset to beginnings as cool and endless as the waters of the lake? The custodian of these myths, who decided if they had Hercules the baby or Hercules the warrior or Hercules the god, was Claudio.

And now she heard him whisper, "I will, I'll make a museum, a really special one. I will."

*

For years, this memory was hidden from her. She did not recall it the day she visited Claudio in what he called his forge, the workshop he'd fitted out by the garage of the lakeside home in Garda. It was summer again, perhaps his second year of university – she'd have been fourteen, making it 1977 – and he was back from Bologna. He was bent over the worktop, dressed in his dirty work t-shirt, but without his apron. There was no sound of scraping or chiselling, no hammering, no sparks flying to the floor; all his tools were in their places on the shelves and wall, and the air was clear of that acrid smoke that usually swirled around his metalwork before getting sucked away by the ventilators. Yet he was bent over, intent, hand moving across something.

"What are you doing?" she asked him.

He spun round, eyes wide, mouth a crooked smile as the words spilled out. "Issa! This is it! Completely new. Every room tells a myth. Look, look, come see." He waved her beside him. She saw a massive piece of blue paper covered in pencil marks, all meaningless to her except that they were an engineer's blueprints, and she swelled with pride at what he had learned at university. At the top was written *Museum of Myth*; *Design*: *Claudio Collina*. "Look," he said, pointing at what seemed to her a random mark. "This is the room of Theseus. You enter here. It is the labyrinth. This way? Or how about...? NO! THE MINOTAUR!" She giggled. "You flee. It comes. But Theseus is here! He slays the minotaur. Now you follow the silken thread. On the walls... Fragments of pottery: the betrayal, Theseus abandons the princess. And... Other myths..." He fell silent, finger running across the page, forehead devouring itself in a frown. The words were buried deep inside him now, and such outbursts were rare and to be treasured. She watched his mouth turn into a soft and timid *O*.

"Papa will like it, won't he?"

"Of course," she said, "but not as much as Mama. She'll love it!"

The smile ran across his face like a flame.

"She'll love it," Melissa repeated. "You must show it to her."

"I will," he said. "And Papa. It will be good."

It will be good.

What did he mean?

She never asked. She wished she had asked. But he was her idol, a demi-god, she could question nothing but wait breathless for his attention to turn to her.

And then, four years later, January 1981, he left them.

It was another myth – Claudio's journey – and the only way she could think of it.

It – that was another part of the myth. *It*, the only word any of them used. It happened, Papa said, because of a malfunction in the ventilator. She didn't understand; she refused to ask. She wanted no more clarity. "It was painless," she heard Papa tell someone at the funeral.

Melissa let flourish another myth, one of an absence, thinking only in the present tense: *Claudio loves this pumpkin soup, Claudio has made me a wonderful necklace.*

She had found the necklace on the day he left. She took it off only when she slept.

*

Weeks passed – this memory had no precision, for even months after *it* had happened, she lived outside of time – and one day Papa burst into her room without a knock. She saw the vast blue paper in his hand and the memory came back to her, of that moment in the car when Claudio vowed to build a museum. She saw that he would never build his museum, and he would never tell another myth, and for a moment she felt the room rotate and she thought she would collapse. She felt for the foot of her bed. She sat down. She would not, she vowed, cry in front of her father.

He did not speak at first. His face was made of triangles that had grown sharper as he aged: a sharp nose, a sharp chin; it was dry and smooth, quick to anger or pride, but no other emotions. He had not wept at Claudio's funeral. It was impossible to feel tenderness towards her father, or even to imagine kissing him. She could hear Mama's sobs from across the open atrium; Papa's jawbone was pulsing. Melissa must be strong so that he would not feel surrounded by weeping women.

He thrust the blueprint towards her. "Do you know what this is?" She nodded. "I see. So, I'm going to build it. A museum for myths."

"Good," she said. She stood up carefully and took the blueprint from him. She found it no more comprehensible than when Claudio had shown it to her.

"Whatever it costs," Papa said. "Any amount. It must be perfect. I will name it after your brother."

"Good," she repeated.

His eyes narrowed as he studied her. "You are interested in this stuff," he said, pointing at the blueprint. It was unclear whether he meant architecture, museums, engineering, or classics.

"In myths," she said. "Yes."

"You will meet someone with me."

Three days later he brought her to his offices, where she met Ernesto Battillo for the first time. Despite her grief, her first worry was for Ernesto's health: she doubted he could survive a month working for her father. He was a young curator from the museum in Napoli, who looked as Melissa imagined a curator should, with thick glasses and a grey cardigan, his pale hair already going grey, his face gaunt. What struck her most was how small and frail he seemed. He was her height, but stooped, with chin lowered, eyes deferential before her father, his voice almost invisible.

"A Museum of Myth," he said. "An interesting idea."

"A unique idea," her father corrected, voice booming. He loved to flaunt his strength in front of people he saw as weak.

"Not unique," Ernesto said. "We recently created an exhibition in Napoli about the myths of Hercules."

"Well that's why you're here," Papa said. "My daughter," he pulled her forwards, "is young, but she knows about this subject. Obviously, the project means something to her. So, I want her input on the – what do you call it? Concept?"

"Conceptual plan," Ernesto said.

"Speak up! We're not in a library."

"Conceptual plan," he said slightly louder.

"Melissa, do you know what that is?" She shook her head. Papa's eyes narrowed again, now judging if she would be a help or hindrance. She stepped forward and shook Ernesto's hand.

"I really like the room of Hercules," she said. She had, by now, made some sense of the blueprint. "I have an idea for it." Ernesto nodded politely. "My father has a Roman second-century Hercules with club. We make a statue of Atlas towering over him, built to hold the roof on his shoulders, looking down, about to pass the sky over to Hercules. That would be the centrepiece of the room."

Ernesto's face lost decades when it smiled. "That is a beautiful idea," he said.

"So it's settled," Papa boomed. "Remember. It must be perfect. Whatever it costs." He stormed out. Melissa heard him barking at his secretary, "The man had better be good; he acts like a timid idiot," and glanced at Ernesto. His face was stern but calm, like marble, and she thought, *I like him.*

They began to work together the next day, using a conference room in Papa's offices.

"Your brother is a genius," Ernesto said as he pinned pages on the wall, careful to mimic Melissa's present tense. "He has designed a whole museum. Now we have to bring the concept to life. Our only limits are our imagination, what is physically possible, and of course, the budget."

"My father said, *whatever it costs*," she declared.

A twitch of disbelief played on Ernesto's stern face. He was close to thirty, a bachelor from Napoli, living in a small rented room paid for by Papa. Reflecting back, Melissa considered how strange this must have been for him, to leave his fellow professionals and find himself in the offices of an industrialist, with only a seventeen-year-old for assistance.

And a spoiled one! Half-crazed with grief, arrogant with the unfinished knowledge she had learned from her mother and brother, she believed she understood mythology. Once, when she was a child, myths had been real to her, but now she knew they were merely stories invented by human beings. She saw myths as works of craft, with components, like a design on a blueprint. It was essential to her that each element of the myths in the museum be accurate. Accuracy tied them back to her brother, the teller of myths. Just as there was no one in the world with the exact same face as Claudio, same smile, same voice, same mind; just as the necklace he had made for her was unique; so there was only one accurate version of each myth to be used in the museum. On this subject, she agreed with Papa. The museum must be perfect.

*

"Why does this say *imprisons*?" she demanded. It was a month into their collaboration. She was at the wall, studying the plans for *Room One: Birth of the world*. Ernesto was bent over numbers at the table. He sat back and adjusted his glasses.

"Saturn," he said. "He imprisons his children and –"

"No! That's not how it goes. Saturn EATS his children." Ernesto did not answer; unlike her, he felt no need to fill silences. "No one says that Saturn imprisons his children. If you look at Hesiod, or Apollodorus, or anyone – he EATS them. Eat is not the same as imprison. Ernesto?"

He took off his glasses and polished them. "The problem is," he said in that quiet but determined voice, "you will have children coming. It is unpleasant to show a father eating his children. Have you seen the painting by Goya?"

"I don't care about unpleasant! That's not what the blueprint says!" She ran over and picked up their copy (her father had kept the original). She found the first room and tried to read.

"What does it say?" Ernesto murmured.

"He says... He says..." She flung it back to the table. "He doesn't. Just *Uranus and Saturn. Saturn and children. Titans fight gods. Jupiter defeats Saturn.*"

"So we must interpret it," Ernesto continued. "Claudio left it for us to decide."

"Left?"

"I mean –"

"He LEAVES nothing," she screamed. "He WANTS no interpretation. He WANTS it accurate. He wants it RIGHT. EEEEAAAAATS."

They were silent. From outside the room, Melissa could hear the mutterings of the secretaries. They were used to these outbursts.

"Saturn eats his children," Ernesto said.

"Yes," she half-shouted.

He came to stand beside her. He smelled of tobacco and a faint musky cologne, like pines, a fragrance she liked. She watched as he crossed out *imprisons* and wrote *eats*.

"Yes," she repeated.

He turned to her, the lines around his mouth taut. "It is important to be accurate in life, Melissa, but myths won't always let you do that. There is no single version of a myth. They keep changing. They evolve. Like genes. Do you understand how genes work?"

She had lost his train of thought, but didn't want to appear stupid, and gave a disdainful, "Obviously."

"Myths are like genes. They come from our ancestors, they are handed down over millennia. Nothing stays the same that lasts so long. Myths aren't just good stories; they are heirlooms, ever changing but handed down from generation to generation. They connect us to our heritage, to our...families."

Something in the way he said the last word made her ask, "Where's your family?"

Ernesto's eyes had withdrawn behind the glasses, and he grew still. She was sometimes this way, communing with her brother, and she wondered if Ernesto was speaking to someone who had gone. Then he shook his head, and a faint smile played on his face, not a fire like Claudio's, but subtler, briefer, almost as precious. "Oh," he said, waving his hand, "all over."

And that was all he ever told her about himself.

His words moved her and Melissa grew a new idea: that there was no definitive myth, and to be truly accurate meant acknowledging this. For what, after all, did a hydra look like? "Some say it has endless snake-heads," Ernesto said, but he showed her fragments of pottery where there were only two heads, and a baby Minotaur that was almost cute, and Medusas with normal hair instead of snakes. "The artists had to adapt what they had learned, and this carried on for centuries, until now, and we too are adapting the myths to suit Claudio's vision, and the limits we have."

Thus he coaxed her, and humoured her, and nurtured the warmth which was buried within, and Melissa became a young woman.

*

For the site of the museum, Papa had chosen a spot on one of the hills overlooking Verona. For nearly a year, Melissa heard nothing more about it. Then one afternoon in winter, Papa burst into her bedroom and told her to dress warmly and come with him. He led her through the streets, wrapped in his thick black coat, feet splashing through the wet pavement in a relentless pace as his breath fogged in front of her. They came to the Garibaldi Bridge. He pointed up. The light was almost gone, but she could just see the hills. "Do you see that little one, that *collina*? They've agreed. That's where the museum will be."

She squealed and jumped up. Before she could think what she was doing, her lips were pressed against his dry cheek.

"Everyone," he continued, as if a kiss from his daughter was a common event, "will look up there and see your brother's name."

They stood in silence, gazing at the hill. It was around the anniversary of Claudio's departure. Melissa looked up at the sky, where the first stars had come out, and then at her father. Small clouds puffed out of his mouth; his hands were in his pockets; his eyes were reflective. She pointed upwards and he followed her finger. "Sometimes I think he's become one and he's looking down at us."

Papa gave a grunt and marched away, down the bridge, so fast that Melissa had to run to keep up.

On the triumphant day that Papa finally approved the plans, Ernesto and Melissa almost ran out of his study before he could change his mind. She watched the sternness slip away from the curator's face, and the years faded to nothing as he smiled.

"I can't believe we are going ahead," he said.

"I'm so, so, so, excited," she said.

He grabbed her hand and took her to a nearby bar. He bought her a cocktail and as she finished the drink, she looked at his subtle smile and thick glasses, and thought what a wonderful mind he had, and how much Claudio would have enjoyed meeting him, and she believed she loved

Ernesto. But she found she couldn't say it, and in her frustration she dropped her head into her hands and began to cry.

"Melissa? Melissa?"

His whispers came from so far and she thought, if he was closer, she could say it. She thought, if she raised her eyes, and he saw them, he would understand without her even needing to speak.

"I am so sorry," he said when she looked up. "This was disrespectful of me. There is no cause for celebration. We are honouring your brother. I am sorry. We'll leave."

He stood up, and helped her up, misunderstanding her touch.

He left the coins, and helped her home, misunderstanding her warmth as she leaned against him.

Finally, at her front door, summoning Violetta to shepherd her in, when Melissa turned and said "good night" with tears in her mouth, still he misunderstood and said, "Claudio would be so proud of you," and she wept herself to sleep because he had got it wrong and it was her fault.

She vowed she would never embarrass herself in front of him again, but she had no further opportunity, for the next day Papa summoned her to his study and announced she was going to university. She knew exactly who was at fault.

"What the fuck is THIS?" she yelled down the phone at Ernesto.

His voice came quietly down the line. "You have done something amazing. Now you must study. Otherwise you'll be wasting your life."

"You're trying to get RID of me!"

"Who is your favourite classical heroine?" he asked.

"I don't know," she fumed, "Medea, Antigone, anyone. Probably Atalanta, the warrior maiden who kills sons of bitches."

"What makes a young woman's life tragic in ancient myths? Is it the length of her life?"

"No," she retorted, "it's like Achilles says, it's not how LONG you live, but HOW you live. A wasted life is...wrong..." Her voice trailed away.

"Enjoy your studies, Melissa," he said. "I hope you will still work with us during your holidays."

He'd outmanoeuvred her, and she wouldn't forgive that, nor would she forgive that he had gone behind her back, to her father, to palm her off to the professors. She decided that her best punishment would be to become such a successful student that he would rue the day he sent her away. She reeled off Latin and Greek translations by heart, and dazzled the professors, and found that the boys who had mocked her at school had disappeared and instead now there were men, the beginning of a long list of men who wanted her, four-limbed men, shallow men with shallow minds and singular passions, none divine enough to understand her and the museum – to quote a single poem of Catullus, to grasp her when she shape-shifted around them like a mermaid.

She stayed away from Ernesto until the summer holidays. When she returned, she found he had a new office and an entire team, including two pretty pouting postgraduates. Her anger bubbled up and she decided it was Medea she liked the best, who slaughtered men and cut them into pieces.

But her anger faded as she marvelled at the immensity of their project. Papa had turned over a part of the Verona factory to Ernesto, and Melissa danced between sculptors and artists and engineers and designers, all making Claudio's dream into reality: here was a minotaur with artificial (fireproof) hair; here was the first idea she had discussed with Ernesto, a vast plaster mould of Atlas stretching up to the ceiling. Melissa played at being the *patron*, crossing and recrossing the factory floor, chastising dirty work benches, pointing out misplaced tools, bantering with the workers, snapping at the postgraduates, delivering curt words to Ernesto.

Thus she alternated for two years: term for studies, holidays for museum. She would think of them later as the happiest years of her life.

*

They finished the museum on schedule, on Claudio's birthday, 22 April. Melissa slept for a night and a day after the work was complete. She came down to find it was dinnertime, and that her mother had resumed her place at the glass table.

"I'm not interested," Mama was saying. Her voice quavered, with frailty, not fear.

"What if I make you?" Papa said.

"I'll scream through your opening ceremony."

Her parents sounded almost smug to be arguing again. It was a feeble echo of earlier years, a pointless sequence of bitter words between two middle-aged people who had failed to keep Claudio alive. She looked at her father, his chin covered in soup, and her mother, with her rolling puffy eyes, and decided that she hated them.

Her father gave a grunt and left the room. Melissa stuffed food in her mouth, the way they all ate in the museum.

"That's not healthy," Mama said.

Melissa stopped. "Violetta!" The housekeeper came in. "Mama wants me to drink a bottle of grappa. Could you fetch it?"

"Stop that," the plump housekeeper said. "Your mother is not well."

"You can go now," Melissa said. Violetta left them with a grumble about spoiled little girls. Melissa patted her mouth.

"Where have you been?" Mama said.

"I was busy the last months, Mama, working on Claudio's project. The museum that you won't go to see."

"The museum of shit," Mama spat.

Melissa thought she would faint with rage. "Your son," she said, measuring each word, "wants the museum. I spend all my time on it. Your husband spends a fortune."

"Oh, a fortune! He can keep his gold shit. Sacrificed his child. Like Agamemnon. What joy is there in a museum? It is STUPID. Where's my Claudio? Why not find a way to bring him back? Study the poet! The poet! *By reason of your death, I have banished from all my mind these thoughts and all the pleasure of my heart.*"

"I know that one," Melissa screamed, "Catullus said it about his BROTHER," and she stormed out of the dining room.

The unofficial opening took place the next day, presided over by Papa, accompanied by Melissa. They passed through the steel gates and in through the sculpture garden, with its bronze nymphs gambolling through strawberry trees and Italian maples, replanted from the hills of Valpolicella. A gravel path led up to the entrance. The building extended upwards from the slope, a cross between the Acropolis and a spaceship. It had white columns and a green dome, and its mezzanine level was completely glass-fronted. The colonnades rose towards a vast pediment, every part of the marble etched with detailed reliefs such as Bacchus wooing Ariadne and Hercules performing his labours.

The assembled group, some fifty of them, watched as her father tugged a rope and the cloth came off the sign on the front. It read:

CLAUDIO COLLINA MUSEUM OF MYTH

Everyone cheered and applauded. Her father said a few words of thanks and the workers dispersed. Ernesto waited, but her father told him to go. "I want to see this alone."

Melissa stayed. Night had fallen. Her father looked smaller, his posture a little stooped, his voice sounding weak in the open courtyard as he said,

"Let us go in."

The doors slid open and the marble entrance hall, now empty, seemed enormous. They passed the guardian statues of Hercules and Venus into the bright main corridor. Booms and screeches filtered from the rooms, the noises of the museum as described on Claudio's blueprint.

Melissa spoke quietly. "We start with the first room, cosmogony, the birth of the world." And they turned into the first room and beheld...

THE UNIVERSE! Sky and earth pairing to create the world, white ceiling and black floor approach each other in the centre, stars swirling. Stepping out of it, a snarling titan turns his weapon to castrate his father: the blood falls to earth to produce the Furies, the genitals fall to water to make Venus, a scallop shell floating in a marble pool of water. Now the water drains, the pool grows teeth, and a circle of screaming god children fall into his mouth. Yes! Saturn EATS his children! But child Jupiter hides, survives, crawls away. Follow round the curving wall and behold: Jupiter, fully grown, bearded, lightning in his hands – a magnificent 2nd century statue, now gods versus titans are projected through the smoke of war, Jupiter hurling the lightning bolts crafted for him by Vulcan and the cyclops, the other gods in a phalanx around him. The titans are vanquished, and we progress to the next room, past Jupiter's mating with mortal women, and all his progeny, those gods and goddesses and heroes, led by the greatest of all, semi-divine Hercules; and to the next room, where Jupiter's brothers rule the underworld and the waves; the next, the gods of the forest; and the next, the gods of the city, Minerva and Vulcan, buildings and fire, all man's industry. And in the next – only the sixth, fourteen more to go – Vulcan's bride, who betrays her husband again and again, this goddess of beauty and love, Venus.

As they walked into this room, Melissa remembered Claudio on that day in his forge, saying, Lissa! *This is it! Completely new! Every room tells a myth!* She looked up at the scallop shells encrusted on the ceiling, and heard the sounds of surf, and saw Venus's lovers scattered around the room in poses of sex and death, and Venus herself, appearing six times across the room, modest, unashamed, naked, clothed, powerful, seductive. She saw her father standing by one of his statues. He reached out and touched it. She heard a small, un-Papa-like noise, like a groan.

31

He turned and marched towards her, frowning, and she felt afraid as he stepped up to her. But he pulled her to his chest, and she smelled his sharp fragrance of leather and tobacco, and his chest rose and fell as he said, "It's so beautiful, Melissa."

It was the only time she ever saw her father weep.

She herself felt no sadness until they reached the Family Room. A full-sized photograph of Claudio looked down at her. It had been taken during his year in London, the year before he left them. He was smiling, but his eyes were frozen, and Melissa clutched at his necklace and reached out for the walls of his museum. Nothing that was solid was real. They had built it, but where was Claudio? Where was her brother? His voice? His love? He was dead. The darkness fell on her, four years of buried denial, and she masked her sobs with coughs.

*

Melissa left Verona a month later after a furious row with her father. She would continue her academic studies, and he would pay, as he had not paid her during her work on HIS museum. For once, her mother was on her side.

She went to Bologna, following in the footsteps of her brother. Her plan was to study anything other than classics, but she ended up writing a thesis on the early works of Virgil. She continued onto a PhD. The covered walkways and outdoor cinema and endless food pleased her, though the men she met still disappointed, and she decided she preferred being alone. She sought another subject – comparative literature, or social studies, many ideas sprang to mind – but mythology was always lurking, waiting to drag her back in, and she finally settled on a study of the Furies in early Roman literature. She was nearly twenty-six, and now looked back with a mixture of awe and disdain at the younger self who had lectured Ernesto Battillo on the importance of accuracy in myths.

She had evolved her philosophy that there could never be an accurate version of any myth. She would ask her undergraduate students to explain the moral of this last story. Justice, they would say – that was why the heroine had to die.

"And what if I tell you that there are multiple versions?" she would cry. "She does not die, gets married, bears a child. What then is the moral? Love conquers all? What if I tell you that myths are fragments of authority? There is no right version, no core, it is like life. We are dancing around the edge of meaning, all of us, and struggling to give it order. The world is beyond understanding! That is the lesson!"

*

The call from Violetta came in the autumn of 1991. "Please, *signorina*, please help me. Your mother is impossible. Another stroke six months ago, and she won't accept it, she won't stop drinking. I can't look after her alone. I beg you."

Melissa returned to find that almost nothing was left of the woman who had inspired her to learn classics, who had told stories of gods and heroes to her and Claudio. Now she was a husk, lying in the shadows, breathing like an animal.

"Mama, I'm here."

A distant, croaking groan. "Poor Catullus, 'tis time – you should cease your folly – and account as lost – what you see is lost."

Melissa sat by her mother's bedside. She intended to go back the same day, but she remembered how Mama had once been a silvery goddess of the dawn, whom she and Claudio would sneak down to watch, bent over her books, translating, and Melissa realised she could not leave. She stayed a year, trying to read, trying to write, but mainly listening to her mother's scratchy breaths.

Her mother said, "Claudio understood. He wrote it all down. He wrote it for me."

"What, Mama?"

Her mother said, "No, no. Forget it. He didn't do anything."

"Who, Mama?"

Her mother said, "Get married."

"Yes, Mama."

Her mother died.

After the funeral, her father spoke to her quietly, almost tenderly. "I always dreamed that Claudio would work with me one day. I know you are not interested in the business. I will sell it. But you helped build the museum. Will you work there? Ernesto will be glad to have you."

She understood that he meant he would be glad, and she nodded, drained from her year, no longer able to remember what she had meant to write about the Furies. She did not even ask what she would do in the museum. She rode up the next day, chauffeured by Roberto, and met Ernesto in his office.

33

He had changed over the years, become more severe, less empathic, he had grown to be more like her father, but a greyer, hunched version that belied his inner strength. His voice had changed from whisper to growl. It had been a youthful infatuation, she saw, perhaps for him as well.

"It is good to have you here," he growled.

"I am glad to be here," she said.

And so she came to work in the museum. She created an education programme that reached out to all the schools in the city. She took over running the academic conferences. She came to know every member of staff, the names of their husbands or wives, their birthdays and favourite gifts to receive. Then she began proposing changes to the rooms.

"Claudio didn't mean for this to become a stale place. It must evolve, right, Ernesto? We say that Hercules killed his family and had to do his labours as penance. But in Euripides, it's the other way around. First labours, then he comes home and kills his family: like a soldier with shell-shock, back from the war. We should find a way to capture that, we could tie it to the war in Yugoslavia."

"That is interesting," Ernesto said cautiously. "Will you speak to Signor Collina about it?"

Her father refused. "The museum is perfect," he said. "It was what Claudio wanted. It's what the visitors enjoy. We won't change anything."

"Papa, perfect doesn't mean unchanging. Claudio understood that."

"You DON'T understand," he yelled. "NOTHING will change."

Melissa was thwarted, but still she gained ever more responsibility, until she was Ernesto's co-director in all but name. Then in 1995, her father told her he was resigning as president and she would take his place.

"When I'm gone," he said, "you'll protect the museum, and make sure it survives the ages."

A small voice in Melissa's head shrieked, *Don't accept!* It sounded like her mother's. She had neglected her doctorate for four years; she'd had so many ideas once.

But who would protect Claudio's legacy, if not her? Who owed Claudio everything she had?

"Yes," she said.

He laughed. "That is the strangest acceptance I've ever heard." He glared at her. "Now, let me explain your duties."

But here too nothing would change, for at every important meeting she was accompanied by her father: with the bald-headed lawyer Caspardi, with the mayor, at the ministry, at press interviews. Her father spoke before her, and stayed behind when she left, and what was discussed in private conversations, he never revealed.

As president, she had thought she could finally make changes. But Ernesto mournfully shook his head as her father said, "I still fund the museum, and so long as I fund it, you will change nothing."

Thus four more years passed. She was president, she was powerless, she was trapped.

*

On Claudio's birthday, April 1999, her father took ill. He went into the hospital with lung troubles. His face turned waxen from his exertions coughing sputum.

"There are many things I need to tell you," he said when she visited. "There's a trust... The ministry..." He coughed. "Get Caspardi," he said.

"You need to rest," she said.

"Get him!"

She left. Her father would not order her from a hospital bed.

In mid-May, they began to apply morphine and the hawk-like face became ever more still. For the first time in her life, Melissa felt she could sit in his company and not be afraid. The beeps of the machines were almost a comfort, playing a rhythm that accompanied his flickering, closed eyelids. She could hear beyond the door the dismal conversations of powerful visitors: executives, politicians, journalists. She went outside to tell them to be quiet. She saw Violetta and Roberto on a bench, patient, elderly, red-eyed; Ernesto sat beside them.

Her father had not spoken for a day, but when Melissa came back in the room, he said, "But no..." Night had come to Verona and outside was darkness; she had extinguished all but one bedside lamp. She saw the silhouette of Mercury, the bearer of luck, a statuette she had brought here. She looked back at her father. His eyes had opened to tiny slits.

"Papa?" she said.

He made a soft noise, an attempt at speech or a clearing of the throat.

"Are you thirsty?" He made the noise again, now impatiently. She leaned closer. "What is it?"

He started to pant, the breath blowing from the back of his throat with the sound of a "Ca" but his tongue was thick and this became an "S". It repeated, slow but insistent. "Ca...Sss...Ca...Sss."

"Mama?" she said, thinking he was trying to say Susanna.

He squeezed his eyes shut and she understood she was wrong.

She took his hand. It closed weakly on hers. "Claudio?" she said, her voice catching. His eyes, fogged with morphine and the dim light, struggled to open further. He shook his head slightly. His mouth contorted into shapes; faint sounds came and she repeated what he had mouthed.

"No. But he knew."

"What, Papa? What did he know?" She had a sudden memory of her mother saying, *Claudio understood. He wrote it all down. He wrote it for me.* "What did Claudio know, Papa?"

Her father swallowed and with immense effort tried to speak. She hushed him but he persisted. Through the painful scratching of his throat came the words, "It was my fault."

She gripped his hand and felt the thin veins and bones press against her fingers. His breath grew shallower. She felt his fingers try to grasp her hand more tightly but he had little strength left. "Melissa," he whispered. She wanted to say something. His eyes closed. His breath grew thicker, then fainter. The brittle fingers on her hand lost their strength.

The air went still.

Machines burst into noise and doctors and nurses rushed into the room. Melissa stood and felt dizzy. She felt a hand on her shoulder and turned to see Ernesto. She gathered her strength and walked outside. The men and women stood stiffly, called to attention by the rush of activity.

"My father is dead," she announced.

Fingers pressed into her arms; there were kisses on her cheek; she heard words of condolence. But she saw only Roberto and Violetta, rushing towards her. She stood stiffly and they stopped in front of her and each took one of her hands and pressed them to their faces as the words of her father tore through her head: *It was my fault.*

He was wrong, she thought, but she could not tell him; there was, now, no one to tell. Her father was wrong, because only Melissa knew why Claudio had died on the shores of Lake Garda.

A day passed. Another day. For what was she living – for whom? The house was empty but for Violetta and Roberto, who tried to offer comfort, and solitude when she rejected them.

On the third day, the bald-headed lawyer, Caspardi, arrived at the door.

"*Buona sera,*" she said. She remembered that her father had wanted him to come to the hospital. He was lean and fierce, one of the most respected men in the city.

"Your father wished for me to dispose of some papers," he said.

"I will go through his papers," she said, "and then you can dispose of them."

"Those were not his instructions," the lawyer persisted.

She slammed the door in his face.

She was alone, the last of the Collinas. As her father's spirit vacated the city, his influence faded from its streets. Only the museum remained, vigilant on the hill, the glass of the mezzanine reflecting the sunset like a lighthouse that broadcast her brother's name to the city below.

Now that Melissa was alone, she began to feel free. She defined her freedom, at first, as a narrow quality: she could finally change the museum. But by early July, she had come to understand that her freedom was something different. She was free to leave.

Last week, she had made her decision. This morning, she had put away her black. On Monday, she would call a board meeting and announce her resignation. She would nominate Ernesto as her replacement. The other board members, hand-picked cronies of her father, could do nothing but submit to the will of Federico Collina's daughter. She had promised her father that she would protect the museum forever, and only Ernesto could carry that burden for her.

She was ready. She knew what she would tell Ernesto. Once he had accepted, she could leave. And she must. If she did not, she would be frozen like the statues in the museum, like the Venus in her father's study, trapped in this house with its dining table that reflected the sunlight onto the empty seats around her.

Sam: The Case Begins

Every detective story needs a hero. It doesn't have to start with him: second chapter is best. The important thing is that the hero be brave, be a boy, and get the girl in the end.

So here he was, Sam Morris, second form, second-born, second row, with thirty minutes remaining in the last lesson of the year and his eyes fixed on the nape of hair at the back of Isabelle's neck.

The skin of his forearm clung to the sticky wooden table as he shifted on the bench. Thirty minutes. A bee was thrashing against the glass of the window, struggling to find the opening that beckoned them all out. Thirty minutes till summer, its vast canopy unfolding before them.

Thirty minutes left in the company of Isabelle Fabron, whose blonde curls spilled back over her shoulders. Sam studied how the dark straight threads by her scalp rolled into ever thicker and brighter waves, spreading out so far that some solitary hairs glinted in the afternoon sun as she bowed her head to write. One dislodged and a breeze from the open window carried it over to his desk. He looked left and right, put his hand over it, and drew it into his blazer pocket.

"Morris?" Mr Roberts barked. The bald classics teacher was a diluted form of Attila the Hun, violence and menace lurking in his classroom.

Sam froze. "Yes, sir?"

"I was saying, you have the list in front of you. Now all of you, stop looking at the clock and pay attention. Time has no dominion here. I decide when your holiday starts." Mr Roberts paused, smiling at them. Sun squashed all prospect of retort.

"Many of these names will be familiar to you. Hands down if you've not heard of *The Odyssey*." Isabelle's hand went up and Sam's did too. "I can wait all day, if you like." All the hands went up. On reflection, there was nothing diluted about the Attila in Mr Roberts. "These books do not appear in the GCSE texts that you begin to study next year. But I want you to read them nonetheless. Especially the two at the top of the list, which are...?"

Sullen voices: "Homer and Ovid."

"Signs of life. Yes, Homer and Ovid. These two are the meat and potatoes of classical study. They are the foundation on which everything else rests, as important to our modern civilisation as the Bible or Shakespeare. Well? Does anyone here agree? Or disagree?"

He glared at the class. No one spoke. Sam could imagine that the rows behind him had fled through the window, and Mr Roberts was ranting at empty benches. He turned around. The lights gleamed and he was conscious of the acne on his face. Fred Chung stuck out his tongue. He turned back. Mr Roberts leaned forwards with menace.

"Your performances this year have bordered on the abominable." Sam felt his skin grow warm. "What is lacking is enthusiasm. Classics, my monkeys, is not a penance you suffer through some fault of your parents. No-o-o, it is a privilege. Now, there are two new translations I encourage you to read this summer. Ted Hughes, before he died last year, released a remarkable book called *Tales from Ovid*. Secondly, Robert Fagles, an American no less, has translated the *Odyssey* and it is very readable and poetic. I think you will find this tale of adventure, sex," giggles, "deceit, fantasy, sex," louder giggles, "families and, yes, Frederick Chung, sex, rather rewarding."

The class had woken up. In the dying moments of the year, Mr Roberts had brought his subject to life. The spirit of the Hun was roused by the sun's rays colliding with his bald head.

"By the way, I am not dismissing the *Iliad*. It is the first great European story of war. Just as this recent war in Kosovo may be the last. Discuss. Hmmm? Very well, do not discuss anything. Now I shall read to you a tale of sex and gods from this Mr Fagles's *Odyssey*. This is the story told by the bard Demodocus in Book Eight."

Mr Roberts began to read. A torrent of voices fell on the room: booms, whispers, wails, sneers. His hands curled into claws as he paced at the front. He whirled on them. Isabelle gasped. Sam watched her golden hairs shiver as the god of War made love to the goddess of Love. The class giggled and War whispered:

Quick, my darling, come, let's go to bed
and lose ourselves in love!

As Mr Roberts spoke these words, Sam saw Isabelle move her hand down to her bare leg and his eyes glazed and mouth fell open, and he rooted for the gods to continue, let their passion spill into the poem as he watched Isabelle's slender fingers scratch her bare leg, and – forget consequences! – he should rise now and fling himself before her and cry, *I am Ares!*

But he had forgotten about the trap of the smith god, Hephaestus. With a thump of Mr Roberts's fist, massive chains fell on the cheating couple and Hephaestus cried to all the gods. He cursed his crippled self, his "shameless bitch" of a wife, and his parents, and the "devastating" god of War. But when he finished his terrible rant, all the gods burst into laughter, and made Hephaestus release the unhappy couple. War fled to his homeland, and Love slipped off with a laugh to Cyprus.

There the Graces bathed and anointed her with oil,
ambrosial oil, the bloom that clings to the gods
who never die, and swathed her round in gowns
to stop the heart...an ecstasy – a vision.

And Sam's eyes were bound to Isabelle's leg.

"Have a good holiday," Mr Roberts said.

He might have announced that the Huns were on their way. Books flew into bags, bags onto shoulders, and the kids stampeded out. Sam watched Isabelle pack and rise. As she shuffled to the door, he broke out of his reverie, grabbed his books, and hurried along the aisle so that they reached the doorway together. He gestured for Isabelle to go first. She misunderstood him and stopped. He stared at her soft pink mouth and imagined diving into it.

"Have a nice summer, Isabelle..." he stammered and she smiled and passed through.

Had she heard him? It was too quiet for her to hear, and yet she had smiled, and perhaps her smile meant he too should have a nice summer. If that was true, what could be nicer than to spend it in her company, in a marriage bed, anointed in oil... But by the time Sam had formulated these thoughts, Isabelle was out of reach.

He stood at the top of the wide staircase that overlooked the yard. Sunlight was breaking on countless black shoulders. Some pupils drifted to benches, others hurried to their lockers. Between them progressed Isabelle, an ecstasy – a vision. Sam smiled dreamily and pulled out the thread of her hair.

"Thinking of Homer?" Mr Roberts asked, appearing beside him.

"Um, sir," Sam said, shutting his fist. "Sort of."

"Good. Read it. Learn it. This isn't just about Greek and Latin, you know."

"Um."

40

"Have a good summer, Sam. Wish Anna one from me too: best of luck to her at Cambridge."

"Yes, sir. Thank you."

The bald warlord surged out, spilling boys and girls in his wake.

Sam followed him into yard. He emptied his locker and set off towards the station and home.

*

It was the end of another difficult year. The teachers had snapped, his father had huffed, his mother had sighed, and his sister had yelled, yet Sam Morris had made it through. He was not academic or sporty, he was not handsome, he was neither cool nor hard. He had got this far because he was a detective. From September to June, Sam had read the complete Raymond Chandler three times. He'd solved cases and cracked codes, and defended the weak against the mighty. Justice was his motto. The Case of the Missing Goldfish: he'd solved that one. The Case of the Weeping First Former: ditto. Summer had arrived and he had vowed to solve his biggest case yet. It would pose a series of ever greater challenges and culminate in glory and no small number of kisses. It was Sam Morris's destiny to be a hero.

On the first Saturday afternoon of the holidays, he sat at his computer in t-shirt and shorts and typed as the world turn to gold. This computer had once belonged to Anna, but she'd been given a laptop for uni. He had created an email address and distributed it to ten people. So far only Fred Chung had emailed him, to say he could type 82 words per minute. Sam was at 68.

He finished typing up his file note. It was closer to home than most of his cases, but justified given his dad's bizarre behaviour in the past 48 hours.

The Case of the Disappearing Surgeon
Date: Friday 2 July, 1999
Time: approx. 8:35am
Location: Gloucester Terrace
Suspect: Chris Morris, 42, 6'1, overweight (over 100kg?), Leeds accent, messy hair
Items: red wheelie bag
Details
Suspect departed with Anna to Waterloo station, then to Kings Cross station and Leeds. Reason given: "training course."

Counter evidence

1. Suspect came home early on Thursday, went to bedroom, didn't come out again.

2. Suspect's wife cancelled suspect's daughter's going away dinner.

3. Answering machine message today: "Chris, this is Thomas Forest again. I spoke to Doctor Loman last night and understand you turned down therapy sessions. I strongly advise against that. You need regular counselling if you are going to be ready to come back to work in six weeks. Consider it, please."

Hypothesis

Suspect suspended from work

Reason

1. Hit a nurse

2. Killed a patient

3. Killed one of the hospital staff

4. ???

Action

Watch and wait

"Good work, detective," Sam murmured. He pictured his father, a face like granite, vast paws for hands, the thick clipped voice that was so quick to tell him off and so curt with praise. The case remained open, but for now he saved and closed the document. What now?

From the street came the unhurried drone of passing cars. Sunlight began to crawl across the window and Sam lowered the blinds. He twirled on his chair. He looked at the ceiling. It was summer, that gentle gloopy slide he had sat on since childhood and slowly, deliciously, sometimes yawningly, descended until he landed in autumn. Summer meant endless nothingness, laziness, and love... Chandler's *Farewell My Lovely* was open on his bed. He picked it up. He read a page. He tossed it back and stood up: he'd get a glass of water.

Sam had lived in the same home all his life. It was a first-floor flat on Gloucester Terrace, a lengthy road that stretched from Hyde Park to Paddington. The pavements bobbed unevenly and crackled in the warmth, and the plaster on the columns peeled. Close-up, the stately terraces turned into either small blocks of apartments with an impossible number of buzzers, or oddly named hotels like the Fitch, the Round, the Prince Gilbert (who was prince of where, exactly?). Sam's flat was towards the north end of the road, facing the large and colourful towers of the Kingsland estate. Further north, the road curled in on itself, changing names several times, never quite saying when it had done so. There was a sense of theatre to the area, that it was makeshift and false, and nearby at 23–24 Leinster Gardens, the buildings were a facade put up after WWII to hide the train station – or so Sam's dad, the surgeon and history buff, had told him. His parents had moved in here in the mid-eighties, that strange period in history when Anna had existed and Sam had not.

This was the first time he would be alone for an entire summer. His parents were rarely home anyway, and now his dad was in Leeds; as for Anna, she had gone inter-railing across Europe all summer with her friends. Sam was free.

This freedom had not always been assured. Only two weeks ago, they'd had one of those rare family dinners, all four of them, which by definition put Mum and Anna in the same room and therefore meant combat.

"Like, Sam's thirteen. He'll survive. He knows where to get food. He knows how to call an ambulance. Don't you?"

Sam had nodded. Anna had become her old self again in those last days before her holiday – supportive rather than sadistic. But that was hardly going to deflect his mum.

"I'm not worried you'll starve, Sammy. But to be alone almost all the time... I could speak to the librarian. A summer job."

"Ugh," Anna went. "So boring."

"This is NOT about you, Anna. You've already got your way."

Anna was off on her European inter-rail holiday.

"I'm just saying," Anna insisted, "if he wants, he can go to the library. He doesn't have to WORK there."

"You need some structure," Mum said. "Otherwise you'll fritter every day by the computer."

"No, he won't!"

"Yes..."

Thus Anna and Mum continued to nag and nibble at each other, barely an argument yet, like the first stab of lightning in a summer storm. The fourth segment of the table held a skulking Dad, head drooped over his plate, barely looking up. Now he gave a grunt and Anna shut up, looking over at him while Mum kept explaining the virtues of discipline.

"What is it, Dad?" Anna asked.

Mum sighed and turned to face him as well. "Yes?"

A low rumble: "What does Sam want?"

Sam was surprised. It was rare for his father to take his side, but here was an invitation for him to speak and share his dreams with the table: how he wanted to read detective fiction and go to the park and find out where Isabelle lived and write poetry for her, he wanted to examine the roads north of the park and meet strange characters, and spend half his days in Whiteley's, hanging out with some of the St. Thomas's kids, and play Championship Manager the other half of the time and take Leeds United back to the top of the Premiership, and he wanted to snog two different girls not counting Isabelle, who would marvel at his maturity, and he wanted to burn all the acne of his face with the hungry sun. Oh, and solve a case.

"Obviously he wants *carte blanche*," Mum said.

"There you go," Anna said. "Decision."

"That is NOT a decision."

"Two to one," Dad said. "It is."

He got up and stomped to the master bedroom. The door closed louder than it should. Mum sat at the table, frowning at Anna in a way that said *this isn't over*. Anna winked at Sam and skipped off down the corridor. Sam was free and it was thanks to his sister.

Sam hadn't encountered any character in Raymond Chandler like Anna.

Until he was eleven, the five years that separated them were a chasm. Anna had prepared his food, helped with his homework, taken him to the park. She taught him about justice: *if someone pushes you, push them back; if you want ice cream, behave well; tell the truth, hate lies, and come here and let me wipe that mud off.* She was his minder, his guru, his nurse, his tutor, more a mother than his mum was.

So it had been until two years ago, when the chasm began to narrow and Sam learned what was on the other side, though he hardly understood it: there was kissing, and drinking, and smoking, and drugs, and possibly even that force which propelled the earth around its axis and on its orbit, whose every movement was curved, and whose every curve presented the budding possibilities of sex. The waves of Isabelle Fabron's hair; the shallow parabola of her smile: these led, somehow, to sex. Sam could not conceive of having sex with anyone, let alone the prettiest girl in class. But it must be possible: the parts existed. Still, how did you get to sex? His parents must know, but the person closest to Sam who could answer (possibly) was Anna. He recognised that such thoughts could be disastrous: his sister's sexuality was protected by ancient barriers. When a boy like George Robinson said, *Your sister's fit*, Sam must screw up his face and go, *Ugh*. But in his bedroom, or past the bathroom, when the shower was on and Anna was humming and the hums vibrated through the water, it was harder to be definitive. Sam's sister was beautiful. It was madness to consider this. It was impossible to ignore.

How fortunate then that she was also a monster.

Anna's wrath had always been directed towards their mother, in clashes that sent Sam and his dad sprinting for their bedrooms. But two years ago, Sam had moved to St Thomas's and Anna had joined as a sixth former. They were locked together in a grey structure where survival competed with intimacy. A month passed and Anna's tender figure grew sinister in the yard.

"Hi, Annie, what you doing?"

Her eyes narrowed as she turned from her shadowy peers. "What do you want, Sam?"

Not a hello, not a *Sammy*. At home, she stopped ruffling his hair. They started going separately to and from school. She got a boyfriend, Jason, whose face always scowled and whose jacket was stained with cigarette burns. Sam didn't like him.

"D'you know what cancer looks like, Jason? It's a big grey swelling in your lungs."

"SHUT UP, SAM!"

Jason broke up with Anna in May '98. She blamed the world but especially Sam, and all her injustices until now proved mere appetisers: the dark ages of Anna and Sam had arrived. She did not speak to him once during that summer. If he walked into the living room and she was on the phone, she'd say, "hang on, my shittle brother's here." The academic year began and Anna bowed into her books, surfacing only to yell at him for coughing outside her door or dropping a shoe in his room. Hope was a distant speck called Cambridge; it grew and shrank according to Anna's swaying confidence over whether she'd get in. When the acceptance letter arrived, Sam was delirious: Anna was going! He was free!

But she still had to do her A-levels. Half a year remained, and it nearly killed him. As the exams approached, the air grew hotter and Anna's stress rose. No word, no sound, not a breath could pass through Sam's lips without provoking a yell of "Shut UUUUPPPP!!!!" His parents spoke only to chastise him. Anna was a princess; Sam was a prisoner. He made a wall-

45

chart and ticked off the days to freedom. He copied Anna's exam timetable and, on nights before her exams, he stayed over at Fred Chung's flat.

Finally the exams ended. Silence fell on the flat. Anna was out whenever Sam went to sleep, and he began to breathe again: soon she would be gone forever.

One afternoon, she came home tipsy with friends and sat in the living room. Sam crept close, drawn by the sounds of bottles clinking and laughs and giggles and, above it all, the melody of Anna's voice chanting and joking. Now he was on the edge of the room and he could see Harry Gordon, the footballer, and Rachel Polk, her best friend, and scary Sumukhi Patel, who knew everything. There was a crowd of ten, drinking alcopops and beer, laughing and beckoning Sam in.

"Don't drink anything," Anna snapped.

But she let him stay. And after everyone had left, she took Sam's hand, even tipsier, and asked, "Which of my friends do you like best?"

"I like Harry," he said timidly.

She ruffled his hair and murmured something warm, and Sam had understood: she was his sister, and always would be. Though he could never match Anna, never get her grades or go to Cambridge, never play the lead in the school play and hang with the popular kids like Harry and Rachel, he resented none of this, he wanted only to be a part of her life. He wanted her to say, *You think Cambridge is something? Wait till you meet my lil bro. He's amazing! He's a detective!*

Alone for the summer, he yearned to be with his sister, out there in the continent where he could realise his greatness, pretending to be the son of a king, or the rescuer of a desperate Isabelle – a hero, as he was meant to be.

*

On this first Saturday of the holidays, on his own, he was free to do as he pleased.

He could sidle down the corridor, as if evading enemies.

He could run up and down, dodging bullets.

He could lie on his belly and pretend to swim in the entrance to Anna's room.

He looked up at the mess: posters, postcards, and photos on the wall; files and books and play scripts on every surface except the floor; where clothes had poured out like lava from her open cupboards to rest beside cushions and teddy bears. It was all evidence of her hurried departure yesterday, yelling *Byeeee!* as Dad led her out.

Sam got up and continued down the corridor. Here was the master bedroom, with its brass bed and Mum's desk. There was a large metal filing cabinet which held Sam's passport. There was also a bookcase. Dad's books were all about World War II, he said home was for *switching off*, as if work was a computer. Mum's books were all medical. Sam had read here that acne was caused by "sebum production" and "follicle blockage." One book warned: "Resolves, but may persist for years. Include psychological support." He hadn't touched his mum's books since.

Coming into the living room, he stopped at the French window. The balcony beyond the sealed doors had accumulated a thick sediment of black gunk which drove Mum wild. Eighties furniture dominated here, a dark blue sofa and beige armchair, also in the dining area with its plastic chairs and a Formica dining table. There was a sense of worn-out-ness that you didn't get in the gleaming apartment of Fred Chung. This continued in the kitchen, where years of Anna's and Dad's messiness had turned the counters a sepia-like yellow.

Sam poured himself a glass of water and headed back to his room. His excursion had killed barely ten minutes of the first day of summer, and he sat down at his desk with a sigh; there is no weariness so great as that of unused talent. He gave the mouse a wiggle. A message appeared on the screen:

You've got mail!

He grimaced, wondering what Fred's typing score was now. But then he saw that the message was from Anna, and Sam's eyes grew wide.

Attention: Gloucester Terrace Detectives.

Hi Sammy – from Paris! It's nice. The sun is massive (behind the clouds).

I need your help. Sumukhi and I are working on this Erasmus essay thing: what's it like to be a student in Europe. We need to include stuff about our families in it. So can you do me a favour?

Can you do an investigation about where Mum and Dad have been to in Europe?

Don't bother Mum, she's too busy. Obviously Dad's away. But go through their files and stuff, and see what you can find. Especially, I'm interested in their student days, cos the essay is about students. Did Mum and Dad meet on a uni trip? Did they send each other postcards? Anything you can find out about those early days might be relevant. UK is part of Europe, after all.

If you find anything personal like a diary, you shouldn't read it, because that'd be rude, but let me know.

Love, A nn A

Sam leapt up, mind racing. An investigation! He would find his parents' passports, and their letters and diaries. He'd dig up photos and postcards from their trips around Europe, and since Anna was interested in their student days, he'd find their old medical notes and – and – and what else? – for this email had burrowed into his brain and sent neurons fluttering in every direction, making him yearn to do still more, because it came from Anna.

She had written to him. Away on her travels, Anna had thought of him and charged him with a mission. He would not fail her.

Melissa: Morning

Melissa picked up her coffee. It was long finished, as was the fruit salad. She glanced again at the note from Ernesto. The headline underneath caught her eye, and she raised the newspaper to look more closely.

Museum of Myth Scandal: Gianluca Strazzo exposes Federico Collina...10–11

She frowned. Since her father's death, the *paparazzi* had been chewing over his life with predictable gossip. But this was the first story she had seen about the museum. She opened the article.

Master of Myth: Federico Collina
By award-winning reporter, Gianluca Strazzo
When Federico Collina died two months ago, the obituary-writers had plenty to say. A millionaire, an industrialist, a political heavyweight, a patriot, a philanthropist. How full his life had been!
No wonder, then, that there was no space for his controversies.

Melissa sighed as she read the usual accusations: the factory closures, the bribery charges, Collina the womaniser, the abandoner of his mother in the *mezzogiorno*.

"But of this Collina," the reporter continued, "we heard nothing." Instead, *Repubblica* called him, "as important a contributor to Verona as Gallienus or Cangrande."

This made him equal to the Roman emperor who built Verona's walls, and the medieval prince who built its castle.

His most famous contribution, of course, is the Claudio Collina Museum of Myth. He claimed that it had revitalised the city. Anyone who spent time in his company was used to grandiose claims. Collina once said the museum had helped bring peace to Europe.

"Collina's great legacy," *Repubblica* called the museum. "A jewel of the city... A noble example of philanthropy."

Hidden until now is a host of problems associated with the museum. They return us to the troubling personality and methods of Federico Collina. He built a Museum of Myth whose own history could be called mythical.

With Collina gone, it is urgently important to start asking questions about the museum.

How was the land acquired? Why did the museum get its own publicly funded road? What was the relationship between the museum and Collina S.p.A.? Why is the museum partly funded by the European Union? How were the statues acquired?

The answers should surprise no one who has followed the ruthless rise of Collina. The museum is built on corruption and fraud.

Melissa's frown deepened as she ran through the journalist's claims: that her father had bribed politicians; threatened them with even more job losses; dodged massive tax bills; misused company funds; and broken a contract with Ernesto's former employer.

Strazzo even attacked the EU funding. It had been one of her father's proudest achievements, a grant to all the city's museums from the European Union. "Further proof," Strazzo wrote, "that this so-called European project is a sham to prop up the elites."

Most importantly, Collina acquired his statues illegally.

At least 150 of the statues belonged to the state and should never have been in private hands.

On his death, Collina agreed that control of the museum would pass to the state. A copy of the agreement, made in 1984 and obtained from the ministry, confirms this.

But Collina's will overruled this agreement. It made control of the museum pass to his daughter, Melissa, and kept the statues under the ownership of the museum.

This ownership is a fraud. Why has the ministry not intervened? Why has the mayor remained silent? It may have something to do with the alleged sums donated by Collina to the political parties. (See the article in last week's business supplement.)

Federico Collina was ruthless and secretive. Even now, many of the sources for this article spoke on condition of anonymity.

But the time for secrecy is done. The museum has been built on lies. The trustees must explain.

It is time to return the statues to their rightful homes. If necessary, the mayor must close the Museum of Myth.

With the crushed newspaper still in one hand, Melissa hurried to the living room and called Ernesto's office. His secretary answered.

"Signor Battillo is in the conference room with our lawyers. I can get him, but he asked if you can join them."

"I am coming." She hung up and called Violetta's name. Her voice sounded to her high-pitched and breathless. "Ask Roberto to prepare the car," she said when the housekeeper came in. "I must go to the museum immediately." Violetta nodded, glancing at the newspaper. Melissa hurried to the garage and paced until Roberto arrived.

Her mind was racing as the car eased onto the road. She remembered meetings with her father, conversations she had barely understood, with the lawyers, with the old mayor. *Federico Collina was ruthless and secretive.*

"What else is true?" she asked out loud.

"Signora?"

"It's a lie about the EU money, because I helped apply for that. And we got the road because of... I can't remember. Ernesto will know. But what about the tax? And the statues. The journalist said – the statues were illegal..."

She recalled encounters with shifty men in Papa's study, each introduced as *mio fattore*: his agent. Crates had poured into the house, to Garda, to the warehouse of the Vicenza factory. Her father would come to see the crate opened, then he'd snap an order for where it should go. He seemed to care little for the work inside. Melissa and Claudio loved the warehouse, where scores of statues stretched out in military rows. While they ran between them, Papa would sit in the corner reviewing his accounts.

"It doesn't matter," she said, addressing the narrow streets racing past. "No one wants to see the museum attacked. This Signor Strazzo has a lot to learn about city politics. The last thing the mayor wants is a battle with us."

"Yes, *signora*..." Roberto kept his eyes on the road. He had long experience of her father's tirades, where any word other than a "yes" or "no" was liable to be attacked.

Melissa reflected on what she had said and her doubts returned; she had not even met this new mayor. At least Ernesto was waiting for her: he had served at the museum through eleven national governments and five mayors of Verona. Between him and the lawyer, they could surely deal with this article. She grew calmer and watched Roberto's bald brown head nodding, as if tied to the revolving wheels.

The car reached the river and the city opened around them. She caught a glimpse to their left of the medieval castle of Cangrande. Invisible behind were the Roman walls of Gallienus. And now, ahead on the hills, like a glittering jewel, stood the museum she had sworn to protect, the museum of Claudio Collina.

*

The photographers were waiting at the entrance.

"Melissa! Melissa! Signora Collina!"

They jumped around her; some fell over, others pressed against her; despite the bright sunlight, the flashbulbs tore at her eyes. Roberto was like a bull, pushing them away, shielding her as she walked straight-backed into the museum. A burly guard blocked the photographers from following. They continued to snap through the glass.

Melissa hurried down the main corridor, hands trembling. She tried to ignore the curious looks of staff and visitors. She was halfway along when she caught the eye of Gina, one of the cleaning staff.

"I am so sorry about this, *signora*," the thin woman said, waving as though she could clean away the *paparazzi*. "Are you all right?"

"Yes," Melissa said curtly and tried to brush past the cleaner, but the faint contact made her stop. "I'm sorry, my dear," she added. "How is your mother? Is she still in the hospital?"

"Yes, *signora*."

"They'll let her out soon."

Gina was shaking her head. "She's a tough one. The doctors can't wait to be rid of her." She looked towards the entrance. "But these monsters. They should leave you alone. I want to see them in hospital."

Melissa thanked her, nearly smiling as she pictured an even tougher version of the dour cleaner. She must remember to send flowers.

Ernesto's secretary was waiting on the mezzanine and led her to the large board room. An alcove at one end held the figurine of Mercury, the broad windows looked east over the hills. Three people sat around the oval table: Ernesto; a chubby woman dressed in black; and Signor Caspardi, the lawyer who had served the museum and her father for many years. They rose as Melissa entered.

"Good morning, *signora*," Caspardi said, intoning every word. His gaunt, bald features brought to her mind an aged Julius Caesar. He introduced his colleague as Signora Vetelli.

Ernesto's grey head turned and sunlight reflected off his glasses. "Are you all right," he asked.

"I'm sorry," she said. "It's just half the city's photographers are outside. What are you discussing?" The lawyers looked at each other. "Of course I've read the article. I meant, what response will we take?"

Ernesto gestured at Caspardi and they sat down. The lawyer unwound the thread clasping his leather binder and pulled his papers out one by one, reviewing the sheets while they waited in silence. Even her father had been patient with the legendary Caspardi.

"We have reviewed each point in Gianluca Strazzo's article," he said. "There are five questions raised about the museum, the land, statues, *et cetera*. The journalist," (he said the word as he might say *shit*), "has drawn many inferences and concluded many falsehoods. It should be possible to ensure at least a partial retraction."

"Excuse me," Melissa said. "Why only partial?"

"Signora Collina, please understand that I accuse your father of nothing. But there are only a few ways to achieve what he did."

"But you're not answering my question."

"Partial is not good enough," Ernesto growled, and Melissa felt grateful. He stabbed a finger at a copy of the article. "The mayor will use this. It's his doing. We have to fight every point."

Melissa frowned. What did he mean about the mayor?

Caspardi's thin hand extended towards Signora Vetelli, who spoke in a crisp voice. "The mayor held a press conference an hour ago. He said he is 'concerned' about the issues raised over the Museum of Myth, but is sure the 'shadow of suspicion' will prove just a shadow."

"Such a poet," Caspardi murmured.

Signora Vetelli continued. "He announced that an investigation would begin next week, to be led by Judge Paoli."

"That could lead to anything," Ernesto said. "I don't like it."

"I believe it is the best way to put such accusations to rest," Caspardi said. "The museum can draw on its friends on the municipality to ensure the findings are fair." Melissa was twisting her fingers under the table. "There's Signor Giorgi. Also that man – Davide something –"

"EXCUSE ME," Melissa called out. "What are you talking about? What do you mean, this is the mayor's doing?"

Caspardi exchanged a look with Ernesto. The director sighed and leaned onto the table, hand against his forehead, rubbing the skin. "Melissa..." he said and fell silent. She waited for him to continue, masking her anxiety with a stern expression.

"Two months ago," he said, "the mayor invited me into his office. He'd been mayor for, what, a month. He said he wanted the museum to relocate to somewhere else in the city. He would cover half the cost."

Melissa's face contorted in dismay. "What did you do?"

"I said no, of course. His first act was to close that bus station where the Roma were sleeping. It was part of his promise to clean up the city. Did he think the museum was a hiding place for immigrants? I told him to piss off. I didn't think of it again for four weeks."

"Six," Caspardi corrected. "It was a fortnight ago."

Melissa's turned to glare at Caspardi. *Everyone knew but her*!

"The mayor called me in again," Ernesto continued. "This time he was less polite. He said we must relocate, willingly, or he would make us do it. I said he'd need Atlas to move the building. Two weeks later, this article comes out."

"Why," Melissa asked quietly, "are you only informing me now?"

Ernesto's eyes were unblinking behind the glasses. "I thought both conversations were nonsense. Plus the first one happened five days after your father died."

She gave a disbelieving laugh. "And? I am the president. First, you do not speak to the mayor without my permission. Second, you do not keep me in the dark about it. You have acted without authority."

Ernesto's face hardened and the lines around his mouth grew taut. "I would have told you, madam president. But you've been impossible to speak to. Screaming at guards, sobbing in the Family Room. Six members of staff have come to me. This week, you told those schoolchildren, *Semele fucked Jupiter*. I tried to speak to you, but you wouldn't listen."

"Go on," she was saying, head shaking, "yes, yes, go on."

"Even now, you're not listening. How could I tell you? I thought it would go away. I was wrong. That's why I called you this morning."

The room was silent. They were all looking at her. Melissa pushed herself up from the table and leaned towards the lawyers.

"Signor Caspardi, it is clear that this problem has NOT gone away. There is a reason why my father never involved the museum director in such issues. Your judgment, too, has been appalling. My father taught me little, but there was one thing he said time and again. *You cannot rely on a politician's friendship, but you can trust in their greed.* You and the director have not tried to understand the mayor's motives, you have alienated him, and if I understand correctly, the outcome is this public relations assault. Now I must stop it. Tell me, in plain language: how serious are these accusations?"

Caspardi's bald head glinted with the sunlight. "The statues are a serious issue. There is a trail of agreements with the ministry. We were drafting a revised version when your father fell ill. The last minister was well aware, but technically, the old agreement remains, that the museum should transfer the relevant statues to state institutions."

"Which statues?" she demanded.

"I don't know. I would need to review your father's files."

"What about the other points? Corruption and bribery? The land? The road? The tax?"

Caspardi smiled thinly. "Your father was a great man, and great men have many ways to exert influence."

"I will see the mayor," Melissa said.

"I strongly advise against that."

But she was already turning away. Ernesto called her name but she continued out the door and towards his office. His secretary was at her desk. Teresa was a small, quiet woman in her forties; devoted to Ernesto, she had doubtless made no protest about being called in on a Saturday. Melissa preferred to manage her own diary.

"Please can you find the mayor for me," Melissa asked with exaggerated politeness, mindful of Ernesto's words. It was true that she had carried her grief in public these past weeks. But that was over. Today she had changed out of black.

Teresa tried the municipality and the mayor's home. She finally tracked him down to a restaurant in the city centre. His smooth voice apologised for being out of the office and suggested they meet at the municipality in the afternoon. "I apologise for the formality, but I must go there in any case." She agreed and hung up as Ernesto came in.

"Are you seeing him?" he asked.

She turned to Teresa. "Please inform Roberto of this meeting. He will take me at two thirty. I will eat lunch downstairs, in the cafeteria."

"Caspardi had some advice," Ernesto said. "We need to call our friends on the city council. You also need to... Melissa, please listen to me."

But she was going out the door. "Tell Roberto," she called over her shoulder to Teresa, "that I'm in the Family Room. I want to see if the director has at least listened to one of my instructions."

In the main corridor downstairs, she could see photographers still lurking by the entrance. The Family Room was opposite. It had been weeks since she had visited here, and sobbed, as Ernesto had put it. She would not sob today, nor call for advice. She was a Collina. Her strength came from her brother; this was his museum. No one could understand what that meant to her, especially not Ernesto, a man with no family. This morning she had planned to nominate him as president, but she saw that she had been too hasty, and now her freedom was one step further away.

*

Large white photographs punctuated the black walls of the Family Room. This was a place for history rather than myth; whenever Melissa came in here, she felt the troubles of her day were left at the entrance, discarded like a raincoat.

She stopped at a photograph of the rascals, her father and uncle, youths in dark shorts and buttoned-up shirts, trying to topple each other into the dirt. Claudio Senior was grinning like a clown while Federico frowned at the camera.

The next photograph showed her uncle, circa 1943, in the hills of Valpolicella, a half-starved partisan, only weeks from death, beaming with pride. A caption read:

Claudio sacrificed his life for others, and the cause of freedom. He emulated the tradition of heroes such as Theseus and Hercules. He took back from the Fascists the right for Italians to be proud of their ancient heritage.

Her brother, her own Claudio, used to boast how he was named after their hero uncle. Sometimes by the lake, instead of gods and heroes, they played at partisans and Nazis, reliving the stories they had been told. Melissa and Claudio could hide behind trees or benches, waiting till the right moment to jump out and go "POW!" Like all villains, the Nazis vanished when the game was over. Then only Mama and Papa were fighting, and the safest places in the world were by the lake or, when they were in Verona, under the white deckchairs of the atrium, where Dio would hold her hand and say, *It's ok,* Lissa. *The Furies are here. But they'll go away soon.* She called him Dio, her own name for him, a divine name – their private joke.

She shook her head and turned away from the first wall. In the centre of the room was a long display cabinet. She saw that it had been changed, as she had instructed: it now held her father's pistol, along with a typewriter and other artefacts from Federico Collina's history. Her father had tried to insist the museum was not about him; this was one argument Melissa had finally won.

At one end of the cabinet were mementoes of her brother, including model bridges from his time in London, and on the back wall, the original blueprint for the Museum. Its pencil marks gleamed under the spotlight.

Melissa walked around the cabinet to study the photographs on the other wall. Most of these were new, including a large one of her parents at their wedding. Her father's expression was sombre, but Mama's mouth curved strangely, as if she was about to laugh or cry. She was barely twenty-one, with a soft face and flowing long hair. Her eyes looked up towards her new husband.

The last picture was unchanged, a life-size photograph of Claudio. It was the only colour image in the room. It had been taken in London, perhaps in a park; there was a fountain behind him. It was a bright day, and his thick black hair reflected the sunlight. A blue collar rested above the elegant *V* of a turquoise sweater. His smile was a restrained version of their uncle's, and in the sunlight, he almost seemed happy. It was why they had chosen this photograph. But his eyes were like their mother's, dark and staring. They turned on Melissa and burrowed into her and asked questions that caused his crooked smile to waver. Eighteen years had passed and still she could not see this photograph without trembling.

"Melissa," a voice said quietly behind her.

She jumped. "Don't!" she yelled at Ernesto. She took a deep breath. "You frightened me."

The director stood beside her and studied the photograph. Traditionally he would not speak first, but she refused to break her silence, and finally he said, "I am sorry." She acknowledged this with a noise. "I see that I should have informed you earlier. I was trying to protect you."

"I don't need to be protected," she said. "And an apology is not enough. You mishandled this."

He folded his arms. "As you say, the mayor ought to have spoken to the president. To be precise."

"Precise?"

The stern face flickered. "Or accurate..."

She could not hide a smile. But she felt sadness as she recalled her earlier thought, that Ernesto could not become the president. He had proven himself unreliable, or worse, weak.

"Tell me," he said, pointing at her neck. "I've always meant to ask you about that."

Her hands reached for the necklace. "He made it for me," she whispered. She felt it running across her fingers like a snake as she unclasped it and handed it to him. He held it close to his glasses, inspecting it as a curator would. Its pieces were of marble, gold, silver, and a darker metal flecked with blues and yellows. Each was a different shape: a gold skull, silver lips.

"Unusual," Ernesto murmured. "What is this one?" He pointed at the hollow marble piece.

"I don't know. There are many that I can't recognise. But this," she pointed at a dark metal one, "is a tennis racket. I used to play. Papa – my father – made me play. So I think, maybe, these pieces have something to do with my life. But I don't know. Claudio didn't leave a blueprint for this work."

Ernesto's throat rumbled, a sound of understanding that recalled her memories that morning, of herself as a giddy youth, of him as a protector who had taught her that whispers could also be strong.

"You've looked after it well," he said. "Twenty years and you have protected it."

Now it was her turn to show she understood: she had also protected the museum. She tapped his hand lightly.

He held the pieces closer. "They are so delicate. I did not realise he had such a skill. And all in that tiny workshop by the lake. But..."

His forehead creased and she knew that he was thinking of Claudio's last day. She took the necklace back and studied it herself. Some of the pieces had been coated with a thin paint or lacquer to protect them, but over two decades, the silver ones had grown darker, and the delicate marble flower was chipped. She had otherwise preserved it well.

She looked up at his photograph and remembered that day she had visited him in the workshop. Lissa! *This is it*! *Completely new*! *Every room tells a myth*! They had fulfilled his dream. She had to protect it.

"I must see the mayor," she said.

"It is your decision, madam president." She nodded and Ernesto walked out.

She lingered a moment. Whenever she left the Family Room, she felt she still had more to learn. It was strange to think *learn*. But she had never forgotten Ernesto's words to her, *myths connect us to our heritage, to our ... families*. That moment's hesitation held all that she felt about her own family, trauma and joy, what remained, what was irretrievable. Their history was like a lacquer on the surface of her soul, and with each visit, she felt she grew one layer more of herself.

Sam: The Evidence

The filing cabinet in the master bedroom was made of grey aluminium. Its drawers opened with Sam's sharp, excited tugs. The top one held the family's current passports. Sam's photo made him look like an idiot: his mouth hung slightly open, his eyes were half-closed. He noted the stamps in his parents' passports: France, Germany. In Dad's were several tantalising blue ones for the USA, where he went for surgical conferences.

The older passports were in one of the brown boxes in the bottom drawer. His mum's photo showed a strange creature with giant hair swelling out of her head. Sam's imagination teased him as he looked at the stamps: had he gone with his parents to France when he was four? Had he rolled in vineyards, had he drunk in the romantic fumes, had he rolled past baby Isabelle and kissed her golden curls?

Anna had asked about postcards. He found a box labelled *Letters*, with postcards and envelopes arranged by year and bound with elastic bands; his mum was fanatically organised. Here was one from Europe – Florence – but it came from Nan and Granddad. *It is very hot. We ate lots of ice cream. There are violinists in the street.*

Sam considered Anna's next question, *Didn't Mum and Dad meet on a uni trip?* He remembered Nan's soft Yorkshire voice telling him a story about his parents dancing as students. He had found no diary or letters that might confirm this story, and could imagine neither of his stern parents on a dance-floor.

Anything you can find out about those early days would be relevant. Sam continued to dig through the drawers and the boxes. He found his mum's neat student folders; photos of Dad in his rugby kit and Mum by the sea; here were Mum's school notebooks, going all the way back to her childhood in Sennen, full of pages that had nothing to do with Europe:

Popular music
Music in the world today is very popular. Peeple like to listen to CANT BY ME LOVE. It is by a band called The Beetles. It means that if you love sumwun and you want them to love you you dont use money it like you do like a sweet in the shop. But the Beetles also have a song calld MONNEY and they say thats what I want. And I think maybe they shud sing one song

60

or the other song but not both. But I think the first song is better because love is speshal.

Sam had grown tired. He jotted down an inventory of what he'd found and began to replace the brown boxes, making sure they were in order as a good detective leaves no traces.

As he knelt, he glimpsed something odd at the back of the bottom drawer. He looked closer. There was a sliver of bright orange behind the brown boxes. He reached in and felt a soft material, like fabric. He banged his elbow as he tried to withdraw it. With a wiggle of his wrist, he managed to extract the strange object.

It was a thin orange box. A navy blue strip ran around the edge of the lid. In the middle was a tiny picture of a man beside a horse and carriage. Below it were the words:

HERMÈS
FAUBOURG SAINT-HONORÉ
PARIS

"Europe!" Sam said.

He opened the box. Inside was a cloth bag with the same logo that held a silk scarf. He felt something else in the bag, reached in and pulled out a leather box. *Boxes in bags in boxes*, he thought. This box held a slender gold bracelet. On it were stencilled the letters: *C – J.*

Sam sat down, cross-legged. A glint of sunlight bounced off the gold and he imagined Dad scowling in his rugby kit as he lifted Mum off the ground; now Chris produced a little box and Jennifer gasped when she opened it and saw the pretty bracelet, but... Sam frowned. His mum never wore jewellery, so why had Dad given it to her? No wonder this was buried in the bottom of the cabinet. If Sam ever gave Isabelle gifts, they would be things she actually wanted, and her name would come first in the inscription: *I – S.*

He returned the items to the bag and saw that the orange box also held a large envelope. The paper had yellowed, the address was handwritten in blue ink:

Jennifer Carter
Bartholomew Road

Oxford OX4
ENGLAND

That was Grandma Carole's address. The stamp was pink and white, with a tiny picture of a castle above the word *ITALIA*. The flap had been sealed shut with tape. Sam opened it carefully and found inside a stack of yellowing pages. The first began *Dearest one*, which struck Sam as odd – it was not Dad's style. He shuffled through and suddenly froze. The fifth page was in Italian. So were the rest. His eyes grew wide. Did Anna know about this? She couldn't! Sam beamed. How pleased would Anna be?

He put the letter to one side, for the orange box was still not empty. Beneath the envelope was a black and white photograph of three people: Mum, Dad, and a dark-haired man. The two men flanked Mum, with their arms around her shoulders. They were dressed for a party. Dad held a mask in his hands, his hair was combed and he wore a bulging black suit that made him look almost respectable. Mum looked even odder: she was in a long dress, one arm dangling, the other rising to her cheek, her eyes half shut, her lips half-smiling. The second man looked foreign. His hair was black and his eyes were dark. He was not smiling like the other two. His suit fitted him perfectly. He looked...

The front door of the building slammed and Sam gave a start. He rammed shut the cabinet, shoved the items into the box, and ran with them back to his room. His heart was thundering. He listened for Mum but the flat remained silent. He laughed. Why had he been so nervous? These were old things.

But they had been buried. Hidden. Secret. They had the smell of a case.

He took the letter out again. He pushed the box under his bed, checking that it was not visible from the doorway. Then he put the letter on his desk and began to read.

Verona, 11th December 1980
Dearest one,
"you who led me into love",
It is a day since I returned home. A day since I left you. I dreamed last night, a dream like eagles that tear at my heart.
I cannot live without you, Jenny.

AAAAAH. When I try to say the things I feel – they come out false, or plain. I am burning with fire, but I don't know how to say it. This is not my language, but even in my language, I could not say:

I hate you.

Odi et amo...

Do you want to laugh? A man on the flight home took pity on me and pressed grappa into my hand. So I was drunk when I came into the arrivals lounge. My mother and sister were crying and laughing as they gave me a hero's return; I felt sick. My father was at home. He has plans for me, he said. I did not speak, fearing what the grappa might say.

I never did tell you about my family. But I wrote it down... Yes... But never shared it...

When my father finished, I went to my bedroom. I closed the door and cried for hours. My mind cleared and I saw you, your curls, the wrinkling of your nose, your crooked hands, your amber eyes. My face mimicked yours, how your smile shifts as you choose to be serious or playful. I pictured you in scrubs, in jeans, in that green dress from the ball.

(The ball we met? The ball we parted? I think it was the same dress. You would do that: rip up my last joyful memory.)

I heard your words. "This is love, what else could it be?" I heard you whisper, "Come back to bed." I heard you say, "NO."

I sighed, and cried more, and finally fell asleep.

I dreamed.

My dreams last night were blurred, no doubt in part by grappa. In the morning, my head hurt and my breath was short. I was in a new terrain, colourless as grappa, bitter, a gift like Pandora's.

There is no comfort in my dreams, but how can I bear to be awake?

12th December

Night-time. Two days since I left you.

Last night, the dream, again.

This morning, I wanted to be alone but my father summoned me to the actuator plant. I am to work there next week. After that, "we shall we see what we shall see." My father's phrases are as hollow as the actuators, as the secret drawer in my desk where I hide these words. As empty as your promises to me. We once made typewriters, but my father sold that division. Now we make hollow valves, works of industry. I hate the factory. Do I hate you?

You often asked about my family. I tried to answer you, but it was with words on paper that you never saw and now never will. You could not have understood them, for they were in Italian. I planned to translate, or find a translator. I planned so much.

It is not your fault. You do not know the pain my family cause me, how I thought you saved me. No, it is not your fault: that I thought, because of you, I was safe, and happy, forever.

These stupid English phrases. Why can I not SAY it, say how I feel?

Say what IS your fault. What you and Chris did. Your betrayal. Your hatred for me. The pain you caused me. You have shattered my heart, so how do I continue to breathe?

It is too much, this jar is full, it has to spill.

The dream is coming: it looms above me; I am Vulcan, you are Venus, HE is Mars, my parents and all the gods dance around me, taunt me, as the gods taunted Vulcan. The dream ends with Vulcan hobbling through black streets. He stares at his hands, he feels the waterfall of Venus's hair on his fingers. He comes to the edge of the darkness, he looks down. A rip, a scream, and the image shatters, the gods vanish.

I am alone and awake, and wondering: was that cry mine, or Vulcan's?

13th December
And if we were gods, would we suffer?
A resolution. A decision. I begin – today.

11th January
Dearest one,
I told you once that Vulcan could make anything in his forge. Yes, anything but happiness.

Some years before I went to England, I built my own forge on the shore of Lake Garda. It became my refuge, and has been since I returned with courage three weeks ago, the day I wrote the words above. I had dreamed of bringing you here and showing you the lake and the mountains, the snow-white church and the restaurants where you can eat fish until you burst and drink Valpolicella the colour of blood. It was courage to visit a place so full of your absence.

My English has improved? Truthfully, I cannot bear to write another sentence, but I will try once more, as I must explain to you my decision. The rest is in Italian.

When I came into the workshop, I found the room was dusty, my red cabinet and worktop untouched. I don't know why I am sharing this with you. Do you care about the firestone and grate, the anvil, the oven? The acids in these bottles, what tools are on the rack: the files, tweezers and saws?

I pulled out a hammer and began to strike an iron scrap. I struck with misery and then with rage. Sweat poured through my shirt.

I did not notice my sister until I heard her footstep close behind. (Only she has not haunted my dreams.) I pretended not to notice her but she touched my back and I stopped. Feeling dizzy, I sat down on the wooden bench.

"Are you all right?" she asked. "Have you been sleeping?"

"No," I said.

She played with the grey fabric of her dress. Her fingers are so restless, always moving. "It's funny, you were only gone a year, but it feels longer. Why are you not sleeping?"

"Nightmares," I said.

She sat on the floor, her dress sprawling across the dust. She has stopped playing tennis and begun to lose her tan, and she may become as pale as you, but her eyes remain dark, her hair black and long as night.

"No one came here when you were away," she said, running her fingers on the floor. "Papa wanted Roberto to tidy it but Mama refused and, you know, she was ill. I'm so glad you're back."

"Really," I said.

Her mouth drooped and her fingers gave a sequence of painful jerks. "But you're here," she said. "You came back because you wanted to be here. So be happy! Don't be wretched like this!" And suddenly she smiled: she is like the sky, clouds and rainbow all in one minute. She rose from the floor, hands never leaving her lap. "Tell me a story?" she said. When I shook my head, she said, "Why don't you make something?"

I too stood up, furious that I could not share my distress with her: my sister is fragile, jealous, I cannot open my heart to her. I wrote her banal letters from London that never mentioned you, still she did not answer. All our lives, I have protected her. Now I spoke harshly: "I can make any THING."

She tried to touch me but I stepped away. Her voice rose. "Don't make a thing. Make a... I don't know. Make a work of love. Put yourself into it. Put love. Please look at me."

I screamed at her. "You DON'T understand, you DON'T care. Just for yourself. GO AWAY! GET OUT!"

She ran to the door and fumbled with the handle. When she was out, I beat at my legs until they were numb. Only I can hurt Melissa the way I do, for only I can protect her.

I began to pace. I could hear the voices of children in the distance. I pictured them running by the lake, in thick coats and black shoes. My sister and I used to crack the frost on the shore. Does your Cornish sea ever freeze? Do you know what it is to touch the cold waters and find them warmer than your blood?

December is a time for heartbreak.

I stopped and held my breath. The forge shuddered with each heartbeat. I felt that I was facing backwards in time. My past was frozen in a sequence of images, like beads, if only I could string them together...

I remembered how, when Vulcan suffered, still he worked. He once made a necklace.

Inside my red cabinet I kept a chain of platinum. I found it wrapped in velvet. I began to work.

That was three weeks ago. The days since have blurred between factory and home and the drives in between, and whenever I could, this workshop where I am writing this now, where your necklace is nearly complete.

It is a necklace of history, its pieces are the fragments of myself, and you, that I give you to preserve. The charms are small, of gold and silver and titanium to represent my metallic family, and marble, whittled with care, to capture our joy and suffering in London.

You asked me once, "Why do you care about myths?" I did not answer because we were in love and I didn't want to speak about hate. I can tell you now that I care – in fact, my sister and I care – because our family caused us to care, our mother in particular – to care and to suffer, to love and to hate. I thought that you would bring me relief, and escape. But I did try to answer you in London, with words on paper; I called this my 'Cosmogony'.

We parted before I could share it with you. I have it here, but it will not interest you, so I will give it to my mother. She called my idea for a Museum of Myth idiotic, but she may enjoy these stories. They are about her and my family, the sorts of stories my sister and I used to exchange when I was studying in Bologna; but I cannot share these with Melissa: they are too true, too painful.

Enough. I am nearly done. The necklace is almost complete.

For you, I have written another tale, which I finished this morning. It is the true story of Vulcan: how he came to England, befriended Mars, loved Venus. How he was betrayed by both.

I know you did not want to learn my language, but I apologise, it is in Italian as I had to be sure of my words. You may not want to find a translator, you may not read it; I don't care if you never read it. More accurately, if you do not translate it, I will never know.

I send the words first, so you can anticipate what comes next: the necklace. I will send it when I finish it.

It is my best work.

It is the last.

It is yours.

C.V.C.

Melissa: Afternoon

The municipal building was near the centre of the city. An attendant led her up the wide marble stairs to the mayor's office. It was an airy room, with parquet flooring and a large wooden desk. Motes of dust danced around a sunlit bust of the Emperor Valerian. Her father had donated it to the municipality in the time of the last mayor.

The current mayor got up from behind his desk as she entered. He wore a black suit that failed to disguise his bulky frame.

"Signora Collina, it is a sincere pleasure to meet you finally." He smiled with the awkwardness of a politician, uncomfortable meeting only one person at a time. His bulbous face had none of Valerian's military strength. "Please sit. I have prepared us coffee – even the mayor must make his own coffee on a Saturday." She sat down, thinking how soft his voice was. She had only ever heard him declaiming at full volume on the television and radio: *one party for one people*! "First, I must offer my condolences for the loss of your father. How often do we hear, after a man's passing, *we will never see his like again*? In your father's case, it is hard to believe that someone of such accomplishment ever existed."

"Thank you," she said, and smiled. "My father certainly lived a full life."

"That is an understatement, *signora*. But I do not mean to correct you. Who knows a man better than his own daughter?"

"Do you have children?" she asked. His sing-song voice irritated her.

He nodded gravely. "Three beautiful children, two boys and a girl. The girl knows me best of all. She's the one who says, *Papa, I think you need to make the schools better*. How old do you think she is? Six! Yes, the girls know their fathers best."

Melissa joined in his head-shaking. She noticed again the bust of Valerian. The marble brow was furrowed, as if the dead emperor disapproved.

"My father was content at the end," she said. "He died knowing that his legacy was assured. It was all he wanted, to benefit the city, as well as to honour his family."

The mayor smiled, teeth gleaming white, his cheeks swelling up around his nose. "Oh, the Museum of Myth is a jewel of this city! How many visitors did we have last year?"

"Close to thirty thousand."

"Thirty thousand. Astonishing. I remember when they were building it. Months and months of work on the hills, and then, finally – incredible! I was a young journalist then. The newsroom was buzzing with excitement. And you, *signora*, you must have been a student? It was... I am sorry – several years after your brother had died. You loved him very much?"

"Yes," she said, fingers brushing her necklace. "I'm curious to know, Mayor, which is your favourite room?"

He spread his arms. "I like all of them! Ulysses, Hercules, Romulus and Remus... All magnificent stories. Oh, but..." His smile faded. "There is a new myth in town. Or a rumour, that the museum is under a shadow. A question about its future. This article by Signor, ah..."

"Strazzo is a non-entity," she said. "His article is nothing. The usual gossip and slander." She took a sip of coffee.

"That is very good. So you are writing to the newspaper? They will retract it?"

"We are looking at various options."

"You must not let these paperboys play with you. I can tell you from my days there, once they begin, it can be hard to stop them. They run with stories. They look for more. They grow vicious." The flesh on his face seemed to tighten as he stared at her. Then he broke into a smile. "But come, who am I teaching? You are the daughter of Federico Collina. You grew up seeing your name in the newspaper every morning!"

"Indeed," she murmured. Near the window was a campaign poster of the mayor. He was surrounded by grinning children. They were attractive, with white or olive skins, glistening hair and immaculate white shirts. The mayor stood in the middle, arms engulfing several of them. She suddenly imagined him as the Emperor Tiberius, who had made slave-children nibble on his testicles in a pool in Capri. She looked back at the mayor. He was sipping his coffee. She smiled politely.

"I think you are quite right, *sindaco*. The newspapers will never stop once they have caught a whiff of scandal." He was nodding. Her voice grew sharper. "This is why it is so important for people like us to be allies. Scandals are – unpredictable. They can spread in all sorts of directions."

The mayor leaned forwards, hands on his desk, his high voice growing excited. "Melissa – if I may call you that – I entirely agree! You must come to me with any problems. Any! There are such sensitive matters in the article. I have actually felt compelled to calm this by calling for an inquiry." He looked up from his thick fingers. "Of course, that will put the matter to rest. We must get on with our lives! You have good lawyers, I am sure?"

"Caspardi," she said.

"Very good." He did not sound pleased. The old Caesar-like figure had a formidable reputation, and for a moment she was glad and could forget that he had helped Ernesto.

The mayor continued as if recalling a distant memory. "As you look at ways to quash these rumours, I wonder if you have considered all possible approaches. I recall meeting your father some years ago. We were speaking about the many depressed sites around the city, and how they would benefit from tourism. It is tragic to see how many of these areas have been taken over by aliens." He took off his jacket, slinging it over the back of his chair and revealing an expensive white shirt. "Please excuse me, but it is so hot. The problem exists even in the city centre. Verona attracts many talented people, but many more who come only to leech off us. Do we really want impoverished gypsies begging outside Saint Zeno's church and living like primitives in tents? If this is the European dream, I am afraid it resembles more a nightmare, or a myth." She did not reciprocate his smile. "Every citizen of Verona should be safe to walk in every part of the city. A simple demand, but not easy to implement. So, you see, your father and I talked about relocating the museum."

Melissa frowned as if confused. "What did my father think of that? The museum is so well-situated. It was part of the design."

The mayor raised his hands. He had gold cufflinks on his sleeves. "True, true. Part of your brother's design, I believe?"

"Yes."

"In honesty, I can't remember Signor Collina's reaction at the time, but I know that he was insistent that we speak again. Unfortunately, the opportunity never arose. By the time I became mayor, he was...ah, unwell."

Melissa took another sip of coffee. She remembered her father shortly before he went to hospital, still railing against the new mayor's party. "Racist bastards. They hate the south. They hate Europe. What am I? A southerner, a Europe-lover, employer of Poles and Tunisians. Bastards won't get a lira from me."

The mayor was watching her, his soft face growing mournful. "I must ask you, *signora*. They tell me I am not the most attractive man in the world, but here I am with my three children. You are, if I may say, a beautiful woman. But I understand you are not married?"

She put her cup down. She crossed her arms. The marble frown of Valerian seemed to deepen. "Correct," she said.

"Please excuse me. I am only thinking how it must be hard to face such attacks. I mean, being on your own."

"Ernesto Battillo is looking after this issue."

"Ah, yes, the director is an excellent man. A little stubborn, perhaps, but excellent."

She gave a rueful smile, to show she was not offended, and to say, *you and me, mayor, we know the world.* She studied his shirt, the cufflinks, the silver penholder on his desk.

"Stubborn can also mean a lack of vision," she said. "The leader of the city should think bigger. The museum's location is more than a luxury. Its presence reminds the Veronese of their classical heritage, and is essential to the design. I wonder, *sindaco*, if there are other ways to help you redevelop the outer parts of the city?"

He gave a business-like frown. "This is an excellent question. It ultimately comes to the issue of finance. The hills, you see, are of great value to Verona. If they are empty, I mean."

Melissa pretended to think. "I see. Though it is impossible to build on the hills."

"Impossible," the mayor agreed.

"But then, impossible usually means very expensive. I suppose some developers would be willing to pay a great deal to obtain a licence?" The mayor's face remained placid, but his eyes narrowed slightly and she saw that her instinct was right. "I wonder... The museum has given considerably to the city, but I sometimes feel it could do more. I mean, financially."

"Financially..." the mayor murmured.

"Yes. A gift, perhaps for the municipality to manage, to help restore those struggling areas of the city. Perhaps you, *sindaco*, would be able to administer it?"

"What order of gift did you have in mind?"

She had prepared her answer. "I believe fifty million lira would be of help to the city," she said.

"Is that so?" the mayor sneered. His face lost its soft deference and grew tight again as his eyes danced across her, face to chest to face. "It seems to me that while the museum is under such a shadow, it must do everything it can to build the people's trust."

"We have the education programme. We offer discounts to local citizens. And –"

"You surprise me," the mayor said. He stood up and walked to the window, shifting the poster so that he could look outside. He turned back to her. "As you know very well, what you are offering is nothing, barely a hundredth the value to the city."

Melissa felt the room close around her. "The museum is not a wealthy institution."

"Unlike you, *signora*?"

"No... It's too much..." She stammered and fell silent.

She had gone through the will a month ago. "Is that all there is?" she had asked Caspardi, who had answered, "There is a great difference between what the world believes about Federico Collina, and the reality." Most of the money had been sunk into the museum, enough to keep it running in perpetuity – and not enough to pay what the mayor was demanding.

"This is illegal," she said.

"REALLY?" he barked and strode back to the desk. The soft face was completely gone. His mouth had curved into a grimace and his teeth were out. "A moment ago you said it was impossible." He sat down with a thump of his fists on the desk. "The museum is accused of illegality. We can pursue that. Or we can reach an agreement. It is your choice, *signora*. The museum, frankly, means nothing to me. It's not even a real museum. It is your father's vanity project, named after your brother. No one cares about it. Thirty thousand visitors? I could speak to that many people in a year! I wonder at your hesitation."

He leaned back, running a hand through his black hair. She looked around his office and saw the poster of the happy white children.

"Let me tell you a myth," she said. "It is one almost all ancient civilisations share." He frowned. "Long ago there lived a race of beautiful humans. They were golden-skinned and white-teethed. They lived in perfect harmony with each other. Then one day, a sin was committed, and the race of gold were wiped away. The gods regretted this and created our present race, the race of bronze, which is weak and ugly, and would not have survived were it not for fire."

"Thanks be to Prometheus," the mayor said.

72

"As it happens, this is a myth that we continue to believe. In every generation, men believe that there was, long ago, a golden age. One, for example, when Italy was peopled only by fair-skinned natives, not a land swamped by blacks and gypsies. Those who tell such myths often present themselves as descendants of the race of gold. They appear so pure and innocent that people look up to them as gods, or politicians."

Little dimples formed in the mayor's swollen cheeks. "Was this one of your brother's myths? I hope you will allow me to visit the museum, before it is closed, to remind myself of it."

"My point is rather different. A myth is something made-up, for a purpose. Like a lie. Now, lies can end up hurting their teller. You mentioned you were a journalist, and I understand Strazzo used to work for you. What further links can we find? Who is interested in a development on the hills? What will it cost them to get it? All this is newsworthy. It would be a pity to lose a new mayor so quickly into his administration. As I said at the beginning, I hoped we could be allies."

The mayor gave a resigned shrug. "If that is how you wish to be, *signora*, when all I am trying to do is help the city, then so be it. It seems we both have plenty to reflect on." He stood up. "Meanwhile, I hope that the inquiry will treat you with courtesy next week."

She picked up her bag and stood as well. She was satisfied. She had not expected to reach an accommodation with the mayor. Now she understood his motive: simple corruption, a desire to be bribed. The large man walked ahead of her and leaned against his thick door as she approached. His eyes danced over her.

"You have surprised me twice today," he said as he offered his hand. It was fleshy and damp. She pried hers away.

"Oh?"

"The first time was with the pittance you offered. The second is your talk of allies and enemies. You sound as if you feel quite safe. I'd have thought someone in your position would not want too much attention. Your family history stinks of scandal, and the journalists have barely begun. Let's see if I can remember. Your father's first wife died in an alleged accident with a pistol. Your mother died from alleged alcohol abuse. Your brother..." Her skin grew cold and she felt faint; one hand darted to her necklace and she forced herself to stand upright, facing the mayor, eyes glittering. "So many myths in the world," he said. "Journalists love myths. We love to take them apart and put them back together in new ways that we can print and call the truth. Do you know that there is new evidence about your brother's death?"

"These made-up stories are –"

"Oh, but that relentless journalist Strazzo has spoken to the company that manufactured the ventilators. They conducted an audit at the time. Apparently, *signora*, there was no malfunction. So, how did he die, exactly? Might he have – whisper it – killed himself? The scandal!"

"Lies," she said firmly.

"Yes, so many stories we could print. I can see the series now: the life and lies of the Collinas. They'll camp outside your house, night and day, Signora Collina, for the rest of your life, they'll haunt you and whatever peace you hoped to have. *Buona sera*," he called as she pushed her way out and hurried down the stairs.

Roberto was waiting outside. "Are you all right, *signora*?" he asked as she sank into the back seat. "Do you want me to drive us home? Or I can get you something to drink?"

"HOME, Roberto!"

"Yes. Sorry."

She took deep, shuddering breaths. "No, I'm sorry. Please, just, home."

The engine hummed. As they sped down the winding streets, she seized control of her thoughts. This man was a journalist and a politician; a liar in a liar's suit. She knew the truth of her family's history: she and no one else was the curator of that history – not the mayor, not any journalist smelling of shit.

What was more, Melissa knew how she would defend the museum. As Roberto drove on, the mayor's bulbous face slowly transformed into the frowning bust of Valerian, and she gave a grim smile.

But then she recalled the history of that emperor. His son was Gallienus, who had built the walls of Verona. Gallienus also had a son, and at one point, all three ruled the empire together. Then the young prince had died, followed by his grandfather, and Gallienus was left alone, surrounded by his enemies. Melissa wrapped her arms around herself and shivered.

Sam: The Suspect

Sam waited two days before reporting to Anna. First he typed up what he had read, for a detective must be prepared and methodical.

The letter was undoubtedly the best thing he had ever found in his parents' bedroom.

It was mysterious: who was C.V.C.? (He pictured the dark-eyed man in the photograph.)

It was sexy: the references to gods fed Sam's fantasies of Isabelle.

Best of all, it met Anna's requirements: it had something to do with their parents, or at least their mum, and it had a connection to Europe.

After he had finished typing up the English, he turned to the Italian pages. These were divided into sections, each with a heading, the first of which was *Casco*. He began to type. There were easier ways to get them to Anna, but these cost money, and he would not risk exposure to his mum, who had hidden the orange box and its strange letter. How, he wondered, had she read the Italian parts?

Typing in Italian proved trickier than English. There were double consonants – *ss*, *cc*, *zz* – which helped with speed, but he couldn't work out how to make a *ù* or *è*, and had to hope Anna would understand without the accents. When he tested himself in English he got 75 words per minute. Getting closer, Fred!

When he had finished the first section, he wrote to Anna.

Hi Anna!

I investigated and found passports, postcards, uni folders, photographs. I put details in this spreadsheet like you showed me.

But I don't think Mum and Dad met while travelling.

It took me so long to reply because I found something. It's an old letter to Mum, I don't know who sent it. It's really long and most of it's in Italian!

I thought you'd be interested so I typed up the first pages for you.

Love, Sam

He did not mention the other items in the orange box, the handmade bracelet, the silk scarf, the photograph. They were his evidence and would help Sam answer his own investigation: who was the man with the dark hair?

Anna replied several hours later.

First, great work, detective.
Second, like the spreadsheet. Exactly what I wanted.
Third, this story is very interesting, thank you muchly. Send the rest?
Your typing is brilliant, by the way!
Love from Par-eee!
ana

Brilliant! His sister was pleased. He pulled out the letter and continued to type. The Italian words danced before him and he mouthed the titles each time he reached a new one: *Casco, Tulipano, Serpente*. An hour passed, and another. He made himself a sandwich. As he typed, patterns began to emerge, repeated words or names: *Chris* and *Venere* and *Vulcano*. He recognised the first word; the last one also seemed familiar to him.

In Anna's bedroom was a colourful book called *Gods and Myths of the Ancient World*. A glowing half-naked woman appeared: Venus, the goddess of beauty. Here was a burly fellow with a helmet, the god of war. And this painting of a man with a hammer, surrounded by fire and metal, was Vulcan, *Vulcano*, whom the ancient Greeks had called –

Hephaestus.

Sam stared outside. The road swayed and blonde curls wreathed the window. His skin tingled as he thought of the last lesson of term, of War and Love and Isabelle Fabron.

He had to know what the Italian words said.

Hi Anna,
Cool that it's interesting.
What does the Italian stuff say? I'm really curious to read it.
Love, Sam

He continued to type until evening, when his mum knocked on the door. He quickly switched off the monitor and grabbed the nearest book – *Farewell, My Lovely*. A curly silhouette appeared in the doorway, framed by the red sunlight coming in from Anna's bedroom.

"Have you eaten?" asked his mum.

"Yeah," he said, eyes blurry from constant staring at the screen.

"Have you gone out at all?"

"'Course," Sam said.

His mum sighed and disappeared. Sam got up and closed his door.

He continued to type, listening for her tread around the flat lest she appear and discover what he was actually doing. He continued nervously for a couple of hours, jumping up again when he heard her approach. But she didn't come in, just yelled from behind the closed door, "Go to sleep!" The whole year she hadn't once told him to go to sleep, but here he was in the middle of the summer holidays and she was telling him to sleep. Anna would call it *typical*. She and Sam's mum were locked in a perpetual war whose battles sometimes dragged him in.

"In a minute!" he yelled back, struggling to type *improvvisamente*.

Now there was silence in the flat, but for the clicking of his keyboard. Sam typed until he felt cross-eyed, until his mind drifted from his body and he felt himself swimming through Italian words. He could not, later, explain the satisfaction he gained that night from typing a phrase like *una porte dolcemente chiusa*. His fingers were dancing figures before him, and the words raced across the screen, words he did not understand.

Finally his eyes were streaming into the darkness and he staggered to bed. He dreamed of words ending in *o* and *i*. When he awoke, his mum had gone and he immediately resumed his typing. He was possessed by spirits, of *Venere* and *Vulcano*, and at three minutes past three in the afternoon, he finished the letter.

"YES!" he yelled, then looked around as if someone else had just spoken.

He sent Anna an email with all that he had typed, thinking how pleased she would be with him, and wandered to the living room for a dazed nap.

Later that evening, he was swaying above his bed when his computer gave an unfamiliar ping. He turned to it and saw that his instant messenger was flashing. It was Anna!

blackeyedpoet
u online?

1093682
HI!!!

blackeyedpoet
hi from Ghent

1093682
:-)

blackeyedpoet
Knackered. Su's out. I'm resting.
THANK YOU SO MUCH
Got yr email. Typing really good!

1093682
is it about gods?

blackeyedpoet
yeah, a little. Boring classics stuff. Tell you when I'm back.
That's all of it, right?

1093682
Yes! Typed everything! Does it not make sense? Can you translate for
me?

blackeyedpoet
think it makes sense.
I'll tell you about it when back

1093682
need to read it now, for an investigation

blackeyedpoet
I can't translate the whole thing, Sam!

1093682
please

blackeyedpoet
I'm travelling!!!

1093682
Mum can lend me money to translate

blackeyedpoet
idiot
don't speak to her about it
maybe I can do it

1093682
Ok

blackeyedpoet
is Mum going on her course? Is she sending a babysitter?

1093682
Yeah

blackeyedpoet
spoken to Dad?

1093682
no

blackeyedpoet
Gotta go. xx

Sam groaned. He didn't want Anna to call him *idiot* and he didn't want her to be secretive and contradictory. In her email, she'd said the pages (she called them a "story") were *very interesting*. In this exchange, she said they were *boring*.

He rubbed his groggy eyes. Then he gave an evil grin. One thing was clear from Anna's behaviour: she didn't want him to speak to their mother.

Hi Annie, nice to "chat"!
Maybe you can find time to translate. I won't speak to Mum about it
for now
Love, Sam

If she wanted him to do things, she had to give him what he wanted. This was the way detectives did business.

Meanwhile, he had two other avenues to pursue.

First, he would trace out all the gods whose names he had typed. He would work out their connections with Anna's book of myths. Venus was the wife of Vulcan, who was the son of Juno, who was the wife of Jupiter, who was the father of Mars... Thus Sam pieced together a genealogy.

Next, he would not disobey a direct command from his sister, but it was clear that he had to speak to his mum: only she could explain who C.V.C. was. He'd have to make an interrogation.

His mother had gone off to a conference and left him in the charge of Maria, a large black lady with a Caribbean accent who smiled a lot and cooked delicious spicy food. She called him Sam, not "Sammy", and took him to the cinema. Her deep laughter bounced inside of him and tickled like the summer breeze, and Sam wished she would stay longer.

Then his mum returned from the conference. She had rung ahead to ask if he could prepare supper, so he cooked spag bol, just the way Anna had taught him, with garlic and smoky bacon from the grocer "and a sprinkle of parsley when you serve it." Mum came home in her posh grey suit, and showered and changed into jeans and a white t-shirt. Sam had arranged everything to perfection: the blue crockery, a glass of water each, a glass of wine for Mum (he had tasted a little), napkins carefully folded, and the steaming pot in the centre, ready for serving.

"Looks lovely," Mum said and they began to eat. Her curly hair was raggedy and still wet from the shower. The skin under her eyes was dark.

"So you liked Maria?" she asked.

"She's nice," Sam said. "She took me to see a movie."

"Which one?"

He'd promised Maria he wouldn't tell his mum about *South Park*, which was rated 18. "*Big Adventures*," he said, making up a name.

"I heard that's good."

So far, so normal. Sam had eaten alone often with his mum in the past year, while Anna studied late with friends and Dad was at work. These were conversations of few words, half-attended, mainly about school.

"When does your report card come?" she asked.

He shrugged. "Dunno. Later in the summer."

She nodded, a faint movement. Her eyes were on her half-finished plate. It was time for Sam to begin.

"Mum..." He waited for her to look up. Slight red veins in the eyes. Pinched mouth, as if the food was too salty. "I miss Anna."

"Oh, sweetie, I miss her too."

"Can we join her?"

One brown eyebrow rose and his mum looked her most doctor-like and professional. "Do you think she'd be pleased to see us coming over the horizon?"

He joined in her smile. "Yeah. I guess not. But it would be nice to see some of those places. Like, she's going to Florence. Did you see her itinerary?"

His mum nodded, unmoved, and turned her attention back to her food. Italy wasn't going to trigger anything in her. He tried a new approach. "Mum..." She nodded. "Can I go to a dermatologist?"

One lip curled up in a withering expression. "Why?"

"Cos my skin's bad, it's got sebum production."

She snorted. "It's very mild acne, Sam. You don't need a dermatologist."

He looked down. "You'd take Anna."

A pause. "I'll think about it," she said and sipped her wine.

He spoke more brightly. "Actually, it's also cos I'm curious to meet more doctors. Cos you know medical school? What was it like? I'm thinking about maybe being a doctor."

The room seemed to grow warmer and his mother more fragile. Her eyes narrowed and her mouth flickered between a smile and a frown.

"I'm curious," he continued. "About what it was like and if you liked it. I mean, was it hard?"

"Of course it was hard," she snapped.

"I know. I meant, like, was it good. Did you enjoy it?"

"How did this idea come up?"

He shrugged. "Just did."

Her eyes danced over his face. Her mouth was still flickering and now her hand moved to her hair, a gesture that reminded him of the photograph, where she'd been dressed for a party. His mum's eyes drifted above him, and the silence grew until Sam felt uncomfortable. Then she put down her fork and her voice was sharp.

"It is work, Sammy. Eight hours of lectures and practicals, five days a week. This is on average, there are harder weeks. Plus four or five hours of studying on top of that. Twelve hours a day, with more studying on

81

weekends. So, yes, it is hard." Her voice lost its edge. "But don't worry. You don't have to make a decision for some time."

"Yeah, that's good, because that sounds like a lot of work."

She started eating again.

"Were there, like, parties?" he said. "Things like that? Like balls."

"Balls?" she repeated. Her fork seemed to hover in the air. She was looking past him. He turned around and saw the blank wall.

"Mum?" he prompted. "Parties?"

"Oh." She shook her head and started rolling her fork through the spaghetti. "Yes. There were parties, I suppose. I didn't go to many."

"Did Dad?"

"I don't know, Sam. You can ask him."

"Oh. Ok."

She leaned forwards. "There's a lot to discover at university. But it's miles away. You've got plenty to enjoy at school."

"Yeah. Guess so." He saw that her plate was empty. "Um... Mum?"

"More cross-examination?" But she was smiling.

"Did you have any boyfriends before Dad?"

Her smile froze. "Why?"

"I'm just trying to talk." He put enough hurt and pleading into his voice that she couldn't avoid looking at him. Now he smiled warmly, to show that she could trust him. He said, "You know how Anna was with Jason and then she broke up with him and now she's kind of interested in Harry? So I was wondering, is that how it goes?"

"Yes," she murmured.

It sounded like this was all she would say. He was racking his brain for more questions when she continued more warmly.

"As you say, Anna was with Jason, and that didn't go very well did it? Well, I had the same thing. I had a boyfriend before your dad. Actually, I met your dad through him. That's how it goes sometimes."

Sam nodded wisely. "What was his name?"

"Claudio."

Sam nodded again.

His mum seemed relieved. She took a deep breath and stood up.

"Right. I'm exhausted. I won't have dessert. Thank you for a lovely supper. It was *de-licious*."

She winked at him and spun on her foot, almost frivolous. Sam had a sudden impression of her dressed for a ball, dancing, laughing. Was it true? Had his mother once been young?

He was still smiling when he realised that her plate remained on the table. She hadn't tidied it away. That was extremely unusual. It was odd for his mother to leave a mess.

So Sam gathered it up: the dirty plates, the half-empty glass, thinking, *Hail, Claudio*.

Melissa: Night

At home, Melissa called the lawyer, Caspardi.

"We cannot reach an accommodation with the mayor," she said. "But it is now clear to me that he wants to push through a development on the hills. The developers will make a fortune, and pay him part of that. Either we match the amount, or he will use this investigation to justify a closure of the museum."

"I have no words fit to describe him, *signora*," Caspardi snarled.

"This is an opportunity for us. It presents so many ways to attack him. First, we must find out about these plans for the hills. Who are the developers? There must be architects, real estate lawyers, land agents. Find them."

"Yes, *signora*," came the deep voice. She could hear that he was pleased.

"There's more. I want you or Signora Vetelli to look for unusual actions by the mayor's office."

"Such as?"

"Illegitimate permits, land grants, licences. Who are the mayor's friends? Who got him into power? We too know journalists. We know most of the influential people in the city, and ministers in Rome. There are thousands of supporters of the museum. The mayor thinks he is fighting one woman, but we are not alone." She thought of Ernesto. "And we have you, Signor Caspardi. Next, we must be prepared for this inquiry. What will it involve?"

"Judge Paoli is coming to the museum on Monday. Not an obvious choice for the mayor, because he is not a complete push-over, but he is enough of a rat that we must be careful." She could hear the pleasure in Caspardi's voice. *He loves a fight,* her father used to say. Whatever her frustrations earlier in the day, she knew she could count on his loyalty. "The museum's representatives," he continued, "that is myself and Signora Vetelli, if you approve, will work with the judge and his clerks to build a complete picture of the museum's history and legal status."

"A complete picture?"

"We must not try to hide anything that the judge could discover on his own, which still leaves room for interpretation. Now, the museum has files, but these are incomplete..." He coughed discreetly. "There are also your father's papers."

"Yes, of course, I will get them for you."

She asked Roberto to bring empty boxes to her father's study. The setting sun pummelled the glass so that the orange and yellow rug seemed to glow as she ploughed through the shelves and filing cabinets. She worked backwards. The nineties. The eighties. She would send anything related to the museum. Folders spilled onto the floor and she stuffed them in the boxes, glancing at some: correspondence with EC officials; statue purchase records; director's reports; correspondence with the ministry; annual budgets. Violetta came in with a cup of coffee. She returned an hour later, replacing the untouched cup with another. The sun went down and still Melissa worked on. Her hair spilled over her face; she tied it back. She felt young and old at the same time, a president with a pony-tail, defender of the museum.

She had amassed six full boxes and was about to call Roberto to transport them, when she realised that it was past ten. She looked through the glass doors. Across the atrium, the lights were off, but there was a spectral flicker from the servants' room: the elderly housekeeper and her husband had retired to bed and were watching television. She could not disturb them. But Melissa felt restless: she had prepared the files, she wanted them with Caspardi.

She dragged the boxes outside and waited for the taxi she had called. It was a rattling brown car, and an old man climbed out of its front. His voice croaked as he wished her good evening, his slow movements grating against her impatience. The car smelled musty. It was the smell of the driver. As they raced through the city night, she opened the window and felt the hot air against her face. The driver's radio crackled without words. Verona in the night was a city she did not recognise. Silhouettes stood or squatted on the street corners. She recalled the mayor's words. *If this is the European dream, I am afraid it resembles more a nightmare, or a myth.* The driver cleared his throat with a tobacco-drenched cough.

It took them less than ten minutes to arrive. Caspardi answered in a dressing gown, and insisted on helping them unload the boxes. She offered to stay and help him sort through the files.

"It is time for bed, *signora*. Please go home and rest. You seem troubled."

They said good night and she climbed back into the taxi with reluctance. They had driven a minute when she realised the driver had said something. She asked him to repeat his words.

"A long Saturday," came the words, slow and scratchy.

"Yes," she said.

"Saturdays are bad days. Sundays are better. I like Sundays." He glanced over his shoulder.

"Please look at the road," she ordered.

"Don't worry, *signora*. You won't die tonight."

He grinned, his eyes disappearing into shadows.

Back at home, she returned to her father's study and its floor strewn with papers. She was still energised and began to gather them up, making a pile of those that might still be relevant to Caspardi.

She was halfway through when she stopped; there was a strange quality to the page in her hand, perhaps it was the thinness of the paper, that cheap Collina typewriter paper they had stocked at home. It had yellowed more than the others. On one side was a pencilled note and she paused to read it.

you won't listen to me
so here – is this
read it
destroy it
but read it
but destroy it

"Mama," Melissa said. The message frightened her. She sat down, body rocking with each heartbeat, afraid to turn the page over. She closed her eyes and let the page fall to the floor. On the other side were typed words.

16 January 1981
Dearest Mama,

Do you remember? I showed you once an idea for Papa's statues, a Museum of Myth. You called it idiotic. Papa said the same. How funny, you agree.

But I am a creator, "the Vulcan of the family," you say. Vulcan the creator – he must create! If not a museum, then what?

What about a story? Here is a story I wrote about Vulcan, and Jupiter, and Juno, and Minerva – a Cosmogony, just for you. I think you will enjoy it.

Are you reading this at your desk? Are your feet on your rug? Look down at this rug. Have you studied it as many times as I, sitting on the small couch beside Lissa, swinging my legs, looking down, waiting to hear your voice?

There is a frayed edge with a thread of purple that stretches onto the wood. Often, when I was so desperately unhappy to be near you but could not bear to be elsewhere, I imagined climbing down and grabbing that thread.

I would tug on it, and the rug underneath your desk would fly away. Beneath the rug was no wooden floor, but a hole where all the myths you had told me lay waiting. With the rug gone, you would fall, as would I, into darkness.

Our falling was not dangerous. You would hold my hand and glowing figures would gather around us. Achilles and Aeneas, grappling with their armour made by Vulcan; Hercules, racing in pursuit of a squealing boar; and high above us, on their mountainous palace, the gods.

The king and his wife look down and beam at us, with their children and attendants, the Dei Consentes smiling as we fall through the universe and you tell me their tales.

This is how our universe began: with the telling of a tale.

This is how mine ends.

C.V.C.

Melissa read the letter twice, then stood up clumsily. She looked about her, at the papers she had not yet collected, and began to pick through them. At first she moved at random, touching every page, then with increasing urgency, finally throwing the papers to one side as she crossed the room, almost running to the telephone to dial the lawyer's house.

"Pronto?"

Her voice was breathless. "Signor Caspardi, you came to my house after my father died."

There was a pause before he croaked, "It is very late, *signora*."

"You said you had to destroy some papers. What were they? Were they among the files I gave you now? What have you done with them?"

"Signora, please understand –"

"YOU WON'T!" she screamed.

"Your father gave instructions. To protect you."

She moaned. Her fingers scratched at the floor and crushed the page. Electric light struck the glass, casting shadows onto the pool. She saw her reflection, her brother's dark eyes and wavering mouth.

She had visited his workshop twice after his return from London. The first time he had been wretched, even hostile. He spoke of nightmares. He cried out, "You don't understand! You don't care!" She had told him to make something, knowing this would cheer him up. He had made a necklace. She found it on his worktop the last time she visited his forge. It had a tiny tennis racket and a gold skull. He had died making it for her.

It was an accident, her father said, *a malfunction*. But he had also said, *it was my fault.*

Her mother had told her, *he wrote it all down.*

Her brother had written, *this is how mine ends.*

This was what they had meant – the words of her brother, hidden from her, written two days before he died. They had lied to Melissa, or in fact, they had allowed her to build her own delusion. This morning she had yearned for freedom, and here it was, on the hard floor, no deckchair to conceal it, no Claudio to protect her from it, no one to hush its accusation. Even the mayor had known. Here was the truth, and she was free to see it:

Her brother had killed himself.

Melissa lay on the floor and rolled her face into the rug until her cheeks were dry. *Hush. Hush.* Her mind stilled, her eyes closed. Her last thought before she slept was strange to her: *How long can a lonely turtle dove live?*

Sam: The Case of the Missing God

Suspects:
C.V.C. = Claudio X
Melissa X? = sister of Claudio
Jennifer Carter
Chris Morris
Main clues:
Verona
Photograph
Scarf
Bracelet (does "C-J" mean Claudio-Jennifer, not Chris?)
Forge – making a necklace (did Claudio make the bracelet?)
Questions to investigate:
Who is Claudio?
What did Mum (and Dad) do to him?
How did Mum read Italian?
Why is Anna interested?

Sam rubbed a finger against a black mark on the screen. He pondered his last question. Did Anna know about the elegant, dark-haired man in the photo? Why had she got him investigating – was it really to do with her essay? If so, why keep it secret from Mum? Why was she so keen to read all the stories?

He looked again at the photo and the dark-haired man with his parents. Was this Claudio? Had he written the letter to Mum? He re-read it and his anger grew. Why had his mum dumped the lyrical Claudio and married dumpy Chris Morris instead? Sam stretched his hand out the window into the evening heat. Out there was Italy, and Claudio, who understood Latin and sex, who could make jewellery, who had wooed his mother and walked with her in the park and told her stories – who had put pen to paper to bring some advantage to Sam. He came from another universe. Claudio was far from Leeds and London, far from Oxford where Grandma Carole brooded in her dark house. He was here, out this window, at the other end of this bridge of a thousand colours that unrolled before Sam and stretched across the waves and glittered with the sunlight. He wanted to go to Verona.

His first step was to find Claudio. He opened the internet and began to search:

Claudio + Imperial College
Claudio + Jupiter
Claudio + Verona

This last combination brought up a link for something called Museo del Mito Claudio Collina. It was full of turquoise and red font, and images of statues and pictures. He clicked on the English version and read:

About Claudio Vittorio Collina
[A photo of a man half-smiling, eyes staring beyond the camera, wisdom, warmth, sadness.]
Born in Verona in 1958, Claudio Collina is named after his brave uncle who died in the War as a partisan defending the nation from evil Nazism. At the age of only 21, Claudio designs the original model for this museum. He is the graduate of Bologna University and the Imperial College in London. His master thesis investigated cantilever bridges. Claudio was a good linguist who enjoyed Latin poetry. The Museum of Myth honours his vision.

Claudio Vittoria Collina: C.V.C.! Sam was nodding, sure that he had found Mum's old boyfriend. He tried to scroll through the website but the links were confusing and most of the pages were in Italian, and there was nothing more here about Claudio. He retreated to his original search. Lower on the page was a link to an article by the Associated Press article. He clicked through.

Collina heir accident a suicide
Verona, Italy, Monday 12 July 1999
There is new evidence about the death of Claudio Collina, son of the industrialist Federico Collina, who was thought to have died in a car accident in 1981 but now appears to have committed suicide.
The reporter Gianluca Strazzo alleges in Il Giornale that the young heir took his own life. Strazzo's research reveals that the coroner hid details of

the death, and that Collina died of asphyxiation in his workshop at the family home by Lake Garda.

A series of articles in Il Giornale have stirred controversy about the Museum of Myth in Verona, which is named after Collina.

Melissa Collina, the president of the museum and sister of Claudio, issued a statement: "These baseless lies are corruption at its worst. The journalist Strazzo is backed by the mayor of Verona who hopes to profit from turning the museum into residential property. The citizens of Verona won't stand by and let shadowy powers tear down the city's favourite institution."

Sam stared hard at the computer screen, trembling with excitement. Claudio Collina was dead! He had killed himself in January 1981; his letter to Sam's mother was dated December 1980. Was this a suicide letter? It must be!

He stood up. He had a case! How did Claudio meet Mum? Why did he go back to Italy if he loved her so much? Did he kill himself because of his mum? And Dad, for he too was in the photograph! How did all this connect to the stories of Roman gods?

Sam realised that his instinct was right: to solve this case, he would need to read the Italian part of the letter. He began to pace, fuming. To do that, he relied on his wilful and erratic sister, who had written *maybe I can do it*. He fumed at his powerlessness, wondering how else he could put Anna under pressure. Or could he borrow money from Mum and hire a translator?

He was still deliberating when his email pinged. "Yes," Sam said when he saw it was from Anna.

Ok, detective, so here it is, Vulcanalia, a work by C.V.C. and Anna Morris, poet and translator extraordinaire and BEST SISTER EVER.

Maybe I enjoyed doing this. "What's that?" you say. "Anna Morris ENJOYS being a boffin on holiday?" Of course she does! She (that's me) is a boffin who is having the time of her life. Yes, all is good out here in Amsterdam, Su and I doing things I won't put in an email to my little brother.

Now I don't need to tell you that what you are about to read is strictly hush hush between you and me. You can hardly imagine that Mum has any interest to know that you've been rooting through her old files, and these stories, as you will discover, are a teensy bit sensitive, and the last thing Mum or Dad need is a teenage boy brandishing Annified Italian stories in their faces. Capiche?

This C.V.C. character, whoever he may be, is an odd fellow. In particular, he paints a portrait of two people we know pretty well – Mum and Dad – in a strange colour palette. e.g. Mum is like "Venus", a goddess of love and beauty, sensitive and tender, anything but the Doctor Jennifer Carter we know. As for Dad, I am not overly fond of C.V.C.'s descriptions of him.

It's also odd because there is no way what he describes actually happened, cos it makes Dad out to be... Well, you'll see.

Now, read, be discreet, stay fit and neat, and await further instructions from the boffin.

Love,

a

n

n

a

He was smiling as he wrote his reply:

Hi Annie, I will do everything you said, I promise. But you also need to know, Vulcan is dead! Look at this article about Claudio Collina.

Now I'll read what you sent. Thank you for translating!

Love, Sam

He opened her attachment. He felt excited, almost nervous, but why? These words were old – corrupted classics – irrelevant to Sam and his quest for love and heroism.

But these old words were Claudio Collina's, and Anna's. They were words of history and love and gods. They were the writings of a dead man. They were evidence.

The case was just beginning.

II – Vulcanalia

Odi et amo. quare id faciam, fortasse requiris.
nescio, sed fieri sentio et excrucior.
I hate and I love. Why do I, you may ask.
I don't know, but I feel it and I suffer.
– Catullus

Vulcan Banished

1972

"I hate tennis."

"It's just the junior 8s, Lissa..."

"I HATE it!"

"Look at this. Don't touch it – your hands are grubby with rubber. Just look."

Sniff. "What is it?"

"A clamshell. It's where I keep my heart. Can you see the fire?"

"I see, sort of, orange on the back. Is that your heart?"

"I found it on the beach one day. My heart is safe here. Where do you keep yours?"

"I don't KNOW. I HATE Papa for making me play. I HATE Mama for not stopping it."

"What about me?"

"You'll give your heart to someone else one day, and then I'll hate you too."

"Don't drown the world with your tears, Minerva!" Riffling through bookshelves. "Aha! Dirty Catullo! Do you know this one?"

I didn't – god help me! – think it made any difference
whether I sniffed at Aemilius's mouth or his arse.
That's not cleaner than this, nor this dirtier than that...

"Ugh, that's disgusting!" Small sob. "Dio? Tell me a story? You didn't tell me about Vulcan for a long time. I want a Vulcan story."

"Ok, do you know how Vulcan was banished twice?"

"I know, when he was born, his mama threw him off the mountain. But... Was there a second time?"

"Vulcan's mama and papa were always fighting."

"I KNOW that, Dio!"

"And he was running between them, trying to make them love each other. But especially he wanted to please Jupiter, because he was the king and he could hurt everyone: not just Vulcan's mama, but the whole kingdom of the gods."

"How?"

"There was nothing Jupiter couldn't do. He cut open his own father. He hurled lightning down at the earth and destroyed humanity, the race of gold. He once tied Juno upside down and hung her from the mountain."

"Nasty Jupiter."

"One day, Vulcan took his mama's side in an argument, and Jupiter was furious. He picked Vulcan up with one hand, just like this... Ugh, you're too heavy now!"

"Hee hee."

"And he FLUNG him!"

"Eek!"

"And Vulcan was banished."

"For ever?"

"No, the gods always come back."

"So there was a happy ending."

"Not for Vulcan. He came back drunk on a donkey and everyone laughed at him."

"Poor Vulcan. Dio, aren't Mama and Papa like Juno and Jupiter?"

"A little."

"And you're like Vulcan. That's why I like his stories."

"That's what Mama says."

"Yes. And does that make me Minerva?"

"I don't know, Lissa."

"But they were brother and sister! Didn't they love each other?"

"Yes. But... Come on, now. Time for sleep."

"Ok. I'm better now. I'm tired."

"Good. Buonanotte, sorellina."

"*Buona...*"

Helmet

VULCANALIA
Words by C.V.C.
Translation and interpolations by Anna Morris
Citizen of the UK and EU
Resident of Gloucester Terrace, W2, London, UK (Europe)
Soon to be resident at Trinity Hall, Cambridge University
Adventurer, translator, student, poet
Sister to the very fortunate (but talented, detective-skills-wise) Sam Morris
Ahem:

It was January. The glimmer of Olympus faded as we plunged through the clouds, the earth rushing up. I closed my eyes. A bump, a sound of tannoy. "Ladies and gentlemen…" Thunder. I was on Catullus's *Ultima Britannia*: the farthest island. I was alone.

In this city of damp and cloud, the fire of my heart cowered in its clamshell. I was in the saddest, wettest place in the universe. I must obtain a Masters to be allowed to leave. Very well. I hurried along strange wide roads until I found the Imperial College; a school for emperors was the only place acceptable to my father.

In the Garden of Princes I found my professor, a civil engineering expert. "I need a Masters," I told him. He said I would have a busy year: I must catch up, my grades from Bologna were poor. I was furious, but I needed the professor. He frowned, anxious, for he needed me: Papa was funding three years of his research.

I told him Catullus's prayer:
may you have a good bridge,
made for you according to your desire
"Bridges, eh?" said the professor. "That will work." We got along from that first meeting.

It was my father's agent who had secured me that "palace" on the Bridge for Knights. He saw two bedrooms and a lounge with a television; I saw a place where I could hide from the damp world. But the radiators did not work every day.

96

This land was full of technology and concrete, yet more primitive than I had ever imagined. The food made me ill. The canteen coffee was transparent. The students dressed in grey and spoke in harsh, guttural voices. I yearned to leave.

I found a *caf* called Jimmy's and began to study there. The food was thick with fat and jelly, the floor was sticky, the air regurgitated and warm, but it reminded me of my forge by the lake and the fire swelled within me.

One busy afternoon, all the places were taken except for the one opposite me. A man approached. He was vast, his bristly face glowering under a helmet of thatched hair. He set down a full plate and pot of tea.

I glared, but the man ignored me. Furiously I opened my book and tried to concentrate on cantilever bridges. Another diner edged behind the man, making him spill tea on my foot.

"Sorry," said the man. His deep voice had a nasal accent.

"Apology accepted," I said.

He gave a grunting laugh and pointed his fork. "What's that about?"

"Bridges," I said.

"Anatomy," he shot back, pointing at his own book.

We scowled at each other and began to eat. My companion tore chunks with his fork and smashed them into his mouth. "Italian?" he said. I shrugged with disdain. "Near Milan?" he added, in mid-chew. I could not hide my surprise and gestured for him to explain, but I was ignored.

The thick face and greasy cheeks were those of a typical Jimmy's customer, but the man's eyes glittered with intelligence. "How did you guess where I'm from?" I asked.

"My dad," he explained. "Went there in the War. First army. Fell in love with the country. He's a history teacher now. Taught me all about it: north and south, Valpolicella and Chianti, Roman emperors, medieval *doh-gees* – is that how you say it?"

And I said:

"Ahh…

I love Valpolicella,"

as I thought of those nights by the Adige, underneath the *castello*, drinking until my friends and I urged each other to dive into the river.

My companion said he loved rugby, drinking, women, and medicine. He invited me to join the rugby medics for an evening "where you can get plenty of all four."

I came and the fire inside the clamshell nearly drowned. I built palaces using pint glasses and forks, and stood on a table and hopped and yelled and waved. I told him that I had planned to leave but now wasn't sure.

He thumped me on the shoulder. "That's right. Stay. We'll look after you. Things can always be better. Like that girl. Prettier now we're drunk." The rugby players joked that "the big northerner" could catch anything, even the ugliest girls, and I feared this drunken medic would be a bad influence.

At the end of the night, we went outside together. An old man walking past us stumbled and fell onto the pavement. In an instant, my companion was there: he picked up the old man, cleaned the knee, and helped him cross the road, murmuring encouragement, watching him hobble away.

Now I understood: he had a heart. It was gruff and protected by vast fortifications but it beat fiercely inside him. He craved love and hid this from everyone. His heart pulsed beneath the bristling iron of his helmet, the unshaven demeanour and scowling forehead.

Chris wanted to heal because he wanted love. I could see this, for I hid my heart in a clamshell. Now I had a friend.

Clamshell

Winter's end approached. The ground was still frozen and the sky remained black, but now I had something to warm me: this friendship with Chris had sparks.

The big medic was determined that no one would laugh at his accent, criticise his upbringing, speak ill of his parents, mock him, attack him, or hold him back. He wore a cheap black plastic watch; he was top of his year.

I decided I too would succeed, and focused anew on my studies. There was a principle of cantilever bridges developed in Holland but not yet tested. The materials were problematic. Might one use a tungsten alloy? "Develop it," went the professor.

Chris had never been to the British Museum. He claimed he'd never been to any museum but now I understood that he played the fool to protect himself.

We stood in front of an exquisite copy of Aphrodite by Praxiteles, and Chris said, "Nice breasts."

"Yes... But observe the chisel marks." Next I showed him a vase depicting the labours of Hercules.

"Twelve labours, eh? Twelve years to get to surgeon, give or take. The War was only six."

Over coffee, I told him my idea for a museum, where each myth would be real enough to touch. "We could make a room for Asclepius, the god of doctors. Zeus killed him for being so good he could heal the dead. His symbol is the serpent. You have it today, on all your medical images – a coiled serpent."

Chris wasn't interested in symbols and myths. "I don't like make-believe."

"It's not make-believe," I said.

"I like history. I like reading about World War II in my spare time. That's what interests me, my dad got a medal, fighting to free Italy. But, yeah, I'd never heard about the snake thing."

I told Chris that my father had also won a medal, fighting as a partisan; so had the uncle I was named after, who had died in the hills of Valpolicella. I knew little else about the war: there were Mussolini and the

Nazis, and then the Allies, and that was it: "there was a pretty girl in my class," I explained.

He scowled and said, "You've got to know your history." I asked him to tell me. He told me how the Allies landed in Italy and crawled up its boot shape, battering against the German barricades. How the Italian army surrendered with empty gun barrels and bare feet, and still thousands became brave partisans. How the Germans raped the land and destroyed its heritage. How soldiers on both sides struggled through mountains and swamps, rain, mud, and endless hours of waiting for death, or engineers to build or demolish. "How do you not know that the Nazis destroyed all the bridges of Verona?" he said in horror and amazement.

We took to visiting museums once a week. This was our only socialising together. Chris wouldn't go to parties; he said he'd rather self-lobotomise than attend something like the Easter ball.

But a group of my fellow engineers persuaded me to go, and came to collect me that night in a taxi clinking with bottles. I accepted swigs and taught them a song from my undergraduate days in Bologna:

Oh partisan, carry me away,
O bella ciao, bella ciao, bella ciao ciao ciao
Oh partisan, carry me away,
For I feel I'm dying...

We arrived drunk. Fire surged to the ceiling and there was an explosion of light and noise, balloons, spotlights, *Rooooxanne*, whistles, plastic glasses, cheap wine, cheap tuxedos, sniffling noses, glittering ball, shiny shoes as, immaculate and embarrassed, the ball-goers paraded through stiff motions with glasses and cutlery, clinking and shifting, turning to one another, beaming with end of term delight, elbow nudging knee, legs nuzzling legs, with me seated between two girls who plied me with drink until I peeled back my lips and became my most Collina-like, whiffs of command and sex, hands creeping towards hands, building bridges out of knives and plates, table roaring, fire surging from my ears as the room crowded around me and I excused myself.

To the bathroom mirror I said, "Ok." The tuxedo: ok. The palace: ok. The masters: ok. I had taken my father's money, I would prove myself my father's son and be a factory man and abandon my dreams of craft and poetry. I saw my mother weeping, her tears running down the walls of the bathroom, but I was past hesitation.

100

This was my promise to Jupiter. So did the king of the gods hear me? Was what happened next a gift? Or a curse? For,

unsteady with
more than alcohol,
I saw you on the floor:
green dress,
marble white skin,
back to the wall, looking up.

"Are you all right?" you asked. I leaned against the wall and slid down beside you. "That's it, sit down. Have some of my water. It's mad in there. I needed air as well."

You smelled like the hills in spring. Words burned a hole in my mouth. "You smell like a flower that grows in Valpolicella, we call it *mughetto*," I said.

"Thank you," you said and smiled.

"I will give you perfume that, when you catch its fragrance, you will pray to the gods to make you nothing but nose."

"That's..."

"It's Catullus. He was Roman. From Verona, near Valpolicella, where the flowers grow. I come from there."

"Um. Water?"

"I remember the flower. In English it is called *lily of the valley*. In German it is *little bell of May*. Valpolicella has wine, lots of wine. And hills. And factories. And guns and partisans."

A group of revellers staggered by, cheering at us, and carried on.

"Your English is fluent," you said. I kept staring at you. You laughed nervously. "I think this corridor is the best place in the –"

"Do you know how Venus was born?"

"Um... No..."

"Saturn cut off his father's genitals and threw them in the ocean. Foam bubbled and made a giant shell and inside was Venus."

Something changed in you. The eyes grew, or the face shrank. Your legs shifted, the green dress rustled. Fire burned my face.

"Who are her parents?" you asked.

I took your hand. "I don't know. She has none."

"That doesn't make sense. Don't touch my hands, they're sweaty. You're not a medic, are you?"

"No, an engineer. Do you know Chris Morris?"

"Yes. He's the best in our year. But he frightens me."

I stroked your hand. "He frightens me too."

"Is that why you're holding my hand?" We laughed. The music grew softer. We were close. We were still. You watched me watch you.

"No," I said.

We danced. You put your hands in my tuxedo pocket and your eyes widened. You pulled out the clamshell. It glowed. You tipped it towards your mouth and fire slipped into your mouth and sprang from your eyes and mouth. I reached out a finger to your lips. They burned.

Tulip

Spring arrived, flowers bloomed, and I, master of bridges, lord of craft, god of fire, prince of Olympus, fell in love. Or, as Catullus wrote:

a subtle flame
stole through my limbs.

We walked in Hyde Park. I told you the myth of Prometheus, who gave fire to man, and of Pandora, who opened a jar. We kissed.

We walked again. We kissed and ate and kissed and lay together. "Tell me something," you said. There was no refuge in my exhaustion. "Tell me stories," you insisted. I told you stories: Theseus, Hercules, Antigone, Aeneas. "Tell me more. Tell me everything." I told you almost everything.

All I had known before meeting you was the lava flow of anger or the trembling sparks my sister coaxed out of me. You released my words. You were beauty. You were auburn curls and shining eyes.

We walked, and you taught me about London: there was a Court for Barons and one for Earls, there was a House of Lords and a Hotel for Dukes. We came to the Road of Kings, with its fading blue signs and tattered glory; its antiques, books, and ageing musicians.

You asked and I told you that my family name was Rossi, the name our father had chosen for us when we were travelling: it was a time of terrorism, of bombs and kidnappings.

"Tell me about your family," you said.

At once no sound of voice remains within my mouth.

"I have a sister and parents," I said, and was silent.

You laughed, you thought I was playing. "Everyone has parents. What do they do?"

I said my father was a businessman, my mother was a poet, my sister played tennis. I loved my sister, but we had parted badly...

"Where does your name come from?" you interrupted.

"Rossi means red. Like the red dust of the fourth planet or hot copper wire. Like sunset on water. Like blood and rubies. Iron. Fire."

"And tomatoes? My, my. I thought you were an engineer. Son of a businessman. Haha."

"And a poet," I said.

But you locked up my family and pushed them to sea. This was part of your power: a short conversation and all could change. So I began to hope, that this meant more than passion, that it was freedom from Olympus. The fire in my clamshell turned pink.

It took me longer to understood you. You had grown up by the shore, and now your mother was moving to Oxford. I thought of steeples and black-hatted professors. You said, "The only reason we lived in Cornwall was because of my dad. But he died winter before last."

"I am sorry," I said. I sought for tears in your eyes, but when you turned to me and said, "let's sit here," all I saw were gleaming hard brown gems. It was warm for early spring and an enterprising cafe owner had put out a table and chairs. You went in to order tea.

"I don't want you to think that I don't care," you said when you came back out. "Dad taught me about love. I'm just not going to cry about him every day. What's the point? He wanted me to be happy."

"You are strong," I said.

"Strong?" Our tea arrived. "It's my...from my mother. She's a...force of nature. Wanted me to be a bloody doctor."

I thought of Papa, who wanted me to be a bloody engineer and work in his bloody factory, and said, "I understand. I don't want to be an engineer."

You shook your head. "No, that's not it. I AM going to be a bloody doctor."

You said many strange things.

You said, "I'm the baby of the family, perhaps that's why I'm so full of questions." I thought of my aunt, after whom my sister was named, the girl Melissa who died in Cava de' Terreni, the one they nicknamed *Why*.

You said, "I like how you answer. No. That's not it. I love it. I love what you say. I love your words."

I grew still as the swell of the Road of Kings roared around us. "It is too early to use words like that," I said.

"Why? I know about love. I know love. It's clear – we're in love." You poured us more tea. I felt afraid. "It is," you insisted, "it's love."

I let the crimson word coil around me and comfort me. What else could Venus call it but love? You planted words in me. You led me into love as if all were safe for me.

I wrote to my sister, being careful with my words. If I said I was unhappy, she would feel wretched for me; if I was happy, she would pity herself.

I wrote, I have a new friend, I call him Mars, he is clad in armour and likes blood.

I wrote, I realise there is a kind of engineering I enjoy – the construction of vast projects. When I return you can help me with the Museum of Myth.

I wrote, Tell me your news. Do not spend too long in the sun playing tennis, it will ruin your skin. But don't spend too long with Mama and her Catullus. Write to me. Send me photographs.

I wrote, of you, nothing.

My sister did not reply.

And then, that glorious day in the middle of May when you moved into the apartment you called our palace.

"Would you change anything?" I asked.

You looked at the grey rug, one eyebrow shivering upwards. "Maybe the rug is a bit dull." (For the English mute their yearnings with 'maybe's and 'bit's.)

We bought a new rug together, pale as marble, and laid it on the floor and rolled onto it and laughed and laughed.

The only thing we could not share was studies. While you were at the hospital, I polished my masters. There were materials scientists to call in America; there was a Dutch engineer to invite over.

And there was Camden, where I rented a forge by the canal. I bought a lump of gold and melted it and beat it and coiled it and cooled it and inscribed our initials on it. I hid it among red and yellow tulips which I gave to you.

"What's this for?" you laughed as I handed them to you. Then you froze, you vanished into a dark silence. You said, "How did you know?" face hidden by the flowers. "My dad used to..." You forgot that you had told me they were his favourites. You inhaled deeply. "So beautiful." Your words thinned into air.

And then you saw the velvet box. "But what's THAT? Oh..." You reached out and opened it. A golden bracelet slipped into your hand. Your hand grew wet and you pressed against me and let me hold you and wept. Now I saw you as you are – the hidden girl inside the woman, the baby that Venus never had been, for Venus was born fully grown in a scallop shell and must never show the frailty of love, only its power – but you were both strong and frail, you were both beautiful and hurt, and I knew I would always love you.

Serpent

Let us live, my Jenny, and love,
for suns may set and rise again,
but for us, when the short light has set,
remains the sleep of one unbroken night.

The sun's daily passages began to lengthen and all in the city except its students cheered. The dread serpent of exams was here. It terrorised the parks and pubs. It crawled across students' beds, rousing them early, and coiled itself around electric plugs and light switches.

There were no nights. There was no sleep. Your eyes turned black. I made you cups of tea in the morning; in the evening I massaged your shoulders and tested you. You coiled against me in the night, sobbing, cooing, moaning.

But in the morning, you turned hard as coal and your voice was brittle. "My friends are not serious. And you're not being helpful. I don't want more tea. Actually, can you leave, PLEASE?"

I fled to the museum. Chris had dropped all pretence at society – no rugby, no drink – but he kept his weekly routine. "Helps to clear the synapses," he explained.

He was fascinated by an exhibition on muskets. "Amazing, the ways man's tried to destroy man. Now it's with the press of a button. Medicine's got a thousand times better, but weapons are a million times worse. What odds we get to the end of this century?"

It was the most eloquent speech I ever heard him give. "How are things with you know who?" he added.

"You should eat dinner with us," I said.

"She doesn't like me."

"She likes you very much. She says you are the best student in the year."

Chris accepted with a grunt.

You were furious when I told you, but then you chewed your lip and nodded as I reminded you: that you wanted serious study partners, that he was the best. And your reluctance fell away, like the robe off a bather.

That first night, the dinner. Chris, who had never been to my palace, inspected the fixtures and views while I cooked. "Your dad's rich, is he?" I was silent; we rarely spoke outside of the museum.

We heard a jet of water and steam poured into the dining chamber. It was violet, heavily perfumed. A voice began to sing, skipping through the room, budding like flowers. We looked at each other. The water stopped and the singing turned to humming. There was a padding of feet, a door softly closed, more humming. The door opened. Footsteps.

And Venus entered the room. She wore a white summer dress, and Cupids hovered round her, stroking her snowdrift arms, kneading her curls. You smiled. Chris's throat rumbled. My heart burned white.

We sat down to dinner: lasagne for food and revision for conversation. I watched your hands chart the course of blood through the body, confident and strong, your frailty hidden again, for me alone to see. I smiled and excused myself to prepare dessert.

When I returned, the two of you had lapsed into silence: you had opened a study book, Chris was still eating.

"As many as are the stars, when night is silent," I said.

"Catullus," you both said.

I wagged my finger at you. "Yes, but have I told you his poem about Thes–"

"Theseus," you said.

"Who killed the minotaur," Chris said.

"Who killed six bandits on the way to Athens," you said.

You both laughed.

I shook my fists at the sky. "Have I taught you everything? Not quite. How about that Theseus was descended from a snake king?" I told you how this king sprang out of the ground when Vulcan tried to rape his sister Minerva, and spilled his semen.

"Ugh!"

"Wish you'd kept that to yourself."

"Where DO these horrible stories come from?"

"It's about control," Chris said. "How you've got to be. Same as the Bible, *thou shalt not rape thy sister*."

"Or corrupted history," I corrected. "Some say these are the stories of powerful kings, remembered as legends. An island king becomes god of the sea. Perhaps there was a hero by the name of Theseus."

"With a pet bull," you added, laughing.

Chris shook his head. "Doesn't work like that. Why'd we want to remember some horny king who raped his sister? People keep what helps them do better. We believed in a god of fire to feel safe with the harvest and volcanoes. Don't need that any more. Got electric lights."

"So you think it's all made up?" I asked.

Chris shoved a fork into his mouth. I could not believe that he was still eating. "Don't know. Doesn't matter. If that Greek guy, Hippo-whatever, wants to help with our exams, that's fine with me."

"The god of medicine was Asclepius," I snapped, grabbing his plate, "and his symbol was a snake."

Mars took one last bite before dropping his fork onto the plate. "All I know is, this isn't relevant any more. We've upgraded. What patient'd want a doctor to use techniques from two thousand years ago?"

"Hippocrates invented two hundred surgical instruments. Do you know what each one did? One may have cured the anxieties of our modern age. Are you certain we haven't lost wisdom?" I glared at Chris, who glared back, and the air was full of metal.

"Look you two, you're both wrong." A sea breeze as you spoke. "Those stories exist for a reason, and it's us: we're always trying to hide from ourselves, we need something to bring us back. That's what my dad taught me, that we're full of delusion, that we hide, we use all sorts of things: amnesia, silence, and lies. But the truth is here, in these myths. They're mad, but they're real. They make us see the world for what it is – the best and the worst in people. So... Why are you both staring at me?" You laughed.

Chris stood up. "Thank you for supper," he said.

"Our pleasure," I said.

*

"He isn't so bad," you said. "He's coming over tomorrow so we can study together. Cardiology." You sighed. "There's so much to revise."

I took your hand and led you to bed. You moved close. I held you. We were one being.

"I wish you could capture a feeling the way you can capture a photo," you said. "The feeling I'd want to capture is this." You sighed.

I sighed.

But in the night, I sat up. There were faint shadows, like snakes, like winged creatures, like Furies.

"Come back to bed," you said.

"But what if I must leave one day?" I asked.

"Love goes where love leads," you murmured. "We will always be together."

Night and day melted into one as you and Chris studied together. Your skin turned pale as marble. Four weeks, three weeks, two remained. You studied so hard that sweat formed on your brows and poured into your laps. You studied by day and by night.

It was the sun that made sight possible; even in the twilight, the moon reflected its fire. But man was impatient and wanted his own fire and made it with dead bodies to create electric light. Electric light illuminated books, days before an exam, when Venus and Mars sat and studied, leg by leg, hand by hand, gold bracelet by black plastic watch, working by electric light to recall every body part every hour of every night and every day.

Sun

You used to bid me trust my soul to you (ah, unjust!),
leading me into love as if all were safe for me...

The exams ended. Chris came top, again. You had done better than before and were delighted. Chris lifted you off the ground and you screamed as he passed you across to me. You kissed me and invited me to Cornwall: it was my last chance to see where you had grown up, before your mother moved to Oxford.

We walked the beaches of Sennen from morning till night, when the sun folds into the water and a thousand colours divide the waves. You told me about your father, and I listened, believing that this too would become a part of my mythology.

You told me how Daddy was a mechanic in the war, how he became an administrator, he was fanatically tidy and yet a wild story-teller who raised you to believe in dreams. "And my dream," you said, "is you."

And I met your mother, who had made you become a doctor. You asked what I thought of your mother. "She is a cross between a Fury and a titan," I said. You liked this description.

It was on our fourth day that I saw the newspaper headline. A bomb in Bologna had killed eighty-four people. I was stumbling by the shore, I could not see clearly, I dove into the sea and pummelled my arms, trying to boil the water.

When I came out, you were yelling, "You're not allowed to swim today!"

"Terrorist fascists! Bastards! Devils!" I rolled in the sand, pounding the earth. You wept before my anger.

"Why did they do it?" you asked.

"Because they are EVIL," I roared. "You would not understand."

"But we have the IRA," you said.

I snorted. "Oh, the British, mimicking Europeans as children mimic adults." The fire in the clamshell had gone blue, hottest flame. I continued yelling. I pounded the earth.

You turned away. "I don't like you like this," you said, "something is missing."

I left and returned to London.

110

I wrote again to my sister.

I read the news. I have called my friends, no one I know was injured, but it is devastating. Are you well?

I wrote, Why have you not answered me? Are you still playing? Are you healthy?

I wrote, I want you to visit me here, I have something to show you. And I want to make something for you. I have already made an item here, a simple golden bracelet. I gave it to a friend.

I wrote, Please write to me.

You returned to London a week later. You appeared at the door of the flat, tentative, nervous, stepping across the threshold as though wild beasts awaited.

My first words were, "I am so sorry for my anger."

You fell into my arms and we were as we had been, lovers, in love. But metal once fractured does not fully mend: a thin crack had appeared. You had seen the fragments of Collina in me.

Chris returned from Leeds and the medics resumed their grind. My bridges also progressed: the Dutch engineer was now sending me letters every week; the professor said my thesis was progressing well, might I consider a doctorate?

Papa had not considered this. He had not anticipated that I might prove a diligent student, that my mind could become inflamed with desire for study, for love of Venus, for freedom.

And I studied.

And you studied.

And Chris studied.

"Let us go out, Jen," I said, "let us go for the weekend to an English castle, let us have dinner, lunch, let's explore London, let's –"

"I've got to study," you said as Chris watched.

Autumn crept in, insidious, bloodying the leaves, and the sun continued to watch the world through clear skies. It tickled my head as I paced the Park, and laughed at me. "Do you not see what I can see?" it asked.

"I see nothing," I said, "but my best friend and my girlfriend."

"Yes," the sun said, "that is what I see too."

*

I came home one day so quietly you could not hear me. I peered into the living room and saw a scene of marble, illuminated by electric light:

My goddess, eyes pressed to paper, forehead creased, a modest sweater. Every paper filed. One hand in the middle of the cream carpet.

My friend, sprawled like a victorious army, surrounded by plates and cups and textbooks. One hand in the middle of the cream carpet.

Finger

touching

finger.

*

October brought the Furies.

Alone one night in bed, I heard the rustle of a wing. I looked up and saw them sharpening their claws. "What are you doing here?" I whispered. "I left you in Verona. Go away."

"Foolish boy," they hissed, "we can go anywhere, we can hurt anyone. Now listen..."

The clouds rolled in and covered the sun and London was darkness. A scream tore through the air, a boom shattered the heavens: "YOUR MOTHER HAS COLLAPSED." And I flew home.

Racket

I went straight to the university hospital in Verona. The doctor said I must not stay for more than a few minutes, but no one would tell me what had happened. The soft body of Violetta, our housekeeper, pressed against me, weeping as she said that Mama would be fine, but then begging me to stay.

I stepped into the room. I was alone with my mother. In the semi-darkness came beeps from machines I did not recognise, and I yearned for you to explain these mysterious charts. A nurse told me she had had a stroke.

I walked closer to the bed. Mama looked like the woman she had replaced – my father's first wife – crooked and grey. She was slumped against the back of the bed.

"Hello, Mama," I said.

Her head moved but her eyes were not on me. "*H-e-l-l-o.*" It came so slowly: it started in the past and ended in the future. Her tongue was massive, it sprawled on her chin. She breathed with pants. "They – are – giving – me – pills."

"Are they?" Throughout my life, she has danced along a ledge, bottle and silver pen in hand, teaching and entertaining, swearing and singing, giving me poetry and myths, a sister, and love and hate.

I took a step back. "I have to go, Mama," I said.

"Don't go," she said. "Don't leave me. Don't go."

Still I heard my mother's voice when I quit the room. Still those silver lips seemed to move.

I went to my father's study. The stormy eyes glowed grey, but I was ready to confront the king. "Why is Mama not well?" I asked. He pointed for me to sit. "Did you hear what I said?"

"You are back," Papa boomed. "About time. I checked with your professor and your work has been fine. Good. Now you will stay."

"But I need to finish my studies."

"You do not."

I stood up. "But I haven't even –"

"YOU WILL NOT!" he screamed and sprang up, shoving a finger to my chest. "For YEARS you have flaunted my will. I gave you EVERYTHING and you spat on me. Even my worst enemies would never behave like THIS."

"I –"

"Have you EVER earned any money? Have you helped look after YOUR mother and sister? Do you know what I have had to DO for the past forty years? Do you know who I did it FOR? Is your family not everything to you?"

"I –"

"You do NOT understand sacrifice. You do NOT understand responsibility. What hopes do I not have for you? What could our business achieve in the next twenty years? Do you know how often your mother speaks of you? Do you KNOW how much your sister loves you?"

"Where is she?" I said.

"I have sent her away so she would not suffer to see you back for so short a visit. But you do NOT ask what I have prepared for you. You do NOT think of love and duty. You will NOT," he gasped, breath expended, storms flagging, worlds conquered, "you will NOT abandon your family."

"No, Papa... But still..." Your eyes, your words, your heart. "My thesis..."

"Very well," he said, "two months."

The Furies gathered in the grey sky above me. Water rolled down my face as I watched them build a vast golden clock. They pushed a button and it began to whirr.

I was hurrying out when I saw a thin young woman standing at the gate. "Going already?" she asked.

I was horrified: my sister was like the string on a racket. "Papa told me you were away," I said.

"I came back to see you, obviously."

"Are you well?"

She giggled without warmth. "Well indeed! I passed out on the court and no longer play tennis and read to Mama in hospital!"

"WHY DID NO ONE TELL ME?" I yelled.

Melissa's giggles were hollow, as from the bottom of a well. "Papa didn't let Mama tell you. He didn't want to disturb your studies."

"What happened to family, and duty, and love?"

"Yes," she said, "and staying, and looking after me always, and protecting me, as you promised, as you failed? What happened to that?

You are yelling at me for your own failings. Let me fetch you a mirror. Would you like a mirror?"

"Please," I begged, "I wrote, I..."

"Do you think your shitty letters mean anything to me? You left me here. You abandoned me with them. Small wonder Mama is maybe dying in hospital."

"DON'T SAY THAT!"

I grabbed her wrist. She stumbled and fell into my arms and sobbed. I led her to the sofa.

"Don't leave," she said.

"I won't," I said. "Or just for a moment, a flash, and then I will return...With..." I hesitated. "There is someone..."

But my sister slept.

Mask

Back in London, I burst into the palace. "We must speak about the future!" I said. "I am building something, a bridge from London to Verona. It will take us to the life we both want. You are the most important part of my life, as I am of yours."

You frowned. "What do you mean?"

"COME WITH ME TO VERONA!" And I spoke for an hour of my research: how to gain an Italian medical licence, where to learn the language, where we would live. You could be a doctor in Verona. I would pay for your friends and family to visit, even your titan mother. I would shower you with love.

"But why go there?" you asked, still frowning.

"You once said love goes where love leads," I said. "I can't live without you. All you have to do is say yes."

There was a silence punctuated by sharpening claws and whimpering Cupids. And then you said:

NO.

But I knew that you loved me. I did. Did I?

I walked often in the park, and the sun looked down and sniggered. One day, I saw you too.

Yes. By the lake, walking, hands flailing, Chris's hand on your shoulder. You stumbled, you turned to him...

Tick, tock, went the golden clock. It was November, yet still a yellow flower grew by the path.

my love, by her fault, has fallen like a flower
on the meadow's margin

It had been seduced by a false summer. It would die soon.

But I would not go without you. I would not lose. This was a fight, my opponent was a master of war, but I had my heart.

*

Tick twenty days.

Your face, when frowning, reveals a coldness I do not recognise. "If it's true that you can't live without me," you say, "then you can stay here."

"But I have no family here," I say.

"What about me?" you say.

"You are not close to your family! You are only saying no out of spite. Or because you do not love me. Because you love another."

You snort. "It has nothing to do with that," you lie. "Look, I've got to go. I've got to study."

In my hands, I imagine holding the instruments of Hippocrates. There were two hundred. What could I find there? Did one cure love? Another loss? Another treachery?

*

Tock ten days.

And Chris dragged me to the British Museum. He strode the marble halls as a conqueror, trailing me behind him like a captive. We came to a display of Roman armour.

"She doesn't want to go to Italy, mate," he announced, "so stop being destructive."

"Hard to make this stuff," I said, "just from iron."

Chris was outmanoeuvred. "Uh... It was various metals."

"*Lorica hamata* was iron chain-mail."

"For the most part."

"Just iron."

"Also bronze," he said. "Whereas segmented armour –"

"*Lorica segmentata*," I half-yelled. "You don't even know the NAME –"

"The name doesn't MATTER. Segmented armour was iron AND steel. It also had–"

"OF COURSE IT MATTERS," I screamed. "EVERYTHING MATTERS."

The hall was silent. Visitors were staring at us. Metal hardens as it cools; what once seemed red and soft proves unyielding and bitter.

*

The night of the Christmas Ball arrived. Chris had once said he'd rather self-lobotomise than go to a ball, but here he was, on one side of you, ridiculous in his tuxedo and black mask. You wore your green dress, the gold bracelet, a silver mask.

Chris leaned back, fat and complacent as a victor. "*Lorica hamata* is iron only. I checked." I did not answer.

"What does that mean?" you asked.

"A secret," Chris said.

You smiled: "I'll get it from you, one way or another."

You both laughed.

We had our picture taken together, the three of us. The photographer put you in the middle.

Now I took your hand. We went to a quiet garden. We sat, wrapped in thick coats. I pressed my hands around your face and kissed you until there was no oxygen in the universe.

"Stop, stop." Your eyes were afraid. Cupids hovered around us, shivering.

I said, "So come now, let us be serious. Come with me to Italy."

"Oh, no. No, no. No." You wept false tears. The Cupids raised their tiny hands.

"I ask so little. I will give you everything. There is nothing you will lack. You will be as free as you wish. You said you love me. All you need to do now is say, *yes*."

"No." The Cupids began to fall, their hands clawing. The Furies tugged at their ankles, dragging them into the ground.

"COME WITH ME!"

You ducked my hands, your green dress coiled around you in protection. "I want you to leave," you said.

I grabbed your shoulders. Your clothes were burning. "You WILL come with to Italy," I cried.

You reached into your mouth and pulled out the clamshell. You put it on the ground, every movement exquisite, and raised your foot. The Cupids gasped. A smash. The Cupids vanished, and I could not see.

I bent down and felt a fragment of the shell. I picked it up. I rose into the air. All was darkness. All was wet. I flew. I wept. Banished. Again. Back to Olympus.

I flew to my forge and withdrew the fragment of shell. It was cold, dead, but I blew on it until it burned again, black, weakest flame, not long to last, but long enough, to make a necklace, for Venus, for memory, for love, one last delusion, and then silence.

III – Amnesia, Silence and Lies

Doctors are just people, born to sorrow, fighting the long grim fight like the rest of us.
– Raymond Chandler, *Lady in the Lake*

Anna: Inter and Rail

2 July 1999

What if in each of us sat a little pantheon, toying with our lives? There'd be a god for travel; a god for study grants; of course a god for good-looking boys; and a god for mums and dads. The dads would be kind and gentle and warm. The mums would be laser-eyed and savage. You'd love your dad, however embarrassing, slovenly, bizarre – you'd love that he saved people's lives. Your mum would be the battle.

Bah.

I'm exhausted. I feel, in fact, ill.

Never mind – FOR I'm on a train, going to Europe, with Su, away from family, life, for six weeks. School? Exams?! No more! WHOOP!!!

Opposite me sits Su, also writing, with a furious frown, deep in thought about some problem to do with Europe. She is formidable, a massive brain, built "like a rhino". (As Sir Nottobenamed said to her at our first party in lower sixth. She cried on my shoulder, and I said, "yeah, rhinos kill twats like him.") Both of these will help her become prime minister of Europe some day, or whatever is equivalent. *Il Presidente*? Watch out world, Su is coming!

I said (how many times? like a thousand?) that I was going to use this trip to finally FINALLY get the Anna Morris diary-writing bonanza out of blocked-up-edness and into forward motion, and when better to begin than on a train? (HULLO? YEAH! I'M ON A TRAIN!)

So.

So, train, train, describe the train. The fields are whizzing by. There is a little boy next to Su, his mum is next to me, they are playing Scrabble.

Soooooooooooooo

So, I am sorry, I know this is not the way to start this journal, but I have got to get it out of my fucking system, Mum and her total commitment to spawning injustices in this world.

E.g. she didn't want me to go on this trip

E.g. she tried to cut it to four weeks, on the basis that I had to spend time with Grandma Carole in Oxford, which is about the cruellest thing she could have said, because it obviously implies that since I spent so little time with Nan before she died, I now have to be with Grandma Carole, who is a medieval version of Mum complete with torture instruments (e.g. her cooking)

E.g. Last night. What the fuck was last night? We were supposed to have dinner *à quatre*, not the most common occurrence in the world, I'd bought beers for Dad, and got Sam working on the sauce, but the moment I came back in Mum was jumping down my oesophagus with a flame-thrower, "GET OFF YOUR PHONE! TAKE YOUR BROTHER OUT TO MR CHU'S! DON'T JUST STAND THERE!" So Sammy and I had to go and eat together like an odd couple, chatting about nothing through dinner, and I didn't even get to say hi to Dad because, quote, "he had a bad day at work and doesn't want to be disturbed."

Whatever. No point in fighting when I had one foot out the door, and the Erasmus money safely locked into my travellers cheques. So I took Sam to Mr Chu's and ordered eggrolls and noodles.

"You'll do a big trip like this one day," I said to him, not quite believing it as he smeared sweet and sour sauce on his chin.

"Yeah," he mumbled.

"What're you going to do this summer? Detective stuff?"

He rolled his eyes but his mouth twitched with a faint grin.

"Don't go finding dead bodies," I warned. "Mum and Dad will lose their licences."

Suddenly his face crumpled up and he looked tiny, a little boy. "I wish I was going with you, Annie." I felt giddy, stung by a little synapse of love I'd forgotten, one that makes me protective to my lil bro.

"Hey, Sammy, we'll go on a trip one day, I promise."

He nodded sadly and I took him home.

Darkness. We're in the tunnel. It's weird being in a train under water.

I got to see Dad only the next morning. He wanted to take me to the station and I pretended to be like, "no, you'll embarrass me," but actually I was glad. With Su watching, I pushed against one of his massive shoulder as he drowned me with another kiss.

"Ok, Dad!"

Now he drew me in with both arms and squeezed till I was gasping. "Just be... Be safe." An alien lilt made me look up.

"Dad?" His face, so soft to kiss, was impossible to read. He ground his teeth and refused to look me in the eyes. I wondered if he was thinking about Nan. Before I could think about it, I was blurting out, "sorry." He grunted and his chest heaved with a deep breath. He stepped back and smothered my hand with his.

"Right, Sumukhi," he called in his hammed-up Yorkshire accent, "take my daughter, and away with you."

She laughed. "Bye, Mister Morris."

I watched Dad walk away, tiny suitcase rolling behind him. There was a roaring in my ears and I felt my breath sink down into my stomach and had to lean on Su's arm so I wouldn't faint. The whole year swept back over me, Nan's death, the Cambridge interview, fights with Mum, Sammy's little crumpled face... I'd lied to my dad.

"Are you all right?" Su asked.

"Yeah..."

In the corner of my vision stood a French-looking boy, slender, in gorgeous blue trousers that I stared at, semi-catatonic. Suddenly he looked over and grinned at me. And I shook off my distress, like water from an umbrella, thinking, *So what if he knows, I've got the tickets*, and pushed myself off Su.

DING DONG. Attention, s'il vous plait!

Sheesh! That was quick. No time for poetry on this ride, just blahblahblahing, but this is the trip for it, for Anna to Annify the world. It is also...say it with a hush...whisper it to the stars (IT'S DAYTIME, ANNA!) – ok, whisper it to the fish in the channel and the waves we passed beneath, and these thin angular Parisian buildings and the tuft of wool poking out of my seat – it is the trip to find *love*.

DING DONG.

The witch is dead! Su is rising! The book is closing. *L'aventure commence*!!!!

*

3 July

Last night, in Paris, in toxic thrilling St Germain, we came to a street where the seats spilled like wicker waves off the pavement. From two sides came Parisian boys.

"Your name, pretty one?" said one. He was pointy and dressed in shades of blue, quick with his gestures. "Anna, Anna!" he repeated, singing. "And you? *Madame, vin rouge*! This is Su... Su... Sumukhi. Meet Anna, *la belle* Anna. And *madame* is the owner."

I was sitting next to a boy called Thomas. Thomas was nothing like the pointy man. He was shyer, larger, softer. Pointy stopped bantering with Su and called to me.

"Hey Anna, she says you are the linguist?"

"*Oui.*"

"Hey everyone, she knows, *oui.*"

I stood up. I put down my glass. I cried out:

A quatre heures du matin, l'été,

Le sommeil d'amour dure encore.

Sous les bosquets l'aube évapore

L'odeur du soir fêté.

The men cheered. *Madame* poured herself a glass and another one for me. I did the whole of the poem, "*Bonne pensée du matin.*" Su joined in, and Thomas came to stand beside me, and I thought again of the line, "*Vénus! Laisse un peu les Amants.*"

"I'm impressed now," pointy said.

"*Grazie,*" I went, "but it's too easy to impress you."

"What did she say? You are speaking in Italian? She speaks Italian too!"

Someone bought more drinks. I had three glasses of wine, four. "Another cigarette?" offered the pointy man. "Look at this gypsy – he comes here every day to play this stupid song on his violin. Hey, *monsieur*, we are not tourists! These are, yes, but Anna speaks better French than you. She is a poet! You ARE a poet? You want to smoke something more exotic? But not here."

But Thomas was so much softer-faced, he had a soft pleasant face, now a fuzzy distance from mine, he was soft and I felt the soft brush of the hair on his arm against mine. I took Thomas's hand and said bye to Su and we walked to a river that smelled like the tears of an eagle.

"I want to write poetry," I giggled.

"What do your parents do?" Thomas asked.

"They're DOCTORS. But I'm not interested in that. I don't CARE. It's their thing. Only thing my mum even cares about. I want to be an artist. I want to write about love and –"

And he kissed me. The water, the river, the ebb and flow of the night: Paris is the truest place in the world to kiss, and I could feel his soft lips, his teeth against mine, his wine breath making the sweet night more sweet, thinking, *Venus! Leave these lovers alone!* I was an adult in Paris, walking hand in hand by the Seine, singing and dancing drunken and giddy around

Thomas, "Look at me now! I am a bird!" Our walking brought us back to the hostel, where we fumbled and giggled as we crept into the girls' dorm and giggled again when a German voice went, "What is this? Get out!" He kissed me goodnight and I went to bed and listened to Jeff Buckley and sobbed, gulping air like it's nectar. It was inverted sadness, an excess of joy, the delicious sense that there are fifty more such nights ahead of me, and a lifetime.

Now – coffee and breakfast.

*

Fuck.

But how to put this?

FUAAAAAAAAACK

Su was still asleep when I finished writing. On my way out, that frizzy red-headed girl at reception called out, "Anna Morris, *oui*? Your mother. She said you must call her urgently. You can use our phone."

No real surprise that Mum's witch instincts had tracked us down. The thick chords of the ringtone reminded me of long evening calls with Harry, or Jason, and I was confused when a clipped woman's voice answered.

"Jennifer Carter, hello?" She must have been on call. "Oh, good, Anna. Are you safe? Are you well?"

"Yes," I said.

"Listen, I need a favour from you. Can you come back next Friday? Just for a few days. I know it's last minute, but I have to teach a course out of town, it'll be impossible to commute up and down, and Sam will be alone otherwise."

The thing about Mum's injustices is that they usually have some logic, but this was completely irrational. So I kept calm as I said, "Why doesn't Sam go to Leeds and stay with Dad?"

"No, he can't. Dad's...too busy. Your granddad can't look after Sam."

I tried again. "Or Oxford and stay with Grandma Carole?"

"Anna, I wouldn't ask you if I had an alternative."

"I don't get it. Why don't you commute? Or cancel the course? Or let Sam cope for three days. Why don't you do anything except fuck with my trip?"

"Stop that language. I am speaking to you as an adult. Sam is thirteen."

"He'll manage much better than I will. I will not come back for this. I'm on an Erasmus grant. I've got a life, yeah?"

"I'm begging you, Annie. Please. This isn't a fight. It's just a few days. It's not against you. Please. You'll still have a wonderful holiday and you can do everything and I'll make it up to you and it will really, really help me. Please."

I looked hard at the counter of the reception desk. The white surface vibrated with Mum's voice; it had an unusual pleading that was strange and intoxicating. I felt myself wavering.

"For once," Mum said, "don't be selfish."

The wavering vanished. "SELFISH? *ME*? Are you even on this planet, Mum? You knew I was going. Dad knew I was going. Why can't you sort your shit out?"

"Your dad decided at the last minute."

"I finished two months of exams. I got the grant. I saved up for six months. Every single thing here – NO, MUM, YOU WILL SHUT UP AND LISTEN TO ME FOR ONCE – every single thing is thanks to me. And it's my eighteenth in three weeks. And I've got Su with me. I can't ABANDON her! But it's you. You haven't done shit to help, you don't give a shit about me, just you and your fucking career –"

"Don't you dare –" she was yelling.

"Your course versus my life. So typical. Dad doesn't want me to come back. Dad was like, *have a great trip*, just before he went away. I'm staying where I am. That's it. Ok? Ok."

I ran out of words and started rapping my fingers on the counter. Mum puffed down the phone.

"Your father," she said, "is the reason for this call."

"What?" I started laughing. "He's in Leeds. Is he like –"

"He's *gone* to Leeds, Anna. He's gone."

It was said so matter-of-fact, so flat and certain, that I opened my mouth and closed it again.

"When's he coming back?" I asked quietly.

"He isn't."

A thing appeared above me. It was black and sticky, unnameable, like a cloud, but worse. I held very still. If I didn't move, the thing would vanish. But then Mum said my name and my ears burned and knees grew soft.

"Are you getting...?" This was hard. "Mummy..." So hard. "WHY?" I was fucking crying.

A long sigh, distant but comforting. "Oh, Annie. This is nothing to do with you. Please come back, we can talk properly when you're here. Please help me. It's not your fault. You did exactly as I asked and of course you must have your holiday, you'll have your independence, you'll be in Italy or wherever you like for your birthday. Just right now I need your help." The voice grew more remote. "You know...it's funny, this is all so old, almost full circle. Your dad was there then. Now I need your help, just for a few days. Please."

"Ok," I said. I put the phone down and leaned onto the counter. When I looked up, the receptionist was there, holding a tissue. I wiped my face, muttering thanks. I touched the phone again, but the girl frowned. "Can I use the computer?" I begged.

A week ago, I'd finally persuaded Dad to create an email account. He'd sent me a test email: *This email is for Anna.* Then he came into my room to check. "Did you get it?" How I'd laughed! I laughed and laughed and...

Now I logged in to stop the tears, typing like a maniac.

Dear Dad, I just spoke to Mum and I don't know what to say. I don't understand, she didn't explain. Can you? She wants me to come back to London to help with Sam. I don't want to do that but I've got to. Please just explain what's happening. I'm sorry. I'm so upset, Dad, just tell me you're ok. This is a dark constellation. Love,

Anna

I deleted the sentence with "constellation." I put "Love" on a separate line. I sent the email.

FUCK

My summer is over.

Jen: Amnesia

That entire month of May was a shitstorm. One of the registrars went on holiday to South America and came back with a tropical disease that would have killed half the kids on the ward; the locum who replaced him was worse than useless, actively dangerous. So there they were, Jen and her fellow consultants, pressing their heads between their knees and hyperventilating. But it was always going to be Jen, being Jen, who would grab the extra workload and shove it into the tiny cracks in her schedule so that, somehow, everything got done.

They finally got the registrar back at the end of the month. The world slowed and that night Jen collapsed into bed, promising herself that tomorrow would be better, she would sleep in, and resume sensible hours, and help Anna with her last bits of revision. As she lulled into sleep, her thoughts grew grander, and she recalled promises to herself: that by the end of this year she'd be up to one day a week of private practice, and three days by 2003, with higher pay, shorter hours, and would that it might begin tomorrow...

She was nodding away, body still rigid, when she felt Chris climb in beside her. He didn't speak and she turned and felt for his arm. She melted and sighed "g'night" and was at peace.

"Thought you were asleep," he said. "Did you read the paper?"

She mumbled a "no", not wanting to lose her doziness, and was soon under.

She was alone when she woke in the morning. There was a copy of *The Times* on the bed, open to page 17. One of the articles was circled. *Death of controversial Italian millionaire*, she read groggily. *Federico Collina. Verona. Museum. Actuators. Claudio.* She read the article again, more slowly. And again.

Chris was late that night too. She was sitting at her desk, erect in full clinician mode, when he came in and closed the door.

"His surname was Rossi," she said. "It's a different Claudio."

"Evening," he said and began to take off his suit. Forcing herself to be patient, she studied the flab on his body and listened to his breathing. She had begun a "suggestive health programme" – suggestions of more exercise, less food, less heart-surgeon hypocrisy – but without progress as yet.

After he had changed into shorts and a t-shirt, he leaned against the door with folded arms.

"Thought so too, at first. But Verona, that was funny. So I checked with Imperial. Turns out he changed names." He looked complacent, almost smug. "Claudio Collina," he said, "was our Claudio."

"But," she said.

She pushed back her chair and stood up.

She bumped her hand against the desk as she walked to their bed and lay down, face in her pillow, still, silent. As soon as she felt the bed move, she burst out, "Why did you DO this, Chris?"

"Sorry," he said.

She smelled his sharp saltiness. She studied the pattern of the bed cover, triangles and diamonds. "You didn't have to tell me." He touched her back. She whirled around. "Did you know already? For fuck's sake! Did you know Claudio was dead?"

Her breaths came ragged as she remembered a ghostly face, its angular lines starting from the nose and dark eyes.

"Thought you'd learn about it," he said. "Better it came from me."

"But you didn't tell me... You just left the paper..." The cruelty of what he'd done – dumping her into this – grew clearer. She sat up. "How else could I have heard about it – who else would have told me? What were you thinking? Why did you do this?"

"Jen," he said. He gripped her arm, she tried to pull away, but he was too strong. "Jen, Jen, calm down, come here, c'mon." Her exhaustion, his grip – too much. She lay down with a sigh. The memories drifted out of her mouth and she watched them sail away.

"Ok," she said.

He stroked her hair and held her and soon she was asleep. She awoke the next day, memory locked away with the others, and life continued as it should, safe in amnesia.

Her nightmares began a week later.

She dreamed that she was on the grass by the Serpentine in summer, the air was warm and a breeze tickled her cheeks. Something wonderful had just happened. She heard a cooing noise and turned and there was Anna, a baby. Jen's heart ached, her daughter was so beautiful. But now Anna was older, and frustrated, clutching her belly. Jen's smile grew: she could fix this, it was just an abdominal pain. She reached out, but Anna started running to university. *Ridiculous*, Jen thought, *it is such a small thing*. She was laughing and jogging after her, pulling faces, making noises, the game they used to play, but suddenly Anna gave a spurt and pulled away. Jen ran faster, every muscle straining. The ground was coming to an end. She would not catch Anna. She yelled, "Stop!" Anna tripped and flew towards the ground, her hands reached out, a shriek filled the air.

Jen awoke with a gasp.

Chris sat up beside her. "What is it?"

"University is dangerous," she said. "Alcohol, ecstasy, unprotected sex... Anna might get into anything, meet anyone. What kind of friends will she make?"

"It's Cambridge," he chuckled.

"Or what if she doesn't like the people in her year? What if she hates her subject? Or her digs?" She knew she sounded ridiculous.

"We-e-ell," Chris said. "Look at you. You got all this out of uni."

She froze. "Got what?"

"I meant –" he said.

She pulled away from his hands and climbed out of bed. Her breaths were short and furious.

"Got WHAT?"

"Y'know, job, me, kids. All came from uni. Not so bad, eh?"

Her husband was a huge complacent shadow in the twilight. She remembered the article about Claudio, and Chris's smug and callous flinging of ancient love in her face. There wasn't a complaint he couldn't chuckle over, nor a problem he couldn't fix.

"Not so bad," she repeated.

"Jenny." He reached out for her.

"NO. This is NOT the life I wanted." His hand dropped. "Did you think you were doing me a favour, leaving that article? Assume you did it out of some odd kindness. Another kindness is honesty, so let me be honest. I am wretched, Chris. Exhausted, unfulfilled. It's a disaster. No, just ignore me. I don't know what I'm saying. But don't you DARE tell me what I got from university. What did I get? Something... I don't know. Ugh. Something is MISSING."

She climbed back into bed, as far from him as possible. He didn't touch her, which was good, because she could have hit him, she was so angry with him for bringing out this bitch inside of her that she wanted to

129

strangle. Even her voice sounded like her mother's. She hated herself. She kept listening for his movements, a slight shake of the bed, a hint of his fingers close to her body, sudden brief warmth gone. Her hyper-attentiveness drained her, and she drifted off within minutes. The nightmare stayed away, presumably cowed by her anger.

But it returned the next night, and the next. She had never remembered her dreams before, now she could not forget:

Dreams of Anna screaming curses at her in Italian; of Chris, leading her into the park and ripping wooden buttons off her coat; she dreamed of dirty orange light bulbs, of bracelets, and tulips, and princes; she dreamed of bath-time with Sam, and yellow ducks, and the waves turning cold, and salty, the spray striking her face and sticking, she could not rub it off; of Cornwall, of Sennen, of sunsets and sunrises; she dreamed of a slender figure, eyes dark and wide, yelling at her as tears slipped down his nose; of pale-skinned Bea, thin, hair falling out, stroking her hand; and still of Anna, chanting in Italian, up and down the corridor of her mind.

When she awoke in the middle of the night, that phrase was stuck in her head, "something is missing," and she mumbled it to herself.

If he was awake, Chris did not reach out for her; he knew to keep away, and she was alone and trembling in the night.

*

She was finishing her shift on the last day of the month when her pager buzzed. She recognised the number for Chris's department. She got through to one of his colleagues, an anaesthetist, who started babbling.

"Jennifer, can you come here? Actually, to the park. Chris is in the park."

"What's the matter?"

"MVR op went wrong. Aneurysm burst. We lost the patient. It was awful. Chris went out, I've never seen him like that. I'm sorry to bother you."

She tried Chris's mobile but it was switched off. She took a taxi to Speakers' Corner and started walking west. There was no answer at home. She hurried on, stones bouncing into her shoes.

She found him sitting on a bench near the horse training ground, head slumped in his hands. As she approached, a couple walked past him, slowed down, looking at him, and moved on. His vast shape was bent into a pinstripe ball. She touched the back of his head. He snapped up with a growl.

"It's me," she said. He didn't move. She cupped his chin with her hands, and pressed his head to her belly. "It's me, it's me." She helped him up. He swayed. His eyes were bloodshot. She took his hand and led him through the park. "Look at the swans!" she said. "Look at the fountain!" They left the park and cut through the small roads that led up to Gloucester Terrace. The white terraces passed in a blur, and still she kept on her chatter: "This is where Sam's friend Fred lives." They reached the flat. She felt him watching her as she fumbled with the keys. "Anna?" she called out. There was no answer. She led him into the bedroom and helped him undress. He lay down on the bed. She lay down behind him. His body began to shake. "That's it, Chris, that's right, let it out." He finally fell asleep.

She went to get groceries. She made lamb chops. He wouldn't leave their bed so she brought the dinner to him, but he lay still and wouldn't sit up to eat. She left the chops in the kitchen with a note telling Sam to eat them and climbed back into bed. They slept through the night: no nightmares, no disturbances. In the morning, they dressed in silence, and she kept looking at him; he seemed as he did before any operation – focused, dispassionate.

"Chris..." No sound. She wouldn't ask about yesterday. "When will you be home tonight?"

"Seven," he said.

Anna was leaving the next day, and Jen decided she would cook dinner for the four of them, a surprise that would please Chris, a goodbye meal to send their baby off. She called Anna from work to confirm this, and when she got home, went first to Sam's room.

"Switch off the computer. Come on. You're helping me with vegetables. We're eating together tonight. I want it ready when Dad gets back."

"Ok," Sam said, standing up. "But Dad's home." Jen went back to their bedroom; she'd not noticed the closed door. She tapped it. "Chris?" She went in. The blinds were drawn. She saw his silhouette, sitting on the bed, facing the window. "Chris?" He didn't answer. She heard the front door slam and Anna's obnoxious mobile-phone-voice. She slipped out.

"Anna, put that down a second, I need to speak to you. Thank you. Change of plan. Here's twenty pounds. Can you take Sam out, maybe to that Chinese place."

Her daughter's dark eyes widened. "WHAT? No way. It's my last night! You said–"

Jen spoke quietly. "Your dad had a really bad day yesterday. I need to talk with him alone."

Anna leaned past her. "DA-A-AD?"

"*Shut up,*" Jen hissed. "If you want to help him, you'll take Sam out for an hour."

The girl shut her mouth in mid rebuttal. She came back with Sam protesting ("but Mum said I need to help") and they stumbled out the front door.

Jen returned to the bedroom. Chris was still sitting upright on the side of the bed. It creaked beneath him.

"Chris?" she said.

"Jen?" he snarled.

She sat at her desk, back straight.

"Tell me what happened yesterday," she said. Silence. "You need to talk about–"

He leapt up. "You WON'T tell me what I need. What you said, *something is MISSING.* Couldn't concentrate. Six weeks suspended. Simple case, and dead. Because of YOU. You – SELFISH – " He thumped the door.

"Chris, Chris, please –"

"Something is missing."

"We need to talk about yesterday," she said. "Tell me what happened."

"You – tell – me."

"Look, you started with that stupid article, I said some hurtful things. I'm sorry. We shouldn't be talking about that, ok? It was just a cock-up."

She heard him inhale violently and realised her mistake too late as he bellowed, "IT WASN'T A COCK-UP!" She plunged her face into her hands, "ok, ok," but he kept on, "NO IDEA! NOT A COCK-UP!"

Finally he stopped; she heard his panting and looked up. "I'm going to Leeds," he said.

"That's a good idea," she said. Her body was shaking. "Yes, Chris, good. You can be with your dad. You can rest. That's why they gave you this time off. Do you have someone up there you can speak to?" She tried to think of friends, colleagues.

"Come with me," he said.

"You need to work through this. I have work, I can't just –"

He pounded on her desk. "I'm asking you ONE thing, Jen, ONE THING." He leaned over her and she pushed him away with a jerk.

"Go, then!" she said. "Go on! Go to Leeds!"

"Yeah. I will." He marched over to his cupboard and started yanking clothes out. "That's it."

She gave her incredulous look but he couldn't see her. She stood up. "What do you mean, *that's it*?" He didn't answer. "*That's it*, Chris?" He didn't answer. "Chris Morris, who'd have thought it! One thing goes wrong and he turns and runs!" She was smiling now.

"One thing?" he said. It was so quiet, like an afterthought, it winded her and she fell back into her chair. She watched without moving as he dumped half the clothes in his bag and went back to bed.

They held their ground, she sitting, he lying. At some point she heard the kids come back and got up and turned off the light so they wouldn't disturb. She felt him watching her, and wondered if he was thinking she might come to bed. She was such a stubborn thing, but if he'd said right then, *come to me*, she'd have done it, just that once, to be un-Jen, because being Jen had helped create this, but he did not speak and she went back to her chair. She wouldn't apologise. He didn't speak. He might have fallen asleep for a little, as did she, but mainly it was white eyes winking coldly at each other through the silence.

Slowly, the blackness turned to sepia. Chris gave a great yawn, got up and mumbled, "Got to take Anna." She watched him crush more shirts into his suitcase; she stood up to help but he had finished. He went out to the entrance and she followed him close.

"How long are you going for? Four days? A week?"

Annoyingly, the kids were there, watching TV on the sofa. Anna was sitting, rucksack at her feet, dark eyes watching them like a predator's.

Chris led her back into the bedroom and shut the door. What should she say? Her mind was wool. She heard some distant words in her mind, faint sounds that she realised might soothe him, and as the words approached her, she felt hope, and looked up at him, and he said,

"Goodbye, Jennifer."

For eighteen years, he'd called her *Jen*, *Jenny*, *honey*, *wonderful*, *delicious*, *beautiful*, *sweetheart*, *angel*. Her tears began. "But... I..." She hated crying, hated crying in front of him. She put her face in her hands and waited for his hand on her shoulder, but it did not come. She raised her head. His eyes were dry, glittering, studying her like a surgical problem. She wiped her eyes and said,

"Goodbye, Chris."

He walked out. She followed him and grabbed Anna at the front door for a hug.

"OK, Jesus, MUM! I've gotta go."

She watched them go down the stairs.

She worked all day and walked back home, body quivering. She hadn't slept in three nights. She wanted to throw up. Only on Gloucester Terrace did she pull out her mobile, but his phone was off.

"This is ridiculous," she said to his voicemail. "Call me. I want to make sure you are speaking to someone. I don't even know that you got to your dad's ok. Call me back, please."

She sounded crisp and unemotional. She lay in bed and waited for the tears to come. As soon as she was crying, she would call him again, and he would hear her voice, and yearn to comfort her, but her eyes remained dry and her bed remained empty. Finally she fell asleep.

The nightmare was waiting, but this time it was a relief.

Chris: Silence

Theatre. The lights above the bed, the smell of chlorine, the humming of the machines, and the room full of the banter that let them ignore that their chests too were mortal. "Nurse, what's that perfume?" "I'm not wearing perfume." "Not shower this morning?" "Why?" "Another smell, haha." "Haha." Sex and blood and electric life were pulsing over the open chest.

Every time in his career that he'd reached this point in the procedure, the first glimpse of the pumping heart, there was a *whoosh* in Chris's ears, like surf, and he'd feel faint, and recognise himself and what he was doing, and think, *this is a human being's heart and I am going to fix it*, then it would pass and he was in, machine-like till the last stitch.

So now he got the retractors out and pried open the chest cavity and there was the throbbing red and white tissue. But instead of a noise he heard faint words: *Something is missing*. He shook his head and pressed on. All was going smoothly, here was the rip in the valve, small enough to close with a patch, or he might use a chordal transfer, and he was making good progress when the blood pressure fell to 90/60.

The technician checked the heart-lung machine while his anaesthetist, Vineet the neat they called him, made small adjustments to the oxygen levels. "BP 85/57," Vineet said, "it's not the anaesthetic, it's something else." *Something is missing*, the voice said. The nurse rotated the display and Chris looked closer and froze. A swelling protruded near the top, choking the aorta. Aneurysm. He looked back at the heart and now saw the tell-tale signs: dark red and white. Everyone in the room was looking at him.

Ice spread in his belly as he gnashed out orders: "Clamp, plasma." The BP fell more. "MI any minute," Vineet said. The machines were furious. *Something is missing*. He shook his head. He was sweating. He pulled out the clamp. His hand was shaking.

"You'll kill him," Vineet said.

"I fucking KNOW."

The BP fell more. He reached out, fingers trembling, metal getting closer, touched the tip of the swelling, *something is missing*, a delicate prod, try to manoeuvre, wouldn't budge. A sharper prod. Another. And the aneurysm burst.

Blood was everywhere, a river, red, wet, sticky, and the machines were crazy, his colleagues moving frantic around him as Chris hacked on, and all he could think was, *The patient's name is Edward.* He had met Edward yesterday, pale and weak but brave as he said, *thank you.* He should not be thinking of this patient for this was pure blood and chest work, blood and blood, it seemed endless, but it must end, and now the reaction Vineet had feared began as the heart attack swept through the body and they electrocuted the body and still the blood flowed and they pumped plasma in but more came out, and it was him, Chris Morris, him, the surgeon, who was doing it, the life giver turned reaper, wrestling with blood.

Ten minutes later one of the nurses was pulling his bloody scrubs off. He staggered to the bathroom, almost composed, even smiling at someone. In the bathroom, he muffled his scream with the sleeve of his shirt. Someone came in and led him into the lift and onto the street. It was hot but he was wearing a coat. He walked to the park dry-eyed. He found a bench and walked past it three times. He was determined to return to the hospital but he sat down, saying, "so stupid, so fucking stupid." All his life had been preparation for this moment and he had failed, he'd failed his mum, and his dad, and the patient. When a hand touched the back of his head he assumed some idiot had come to speak banalities and he looked up but it was her. She grabbed his head and pulled it to her belly. He thought, *Who did this to Edward?*

"It's me," Jen said. "It's me."

*

Chris woke and saw himself reflected in glass. Beyond were flying trees, a line of grass and crops rising up and down, glimpses of slats and chimneys, and he recalled where he was: on a train, on his way home.

Home.

A taxi home was a luxury he'd earned. Soon it was his street: red bricks, brown and white lattice fences, half-grass pavements, windows patterned like that artist Anna liked – Mondrian, that was it – Dad's little blue car, and home, with its flaking red front door. He'd promised last time to sort it out; he'd do it this time. He walked down the narrow path and the door opened.

"Afternoon."

He was a little shorter, skin a little saggier, but still Dad: vast, mighty, thin of hair and thick of handshake. Morris and Morris, the big lads, together.

Chris went into the living room without a word. He looked for traces of Mum in the wicker table-mat, and the tartan sofa, and the photos of their wedding. Here she was, a schoolgirl before the war, next to the photo of Dad in uniform. The room smelled of polish and fresh hoovering. Dad was watching him with nervous nodding. Chris spotted dust on the TV and a cobweb by the window, but he was sensitive to dirt after twenty years of medicine and Jen.

"Tidy," he said.

"Go on," Dad said, sounding pleased. "Or don't you remember where?"

Chris went up the stairs and into his old bedroom. It was now a study, with a computer and large print-outs of family trees on the wall to replace his old rugby pics. But his bed was still there, with clean sheets: Dad had gone all B&B. He dumped his suitcase and came back down to the kitchen. The kettle was boiling.

"How long you with us?" Dad asked.

Chris leaned against the fridge, arms folded. "Dunno. Few weeks."

"Long as you like. *Me casa, soo casa.*"

They laughed and ate a quiet supper of frozen pizza. He went early to bed. His bed was too small and as his eyes adjusted to the darkness, he saw generations of happily married ancestors scowling down at him.

He switched on his mobile in the morning and got Jen's voicemail. *This is ridiculous*: her favourite expression. She wanted him to *speak to someone*. She was as compassionate as an insurance form. He came downstairs feigning a grin at the smell of breakfast.

"Yum yum," he went through the burnt eggs that stuck to his teeth.

"Not finished yet," Dad said, coming back with buttered toast and runny beans. He sat down opposite and pretended to read the paper.

"Yum yum."

Dad looked over the paper. "So, what's got you up here? Visiting Jimmy's?"

Chris nodded and hoovered up the rest. He stood up with a groaning pat of his belly.

"Delicious. See you later?"

"Aye." Dad watched with a puzzled frown as Chris sauntered out in a tracksuit.

It was a tidy street, safe and quiet, but some years ago Mum had begun to conspire with him about moving to the countryside, near London, near the grandkids.

Round the corner the road widened, and below was the sprawling city centre. Chris could just make out a corner of St James Hospital, aka Jimmy's. He thought again of Jen's voicemail and her *speak to someone*, and as he walked, his mind drifted to the day after Edward's operation.

*

He'd gone back to work determined to keep on, but the head of surgery, that smooth old shit Thomas Forest, found him at lunchtime and said he was booked in to see the resident psychologist, a Dr Loman. The so-called doctor turned out to be a tall woman dressed in black with a low, thick voice.

"Tell me what happened yesterday, Chris."

He picked at a wedge of black leather on the sole of his shoe. "Patient came in after a massive MI. Partial rupture of the posteromedial papillary. Began the chordal transfer. Sixty minutes in, found the aneurysm."

"And?"

He splayed his hands. "It burst. Nothing we could do."

"How did that make you feel, that there was nothing you could do?"

Silence. Her voice was strangely comforting. He wondered whether she could just talk for an hour and let him get back to work. He shrugged.

"I understand that you recently lost your mother," she said.

"What?"

"Chris, my job is to make sure you are fit to work in surgery. You can feel comfortable –"

"YOUR JOB IS SHIT."

"Chris, please sit down. Chris, please."

He imagined her speaking to Jen like that. He sat down.

"Chris, I'm trying to help you. You can tell me anything in strict confidence. My report will discuss your readiness for work, but what you say here is strictly between us."

He smiled. "Unless I've killed someone, right?"

She raised an eyebrow.

He thought about his joke. He'd only meant... His face melted. He took long, deep breaths.

"Have you had any difficulties at home?" she asked. He made a noise. "Such as what, Chris?"

"It's nothing," he said.

138

"I've looked at your records, Chris. Over two thousand operations. Mortality rate of 1.3%. One point three! That must be one of the best records in the country. You are an extremely accomplished professional."

His mouth twitched. "So?"

"So, Chris, as one professional to another, you know that mistakes are a natural part of human activity. You can't help them. They happen at work and at home. What I'm getting at is, if you have something on your mind that you're not sharing, that could be affecting you. How can you be truly professional then?"

It was a point, and he'd thought about it. But he said nothing more of substance and the psychologist let him go after thirty minutes. He went home, drew the blinds, sat on the bed, and waited for Jennifer. First the phone rang.

"Chris, this is Thomas Forest here. Take six weeks off. We'll see you end of August."

"No need," Chris began, but Forest had hung up already.

The psychologist called next. She recommended two meetings a week for six weeks.

"No."

"Chris, you're blaming me for suspending you, but you've focused only on what's gone wrong. You need a sense of balance. You can't be in theatre without it. Your mind and hands both need to be in complete control."

"Want to re-train? There's a vacancy at Mary's."

"Please listen to me, Chris. See someone. Speak to them. Anyone. You've got too much in you to keep it locked up. It's not going to come out over pints on your own."

"DON'T call me again."

Thus he'd told her, the bitch, thus he'd told them all.

Bitch, bitch. The psychologist's features faded and were replaced with curly hair and false tears. And still he thought, *Bitch.* The phrase looped in Chris's mind as he stomped down the hill and into the city centre. He'd reached the part of Leeds that was all granite and concrete, black and grey stone looming above him. He found the bookshop, *Specialists in medical and legal textbooks.* He found the cardiothoracic section. They only had the standard text on MVR, the new edition that he'd already devoured in the hospital library. (Always advancing, medicine; got to stay ahead, Chris Morris.) *Aneurysms... Serious complications...* It covered everything that had happened that day, except one piece: the words that had disturbed him, *Something is missing.*

He continued his walk. He walked over to his old school, and the rugby club, and over to the Chester Arms, and found that hours had passed and his feet were sore and he was back home. Dad was in the study-bedroom, leaning towards the computer.

"Need to get your eyes checked."

On cue, Dad went, "I don't need bloody glasses!"

He gestured for Chris to come closer, and pointed at the screen where there was a digital version of the archives on his wall.

"Amazing, this software. And what she did. Three hundred years of Morrises, Berwicks and Smiths. A bloody chemistry teacher!" Dad's eyes wrinkled at this last phrase. He traced a finger along the screen and jabbed. Chris leaned in to study the spidery lines. "Look. Your mum's great-great-great grandfather, Henry Berwick, born 1815."

"Battle of Waterloo," Chris said.

"Aye. And died 1870. Well?" Dad looked up sharply. When Chris shook his head, he tutted. "Franco-Prussian War! Man of his times." Dad laughed.

When he left, Chris switched on the internet. In his wallet was the piece of paper with his email password. It took him a while to work out how to log in: this was one innovation he'd avoided longer than most, but had finally succumbed to his daughter's accusations that he was a caveman. He logged in and then repeated it three times, until he had the method right. (Always got to look ahead, improve, got to...) He had one new email, and when he saw it was from Anna, he grinned and clicked on it.

Dad, I just spoke to Mum and I don't know what to say... She wants me to come back to London... I'm so upset, Dad, just tell me you're ok.

But this was NOT how she was supposed to find out. The floor shook as his legs jiggled and he pounded the keyboard with his fingers. *No, everything is fine, I love you.* He wracked his brain for ways to make it lighter, but he was too angry. He should call Jen, but he feared he'd start to shout again. He recalled how Anna had shown him his "contacts" list. Daughter, son, WIFE. He started writing.

You know what's ridiculous?
Interfering with our daughter's summer.
I cannot believe you told her.

I am disgusted. I will not let you ruin her summer. She is going to keep travelling.

If you want to discuss this, you can do better than leave a shit message.

"*Ha-huh,*" Chris grunted. It seemed that anger made him eloquent.

Now he turned to Anna. Chris imagined all the places she'd visit. He grinned as he typed, and signed off, *Don't do anything I haven't heard of!!* He was chuckling as he came downstairs.

Dad was reading in his armchair. "What's so funny?" he asked.

Chris sat down on the sofa. "Just sent an email to Annie."

"Where is she?"

"P-ris. Ahem. P-ris."

Funny. That word was coming out wrong. Garbled in the first syllable. Try again.

"Puh-ris."

"Aye," Dad said.

It wasn't right yet. Chris's smile was wavering. His chin felt heavy. He tried again. "P..."

"Yes," Dad was saying, and sitting down beside him, and taking his arm. He said the name of the city again, or tried to, but instead of words he just heard explosions of wet air coming from his mouth and high-pitched whining inhalations and he knew that he was sobbing in front of his father while Dad patted him, saying, "C'mon, 's ok, 's ok."

Finally Dad got up and went out of the room. The kettle boiling. The smell of tea. Chris didn't move when Dad came back in and put their cups on the brown and white wicker mat.

One biccie only, Chris!

He put his head down at the memory of Mum's voice.

"What's the matter?" Dad said. "Work? Kids? Jennifer?"

Chris pinched the skin on his leg until the pain was worse than the memories and sat back up and wiped his face roughly. Dad had a mug in his hand. He was a sad old widower, alone in a chair, grey, shrinking. How to begin to tell him? How to put this weight on him?

"It's your home, Chris," Dad said. "It's safe here."

"Safe?"

"To speak. About whatever. Your mum and I never used four words if two'd do. But once in a while, you need to. That was it, back from campaign. Took a long time. A lot of silence. But the right kind: together.

141

And sometimes, speaking. If you've been in the wars, you need to speak about it."

Chris shook his head. "Too late for that," he said, and went to bed.

Anna: Arms and Armour

3 July cont.

I must look ill: Su didn't take much persuading to leave me alone and go to the Louvre. "Just stay in bed, and I'll be back in a few hours."

It's started pouring outside. Poor Su. The dorm is empty, I am alone. It wasn't a total lie about feeling ill, I feel dizzy, a sad little moon spinning around the planets. All I can think about is Dad.

I remember him one evening, coming back from work, "SURPRISE!", flowers in hand, presenting them to Mum who rolled her eyes, but Dad swung her up and she shrieked and they kissed as I fled to my bedroom yelling, *YUCK*!

I hear Mum's cold voice: *He isn't coming back.* I see Dad's wretched smile at the train station; I feel him wrap his arms around me and squeeze.

The window darkens. Outside is a black sky, thick drops of rain explode against the window. The hiss of water. Paris is drowning.

Sudden cold memory: last September, when Nan fell ill, only a few weeks after we'd been to visit her and Granddad. Dad went up, came back, said it was nothing. But he started going every weekend. "It's in the spine," he finally told us. His eyes became this weird colour, like mud, dark and unreadable, riddled with scarlet branches. I kept meaning to go, but the more Nan got ill, the harder I worked. Nan's dream ever since I was a baby was for me to get into Cambridge, it was she who showed me the whole thing – St John's, punting, Fitzwilliam, fudge. I knew she'd be upset to see me. So I stayed down, and Dad said that was good, and I knew it was good, and I knew it was wrong, and I knew how upset he was, and I cried every night.

Selfish, selfishly revising, selfishly celebrating, doing nothing to help, or worse, making it worse, cheating, lying, *Anna, Anna, Anna.*

The rain pummels the earth and calls my name and curses me. *Selfish bitch you lied to your dad.*

A punch of heat on my head: the sun has broken through the clouds.

Above the buildings opposite the window – a rainbow.

So what? Just water particles and sunlight.

*

Dad's replied.

Darling Annie,

Keep travelling! This is nothing to do with you, just history. Don't worry!

Do me a favour? Some mates who never left Leeds need your eyes and ears. They're godshonest Yorkshiremen, so forgive their simple questions. Here goes:

Is it true about drugs in Amsterdam?

whats the best route into Germany these days?

Is it true about the red light district in Amsterdam?

Wheres the best place to go clubbing in Rome?

How much grappa can you smuggle back to England?

Dont do anything I havent heard of!!

Love you,

Dad

Bullshit, Dad. There is no way he would write so much, no way he'd try so hard to make me laugh – unless something is wrong. No WAAAAAY, Dad!

I need to calm down.

I need to be practical. What is happening? Mum's saying Dad's gone, Dad's saying nothing is wrong. Typical. Mum made it sound like dad had left her, but that makes her sound vulnerable, Mum, aka Dr Carter, the paediatrician who frightens cancer away. Mum has sent him packing.

Questions:

Are they getting divorced?

Since when?

WHY?

Just history, wrote Dad.

This is all so old, Mum said. Now I need your help.

What is this about? All I know about the world before I was born comes from what other people've told me. Like Nan, when she took me to Cambridge, I was 13. We were on a punt and she pointed at some students and said, *Your mum and dad were so sweet. Fresh-faced students like those. They danced at the wedding. It was so beautiful, Anna. Your mum wasn't sure at first, you know, and I don't blame her. Our Chris wasn't the best-groomed young man in the world.*

And I was like, Dad's the best dad in the world!

Nan smiled and said, Aye, But she couldn't know that then, could she? No, she wasn't sure, and she took a long time to decide. And you make sure you do the same! No need to rush, and you're more certain after you've hesitated.

So Mum hesitated. I can believe that. But Nan was wrong that this would make her more certain, since Mum has now thrown Dad out.

I can't go home. All I'll do is scream at her, and she'll scream back... Pointless.

I can't go to Leeds, either. Dad will just make jokes, and Granddad won't say anything. Look at how they dealt with Nan's illness. "She's poorly."

But what can I do?

Just history.

Mum's got all those files in her cabinet, the old photos, she once showed me she's even got her medical files, school notebooks, stuff from Cornwall; always going on about Grandpa Peter who was like her, a fanatic of tidiness, the filing Nazi. So yeah I could root around and see if

WAIT!

Sam is there!

Detective Sam! I taught him to be one, out in the park, on the grass near the fountain, scrabbling in the dirt until we found a funny-looking stick. "This is evidence," I'd say.

"Of what?"

"Baddies, Sammy. They're hiding from you! You've got to find more evidence"

His eyes wide, his mouth open – my baby brother was a joy to tease when younger. I'll write to him.

*

4 July

Who the F is C.V.C.?!?!

My dense brother has actually found something.

It's a letter from 1981, from a guy called C.V.C. He loves Mum. He writes, *the way your smile shifts as you choose whether to be serious or playful*. I can't picture Mum as a young woman who inspires an Italian to fall in love with her, but no doubt about it – it's her.

I don't get all this ancient gods stuff. Apart from Pandora: that's the story Mum used to tell me when I was little, the woman who released all the bad things into the world. (A bizarre story for bedtime – but that's Mum.)

He also talks about Dad. *What you and Chris did. Your betrayal. Your hatred for me.* He can't be talking about the same Chris, surely?!

Sam says there's more, in Italian. He sent the first part, which is all about the narrator coming to London and meeting Dad. Why has Mum kept this? How did she read the Italian? And how did Sam type it up without knowing a word? *Bla bla blaci bla.*

I can't go back to London. How would I confront Mum? *What is this, you never told me you knew an Italian, rantrantrant.* No, I need to read the rest of this first.

FROM: Anna
TO: Mum
Sorry
but
I'm carrying on with my holiday.
You created this mess, you can sort it out yourself.
It's the most selfish thing you've ever asked of me –
and you're supposed to be the grown-up
Get a babysitter.
Anna.

[Deleted "And stop fucking around hurting other people."
Added a full-stop at the end of my name.]

FROM: Anna
TO: Sam
Great work, detective.
Send the rest.
Yes, I feel my strength returning. This C.V.C. has given me armour.

*

5 July – Ghent

Ghent is much smaller but more beautiful than Paris, more medieval, with more cobbles, more castles, and many more little Belgian pubs. But it also has ugly glass buildings and angry cyclists who yell at me because I keep stopping in the middle of the road. I feel weary. Dizzy and tired.

Oh, stop pitying yourself, girl.

6 July

Sam has sent the rest of the stories! I told Su I wanted to spend the afternoon in an internet cafe, catching up on emails, so she parked herself at the terminal next to me while I read the history of Vulcanalia.

What to make of this madness? First of all, I am clearly a genius, because I understood everything (almost everything) he wrote. In fact, C.V.C.'s language is not that difficult, kind of stilted, like his stories are notes for something longer. Given what he says at the beginning of the letter, I guess he didn't feel he had much time to write this. I wonder who he is, and where he is now.

As for the stories themselves. Mum comes out smelling less sweet than dead roses. She messed around with this guy's heart, and had this bullshit "I don't know what you're talking about, I just don't want to go to Italy" line which Mr C.V.C. saw right through. This is an apt prelude to her treatment of Dad eighteen years later. Still, it does show something good about her: she chose Dad over him.

Dad's role makes no sense. I cannot see him cheating on his friend with Mum. Dad is Mr Loyalty – won't even shop at a normal supermarket because "we've been doing our groceries with Khaled for years." But C.V.C. gets Dad right in that he's a softie; if Mum sent him packing, Dad would pack and go.

How I can use this? Is there a way to remind Mum that she made her choice, that Dad is the best man she could ever be with? Now I've dug up this past, I'm worried about waving it in front of Mum's face. I have to tell Sam to keep it secret. If part of this history they both talked about is this guy, C.V.C., I don't want Mum suddenly going gooey over some ancient crush.

7 July

Now Sam is demanding that I translate what he sent. He'll tell Mum if I don't. Blackmail! What are they teaching kids these days? I've printed off the pages, which cost a godawful 140 francs, but I can't translate. I'm too tired. What to do?

Afternoon

Su and I were passing a canal when I spotted a massive statue of a muscly man with a trident bobbing in the water. I asked Su what it was, "Neptune," she said with that eye-rolling thing that means utter disappointment in the world's ignorance. Sunlight was dancing around the plastic god. I felt dizzy again and said, "I need to rest."

So we've plopped down in the café, in the heat, nursing tap water. Su has her notebook with the Erasmus essay, the one I am also supposed to be writing: "Participants in the grant programme will write a 3,000–5,000 word essay relating to their travels on the theme of 'Growing up in Europe'." They should try growing up in Gloucester Terrace with two crazy doctors and a detective, you'd need at least 10,000 words for that.

Ok, so, actually, it seems I have a little spark of energy. I wanted poetry, didn't I? I have Vulcan, don't I? Shall I give it a try, a little bit, a little play with C.V.C.'s words?

Yes, Anna, try and get it straight, this story of Vulcan, Venus and Mars.

Jen: Pandora

She spent every waking hour that first week of July in offices and hospitals. There was no pause for breath, no moment of reflection, and when she came home, she was too exhausted to eat. At least her brief hours of sleep were no longer disturbed by nightmares. Instead she was occupied with fury, at Chris, at Anna, both of whom had gone to the same school of email-writing. They would have, she vowed, no response from her.

She never saw Sam, but she still needed to sort him out, since no one was going to help her. At the last minute she discovered that one of the nurses, Maria, babysat part-time.

"Sam's a good boy," Jen told her. "He won't be trouble, he's pretty much self-sufficient. I just can't leave him on his own for three days. Ok? I've got to go."

"What is he like?" Maria asked in a thick Caribbean accent: *lay-ak.*

"Um, he's nice. Very nice. A little erratic. But he'll be no trouble."

"What is he interested in?"

"Oh, I don't know, films, and detective stories."

She raced off to Cambridge, to teach a three-day course for new paediatricians. It went well; the group was young, bright and attentive; she could see that Mr Hussein, the surgeon who had organised it, was impressed with her, and she was pleased.

Her carriage on the train back was full, a hundred bodies inhaling each other's carbon dioxide. She wanted a glass of wine, but no trolley would get through this crowd. A cough came from the row behind her, another cough in front; summer coughs, littering the silence of the carriage. It was important to impress Hussein, she reflected, because it meant she might be invited again to Cambridge, which meant she could be near her daughter.

The thought of Anna made her clench her fist. "Shit."

A man opposite her looked up. His jowly face smiled, as if the diagnosis was easy. She turned to the window; the fields were sharp in the evening light, as if seen through a magnifying lens. She thought how she had just wanted to hold Anna, her baby and monster, for one second; one squeeze and release, the poison in her body flowing out until she was fine. But the cord between them was too taut, threatening to strangle, and Anna was too strong-willed. Jen could hear her mother proclaiming: *What you learned from me, she learned from you*. True, the stubbornness may have come from her. But Anna got her too-quick-to-be-cleverness from another source: Mr Bloody Morris.

The bowels of London were sweaty; her skin felt caked by the time she arrived home. She prepared herself as she opened the door, and when Sam called, "Hi Mum!" she put on her brightest smile and came into the kitchen.

"I made spag bol!" he said proudly. "And I poured you wine. And I put music on."

A good boy! she thought. She studied him. He hated his acne, but it was mild; he was growing taller, and a little podgy, like his dad. She should encourage him to go to the gym, perhaps they could go swimming together. All she had to do was ask; he was so much easier than Anna, so happy to spend time with her, could always make her chuckle. She remembered his yellow ducks in the bath: *they aren't very clever, Mummy*. She was freer with him; with Anna, who was more accomplished, the stakes felt higher.

But he was saying something. "Sorry, love?"

"Did I make enough?"

She realised spaghetti bolognese was the last thing she wanted to eat. "Lovely!" she said. "Just give me a minute."

She dropped what Chris called her Power Lady suit to the floor. The water in the shower pierced her skin and ran toxins down the drain along with the memories, the flirty smiles of the males SHOs, Hussein's nodding, Anna's yelling, *independence, sacrifice, discipline*, the rush of water against her ears, the steam in her eyes, and now she pressed her head against the glass door until it hurt, and she saw Chris, and felt pain, hair clinging to her neck, hands gripping the handle, a sob, another, and she switched off the water with shuddering breaths.

In the dining room, she half-listened as Sam's skittish brain leapt from topic to topic. He wanted to go to Italy. He wanted to see a dermatologist. He wanted to learn medicine. She hardly understood what they were talking about until he asked:

"Did you have any boyfriends before Dad?"

She felt the past month close around her. "Why?"

Sam dropped his head. "I'm just trying to talk." He sounded pitiful.

"Yes," she said, trying to collect her thoughts into something rational.

"What was his name?" Sam asked.

An invisible Chris appeared at the table. He was scowling at her. "Claudio," she said. Chris's face blanched, his chest ached.

Then he vanished, and there was Sam, nodding, which was wrong, he should not know about Claudio.

Jen's smile grew. She stood up. She put her hands against her cheeks and felt the heat. "Lovely!" she said, not quite looking at her son, and hurried to her bedroom where the memories could not follow.

But the nightmares could, and that night she dreamed of Italy: yellow hills, vine-leaves, wine-red light falling across the white walls of a church; when she reached out to touch it, her hand plunged into the wall and ripples spread, and she was watching the sunset in Sennen. "Princess?" She heard her dad's voice, and she awoke with a gasp, alone. The night was quiet, just a distant siren. "Something is missing..." she murmured. She grabbed a pillow, thrust it under her armpit and crushed it.

She awoke the next morning with a plan. She was always one to face forwards, but something was missing; not Chris, whom she must let recover with his father, but something from her past, and she must find it.

She started that morning: she went swimming for the first time in a decade. She just fitted into her orange bathing suit. The smell of chlorine prompted memories of the swim centre near Sennen, and the bald coach, his name forgotten. The plastic matting bit at her feet. A ticklish splash on her limbs as she dove in. She bobbed up and down; the water made the elastic less tight. She grinned and began to front crawl, arms motoring, legs pumping. *Kick, kick, kick!* came the ancient yell. Bryant: that was the name of the coach.

She came home bouncing. "Come on," she called, flinging open Sam's window, putting her hands beneath his shoulders and lifting him away from the bloody computer as he whined, "I don't want to!" She dragged him outside and into the Park. "I'm tired!" She pushed him onto a bus and they rode over to the National Gallery. "Your grandfather took me once," she said to Sam as they stood under cooling marble and maple and oak.

"I'm bored!"

But here was what she wanted: a painting by Turner. "Look, Sammy! Isn't it beautiful?" And she thought of Sennen, evening light draping on the sea, Daddy coming to get her for supper, and that evening she had walked the beach with Claudio, when there was no end to sand or energy, and they giggled, and lay...

"Yeah," he mumbled.

"Come on. One hour and I'll buy you an ice cream."

He rolled his eyes, but grew more compliant. Always so easy with Sam: second child, boy, son of Chris; how many ways there were to explain why he was the anti-Anna!

He stopped at a painting. A pale chubby woman, with her back and buttocks to them, was leaning over a man who was naked except for a bed sheet covering his crotch. At the man's leg was a small baby who seemed to be gnawing into the man's shin. She leaned into the plaque and read, *Mars and Venus* by Palma Giovane. "Did you study this at school?" she asked. Sam's head jutted back into his neck, eyebrows flying up: *as if.*

Outside, he reminded her about the ice cream. She bought him a cone. "You know," she said, "that sugar and fat increase sebum production?"

"Yeah," he slurped. "But it's important to treat yourself once in a while. The best ice cream is in Italy. It's called *gelato.*"

"Yes," she said.

*

She swam the next morning, and the next. The bathing suit began to fit. The weekend passed, another week came. She saw patients. She saw old friends. She stuck to her propaganda: *Chris is shell-shocked, gone home to recover, he'll be fine.* She called him twice and left him messages but he never called back, and she decided that this meant he was healing. She cooked dinner again and again for Sam. She ignored Anna's strange emails: *For the Erasmus essay, there's this classics stuff, can you help?*

She began to face forwards again. There were no nightmares, no thoughts of Claudio, or her father; her mind was clear of this self-pitying backwards-facing history-sucking nonsense. Her plan had been perfect in both conception and execution.

Then Friday night arrived.

It was the third week of July. She left Sam to wash the dishes, went to her desk and found an email from her daughter.

What's that classics story you used to tell me when I was a kid? Anna asked.

Pandora, she replied.

She switched off the lights and lay on the bed. In the twilight she saw a pillow that made her think of Anna as a toddler, playing with Mummy's curls, unrolling them with precision while Jen closed her eyes and sensed the tiny fingers learning to grasp, eyes coordinating with digits, the physics of curls embedding itself in Anna's plastic brain: down, up, down, up. On

152

weekdays, if she came home early and Anna had just gone to bed, it was story time. *Did you know...?* It was always an explanation of things, because a good mother creates the desire to learn. *Did you know how fire came into the world? Prometheus stole it. The gods punished him. They punished man as well. They sent Pandora with a jar. And when the jar opened all the bad things of the world came out and all the humans screamed.* Mummy stopped here and Anna looked ready to burst into tears. So she added, *And all the good things came out too. Like kisses* and she kissed *and hugs* and she hugged *and cosy blankets* and she tucked her in and rolled her up and Anna slept.

But Jen could not sleep. The waters in her mind began to rise. Darkness was around her. Her breaths grew short. She recalled saying to Sam, *Claudio.* The story of Pandora was his story. The words of Anna's email swelled and she remembered her nightmares. The waters kept rising. She had opened forbidden doors, wretched things were crawling out. Chris was yelling, "*Something is missing.* That's what you said." Three weeks, alone in bed. She was shaking. She pulled the blanket over herself. She gripped her knees and curled up, head pressed into the pillow. A low moan vibrated through the bed. There was a pain in her belly. Onset. When had this started? Was it three weeks ago? No, earlier: three months – that first nightmare, repeating for weeks after. But, no, earlier, when Anna got into uni. And still, the waters rose, her head flooded, and she recalled last year, when she had sobbed and hugged her kids, tearful over Bea, Chris's mother, but not wanting to frighten them, inventing work problems, fictitious leukaemia cases; but still further, two years ago, when they'd gone to Cornwall and she'd seen her entire childhood in five minutes and slipped into a waking nightmare, terrified of being with her family, and walked all day and night, falling to the ground and crying, rising again, and, no, what was that? Where did it come from? *Something is missing.* She was crying freely into her pillow, hoping her moans were masked by the door Chris had pounded. What did she miss? Claudio... Her stomach clenched. Dark eyes, slender nose... But so long ago, so ancient. And still her thoughts would not stop, memories swept past her, further back, to Sennen, and *DAAADYYY...* She rolled and wept and no longer cared if Sam heard her.

She had grabbed at the jar of her life and tipped it over. Something was missing, an absence she had clung to all her life, a perversion of comfort that she could not hide behind any more. Something was missing. What?

Chris: Hercules

They tried cooking together on his tenth night up. Chicken shouldn't be that shade of black. So they went for curry.

Dad asked, "Sam going to visit us this summer?"

Chris said, "'Course, just working out when's best."

Next morning, he tried London.

"Morris residence?" went Sam's voice. It was funny, Chris thought, to hear that from Dad's house.

"Hullo, Sammy. How's you?"

"Ok."

"Doing anything fun?"

"Yeah." Sam seemed to think about this. Then: "Not really."

Chris wondered how dentists got their patients to speak, even with shit in their mouths.

"What you been doing?"

"Dunno. Watched a film."

"What film?"

"*Big Adventures*. It's this cool movie about, um, Greek heroes. There's this hero who, like, gets betrayed but then he finds the people who betrayed him and he gets them."

"It's lovely up here. Granddad misses you. Love to see you." Silence. "Want to come up on the train? That's a big adventure."

"Um..."

"Reading those Chandler books I got you?"

"Yeah, The Long Goodbye."

"Got to the bit where he meets the dodgy doctor?"

"No! I'm still near the beginning. He's just taking Terry Lennox to the train."

"You could read that on the train."

"Oh, yeah, but, um, I've got this stuff to do at home. I'm helping Anna with her project, and she needs me here, to go to the library, and I've got all the notes here, and it's complicated."

"Ok." What else? "Report card?"

"It's coming in a few weeks, I think."

"Right. I'll call soon."

Chris hung up, giving the Morris grunt, two parts descending, *Ha-Huh*.

Dad cooked their tea that night while Chris sat with his *MVR* book, grunting whenever Dad made a comment like, "good, this tinned tomato." He wanted to get into theatre and operate. His fingers were twitching, his eyes felt dull from lack of action. Somewhere in the country, he thought, right now, there was a man, fifty-something, overweight, maybe watching a film, suddenly feeling wrong, standing up, sweating, chest tightening, kneeling down, breathless, now he was racing in an ambulance to Jimmy's, his chest needed opening, there were chordae torn and muscles ruptured and arteries blocking up, blood was washing back up the system, and who was going to save him? Who was better qualified than Chris Morris? Well, he thought, well then – why was he good? Because he always looked ahead. So, to spite them all, he'd know every bloody word on every page of every recent cardiac surgery journal and book by the time he came back.

"Go on then," Dad said, settling down with their spaghetti and sauce and pointing at the book. "I'll test you."

After supper, Chris went out into the messy backyard and kicked at the grass. He wondered what his Dad thought. He hadn't asked a thing: *why are you here*, *what are you doing*. It was a relief, Chris reflected, but then it was how they were – how had Dad put it the other night, *Never four words if two'd do*. Chris tugged at the broken frond of a bush, trying to release it, and gave up, slunk back to the easy chair with an *oomph*. It was a cooler evening. Chris felt old in this little fold-up chair, knees to his chest, book on his lap, looking up at the twilight. A bright light was winking, and he tried to count its pulses. Did that tell you how far away it was? He tried to remember Anna's physics lessons.

Later he logged on and found another email from Anna. He waited with his smile this time, and was rewarded.

Sorry about my last email, Dad, I get I totally misunderstood. Anyway, Mum and I chatted and she'll sort out everything her end.

Your requests are very strange and I hope I can answer them, apart from the ones about Amsterdam because Su and I are only going there to visit the museums and if I see someone doing drugs I will have them shot on sight.

Because your requests are so strange, I hope it's ok if I send some strange ones back, courtesy of Sumukhi. She wants to know "how long does it take to become a surgeon from the moment you start medical school". I said it was twelve years, like the twelve labours of Hercules, and she was like, "don't be pretentious, Anna," but anyway, please help us because we are at a terrible impasse.

Speaking of Hercules now Su and I are trying to fit his labours into this essay I'm writing about Europe but we can't remember them all. Can you help with that too please?

He was beaming as he stood up from the desk, but then he saw he had another voicemail message from Jen.

"Maria looked after Sam well. He misses you, though he probably won't show it. I hope you're ok. Everything is fine down here, I've been swimming. Anyway, I'll leave you alone for a bit, because I see you aren't in the talking mood. Call me when you are."

He walked quietly downstairs, and went onto the street. Why was he feeling so angry? He walked past the Chester Arms and its familiar faces, got to the Spread Eagle, and ordered a pint. Muttering: "Because it's a lie." Pint, laughing at the children dancing on the TV. Pint. "And she doesn't give a shit." Laughing at the old man with his big bum hanging off the chair. Pint. Swaying to the bar.

"Had enough, pal?"

"'nother." Pint. Swaying back to his corner, saying, "It was a test." Jen'd failed. She'd not come with him. Didn't love him. One thing he'd asked her to do. *Goodbye, Chris.*

"Pint." Pint. Everything he'd done for her. Eighteen years. She'd said: *Something is missing.* Clawed at him each night, dragging herself out of sleep, nightmares, striking him, saying it over and over, something is missing – he'd done all that, "and she never says I LOVE YOU."

"Come on! I told you, enough! Go on!"

Into the streets he marched, Chris Morris, left foot and right, forming up a chant: *Jennifer Carter! Lying bitch!* It sounded great out loud. He added, "A FUCKING BITCH!"

A voice from above: "Shut it, you twat!"

"LYING! BITCH!" All he'd done. "SHE NEVER GAVE A SHIT!"

"Shut it! Bugger off!"

Panting up the hill. "NEVER SAID IT! NEVER! NEVER!"

He crashed into the cabinet in the corridor at home and knocked over some plates but nothing broke and Dad didn't stir. He climbed the stairs cautiously, one a minute, stumbled to bed, and collapsed face down, saying,

"I bloody love her, I love her – why why'd she do it, why'd she hate me?"

*

He made himself a routine: university library, diagrams and formulas, nine to five, break in the canteen. He went to Jimmy's and played sycophant with the head of surgery, "Heard you lot were doing amazing things," and was allowed to observe operations, his fingers burning, god how he wanted to hold steel. Saw so many mistakes. But he couldn't completely lie to himself: every time he put on the gown, his hands began to tremble. He remembered how the whoosh hadn't come, how in that moment instead he'd heard *Something is missing.*

He went downstairs. He felt shaky. He drank. Dad's beer, and Dad's whiskey, and when he'd finished that, he went down to the corner and bought wine and whiskey and brought it back and drank more.

He was lying in the garden when he felt his body being shaken.

"Chris? Chris?" Dad loomed over him. "Look..." He squatted down awkwardly and settled for crossed legs on the grass. "Let's leave town for a day or two. Go to the lake. Have a talk. You've got to tell me what's going on. Come on. Say yes. Please."

Chris felt the spiky grass against his hands. His mouth tasted of spirits and mud. He felt like a kid, looking up at the familiar shadow, saying, "Ok, Dad."

Anna: Symbols and Words

11 July – Amsterdam

Nearly finished!!! I've spent about 10 hours on these translations. "You're writing more than me!" says Su. I've promised to share this when I'm ready. I wonder what she'll make of it. Meanwhile, she's beavering away at her essay, it looks like she's writing the history of Europe.

C.V.C.'s writing isn't poetry, not the kind I want, so I've begun to insert my own touches, ripening the language, lengthening the sentences, until we get what C.V.C. missed, a cadence, a rhythm that is mine – we can call it an Annification of the story. Or a collaboration: *Mr C.V.C. + DJ Anna Morris. Tonight from 22:00.*

He is pretty weird, if not crazy. Mum choosing Dad over him makes a lot of sense, and represents perhaps the first (and only good?) decision she's made in this department. She might say it was *practical*; not an ounce of romance in her body. That's another part of C.V.C.'s weirdness – he thinks Mum is a love nymph or goddess.

I've gone back to the English part of the letter to try to work out why he's sending her this.

He writes: It is the true story of...how I was betrayed by [Mum and Dad].

He writes: If you do not translate it, I will never know.

He writes: I will send [the necklace] when I finish it. It is my best work. It is the last. It is yours.

This sounds kind of dark. What does he mean by "the last"? What does he mean by "I will never know"? I wonder if he sent the necklace. I should ask Sam if there's anything like it in Mum's stuff.

*

Hair interlude

In this city of water and bicycles and sharp angles and narrow buildings that lean towards each other like drunks, I've decided it is time to become my TRUE self. So I grabbed Su and dragged us to a hairdresser.

"All of it?" asked the young woman with the piercings, in fluent dismay.

"No," Su said.

"No," I agreed, "but much shorter." The long black strands tumbled onto the floor and my head felt ever lighter. I babbled: "All my life I've had this long hair. My mum never let me cut it shorter than this... AND NOW!"

"Careful," the hairdresser said, snatching back her scissors as I sprang out of the chair.

"You look like a lunatic," Su said.

*

12 July – Hanover

I've sent the translations to Sam, and he in turn has worked out who C.V.C. is: Claudio Collina.

Who killed himself soon after sending this letter.

Ugh.

It's a suicide note. I feel grubby, a bit sad. This was meant to be a neat way to get under Mum and Dad's skin, but it's opened some uglier vistas.

Basta diary for today.

*

13 July

The more I've translated, the more I've felt like I was in Claudio's head.

I like some of what I see there, but only some. He has this avoidance technique, not talking about his family, making these fantastical things appear like Cupids, like he doesn't want to face the life he's been leading. I get that he sees parallels between real life and these ancient myths, and I like it (otherwise I wouldn't translate it), but I think he needs to grow up.

One thing I can give him credit for, though: I now know more about my parents than I did before. Only nan ever told me real stories about them, Dad just made jokes and Mum avoided the question. I wonder if it's because she feels guilty over how she met Dad.

Speaking of guilt, let us turn our laser beam to Mum. I've written to her about Vulcan. I kept having weird flashbacks, of Mum sitting on the end of my bed, telling me stories. Not just about Pandora. I think I remember the story of Vulcan. It's weird – I know it must have been Mum telling me the story, but I can't picture her doing it, can't remember her voice. I don't get when she would have had time, between working and telling me off. Maybe I should mention Pandora to her.

And Hercules to Dad.

Why? What am I doing? I'm trying to get them to think about how they met, and who they really are.

*

15 July, Berlin
FROM: Sam
TO: Anna

159

Hi Annie,

I really like your translation! I read it three times already!!!

Do you think Mum ever read them if they're in Italian? I don't think she did. But then why did she keep them?

Meanwhile I've done more research about Claudio. (Maybe this is useful for your Erasmus essay?) His father was rich and powerful. Federico Collina was born in Cava de'Tirreni. He ran a big company that made typewriters and then actuators and steel and all sorts of things, it's called a "conglomerate", but he sold it. He died only a few months ago, this year. (I didn't know what actuators are, so I looked them up. They're like valves that you use in waterworks. Actually, I still don't know what that means.)

Federico Collina owned a lot of statues and these got put into the Museum of Myth that Claudio mentions. It was Claudio's idea and they built it after he killed himself. Here is the link to the museum website.

I've tried to find the necklace Claudio mentions in Mum's things, but it's not there. So either Claudio never finished it or he never sent it, or maybe Mum didn't keep it?

I really hope we can visit Italy, and go to Verona to see the museum. Claudio died after he wrote to Mum and he never saw the museum, which is sad.

Do you think Claudio kill himself because of Mum and Dad?

Love,

Sam

Yes, it is sad that Claudio had an idea for a museum that he never got to see, but I'm not interested in Sam's little detective story, I don't care why Claudio killed himself. I have to make sure that he doesn't let his inquiries take him into the present shit-storm, the key question, which is what does all this have to do with Mum and Dad *now*?

But I did look at the website Sam sent, and showed it to Su. She was interested.

"I don't think anyone has ever made a museum for myths," she said.

She's particularly interested in the whole Roman gods/Europe connection.

"Remember, Anna, how Mr Roberts was saying the new European currency was like the old Roman *sestertius*, a new way to bind the western continent. Old Rome, new Rome." She drifted off, looking at a particularly good-looking American boy who had sat at the table next to us. (I've kissed three boys so far, Su has snogged none.)

"Very interesting," I said, totally disinterested. But it never hurts to be polite to your friends if they might one day be President of the Continent. "What does this have to do with the gods?"

Eyes rolling wildly: "Think about it like this. The last time we had a single currency for the continent, we had lots of Roman gods. Then we had lots of countries all believing in one religion, Christianity. Now what do we have?"

"Nothing?" I was getting impatient. Su thinks she's Socrates.

"Now we have new gods, little 'g'. Like a god of justice, of equality, of democracy. Maybe to have a unified continent, we need a fragmented religion. Maybe, the European Union will succeed because no one believes anything any more."

She nodded at her own words and began to write furiously. She scowled when I said, "But didn't the Romans believe in their gods?"

"Oh, maybe, I don't know, but it wasn't *serious*, it was like a transaction. Take Vulcan. They had this festival every year, Vulcanalia. The Romans would go to Vulcan's altar and burn fish to please the god. It was like a commercial deal. *Oh mighty god, please spare the harvest, and in return, we burn these for you.* Why don't we do that anymore?"

"Cos it was bollocks," I said.

"Yes, it was bollocks," Su said, "but if you were a farmer today, you wouldn't want a fire to destroy your crops."

My mind lightened and for a micro-second I almost understood what Su was talking about. "So was it like taxes? We pay the government to put out fires, the Roman citizen paid the gods?"

"Correct, Anna," (SO professor-in-waiting) "the state replaces Vulcan. Is that so different from worshipping gods? Do we even see the state? Look at Europe." (She waved an arm towards the American, almost knocking my sunglasses off my head.) "I mean, what is Europe anyway? It's too big to see it all. There's no one alive who's seen the whole of Europe, and there never will be. So how do we know it exists?"

"That's just nihilism," I said.

"No. I'm saying, we have to believe in it. It's not enough just to say it's out there. We have to believe in things for them to be real to us."

"Right..." I said, adding quietly. "I tell you what I believe. I believe in a thing called love. And that boy over there, no there, is looking at you with a lot of interest."

Su scowled at him and rolled her eyes at me. "My point is, Anna, without gods, what symbols do we have? Take Vulcan, he symbolised fire and industry. Or the sun, it symbolises light and understanding. What does Europe symbolise?"

"I. Don't. Know!"

She scowled at me, but then suddenly her eyes brightened. "You're right, Anna. No one knows. Haha! No one knows what Europe symbolises! That's the problem!"

I'd think she's mad. But then, I'm the one translating the Veronese boy who thinks he's a god, while I have no idea what my parents are doing...aaah.

Vulcan Revenged

1975

Scrape, scrape, scrape.

"But why can't you study HERE, in nonno's university?"

"It has to be Bologna, Lissa."

"But WHY?"

"I have to study engineering. Bologna is the best for engineering."

"Mama says you're only going because Papa forced you." Scrape. "She says engineering is for beavers and monkeys." Scrape, scrape. "But what KIND of jewellery are you making?"

"You'll see."

"Mama is translating Catullus's poems. Do you know that? And she's writing a commentary. And I memorised some of the poems. One bit goes:

a maiden untouched is dear to her own;

but when her body has lost its flower,

she is not lovely, not to boys nor to girls."

Pause. "That's an...interesting choice, sorellina." Scrape, scrape.

Footsteps.

Tinkle.

Creak.

CLANG.

"ISSA! Don't touch anything!"

"Sorry. Are you making a present for me or not?"

"We'll see who it's for."

"Mama says Vulcan was the god of the workshop. She says he could make anything."

"Like what?"

"He made Pandora's box."

"It wasn't a box, Lissa, it was a jar."

"Oh."

"You have to be accurate about these things. He also made Pandora herself. She was the most beautiful woman who'd ever lived. Vulcan got all the gods and goddesses to put the worst things into the jar and then they sent her down to earth to release them so that mankind would suffer."

"Why would Vulcan want mankind to suffer?"

163

"He didn't. It was the other gods. Especially Jupiter, who loved to punish everyone even though he was the worst criminal of all. Whereas Vulcan was happy as long as the Romans burned live fish for him."

"Please don't go, Dio."

"I promise I will make something for you."

"So you can stay?"

"So you can remember me."

Sniff. "Don't be late for dinner. Papa is angry; he says he has to sell the typewriter business and no one is here to help him. And Mama is... Mama loves you too, Dio. And I..." Kiss. "Make me something special."

"I will."

Footsteps. Creak. Slam.

Scrape, scrape, scrape.

Jen: The Jar

Saturday morning. Jen stood in front of the mirror. She stuck out her tongue, she pulled at her hair. She lifted her shirt and looked at her belly, straight on, sideways. She took off her pyjamas and stood naked. She tapped her knee. She blew up her cheeks and bent her mouth into a smile. She did not look at her eyes. That was where the memories hid.

Her appearance was composed and professional. There were some lines on the neck but no grey in the hair. When she'd been young, she'd not appreciated her beauty. In her filing cabinet were photos of her, in a dress, in a bikini. Ugh. Gorgeous! Wasted! She looked back in the glass and here was the sheep they'd no longer shear.

Patient "E", 42, female. Presenting distress, guilt complex, Elektra complex, emotional repression, amnesia, and...

"Something is missing." She nodded.

She checked her pulse. She breathed in. She breathed out. This examination was ridiculous. How would she find what was missing? How did you treat an adult?

Same as a child: take a history.

"I'm off to the Park," she called to Sam's room. "I'll be a while."

*

1957–1976

Cornwaaaaaaaaaaaaaaaaaaaaal

Running ahead of her daddy, down to the beach to take in the salt air and sun, ducking their endless contest where she was the prize, skipping on the sand, skimming to the water...

"Don't go too far, Jennifer!"

"She's fine – let her explore."

She was the youngest, the only girl. She was playful in the way of underwater currents. Her brothers wanted to catch her but she was the littlest girl with the blondest curls and would be caught by no one. The water was her friend. She swam and swam until they dragged her out.

"Don't want to. No, no, no!"

She was

"stubborn as hell,"

"a determined little girl."

165

She stood above a rock pool and looked down at an immobile starfish: sunset orange, barnacles of white on hard skin. A tiny movement in one of its fingers, a sullen lifting. She crouched down, tiny bottom on tiny heels. The starfish was stuck in this rock pool. *Stuck*! She giggled. If she lifted it up like this, slimy life pulsing in her hands, and walked past the rock pool, and tossed it into the waves...

"What are you doing, Jenny?"

"I made the little star fish free!"

Out there, in the ocean, something was waiting for her.

She'd learned this from Daddy. He too was stuck. He had been an engineer in the RAF and was now a manager within the NHS. Obsessively tidy, surrounded by files, his heart craved water and stories. He took the boys on adventures, "but who's my only princess?" His stories were gospel. They were the spirit in her soul, like the wind that patterned waves and sands; they were among her earliest memories, as strong a footprint as her genes.

Half of Daddy went into her and half of her mother. "Carole with an 'e'," not tender but involved, not beautiful but striking. She came from Oxfordshire and wanted to return – she didn't like the sea. Carole had wanted to be a doctor; the war came and she could be a nurse. She told her daughter no stories, just the reality of blood-and-sweat canvas floors. She chanted mantras at her daughter: "Independence is the goal. Medicine is the best. Be a doctor. Let no one tell you that because you are a woman you cannot do anything in this world."

So boring to a girl of sand and sea and stories. Yet:

"What do you want to be when you grow up, Jennifer Carter?"

"Princess and a doctor! Princess and a doctor!"

"Princess OR doctor?"

"And! And! And!"

Though what she wrote was:

When I grow up

When I grow up I want to be a Princess. Altho this is wat many peeple want to say I think my plan is better wich is to marry a Prince! Here is what a Prince looks like. He is very tall and strong and he rydes on a horss he wars a crown and his eyes are very bloo. A Princess duz many fun things like go to Balls like Sinderela but she duznt do nuthing els this is also for she duz important things like open hospitals and help the needee. So I think it is important. And also fun.

The air sucked at her infant hair and she grew into a brunette. She became proud and wanted to conquer every class, even those where she had little aptitude, such as languages. She yearned for the outdoors. But adolescence is the rejection of childhood. Her mother, once a dull enforcer, was now who she wished to be. Daddy was just tired, a facilitator for the doers: he had not fought in the war but repaired planes; he was not a doctor but a manager.

"Come on, princess, let's go for a hike."

"Jesus, Dad! My exams are in a week."

Whereas it hurt to think of her mother's ordeals. Alone and exhausted in her bedroom, she could cry among the files, exhorting herself – "What are you? some shitty failure? will you make her proud?" – and pretend that she too was a stubborn young nurse shipped over with the Queen Alexandra's to Juno beach, wading through blood-thickened canvas and the stink of splinted flesh and unwashed uniforms, among men without legs and arms and jaws, lungs, kidneys, eyes, but with life and the prospect of life for there was someone there to save them, and nothing was more necessary in the universe than to save them. What was missing? To be a doctor. When? Immediately. Where? London is best. Which...? Enough questions! Go, girl! Go, go get it!

*

1976–1978

London in '76 stank. Dirty streets, Dickensian belchings of smoke. She went to her digs and unpacked her meagre warm clothes. The endless pulse of the city outside was intoxicating, but she had to study.

"Carter?"

"Anterior."

"Thank you. Now will the rest of you pay attention?"

There was no way they were going to treat her as some backwater girl. She may not have had the best grades but she would work harder than any of them and she'd be an excellent student, though she had no ambition to be the best. It baffled her that everyone gave that title to the monstrous northerner, Chris Morris.

"Help you with that, Jen?"

"No. Thank you."

Fumbling. Bloody knives.

"Here, you want to –"

"Piss off, Chris."

She tried to match her propaganda: that she was respectable yet ambitious, civilised yet tough. Her friends were earnest middle-class kids from London. The best was a sweet girl called Sarah (*now a GP in Ipswich*). She gave herself to medicine, and medicine gave her power.

"Learned anything yet?" One of her brothers, probably Richard, Christmas '77, the last time they were all together.

"Yes."

"How to tie your scrubs. Haha."

"Haha. How's your food? Is it past your pharynx yet?"

"What?"

"If so, it's moved into your oesophagus and stomach sack, and later your colon, where *E. coli* produces methane, which is why you stink so much. The waste will pass through your rectum and into the anus, where we hope your voluntary sphincter will stop you from defecating."

He: Gagging.

Mother: Smiling.

Daddy: "Jesus, Jenny."

*

February '78

"Your father is ill."

She sprinted for the train. Daddy had kept quiet for weeks about the pain in his lungs; Mother "didn't want to disrupt your studies."

He was gone when she got there.

The sea was bitter cold as Jenny spat her tears into the wind. Her yells drowned in the waves, she hurled curses, begging questions, the ebb of childhood joy, the flow of smoking London: *your career is meaningless*, roared the waves, *you couldn't even save your daddy*.

Mother didn't wait a day before talking of moving back to Oxford.

There was nowhere to escape to. She fled to London, disembarking at every station on the train back to the capital, sobbing, furious, demanding, *Why doctor? Whose idea? Another's fantasy.* Who hated the sea? Who hated her? Only one person had worked so relentlessly to undo her happiness. "Bitch! Make me lead your life?" Whereas only one person had told her that she was a princess and the world was full of dreams that were hers to shape. But she had not listened to him, and now never could. A furious whistle and she climbed back on – each station, again.

That night in London was the hardest: meter broken, shivering under the duvet, swearing oaths she couldn't recall, a memory in black and grey, surrounded by somethings that were missing – her daddy's stories, his smile, his testing an apple's ripeness by tapping it against his teeth.

Her friends found her and fed her, they led her, talked to her, listened to her. Her grief was a snowball. Winter passed, a year passed. She studied, avoided home, took solitary walks. On the anniversary of her father's death, the snowball of grief returned and she lay in bed and sobbed and swore new oaths: yes, she would be a doctor, but no, life would only begin with sex and marriage, a bundle of firsts to be met by One Worthy Man, who would be a prince, who would be the great story of her life. That was what she missed.

And the snowball began to roll.

*

Mar–Sep 1980

She was a doctor-in-waiting, waiting at a ball, and staggering along the carpeted outer corridor was a drunken prince. Ridiculous.

"Are you all right?" she asked.

He leant against the wall and melted into a sitting position beside her. She reached behind and presented a glass. Drunken handsome idiot.

"Have some of my water."

She must guide the patient through the steps. She watched him study the glass, taking it by the tips of his fingers as if it was larger than it appeared. He raised the rim to his lips. His hair was very dark. He looked up. His eyes were very dark. He handed the glass back to her. He spoke in shy English, Italian-flecked but fluent. "You smell like a...we call it *mughetto*." She made some comment about the air.

Mother had not considered this. She had not conceived of the risk. She had not taught that simplest of rules: do not fall for a dark-haired Italian stranger.

He said she smelled like a flower, quoted Roman poetry, spoke of war, and wine, and told her a story about a goddess. This was an avalanche!

His eyes were sad like Daddy's, but he was a prince. What was a prince? Exotic. Rich. A good man. A fragile man, needing protection, needing a princess. What was a princess? The woman for a prince.

And they danced.

But no, no, no, she was a *doctor*. She fled. She hid.

Three days later, her flatmate Sarah handed her the phone without explanation. It was him, and she could not hide a vocal blush. A meeting in the park? Unusual and ill-conceived given it was still cold, but very well.

This park. This bench. That path. This pool. Prometheus. That fountain. Pandora. (*Hasn't thought of that in years. Funny, Anna's email – asking about...*)

She kissed him.

Go, girl!

She slept with him.

Go, go get it!

She moved in with him.

She'd fulfilled her oath, Claudio was the worthy man, the One, now just marriage left to do. And so she turned to prophecy: she would finish her studies; then they would marry; there'd be career; then babies; she even pictured grandchildren, running in little red boots. She made this prophecy when Claudio's hard face was caressed by sleep, when she yearned to share his dreams and imagine that they were hers.

She skipped steps. What would he do when his year at Imperial was over? Where would they live? But that is the nature of prophecy: implementation is an after-thought.

With Claudio, she made new friends. They were wilder and brighter. Chris Morris, still top of the year, was closest to Claudio. They visited museums together, an odd couple. What did they talk about? She wanted to fly above them, hide behind a statue, ears craning round the marble and armour. Claudio told them to study together. Chris proved a perfect study companion; she was the organised one, he the knowledgeable.

In everything he did, Claudio was perfect, and nothing was missing. Except...

He had, like her, a Mother, or rather a Family. "Won't you tell me about them?" Claudio's slender face never ceased dancing, eyes darting, lips jumping between half-smiles and semi-smiles and half-frowns. But when she asked about his family, he froze.

His father was rich, that much she could guess from his digs. His mother, he said, was a poet. He had a sister but said nothing more about her.

"Ok," she said. She felt a dark weight upon him, a something that was missing, that he wouldn't share, but ok, and she held her tongue.

In the summer holidays, she took him to Sennen. After he left, she spent a week alone, walking the beach, communing with Daddy's spirit, telling him about Claudio. She decided that he adored Claudio as she did. She decided that she would be happy with him. She wore a bracelet that he had made her and their song was "Romeo and Juliet" by Dire Straits, and they shared a bed, and were perfect in the day and in the night.

*

Oct '80

And in the night they held each other
missing nothing.

*

Oct '80–Dec '80

The truth of hearts beating chest against chest is vital and quick and then quickly lost.

Claudio went to Italy in October and came back haunted. "My mother is sick," he said. But he had good news. "Come to Italy."

"What?" He'd stunned her. "Um. Wow. Let's discuss. Think it through."

"No! NO DISCUSSION! I need you to come. Come with me! I beg you."

Before his sudden, unfamiliar anger, her stubborn self rose up and lashed out. "No," was her first instinct. But rather than talk it through, he ran off, furious, himself crying, unable to express himself. When he came back, it was to ask the same question. It was as if he believed that, with enough kisses and pleas, he could change the functions of her mind. But she needed explanation. She needed to know more about his family. That wasn't all. She needed to finish her studies and have some idea about the future, and they weren't such big things to ask for, were they? (But she was such a perverse, stubborn little girl – oh, if he'd said, "I'll stay," she might well have gone.) He offered no answers, only solutions.

"You will learn the language easily. You can practice medicine there."

He pulled such thoughts out of a magic hat: everything in life was easy for him. He would neither listen nor understand. Every conversation ended with a grab of her hands, lips pressed to her cheeks or lips, his hot breath on her face, the passion almost overwhelming her, the spell undone as he said, "Come with me, to Italy." She hated crying but she became a sobbing child in front of him, tripping over one-word sentences. "Please. Claudio. No."

She turned in desperation to his best friend, Chris, who offered to bring it up with Claudio. Her mind floated about the corridors of the museum they went to every week. The default for this odd couple, in her presence, was silence, and she wondered how they communicated about something like this. Chris reported back in his thick accent.

"Wants you to go to Italy."

They were sitting on Claudio's cream rug, surrounded by books of pathology. "I know that!" she said. "But I don't understand why it matters so much to him. He NEVER explains."

"His family."

"But he doesn't TELL me anything! He CLAMS up. He talks even less than YOU do."

It was useful to yell at Chris. She couldn't yell at Claudio, he was too fragile, too furious, she wanted only to hold and be held by him. Chris was a rock, somewhere to direct her anger. They took to walking in Hyde Park, clearing their minds, splitting their conversations: outdoors for relationships, indoors for medicine. Autumn dyed the leaves ruby red. She started each conversation hopeful but ended each one in despair.

"Have you told him that I can't go? Have you told him that he's being cruel? Does he not understand? Chris, what does he say? What do you tell him? No, don't look at me."

After her sea-and-sand-storms, Chris would pick himself up and say, "It'll be fine."

Funny how she always believed him. She didn't want Chris. You could not want a Chris. The best you could do was marry one and build a civilisation on his broad forehead. Or let him hold you in the park.

It was early winter and the sun was close upon them. She tried to take off her coat. One of the thick wooden buttons got caught on her hair. Chris tried to help and was leaning close to her, and she turned her head and suddenly his lips were against hers. It was almost pleasant, and then it was over. Chris staggered back, saying, "sorry, sorry," and she'd got her coat off, and she said, "no, no, it's all right" as if he'd broken a mug.

She didn't want a Chris. She wanted a prince. But through November and December, her prince turned to accusations, as if he'd been there that day. "Jen, my Jenny, please, you must stop seeing Chris."

Each night with Claudio felt like the last. He was evaporating, destroying the prophecy. "If you don't come to Italy, you are betraying me." She learned to hold back her tears.

172

At the Christmas Ball, he dragged her to a small garden. Her skin was frozen.

"So come now," he said, "let us be serious. Come to Italy."

She thought of waves and sand and cried. Life had promised her a prince and given her a prince and the promise was a lie because the prince would go and she cried. She said "no" a thousand times and cried and cried and he said, "Then there is no reason for me to stay."

Grain by grain, she rebuilt her fortifications, until finally she could say, "Fine."

He turned and left. When she came back to the flat, she found that he had gone. There was a letter advising her that the lease would expire in a month. He hadn't even signed it.

He took something with him that day, something of hers, something she'd never have again. But that couldn't be what was missing, because it had been missing before she met Claudio, and it would be missing after Claudio was gone.

*

Dec '80-Jan '81

But something remained.

She found out at Christmas, at Mother's new home in Oxford, getting teased by her brothers who feared the unmet Claudio. She sat down at her childhood desk and wrote a letter.

My darling Claudio,

I think of you every day. I think of us.

I remember…

I remember so many moments but they are too raw. I cannot bear to think of any except two.

One is walking with you in Hyde Park, that very first time, when you told me the story of Pandora.

And here is the second I allow myself: Walking with you on the beach in Sennen, and the old man who tried to sell us an ice lolly that he'd been given by some stranger, and you telling him that you only had a ten-pound note, and then giving it to him. And I thought, this is the mad generous man who I want to be with for the rest of my life.

You left and this has been the hardest month of my life.

I am not like you. I can't say things in the way you like to say them, and perhaps hear them. I am too pragmatic. You called me a princess once,

and I told you to bugger off. But that is what I always dreamed someone
would call me, and so now I have to tell you: I am pregnant.
 You said things when you left that I didn't understand and still don't.
 I want to be with you. I need to speak to you.
 Please come back to London.
 You have it – you have my love,
 Jennifer

She took it with her back to uni. She knew what it meant to send the letter.

There were five months left until their final exams. She lay on the sofa in Sarah's flat, lonely, homeless. She walked the streets of Paddington and the paths of Hyde Park. Step by step, she tried to make a decision. She stopped to cling to dirty black railings or lean against columns with cracked paint. She got offers of help which she waved away with a wretched smile.

On the first ward visit back, she leaned against anything that would support her weight, hiding shaky knees. It doesn't take twenty medical students to guess. She managed it until Chris came to visit with flowers.

"That's sweet," she said. She laughed and stumbled. He caught her. She began to sob.

"You're pregnant," he hushed.

They sat up all night. The bulb in Sarah's living room was dirty orange, shuddering occasionally with the nearby trains, casting hulking shadows of Chris's thick legs sprawled out from the sofa and her glass that he endlessly refilled. She went to the loo every hour. Each time she returned the room was a little softer and he sat a little closer; finally she was bent over her knees and he was stroking her back and saying,

"Send it, or you'll regret it all your life."

The reply came three weeks later. It was mournful, full of self-pity and recrimination. It spoke of the myths Claudio had always enjoyed telling her, but more darkly, with glimpses of the family he had hidden from her, especially his sister. It was fascinating to her, and upsetting, and she read it several times, trying to glean more meaning, always arriving back at the moment when the English ended and the Italian began. What was she supposed to do? She was pregnant, she had finals, she spoke no Italian, she knew no one who did. She had asked him to come to London. She should have guessed that Claudio could not take a simple letter and reply simply.

This was his answer: he was not coming. She was meant to translate his life story, or his mythology, or whatever it was he had sent, and be grateful for what he had shared. Instead she filed it, intending to destroy it.

But at that moment, her mind was clear. Nothing was missing this time, rather the opposite.

*

31 July 1981

PainnnnNNNnnNNNNnaannnnannnnannannnnannannnnnnnnnaannnnnna she was having a baby why was she having this baby whose fucking idea was it no why had she done this to herself no Claudio had done it no she wasn't allowed to think his name no it was Chris who had stopped her going out the door to the nearest abortion clinic he'd said think about it so she'd thought about it for a day and a day became a week and a week became a month and she had to tell her motherrrrrrrrrr you knew where you stood with Mother and the moment Mother's tongue started clicking against banalities Jen knew that only one thing here was irrevocable if she killed his no the baaaaaaaaaaaaby but that left her with this fucking pain which made a joke of the inconvenience of the past months explaining to everyone what had happened preparing for exams with half her brain focused on keeping this thing in her belly aliiiiiiiiiiiiiiiive and they'd had to make arrangements because of what they called her special circumstances and she'd had to sort out where she'd live and how and none of it would have been posssssssssible without that fucking fucker fucking amazing Chris Morris whose baby they said it was and he was standing outside now because she'd cried "THIS ISN'T YOUR BABY WHYYYYYYYYY ARE YOU HERE?" but the answer was he was her boyfriend no surely more than that and he was out there with her mother which must make for interesting conversation buuuuuuuut she'd passed her exams she was a doctor a doctor on a bed on a BED with a midwife beside her a difficult cassssse she was the difficult case "whyyyyyyy are you so stubborn" Mother said "whyyyyyyy don't you listen" but she didn't have to listen anymooooooorrrre she was aboooooooout to beeeeeeee a moooooooooother herself aaaaaaa she was aaaauauahanana she was

*

1981

A mother.

To keep the child was the most sublime decision of her life.

175

It was also the stupidest. The child was not only hers. But the father had abandoned her, and rejected her plea to come back, and sent her a mad and angry letter, and before this, insisted that they go to Italy – with him as the absent father, what kind of life would she be accepting for herself and her child?

Well, what alternative did she have?

There was a myth that Claudio once told her: it went, Jen cheated on him with Chris. Now Claudio was gone, and here was Chris, a brilliant medic, a loving son, a family man, a man to build a life with.

She was mad.

Not least to think that Chris could have any interest in this idea. And yet, one day in the park, her bulge long past "starting to show", he put his hand out to her. "I'll be the dad," he said.

That was the first step. He didn't wait for her to give birth to propose the second one. It was the day after medical finals. He took her to the park and smashed a bottle of champagne against a tree. She yelled about the waste, he noted that she couldn't drink it anyway, and as she was working up a retort, she saw what was on the ground: a gleaming wet golden ring.

"What?" she said. Then: "Yes. Yes, but... No, Chris. This is not a good idea. We're not at all alike. And you gave me terrible advice: you told me to wait. I should have just done it. Now look at me. I'm a blimp. And it won't work, us being married. I don't want to play second fiddle to anybody. No. I won't marry you. I won't do it." He held her close. She squirmed but couldn't undo his grip. "You're going to be some top surgeon. I don't want to be a bored housewife."

"Mum's a teacher," he said.

"I am not your mum." No, indeed: she was a brat, whereas his mum – Beatrice Anna, "call me Bea" – was tough and tender, watching her with careful eyes but welcoming her into the fold with a hug. She liked his mum. "Anyway," she snapped, "I have to marry you now. Claudio's gone."

Chris's shoulders slumped; his chin drooped. And she understood. She could attack Chris, she could beat him, berate him, but she couldn't say this ever again. He was not Claudio's replacement: he was Chris, a man to marry willingly, or not at all.

"I'm sorry." And she kissed him. Not a stolen winter kiss to puzzle over and lie about, but a true one, tender and summery: a kiss of their own. Chris had thick lips and a great gentleness for a man so large. He had a rich, salty fragrance. He came from the hills of Yorkshire but he smelled of the sea. She could live like this, held by him. She could embrace this life.

He would only ever treat one person with more tenderness than her, and that was her daughter. Their daughter. He was husband, father, surgeon, man. Chris: he was the man she had chosen. She didn't have to. She chose him.

But...

Even then, there was a hesitation. It had nothing to do with the lie, nor the way Claudio was pushed to one side. She had learned to live without her father by forgetting the hardest parts, the deepest pain. She would do the same with Claudio.

But something else was missing with Chris. He wasn't perfect. Because she didn't fancy him? Because he spoke so little? Because he truly was brilliant, and she knew no matter how hard she'd work, she'd always be in his shadow? Or was it this: how often had she heard her mother rant about the primadonna surgeons, who think their family and hospital and the entire world should accommodate their every need? Chris Morris might become one of them.

"No, I won't," he said.

"He says that now," a little voice told her, that might have been Daddy's. "But give him five years. Ten."

Eighteen...

And what of all the challenges she faced and overcame in those years, how she raised her kids, how she was a good mother to them, she was a good wife to Chris, she never went back to the sea that called for her, she brought them up in London though she hated London, she chose the best life for them all, and for eighteen years, she was an excellent woman? How she tried to please Anna, to steer her daughter out of girlhood to become the young woman she must surely be. "That's not the way to sit. That's not the way to speak. Be kinder to your brother." So she found herself a Mother, chastising her daughter, fighting her baby, trying to control her, though she didn't want control! She wanted Anna happy, and covering yourself in sunburn and tears is not the way to do it, so Mummy does insist on suncream before you go to the park. And Mummy doesn't think Italian is a good language to learn, "but Nan and Granddad do," so Jen won't fight, but even so it becomes a fight, why won't you listen to me, "I FUCKING HATE YOU," why was she always wrong and Chris always right – but Chris got it wrong, Chris insisted too, Chris the penny-counter,

Chris had hurt Anna as much as Jen had – but Chris had chosen Anna, as he had chosen Jen, and...

*

1981–1999

That bench. That statue. That stroller. That child. That wipe of the nose. That game of tickle. That game of chase. That fountain. That bathtime. That ball. That lecture. That yell. That hug. That kiss. That tying of the shoelace. That sob. That look of disappointment. That ice cream cone. That "don't want to!" That "no, no, no!" That yell of the name. That hug. That trip. That scream.

These cases of sore throat, of pneumonia, of mumps, of rubella; of cough and wheeze, of bronchiolitis, of streptococcal pharyngitis; of rhinorrhea, of sinusitis. Of rash, of viral exanthem, of Kawasaki's, of pyloric stenosis. Of fractured hip and leg and wrist, of bruising, of social workers, of police. Of septic arthritis, of transient synovitis, of petechiae and purpura, of trauma, heart murmurs, and lymphadenopathy. Of leukaemia. (*Patient R. has hemolytic uremic syndrome?*)

Those words of comfort. Those long walks. Those mornings in bed. Those (rare) holidays. Those giggles. Those stories. Those gifts. Those tender words.

Two years ago: Cornwall. One year ago: Bea's death. Six months ago: Anna accepted to Cambridge. Three weeks ago: "Goodbye, Jennifer."

Something is missing. What?

Something is missing. But now she's taken the history and has no diagnosis.

Perhaps that's all you can expect when you take your own history: shake a box and watch everything come out. And now to pack it away again.

All but what is missing.

Sam: The Plot Thickens

Sam's dad, whatever his faults (and, indeed, crimes), had one redeeming quality: he was an expert recommender of detective books. Every summer, apart from this one, he had given Sam a bundle of good books to read. Last summer, along with Raymond Chandler, there had been *Fatherland*. Sam's first reaction had been, *here's another one of Dad's WWII-obsession books*, but it had turned out to be an excellent detective story; moreover, the stubborn, methodical detective had taught Sam that one of the things a good detective must do is make a chronology. *And so...* Sam thought, as he opened up his case file and began to type.

Case of the Missing God (cont.)
Chronology:
Jan 1980: Claudio Collina arrives in London
Mar: meets Chris Morris (at "Jimmy's caf")
Apr: meets Jennifer Carter (at April ball)
May: Jen moves into Claudio flat
Aug: Claudio goes with Jen to Sennen
Sep?-Nov?: Jen and Chris cheat on Claudio
Oct: Claudio return to Verona to see ill mother
Nov: tries to persuade Jen to come to Italy, fails
Beginning Dec: Christmas Ball (see photograph)
10 Dec: Claudio returns to Verona
12 Jan: finishes letter to Jen
18 Jan: Claudio kills himself
Questions:
Do Mum and Dad know that Claudio killed himself? Unlikely (only reported in Italian press)
Why did Mum keep Claudio's letters? Guess: still loves Claudio
Original questions to investigate:
Who is C.V.C.? Claudio Vittorio Collina.
What did Mum (and Dad) do to him? Betrayed him.
How did Mum read Italian? Guess: she didn't
Why is Anna interested?

The pieces were falling into place, but Sam still did not understand why Anna had wanted these stories in the first place. Why had she been interested in finding out more about Mum and Dad?

He re-read their most recent emails.

FROM: Anna Morris
TO: Inter-rail Envy (group)
Hello all,
I know, I know, I'm sorry, I promised regular emails, daily, weekly, monthly, whateverly. Sorry sorry sorry, but I've finally managed to snatch some time to bring you all the news.

So far we've been to Paris, Ghent, Amsterdam, Berlin, and are now in Prague. Holy moly! Highlights of the trip include:

Paris: Louvre, Notre Dame, day trip to Monet's house, Su's new husband/Email stalker

Ghent: The beer, the castle, the beer,

Amsterdam: Remember nothing. But, seriously – Van Gogh museum is amazing

Berlin: Here we really had some wild times. Su now has four husbands and I have four piercings. (Half of this sentence is a joke)

Prague: Castle, bridge, museums, park, exhaustion, internet cafe.

Phew! If you're still with me, we're leaving in two days for Vienna, then into Italy on the same route as Hannibal (that's the Carthaginian general, Tabs, not the cannibal).

For those of you interested, Sumukhi and I are developing what I can only describe as an UNUSUAL essay for the Erasmus grant about the parallels between the EU and ancient mythology. I expect it will make a few geezers in Brussels scratch their heads.

Love, Anna
A few personal PS's:
Mum: The joke about remembering nothing in Amsterdam was a joke.
Tabs: details to follow separately
Sam: I met a girl in Berlin who is a huge Raymond Chandler fan. There is hope for you yet.

FROM: Sam
TO: Anna
Hi Annie,

I hope Prague is really cool. I wish I was there now and then going to Italy!

I worked out the chronology of what happened to Claudio. He killed himself thirty-nine days after he came back from England, which was just enough time to write the letter and make the necklace. His letter to Mum is definitely a suicide note.

But I think maybe she didn't know, and maybe Dad didn't either. That doesn't make it ok what they did.

Do you think Melissa Collina would be interested in these stories?

Love,

Sam

FROM: Anna

TO: Sam

Oh, lil bro, you are too much. This is not a murder investigation. Mum and Dad were young, and in love, and this is what happens sometimes – people move on from each other. Claudio wanted to go back to Italy, Mum didn't have to go with him. I don't expect you to understand all this yet, but please store it in your brain for when you are fully grown.

Now THAT'S done, let me fully reciprocate and say, it would be hilarious if you were here, you and Su could debate Roman gods to your heart's content.

Ok, she's waving at me, I've been spending too much time at the computer TRANSLATING (ahem) and now we must go and enjoy dinner Prague style, which presumably means dumplings and red wine. (Though I don't drink, being underage.)

Love,

AnA

Shaking his head, Sam asked himself once again: why did Anna want to know about his parents? His mum had been behaving very oddly since he'd mentioned Claudio to her. Guilty conscience? And yet, he was sure she did not know Claudio had killed himself. What was there to feel guilty about?

He went back to the photograph of Claudio and his mum and dad, looking more closely at the man in the middle. Something about his face was strange to him – strange because it was familiar. He opened the internet and went back to the Museum of Myth website. The photo there was clearer, but from a different angle, and the familiarity faded again. He went back to the polaroid, staring at it, willing it to reveal his secrets the way he used to look at Anna's photos from holidays with her friends, trying to deduce their debauchery.

And then he froze.

He knew what his mum felt guilty about.

Chris: The Labours

Clear sunny day, northern sky, a vast open blue. They filled the car with equipment and drove to the lake. There was heavy traffic on the motorway but they knew how to find the quieter spots off it. No conversation. Dad was driving; Chris had fumed at first, but now he had relaxed, slipping into childhood habits, watching the world slip by as they listened to Radio Gold. *Can't buy me love...*

After two hours they reached Fordham Park, the campsite they – his own family – had visited a few years earlier. The tents were stacked almost on top of each other near the water, but close to the trees there was space. They set up the tent and strolled down to the lake.

"Remember when we used to come here?" Dad said.

"Yeah. Brought the kids here, few years back."

Dad was looking at him. "We came here when you were thinking about Imperial. Remember? Why didn't you want to go?"

"Dunno."

Dad gripped his shoulder. "Your mum. What would she say?"

Chris kicked a pebble. "Dunno. Something poetic and practical. Speak to the water, it'll wash your words." He chuckled coldly. Dad sighed.

They sat down on the ground, dry and pebbly. Chris lay down and looked at the sky.

"What'd you want to be when you grew up?" Dad asked.

"A doctor."

"And...? Come on. You said we'd talk. Just tell me about that."

And Chris thought... how once... "Once..."

"Aye?"

...he'd been...

"Go on!"

...SUPER KID! King of the jungle! Lion slayer! Dynamic, gregarious, mighty Chris Morris: tease him, prod him, copy his exercise books if you can, but never piss him off. Chris the just! Chris the defender of the bullied! "Look, Mum, look at this!" Charge, thunk, zoom, biff – the ball hits the tree. "Goal!!!"

In the car, ten-year-old Chris, face suckered up against the glass, looked at the hulking building they passed to and from the park. "What's that, Dad?"

"Jimmy's, love."

"Who's Jimmy?"

Mum laughed. "Jimmy isn't a person, that's the name of hospital."

"I want to go there."

"Hey!" Dad scowled. "We don't make jokes like that."

"I want to be a doctor!"

The heads turned towards each other; the sunny ellipses of their mouths: he'd said the right thing. How had he thought of it? Was it that story of Gunner Reynolds, marching beside Dad, whose knee was poking out like a stone in a quarry? The doctor came and jammed it back in. Doctors were fab! Doctors whacked things!

"And help people, Chris. But you'll need to study hard."

So he did. Bunkered down, wrapped up in winter, bare-chested in summer, devouring biology and chemistry. Teachers never believed he'd make it. "You're a bright student but medicine's hard. You'd be happier as a teacher like your mum and dad. Or use your hands, take an apprenticeship. Be a welder, a carpenter." Yellow-skinned doubters! He'd slay 'em all! He'd show 'em all!

"That's right, Chris." Mum. "Don't you listen to any of 'em. People can't look outside their own little worlds, they're petty, they don't want you to succeed. You will, my love."

Leeds Uni answer came first: Sorry, no place for you. No, said Edinburgh. No, Newcastle, Manchester. Where were those welder-application forms? Dad dared not say a word, thinking it his fault ("*I did*"), should have tried harder to get his son into a grammar school. Mum hugged him and said, "There's one more." Yeah, bloody right, the hardest school of all. What'd la-dee-da Imperial College want with some grubby Yorkshire lad? But the posh voices harrumphed and a letter flew north. "Chris Morris, come on down."

Yes, Imperial College wanted him, and he was miserable. Dad took him to the lakes. Dad was broad-shouldered, tall, thick grey hair combed sideways, moustache, huge granite hands; Dad the war veteran who said nothing about the War except as a teacher; auto-didact; son of a miner. "You can always come and work here later on." But Dad's cheer-up-lad plan went awry: his voice broke and Chris was more miserable than before.

Then came a knock on his door. "Go away!"

"Chris." Mum. He let her in. Round as a plum, pale as an apricot, softest voice in the world; heart of gold but tough as steel; chemistry teacher, best biscuit-manufacturing one-woman division in the world. She sat on his bed and stroked his feet.

"You're going, my love, because it'll be the grandest thing that'll ever happen to you."

He cried and went.

And it was all that she promised.

("*Aye.*")

And it wasn't.

("*Why not?*")

Because he always missed home. Always. And he promised himself, that when he graduated, he'd be going back. Yet six years on, he found himself a doctor with a marriage certificate and a baby and a WIFE, living in a flat in West Kensington.

One evening then, he crept in and watched Jen. She was rocking Anna in one arm, pouring over hospital application forms on the kitchen table. What did he love more: her grace in rocking the baby, or her precision as she studied the forms? One knee jiggled up and down in tender chaos; one hand moved meticulously along the form, making careful notations. Organisation and wildness, delicacy and strength: this was Jen. She was, also, beautiful, but she didn't want him to love her for her beauty and he didn't – he loved her for everything.

"Does it have to be London?" he said.

Without stopping her two activities, "Where else? I don't want to go home and I don't want to go somewhere new."

"Well, there's..." He paused to let her fill in the gap. "Y'know, there's my way. Mum and Dad'd love that. Help look after Annie."

She didn't think long. "I'm sorry, Chris, but it wouldn't work. Our careers, Annie's education: it'll be much better down in London. And, your parents really are lovely, but they're the only people I'd know."

"You sure?" He asked it only once.

Now she stopped. Looked up at him, eyes scanning him from head to foot and back. He thought, *it's with love.* He thought, *whatever she says now, it'll be the right answer for both of us.* She said, "I'm sure."

So they stayed. They stayed in London for another seventeen years. They moved further out, towards Uxbridge, to be near his first hospital – a concession to him, she pointed out – but then they were right back in the centre, north of Hyde Park. He watched his kids grow up with posh London accents. He took his family to the Lake District every summer, and his kids loved their Nan and Granddad, but they were Londoners. As Jen became. As, in the end, he would become. With a flat on Gloucester Terrace, and a good job at St Mary's, and this wonderful life in the heart of the city. That he had. This fucked-up repressed London existence.

("But you came back every year. Kids loved it. Jennifer too. She and Bea were friends, giggling all the time. I was bloody glad each time you left. Come on, Chris. What did you miss? Your friends?")

Well, his first friends were lads like Stu and Bill. Ok, bad influences. When he was fourteen Dad took him to the amateur rugby club over on Richmond Hill, under Mum's instructions to get him with another set. He was hooked playing hooker, getting yelled at by that mottle-faced half-Dutch coach, Hendrik. Even then, in the happiest part of his childhood, he didn't linger after matches: he had too much studying to do, he wanted to succeed, burning with desire and ambition. Among this motley collective of amateur rugby players, he was still an outsider.

Down in London, he picked a stereotype, or it picked him: Me big northerner like rugby beer women. Far away from Mum and Dad, he made new friends, rough lads like Charlie and Fred and Patrick Anderson. They were middling at studies but good at rugby. Companions rather than friends.

He only made one real friend.

("*Aye?*")

He met Claudio in his fourth year. It was in that café he often went to study in, Jimmy's, a little nod at homesickness. The man's lilting voice made him think of Dad's old stories. He was prepared to patronise this charming Italian, who was clearly in the wrong place – should go back to Milan or wherever and enjoy the sun. But then he got a surprise. This man's passion was angry, not dreamy; and he was practical, studying bridges; and he was intellectual, knew all about classical mythology and sculptures. This was the first intellectual Chris had met apart from his parents. Like Chris, he missed home. It should count against him that he was the son of a rich man, but somehow that only brought him closer to Chris, two young men with too much to prove to the world to care what it thought of them, both wanting to be – better. That's what those trips to the museum were about. Chris joked about the statues: "look at this bum", "look at those tits". But he wanted to understand, and Claudio saw that. The quid pro quo is he educated Claudio about anatomy – which these Greeks and Roman sculptors understood bloody well – and about the War. Claudio's dad and uncle, it turned out, were partisans. Chris told him about his own Dad, who never spoke about the War.

Not ever.

("*Go on.*")

Claudio was interested in how things were made: this statue, that pair of earrings, this building, that medical device. "Myths too are tangible," he said, "they have components." He liked to take them apart in conversation.

"What does it mean, Chris, that Hercules kills his wife and family?"

"WHAT?"

"That is the story. He must go mad so that he must do his twelve labours. The madness is a gift of the gods. But what is the psychiatric explanation? Why does a hero do such a thing?"

"No clue. Horrible shit. You can't explain things like that. It's just stories. That's the problem with your myths. Life's not like that. You have to make the best with the cards you're given."

Claudio shook a finger. Funny what stays with you all your life: that gesture was just him, professorial yet childlike. Also his voice: hard, dancing, hesitant yet insistent. Some people get seared into your memory and never fade away. "You always say, make the best. But you have to accept that we do not start with a blank piece of paper. Patterns repeat and stories are guides to these patterns. Myths help us understand what can happen again."

"Yeah, yeah. So which patterns will we repeat?"

Finger again. "I am not a soothsayer. But I think you are a man of the heart. So you will be a heart surgeon."

Funny. Yes. It was Claudio who said that first.

Later that year, his fourth, he was summoned by Dr Fitzborough for a commendation and a chat. "Christopher, you should start thinking about what kind of medic you want to be. Now, it's less about the medicine and more about the people you want to work with." The beard waggled up and down, hilarity at what its owner was going to say. "It goes like this: orthopaedic surgeons are arrogant wankers, heart surgeons are extremely arrogant wankers, brain surgeons are freaks, other surgeons are straightforward wankers, radiologists are geeks, paediatricians are soft, obstetricians are soft wankers, GPs are paediatricians without balls, oncologists are perverts."

"Uh... I was thinking about heart surgery..."

"Ah, yes, I guessed you liked to masturbate. Cardiothoracic, eh? Hardest job. Every day you're on the front-line. That's where you want to be, is it? You might just be capable enough, Morris."

And so Chris began his journey into the heart, where he discovered the most god-like medicine there is. Heart surgeons were true mythological characters, people like Gibbon, who invented the heart-lung machine so you could keep the blood flowing while you were fixing the pump, or Barnard who carried out the first heart transplant in a small hospital in Cape Town. All he ever cared about was the next case, the next patient's life. Isn't that why he went into medicine? Ah – but he wanted more! He wanted to win the war! And Claudio understood that! He understood that Chris wanted to be a hero!

It's funny how, years later, he could still think of Claudio as a friend. How much did Claudio give to Chris, yet what did Chris give back? All he did was send a letter – around when Jen sent hers – offering unconditional friendship. That took something, to send a letter like that, when the boy had left England without a goodbye. He never knew if it had reached him.

Claudio gave him so much. Chris had to surrender only two things in return.

One: their friendship.

Two: the hope that, one day, Jen's adoration for Claudio, her doting on Claudio's every movement, her love for Claudio, would be replicated with Chris.

("Go on. Tell me about her.")

He loved her from the moment he first saw her in Doctor Fitzborough's class, October '76. It was a rainy afternoon as they filtered into the classroom in their white labcoats. Everyone was sizing each other up: who'd be fun, who'd be proficient. And he saw this otherness, the curious eyes beneath wild curls, arms folded across her chest, timid yet strong, he saw the same fragility he felt inside himself and he wanted to protect her straight away. They filed into rows and he found himself behind her. They were instructed to write their names in their notebooks and raise these when they were called on to speak.

"Well…Miss Carter?" Rows of brown plastic chairs stretched up from the white-coated old beard, grim-voiced, challenging the girl he'd already decided he loved.

"It's a…um…rupture," she said.

"Foolish answer." The class giggled at Dr F's brusqueness. Chris raised his hand. "Yes, um, Mr Morris? Terrible handwriting. You might just make it as a doctor. I suppose you know better?"

"Embolism, sir."

"Well done."

The class took turns to look over at him. In front of him, the curly head was motionless, and he added, conciliatory, "Sort of like a rupture."

"Very gallant," Dr F pronounced and the class giggled again. The auburn curls shivered as she turned her head – towards him? No, she whispered instead to the girl beside her. He yearned to reach out and grab hold and gently so gently shake her till a golden apple came falling into his hand and he'd caress it.

This first non-interaction set the pattern: he was here to help this girl succeed. She seemed nervous around bodies so he showed her how to slice open a knee, lingering until she snapped, "all right, I understand now." She struggled with chemistry formulae, whereas he was swathed in Mum's knowledge, so he offered to teach her, and she snapped again. "Look, Chris, I'm grateful that you want to help me, but I don't want your help, ok? I need to work it out on my own." He started to back away as she added another passive-aggressive, "Thank you." She was fierce and fearsome and he didn't dare go up to her again, especially not when he saw her laughing gaily with handsomer boys than him – which was every boy in the year – and gladly accepting their counsel. He just wouldn't go up to her. He wouldn't speak to her. Was he afraid? He hovered close enough to hear her, far enough not to be creepy. Her voice was pressing, confident, yet with a catch, as if she was about to laugh or cry. Was he afraid, or something else? Even when her dad died, and she turned ashen overnight, and accepted hugs and kisses from anyone in the year, he found no way to approach her, not even to say "sorry", just constructed an apologetic downwards smile around her. He was respectful. Or was it coy? Maybe shy. No, he was cautious. That was it: because he loved her, he must be careful. So long as he didn't approach her, his love was safe, for he couldn't control how she'd react, but she couldn't take his love away if he kept it hidden from her.

189

("Bizarre logic.")

And that was how it might have continued, till they'd left university and he'd go back to Leeds. But he was at rugby practice one day in April '80 when Anderson said, "Hey, did you hear about Jennifer Carter? She's going out with that Italian bloke." His heart turned to ice and the ball struck him on the chin. "Wake up, Morris!"

He went to find Claudio.

"Hear you're seeing someone."

"Yes, Chris! A medic, like you. Jennifer. Jenny. She is amazing. It is love. She is so passionate and interesting – so different to what I expected of an English girl. But she is practical. She doesn't want me to call her a princess. But she likes mythology. I think you are not friends? But you should be!" So Claudio was in love. And, it seemed, Jen was in love. For a day, he was in a nightmare, then he woke up: Chris couldn't be with Jen, but he could be the friend of her lover, and so her friend by default.

So now he was in an orchard and golden apples danced around him in perfect triangles: two lovers and a friend; two English medics and an Italian engineer; two men and a woman.

"You should study with her!" Claudio's dark, insistent voice: how could Chris resist it? Why should he resist? It turned out she'd admired him since the first year, always felt intimidated by him: he could have approached her at any point! She missed the sea and her dad. She was so – find us a word – what to call her? – alive. She was alive: even at her stillest, lying on the sofa, asleep, every movement contained energy and passion. And she was so organised, she amazed him, making little study timetables that she stuck to rigorously. He'd never been an organised sod, just ploughing through everything till he understood it, and this idea of organisation appealed. As did sitting on Claudio's rug beside her. He took her hand and showed her the flexibility of fingers, the whorls of fingerprints, the warmth of hand to hand.

"Talk me through the pyloric system."

"Fetal defects: three months. Go."

"I can't remember what atropine is."

They grew closer and he couldn't help it, could he, his love was growing, past infatuation and into truth. And still, he was Claudio's friend. There was nothing for Claudio to fear.

Until Claudio invented a myth: that Chris and Jennifer were betraying him.

"You should stop now studying with Jennifer. I do not feel comfortable that you are studying together all the time, alone."

"What do you think? We're fucking on your rug?"

"If you can speak like that to me, Chris, then how can you be my friend? I am asking you to stop studying with her."

"Isn't about your paranoia, friend. It's our careers."

The triangle began to fracture, Claudio growing miserable and brusque, Jen suffering. Chris had something else going on in his head: Claudio's accusations, which rang so true. Since he'd been accused of it, let him love her! How could he resist, when she turned to him for support, wailing and gnashing her teeth, battering his chest, begging him to help her, then pushing him away, wiping her eyes, saying, "Ignore what I said. I'm a nuisance."

It was the start of a pattern they had to the present: Jen was quick to fragment, Chris was quick to help. He'd protect her from the universe itself! He started smaller: he'd help her study, he'd help her talk, he'd walk with her in the park. Her attention on him was – that word again – a wonder.

One day, his clumsy arms fell about her shoulders, she stepped closer, they half-kissed. It was just a stupid thing that happened... But you make your own fortune. And he'd started to realise: for love, he'd do anything.

("That stupid song Anna used to like: 'I would do anything for love, but I won't do that.' I would. I'd do THAT as well.")

Claudio left but a part of Claudio remains. Jen was pregnant. She was shattered. Weeping. Chris felt confused, honourable. He told her to write to Claudio. She did, and got no reply.

It was clear what must happen next. She'd either lose everything and certainly fail the exams; or keep the baby and probably fail the exams. Faced with two options of great risk, the surgeon must choose the more likely path.

There came a day, oh, a month after Claudio had gone, mid January '81. Her belly was still flat but it was time for a decision. No one but him knew – she'd made that clear, she couldn't trust her friends, and as for home – nothing made her tremble more than the prospect of telling her mother.

They'd finished pathology revision. She had her eyes on the ground. He said, "sunny," and she said, "can we walk to the park?" with a delicious widening of her eyes that made him think of sex, so inappropriate but

191

that's what he thought of – holding her definitively fertile body – and he nodded.

She sighed. She cried. He shortened his strides.

"What is it?" he asked, though only two things were on her mind these days: Claudio and Claudio's baby.

She unfolded her arms and began to wave them. "I have to decide. Otherwise biology is going to decide for me. My head hurts, it's like there's a flock of birds flapping in it. To keep this child is madness: exams, qualification, practice. We have five months till exams! I'm twenty-bloody-three! I must be mad, Chris. Mad." He reached out to touch her. "No, listen. If I don't keep her, I will regret it all my life. I'm not mad now. I'd go mad remembering the decision. And wondering. This is a decision. A huge decision. It is not about convenience." Her voice turns sour, her teeth grind. "My fucking mother does not get it."

He tried to get it. Gave up. "How do you know it's a girl?"

From tears to smiles in one easy step, and Jen patted her belly. "It's not a monster."

The previous week promised early spring but winter was back. The hoary grass looked sharp enough to cut through dreams. Still he dared to dream. If she had madness, couldn't he?

"If you have her, and keep her – what'll you do?"

She yelled, "It won't be easy! Do you think I don't know that?"

He could take it. If birds were flapping in her head, he'd clear them. She looked at him, a long stare, judging and inviting, and he wondered if she'd looked at Claudio in this way.

"I'll need help," she said. "But I can't use *her*. I don't want her involved. My mother is a cross between Genghis Khan and that martyr who died with arrows in his body. But nursing care is expensive or bad. Or both."

He pointed at the swans on the serpentine. "Doesn't have to be."

She ignored the swans. "What do you mean? Where else am I going to get help?"

He was silent.

Her voice came with waves of emotion. "When I was a kid... My mother and I... We were always at each other. If it was just me and her, I don't know how I'd have coped. It was my dad. Daddy kept us... he kept the family together..." She stopped speaking.

"Yes," he said.

Children ran past them. She looked up at the sky. It was cold blue, clear. Chris wondered at her thoughts: was she thinking, this is the same sky that hangs over Italy?

"I miss him," she said.

"Yes," he said.

"I mean, my dad."

He stopped abruptly, so that she had to turn back to face him. Sunlight surrounded her. She was glowing. He screwed up his eyes. If she ran at him, he would stop her. If she punched his arm, he would smile. He was strong. He looked down at his hand.

He raised it towards her.

("Brave, you doing that.")

When Mum and Dad came down to London to discuss his decision, he was steeling himself for confrontation: *you're too young*, *you hardly know this girl*, *this will trap you in London*. He wanted them to attack, so that he must fight for Jen, and harden his resolve in battle. But they upset this plan. Dad just asked where they'd live, his flat voice giving away nothing, no word of encouragement nor rebuke. Mum was worse: she kissed him and said, "I said you'd find someone special."

He was leaning forwards, hands ready for fists, and was caught off-balance. He blurted out, "I'm going to be the dad. On the birth certificate."

His parents looked at each other, and he felt the tension between them.

"It's sensible," Mum said, but her voice was harder. "Your idea?"

"No," he said, honest as always.

That was the only moment he caught something in her eyes, like the hooves of wild mares, a surge of anger towards the young woman she had met once so far. Mum turned and walked out of the room. They heard the bedroom door close, and then silence. Dad was craning back, trying to see where his wife had gone. *Don't leave me alone with our crazy son!* Two minutes passed. Mum came back in. Chris looked for red in her eyes but she swept in too quick, giving him a hug, a kiss on the cheek, and went to the sofa, meaning, this was his decision and she would not try to stop it. After all, he was the medical student; biology and reproduction were his domain.

They came back for the birth. It was the summer holidays and they stayed with a cousin of Mum's in Wandsworth. Every day, they telephoned to ask how Jen was. She invited them often, partly as a foil to her mother who was sleeping on the sofa, and partly because Jen and Beatrice were discovering they liked each other.

Now the three parents were sitting outside the delivery room, and he was inside. Now Jen was crushing his hand. Suddenly she whimpered and he was whispering in her ear, "It's ok, you'll be ok," and she crushed it and shouted, "What are you doing here? GET OUT!"

He ran out of the room. Mum and Dad and Carole all wanted to speak to him so he had to pretend he was going to vomit and ran to the loos.

He took deep breaths and looked at himself in the mirror. He was about to cry.

"But I'm a doctor," he said first.

"And I'm going to marry her," he said next.

And then, twenty times: "This baby's mine. This baby's mine. This baby's mine. This baby's mine. This baby's mine. This baby's mine. This baby's mine. This baby's mine. This baby's mine. This baby's mine. This baby's mine. This baby's mine. This baby's mine. This baby's mine. This baby's mine. This baby's mine. This baby's mine. This baby's mine. This baby's mine. This baby's mine."

He scrubbed up and went back into theatre. Jen was panting. Halfway out. She took his hand again and they were a team, him and Jen, the midwife, and the baby, which was out, and he was out in the corridor crying, "IT'S A GIRL!"

He ran up and down corridors, yelling, "IT'S A GIRL! I've got a girl! And she's called ANNNNNNNAAAA!"

They chose the names before: Sam if a boy, Anna if a girl. Samuel was her dad. Whereas the lady of Richmond Hill, so-called by the policeman, postman, GP, other mothers, pupils, as in, *you be good to your ma, Chris Morris, she's the lady of Richmond Hill*: that is Beatrice Anna Morris née Berwick. And Jen gave him that. She gave him Anna.

("Aye. She did."

"I want to talk about Mum."

"*No.*"

"I'm going to talk about it.")

He got Mum's call last September. "GP says I have to go in for a scan."

He didn't know the radiologist, but Jen's colleague did and said good things. He came up to be with her and Dad when they met the oncologist ("perverts, the lot of them" – Dr Fitzborough) to learn the cancer was in her spine.

He began to pray. For the first time in his life, he called up to all-mighty God.

But prayer was all he had. Chris Morris the surgeon had lost control. He was as useless as Mum and Dad, herded like cattle from room to room, ward to ward, for scans and blood tests and chemo.

He shuttled between London and Leeds. Jen insisted on coming up with him, crying all the way up and down, so that he was comforting her, which was good for him; it gave him something to do.

When Mum began chemo, he told the kids, in short, plain words, with a final exhortation: "Your nan would survive anything except a direct hit from a meteor." Jen didn't want him to tell them. Now Sam was crying. Anna was crying. And Chris was lifting them up, raising morale. *Come on, troops, I need you behind me! We're going to war against cancer!*

They had to win. Not just because Mum was Mum, but for all she had become over years of study and gracious behaviour. All that wisdom is acquired painstakingly and then it's gone, with nothing left: the body betrays us, we die, and some say it is a necessary exit to clear the way for the blank slates, the purest young minds, but he, a surgeon, could not accept that, for death is the enemy.

He was a surgeon. He wanted to rip out those tumorous cells and shove them in the incinerator. He confronted the oncologist, the radiologist, the GP, the nurse, anyone he could shove a finger into their face and demand, "Why? I mean, why hasn't it gone down by more?"

He kept saying, *I mean*. He kept asking, *why*.

Mum was pale as an apricot, thin as a plum core, shaking with cold, paper-thin words, not wise words, not warm, just the words of someone dying: "Look after your dad. Be kind to your family. I know you always try, Chris, but sometimes you have to be strong. You're stronger than you realise. Be a good boy. I know you'll be a good boy."

Each day in London, at work, before he went into theatre, he looked in the mirror and said to himself: "My patient has a family. My patient has a life ahead of them. I will save my patient's life. I am privileged to help others. I will work well today."

Sort of took its toll, didn't it, lying to himself like that, every day, for weeks?

And when Mum died, sort of carrying on.

Sort of hiding away.

Sort of silent.

Sort of buried...

"Come on, lad." The thick arm on his shoulders rocked him and Chris looked up at the red water. After two days by the lake, his mind was empty, his mouth exhausted. He got up to follow Dad to the car. Then he grabbed Dad's arm and stopped him.

"You and Mum raised me so well, but I've never done anything like you. Italy, the Hitler line. I never had your courage. You won't tell me what your medal's for, but now I've told you everything, what am I supposed to do? Live a lie? Will that win me a medal?"

"Medal..." Dad's voice was thick and low. "You know what a medal is? Piece of bronze I got for pulling a couple of lads out of a tank. That was the only thing to do. No courage, just instinct, training. We all got the maple leaf for helping the Canadians that day. Germans firing down at us, what were we to do? Keep driving, keep firing, praying..." Dad picked up an orange-grey pebble and rolled it in his fingers, looking down. He squeezed it tight. "I'll tell you what courage is, Chris. A man who goes to work every day, knowing there's a chance he'll kill someone. But if he doesn't show up, patients will die. The man who knows this, he's got no one shooting at him, he chooses to go in. Every day he goes in. That's courage."

"Just training..."

Dad's vast hand on his shoulder, squeezing it, his eyes reflecting the fading light. "You've no idea how proud I am."

And Morris and Morris, the big lads, turned away from the lake, into the car, back to Leeds, back home.

Jen: Skin

"How do you think Sam will feel? He can't go back to school and report that the biggest event of his holiday was a fortnight with his grandmother... No, you are not going to transform his academic potential, Mother... No, I am not stressed, I'm in a hurry, I'm taking Sam to a dermatologist... No, he's fine, just worried about his acne, and he needs someone who isn't me to tell him it's ok... No, someone professional... Because you're not a specialist, Mother, and you know what Sam's like – he'll query every bloody detail... What about Chris? I told you, he's recovering in Leeds... For the last time, I am not fucking stressed... I said, I've got to go, Mother. Goodbye."

She took Sam in the car as she had to go to Great Ormond Street afterwards. He could take the Tube home, he was an independent boy, a good boy. He kept shifting in the seat and picking at the seatbelt. He seemed nervous.

"Um... Do I... Is Doctor Anderson good?"

"Yes," she said. How to put it? He was the most successful mediocrity she knew. He'd been nothing in their year, a bit of a rugby lad and a friend of Chris's, but had made his way quickly into private practice. That wasn't hard when your work only went skin deep.

"Do..."

"Let's see what he says, Sammy."

The morning traffic was heavy. This bloody city was a nightmare. At least she lived within walking distance to work.

"Um, but Mum..."

It was hard to concentrate with Sam stammering in the corner. "Just wait!" she said. He shut up.

Harley Street was full of lithe black Porsches. Patrick's office smelled of the roses he kept in a porcelain vase on the sill. The carpet was thick, the chairs made of leather. The art on the walls looked expensive; certainly it hadn't been made by sick children. Patrick wore an immaculate pinstripe suit and gave her an awkward half-shake, half-hug, before turning to Sam.

"So this is the young man with medicine coming out of every pore."

"And sebum," Sam said.

Patrick laughed. "Not exactly. Your problem is that the sebum is getting clogged."

At least Patrick remembered something. She settled in a corner with a medical journal as he started plodding around Sam's face with a metal rod.

"And how is hospital life?" he asked in his slow, drawling voice.

"Overworked," she said.

He chuckled. "And Chris?"

"Same old." She started leafing through the pages but sensed him glance at her and understood that he knew about Chris's suspension.

He finished with Sam's face and leaned back. "It's very minor, young man."

"What does that mean?" Sam demanded.

"Nothing to worry about. Completely standard for your age."

"But how long will it take to resolve? Do I need psychological support? If it's standard, does that mean it can get worse?"

Patrick chuckled and looked over at Jen. "Been training him?" He turned back to Sam. "I'll give you some benzoyl peroxide."

"What's that?"

"It's a cream. I'll give you literature to read about it. You apply it every evening for two months. We'll see if things don't start to improve. All right?"

"Yeah," Sam said sulkily.

"Are you eating healthily?"

"Yeah."

"Is he?"

"Yes," Jen said, and realised that, for once, she knew this to be true.

As they stepped out, she took the prescription from Sam. "I'll bring the cream tonight. Do you have coins for the underground?"

He nodded glumly. He missed Anna, and she wanted to tell him she did too, but feared that would only make him more upset. She felt a sudden urge to hug her son; he carried the load of his upcoming adolescence with such little complaint, he was a brave boy, independent and strong, and she was proud of him. But she didn't want to embarrass him, and allowed herself only to ruffle his hair before turning towards the car.

"But don't you want a croissant or something?" he asked.

She stopped and opened her purse, handing him a fiver.

"But don't you want to eat something?"

"I've got to go," she said. She turned again.

"*I've got to go,*" she heard him say. "*I've got to study.*"

"What?"

The sunlight in her eyes made it hard to see her son. His silhouette looked strange: feet planted apart, an aggressive pose, like Chris's the night before he left.

She spoke slowly. "I've got to go, Sam. I've got to work."

"I found Claudio's letter," he said.

"Claudio," she repeated. "Yes, I told you, he was an old, you know, friend."

"The stories are in Italian." He pulled crumpled pages out of his trouser pocket and waved them at her. She felt faint. Sam's voice wavered between registers as the words poured out. "I got them translated. You never read them, did you? You don't know what they're about. How you led him into love as if all were safe for him. How he loved you more than his own life. And you loved him."

"That's ENOUGH, Sam. You had no right to go into my filing cabinet. And how dare you read those papers? You had no right at all."

But it came out weakly, the volume dropping. She couldn't yell at him. It was too strange. He was right: she'd never read them.

And what was that he'd said? They were about love. She felt her toes, curled in distress, release; her mouth fell open. What was missing, if not that? She must speak to...

But Sam was waiting for a response. She couldn't think of what to say to him. It was too vast a moment to discuss with her son. She was reaching out to take the pages when a thought struck her.

"How did you get them translated?"

"I gave them to Anna."

"WHAT?"

It was faster than light, the transition unseeable: one moment she was facing her son, the next she was leaning against the car, hand stinging, a thin trail of water bleeding onto the car. She heard him gasping. She pushed herself up. He was running away. She tried to call his name but nothing came out; it was her nightmare again, and now she understood: she had been right to be afraid. She had to see Anna. She had to tell her.

Chris: Heart

The day before Anna's birthday, four weeks after he'd left home, the phone rang.

"Morris," Dad answered. "Oh, hello love." Chris's heart started thrashing in its cage. "He's just stepped out. See if he's in the garden. CHRIS." Hand cupped over the mouthpiece, Dad mouthed her name.

Chris took the phone. "Hello."

"Hello." She was neither warm nor frosty, balanced on an edge. He must keep his voice there too, not be flippant, nor rough. And he must speak, not be silent.

"How you been?" he asked.

"Yes. I'm all right. I left you alone, I hope that was the right thing to do. How are you? How are you feeling?"

"Ok," he said.

"How's your father?"

"Had enough of me." What he wanted to say was, I've realised something since coming up here: I'm not ready to go back to work because I've been palming all the blame away from myself, onto the nurses, psychologist, my boss, my wife. The truth is closer to home, that something has got stuck in my gut in the past nine months, since I lost Mum. It's taken me this long to understand that, but now I do. And I'm sorry. And I love you.

"Good," she said. "Because I've decided I should really see Anna for her birthday. I was going to take Sam but then I thought, actually, it might be nice if you come back to London and be with him. I'm going to be away for two weeks, and can't handle the idea of him being with my mother for that long."

"Italy?"

"It's been a real month. Year." She laughed uncertainly. "I feel like a proper holiday."

"You've earned it. But – Italy. You don't want us to come with you?"

"Look, Chris, it would be good if you were here with Sam. He's been out of sorts this summer. You can spend some quality time together, and I can with Anna. And then... we should talk when I come back. There are things

I am sure you want to say. And there are many I want to say. And I think a talk would be healthy. And helpful. And good."

"But you're sure?"

"Yes. Anna's birthday is tomorrow. I'm flying in the morning."

"Right." He paused, thinking about Italy, trying to find a way to stop Jen going alone. It made him uneasy. But all he could manage was, "Send us a postcard, eh?"

After they hung up, her words danced around him. *There are many things I want to say.* What kinds of things: the ones that make us whole, or the ones that break the heart?

"Going back to London," he answered Dad's quizzical look.

"So soon," Dad said, and laughed.

That was it, parting always easier than arriving. Even that first time he'd gone to London, they'd sent him off with a brisk handshake and a kissed reminder to sit facing forward, so he'd had this trivial detail to worry about, his mind so preoccupied with logistics that he'd forgotten all about home until he'd settled in the train.

*

The white columns of Gloucester Terrace looked massive after a month away. The stairwell had that familiar smell of vanilla and wet carpet. The front door had no cracking paint, and Chris realised that he still hadn't painted Dad's door. He came into the hallway.

"I'm home! Sam!"

The boy slunk out of his room, slightly stooped, face dark from sunshine, voice crackling between registers. "Hi."

Chris raised his arm for a hug. Sam stood an awkward distance away, half facing him, staring at his feet. Chris lowered his arm.

"Still on the *Long Goodbye*?"

Sam narrowed his eyes. "No. Finished that a week ago. Now I'm reading *Lady in the Lake*. And other stuff," he added in a mutter.

"So. You and me. For a fortnight."

The eyes narrowed further, till they were almost closed. "I'm busy," Sam snapped, and turned to go back to his room.

"Hey!" The door closed. This would be a long fortnight.

Chris went into the bedroom. Jen had smoothed out the duvet, left her white desk immaculate with a small pile of papers by the computer screen. There was no sign of his wife's recent departure, and certainly not of their last encounter here, his bellowing, their furious cold goodbyes.

He unpacked everything before he let himself sit down at her computer. His first attempt was a thousand words. He deleted it all and started again.

My darling,

I am going to celebrate with you properly, and give you a proper birthday card.

For now this is to wish you a very happy birthday. Eighteen is an amazing moment in your life. I am sorry I can't be with you today but I will be soon.

And I have a very special present for you.

All my love,

Dad

He'd found it months back, after a visit to the British Museum with Sam. She liked to call him a caveman. Well, that made her a cavegirl, didn't it? The flint had cost a small fortune but he knew Anna would appreciate it.

She replied two days later.

Hi Dad

Mum, Sumukhi and I are just chilling in our palatial B&B headquarters in Florence. Are you jealous? Well, here's an idea. We'd love you to come out and join us (sans Su) in Bologna. Bring Sam. (If you have to.)

Seriously, I am not drunk (I don't drink) but Mum says that it's a great idea (of hers) and I concur. You see, it'd be like a family holiday. In fact, oh my god! It'd be exactly that! e perché parlo correntemente l'italiano, we could do all these brilliant things that tourists can't, like go to the really good authentic local restaurants, find out the real authentic history... Do I have your attention yet?

Please come.

Love,

anananananananananana

xoxoxoxoxoxoxoxoxoxoxoxo

It felt like the first time in months that he'd smiled.

"Hey, you," barging into Sam's room. "We're going to Italy."

Sam jumped up from his desk. Stale smell: this room needed airing. The computer was on. This was not where a boy should be in summer, but now was not the time to mention it.

"Really, really Italy?"

"That's right. Land of pizza and *gelato*."

"And Roman emperors," Sam said.

"And opera."

"And gods and goddesses."

"And sunshine."

"And Hercules. And Juno, and Jupiter, and Mars, and Venus, and Vulcan."

The room was silent.

"Is that your new thing, then?" Chris said weakly. "Classics?"

"I'm not that interested. But did you learn about that stuff, Dad? At school? Or was it at uni?"

Chris laughed uncertainly. "Yeah. Like Hercules. Killing the hydra, cleaning the stables. It's – what's the word – *apt*. Medicine is Herculean." He didn't know what he was saying.

"And Cerberus," Sam said. "The dog who protected Hades. And didn't Hercules get helped by Vulcan?"

"Dunno. Anyway, I'm knackered." Hands clenched, Chris hurried away.

He spent half the day calling travel agents. You couldn't get a flight to Bologna for less than four hundred quid. "What if we fly to Milan and take a train?"

"Sir, as I've explained to you, all flights into Italy at the moment are expensive, especially if you're booking five days away. The cheapest flight within five hundred miles is into Zagreb." Chris considered this, but then, he was trying to make good with Jen, and driving her son through a recent war zone was not the way to do so. He gritted his teeth and paid for two tickets to Bologna the following Monday.

*

Sam kept himself locked away over the next five days, while Chris read his books on surgical procedures, smiling at the idea of sending Dad a postcard from Italy. He called to apologise about the flaking front door.

The day before they left, the sky turned black and demonic, and clouds swirled above Gloucester Terrace. A boom ran through the flat. Chris looked quietly in on Sam. His son sat at his desk, clutching that book he'd seen lying around: *Bumper Book of Myths*. The window was half-open, and rain splashed onto Sam's desk, ignored. He was reading something on his computer, occasionally looking down into the book. By his feet was his backpack, fallen over, some of its contents spilled out, a lot of paper. Why so studious suddenly? Trying to impress some pretty girl in his class? Chris could understand that! He could talk to his son about that – in Italy!

What else would Italy bring him? His wife! Did he dare to hope? To dream again?

Above all: his daughter! The best tour guide in the world! The best girl. How much he had to tell her! He went back to their bedroom and carefully packed Anna's present in tissue paper, a pre-historic flint knife, unusual gift for an eighteen-year-old, but then she was unusual for eighteen (eighteen! adventure! how he'd slunk out of Leeds head down never looking up till he found himself at uni in London and all he knew was how to throw a ball and not throw up after eight pints *haha joke, Anna, love, but this present is for your struggles, and I know you'll make it, whatever you want to do, you'll be great, that's why this flint is strong and multi-purpose, they'd have used it for curing meat, for war, like your granddad might've used, even a surgical tool, and I know you don't want to be a doctor, and I know it won't help you much up in Cambridge, but maybe it'll make you think about those early humans who spoke the first language, what they had to say about themselves, how maybe they loved their mums and dads, and why they spoke and how they spoke*, and he imagined her answering, *With grunts*) and he smiled.

IV – If We Were Gods

HEPHAESTUS: The ties of birth
and comradeship are strangely strong.
– Aeschylus, Prometheus Bound

Vulcan Loved

1979

"So that's it? You're going again? And to London!"

"I tried to stay."

"You were never going to stay." Silence. "Silly Dio."

"I'll be back."

"Don't waste your breath, you need to hold it there, for the stink. And it's always wet. Go and practise your English. Go and live, 'you who were once my brother', be happy. Go on! Get out!"

"Say goodbye first."

"Do you know about Vulcan and Minerva, Dio?"

"Yes."

"Minerva was born in her armour, and she came out of the head of Jupiter. And it was Vulcan who chopped open Jupiter's skull so Minerva could step out."

"I know."

"So then Vulcan tried to rape Minerva."

"That's a Greek myth."

"So? They're the same thing. He tried to rape her, but he failed. I don't know if that's an unhappy ending or a happy one. What do you think?"

Silence.

"Vulcan's semen spilled on the ground and that was how the kings of Athens were born. Minerva became the goddess of Athens and Vulcan was the forefather of its kings. A nice coincidence."

"There are no coincidences in myth, sorellina."

"What are you still doing here? I thought you were going."

"Tell me, Lissa, where does your story talk about how Minerva hated Vulcan's girlfriend, and laughed at her, and spilled wine on her at dinner, and called her a bitch, and made her run away?"

"That doesn't sound like a myth to me. Haha. Anyway, he never abandoned his sister. He went because he had to."

"I have to go."

"You have to protect me."

"It's not for ever, Lissa."

Tears. "I know it is."

"Don't be silly."

"Buonanotte, fratello mio."

"Buona…"

And in the house, silence.

Melissa: Forge

The sound of turtle doves and rain guided Melissa awake. She lay in the half-light, savouring the haze that was no longer dreams nor yet reality. In the night, mighty beings had chanted her name, angry, powerless, imploring her. Today the judge would issue his report on the Museum of Myth.

She rose and put on her necklace. She watched herself dress in the mirror, each arm slowly filling a sleeve as she recalled the past month. The lawyers had prepared their submissions; the newspapers had printed their stories; Ernesto had raised an army of supporters. Melissa had been tireless, speaking to magnates, ex-civil servants, councillors, citizens of Verona and beyond, the press, the academies, making good her promise to the mayor to publicise his own corrupt dealings. Now they must wait for the outcome: would the mayor condemn the Museum and damn his own administration, or would he surrender quietly?

She caught a glimpse of the necklace in the mirror and looked away. She had also, this month, accepted the truth about her brother and his death. A month ago, she had found his letter to her mother. Since then, her sleep had been fitful, disturbed by nightmares, memories of her brother and his stories, dark dialogues where she never saw Claudio's face, only heard his lilting words. Her furious activity during the day drove her to exhaustion, but she was never so tired that the dreams did not haunt her. Her thoughts of leaving the Museum were cast aside: she had accepted her duty as her fate, and was now bound to it.

She went downstairs. The entrance hall was dim with the overcast light. When she switched on a light, she was surprised to see Violetta standing by the door, coffee in hand.

"I'm sorry," Melissa said, "but I don't have time." She started past the housekeeper.

"There is always time for an espresso." Violetta thrust the coffee towards her, and Melissa sighed and took the cup. "I know I irritate you, *signora*, but many years ago I promised your mother that I would look after you and god knows someone has to, you take so little care of yourself." Melissa was about to retort but Violetta continued, "You are the way you are, for good and bad, like all of us. I wish you cared more for yourself, but this is not the time to change how you are. Today you are looking after the museum, and what is my job? To look after you. Isn't that fair?"

Melissa smiled faintly. "A division of labour."

"Exactly, *signora*." Violetta leaned forwards and pulled Melissa, cup still in hand, towards her, thick arms engulfing her in a hug. Melissa felt herself pour into the warm, soft body. She yearned for sleep.

"Thank you," she said.

"Now finish your coffee," Violetta said, "and tell the mayor I'll make him into soup if he puts another foot wrong with the Collina family."

In the museum, Melissa walked without hurry down the corridor, passing visitors for whom this was an ordinary day. She stopped in *The Olympians* room. The bulky figure of Vulcan stood high above her, distracted, his mind on some task left to do. In one hand, a giant hammer, in the other a ball of clay that might become a thunderbolt, or figure of Pandora, or indeed a museum.

She climbed to the mezzanine. She had an idea to say some words of encouragement to Ernesto but he was on the phone when she came into his office, and waved for her to sit down. She studied the cabinet lined with small replica statues, and noticed that the statuette of Mercury, the bringer of luck, had been moved in here.

"Tell Signora Collina directly," Ernesto said. She noticed a faint stain of shaving cream on his neck as she took the receiver.

"I have spoken with Judge Paoli's office," intoned the deep voice of Caspardi. "The report will be issued at the end of today but its contents were disclosed to me. The judge has concluded that the museum has violated multiple laws concerning charitable institutions and public venues. His report is considerably more damning than an independent judge's would be."

"As you told us," she said, "he is as corrupt as Caligula. Now we must wait for the mayor's next move?"

"I am afraid not, *signora*. I have also spoken with the municipality. The mayor will announce shortly that he is invoking a law concerning municipal museums. It dates back to the post-war era and allows him to close with immediate effect any institution that has broken charitable law."

Melissa looked out the window. The grey clouds pressed close to the city. She observed, as if for the first time, their great height above the Adige. If a strut in the building gave way, they would slide towards the water.

"I don't understand," she said. "You told me that the worst outcome of the judge's report would be a court battle, that in a worst case we would have months to fight it. Surely we can appeal?"

"There has been no trial, so there is no appeal."

"Then we must sue them."

"It is a case we will lose. It is not the mayor and judge who have acted illegally. We will be putting Italian law on trial in an Italian court. Your only choice is whether to anticipate the mayor by announcing a closure, which may allow you to negotiate certain settlements. Either way, there can be only one outcome. The museum must close."

"Signor Caspardi, please, you have to advise me. I cannot let the museum close. Please."

"Melissa," he said, sounding suddenly like the relative she never had, an uncle, "let us be honest with each other now, for I did not dare to say it earlier. This was always the likeliest outcome. You have fought valiantly, but you must accept reality. You must find a new purpose for your life. You have carried this responsibility from an early age, now you can care for your own person."

She was silent.

"Please excuse my talking beyond my remit. I will leave you to discuss with the director how to manage this."

She held the phone, staring at the city. The river was a brutal grey, the colour of the castle stones. Ernesto leaned over and took the phone from her.

"What do you want to do?" he asked. "Did Caspardi say there were any other options?"

"I have to go," she said.

She stood up and left his office. The corridor's walls were white. She went down the stairs. She saw anxious expressions on the staff's faces. She gave a failed smile to Gina the cleaner and hurried outside. Roberto drove her home.

She sat in the living room and watched the grey light play across the statue of Venus, stooped in forgotten modesty, missing the hands that had once covered her nakedness. When the light had gone completely, Melissa still sat facing the frozen goddess, looking beyond at the hills, but seeing only darkness.

*

Ernesto rang the next morning. "It is a disaster. Have you read the newspapers? The mayor says, 'The Museum of Myth was built on corrupt foundations. I have little choice but to accept Judge Paoli's recommendations and close the museum.' The journalists are ringing non-stop for comments. What do I say? What do we do now?"

"I trust you to say what is best," she told him.

"You should come here."

"The photographers have been outside all morning."

"Yes..." He sounded doubtful. "The mayor's office called. They want us to close the museum ourselves. To avoid further difficulties, they said." His growling voice turned furious. "I want to burn down the mayor's office." He paused and she heard his scratchy breathing. "Is there no way to fight this?" When she did not answer, he sighed. "We must announce the closure. In two months? That will give us time to prepare a transition plan."

"Very well."

Melissa did not read the newspapers. She did not let Violetta switch on the radio or television. She sat in her father's study.

The telephone rang again after lunch. Ernesto was spitting.

"They are saying that the museum must be closed tomorrow, and the site cleared for demolition in a month. They say that any delays make the issue seem unresolved. What – do – I – do?"

Melissa hesitated. She shut her eyes and imagined the many conversations she and Ernesto might have held. Might they have spoken of statues and museums, or children and weather, and the ancient poem that captured these ideas? He would tease her knowledge, and she would say that he had taught her that poem, and he would pretend to have forgotten.

"We must do as they wish," she said.

"Are you all right, Melissa? Do you have company?"

"Thank you, Ernesto."

Now she felt ready. She sat behind her father's desk and summoned Violetta and Roberto. His blue eyes were wet with distress and the little tufts of grey hair on the side of his head were unkempt. Violetta was in her tent of black, her thick face dense with lines.

"Well, *signora*," Roberto said, "it is a heavy blow, but you have a hundred ideas to beat them, eh? This mayor is an idiot. Everyone thinks it is ridiculous. What will you do?"

"There is nothing to be done," she said.

"What do you mean, *signora*? They are going to close the museum? But this is the biggest shittery I ever heard! Pardon my language. Your father spent years building it. And you, *signora*, I feel so sorry for you, you dedicated years to it. No, *signora*, there must be something – what can we do? Please tell me."

He started to cry. Violetta held his arm and murmured into his ear. He wiped his eyes and lowered his face.

"I am afraid I have worse news," Melissa said. They stood before her, hands clasped in front of them. "It was a shock to me, I imagine it will be the same for you. My father left me limited means to support myself. This month's pay is the last I can afford to give you. I am sorry."

Roberto waved his hand. "So what, *signora*? I'm not worried about that."

"No, you don't understand..."

Violetta took Roberto's hand. "We know you'd feel too obligated, *signora*. It will be difficult..." Her voice faltered. "So, then. Our children can look after us. We are old, isn't that right, Roberto?" Melissa looked down, at the purple rug. "When do we stop? The 31st of August?" Melissa still could not speak and Violetta repeated the question.

"Yes," Melissa said, "yes, that is fine. Oh, I am so sorry..." She stopped herself. They hardly needed her tears, and she imagined Roberto and Violetta receiving Caspardi's phone call, their shock, their grief, both overcome as they returned to this house, now its owners. How happy she would make them!

They began to leave, but Melissa called Roberto back. "I'd like to go to Garda."

"Now, *signora*? We will need to be careful with the journalists. But ok, don't worry about that. I'll get the car ready, and Violetta'll pack a bag. Do you want her to come?"

"No. Thank you."

The press were waiting when they pulled out of the house, but Roberto was a veteran evader and soon lost them in the maze of Verona's streets. They drove north and entered the countryside. The rain had long stopped, and in the golden light of evening, Melissa could see the hills rising into Valpolicella, dense with vines. Her uncle had fallen on its rich soil. They passed through villages and drove by the water's edge. Heading up the east side of the lake, they passed stone walls and steel gates, and finally drew up at the familiar outline. Here was sanctuary: the walls were high, no intruders could disturb her.

The house was not ready for a visit, but there was little to do: Roberto switched on fans and checked the lights were working. He inspected the larder and noted a spot of mould on the outside wall. He would deal with that on his next visit. Autumn was not far away, so he'd get the storm shutters out next month. He had forgotten he would not be there the next month. Melissa went to the porch with a glass of wine and a book; the evening was cool and pleasant. She pretended to read until Roberto came to say goodbye.

"When do you want to go back, *signora*? It'll take me an hour to pick you up. Are you sure I can't stay?"

"I will call you when I'm ready," she promised.

She waited until his engine had faded, then she took her book and drink inside and placed them carefully on the big wooden dining table where her father had hosted great parties. Hordes of children had run after Melissa and Claudio, sprinting by the lake.

She went to the garage; the back door led into Claudio's workshop. She had to shove it hard with her shoulder, and with a noisy creak, she stumbled into her brother's workshop.

It was dim, with only the light from the garage to illuminate the stone floor and the objects around her. The air was cool but clean; small vents, and Violetta's monthly visit, had kept it free of dust and fungus. To her right was the worktop, a sloping wooden desk with a half-moon cut into the front. Beside it was the old-fashioned anvil, and next to it the small oven with a furnace. She took a step and heard a clatter of a small piece of metal, kicked by her stray foot. She could make out faintly the ventilation pipes on the walls, but not their colours; she knew they were yellow and green. Another step, and there was the red cabinet, which had once seemed to her a treasure chest. Now it reached her shoulders. She tried a drawer, but it was locked.

Melissa closed her eyes. Her fingers felt for the necklace. She tried to hear the falling pitch of hammer striking metal. She listened for a solid gait, pacing, pondering. She inhaled and noticed the faint metallic trace in the air. She raised her hands, fingers stretching to the corners of the room. They touched nothing. They felt cold.

Like winter.

And she thought of that day.

*

213

It was a Sunday – January 18th – a day that passed much like any other. The most important moments in our lives only appear so in retrospect. We eat meals. We yell. We lie. We deceive one another. Afternoons come and go, nights fall.

On that night, Claudio still had not returned. Papa had forbidden him from staying overnight in Garda anymore, and it was almost time for dinner.

"That's it!" Papa snapped. "I'll lock him in his room if I have to." He drove off with Roberto. Mama and Lissa waited, reading in the living room.

"Let's make cod," Mama mumbled. "It's Dio's favourite." She went into the kitchen and tried to explain to Violetta what she wanted.

Issa thought how clever she was. Dio was staying in Italy and going nowhere else.

Two hours passed and they still had not come home.

"Where are they?" Mama asked. She had begun to ask it every few minutes.

Her anxiety seeped into Lissa, who tried to project calm, as Mama was still fragile from the stroke. "It's fine. They're probably arguing. There's nothing to worry about!" But she began to pace up and down.

Violetta stood in the corner, looking out the window. "Should we call, *signorina*?"

Lissa called Garda but no one answered. "I'll go there," she said.

"Don't leave me!" Mama begged.

She ran outside and into the car. She had learned to drive last year. Forty minutes of the motor and the wind rushing outside, darkness, winter night, the roads icy, and Lissa knew she must drive carefully, but she accelerated instead. What argument might Papa and Dio be having? She must stop it, she must protect him. The lights of her car devoured the road.

She arrived at the house. Lights were everywhere, in the house, in the garden, floodlights, flashing lights, and as she drove closer, she saw an ambulance and a stretcher.

Papa was sitting on the ground, his head in his hands. Roberto was trying to lift him up.

"Where is Claudio?" Lissa asked the back of a stranger, a man in a medical uniform. He turned. His face was a mask. She shrieked and ran away, towards the workshop. The door and windows were open. Men were inside, wearing masks.

"Don't come in!" one yelled.

There was a bitter smell in the room. She felt faint. She called out, "Dio? DIO?" She ran to the worktop. There was a necklace. She picked it up. She wanted to vomit. They were grabbing her. She ran outside. "CLAUDIO?" She saw a stretcher, a sheet, a bulge. She ran to it. She tugged the sheet.

Darkness.

And when she awoke, Claudio had gone. That was the myth, the one she had lived for two decades. But he had not gone. He had died.

She had always understood, truly, what myths were. They were lies.

Picture Olympus, where the gods dwelt in infinite pleasure. In modern times, climbers had scaled its peak overlooking the Aegean Sea. Their reports came back: there was no ambrosia, no nectar, no unwrapped togas, no thrones or palaces, no naked divine bodies. The gods were not there, they never had been.

Melissa dragged a foot along the floor and opened her eyes. She saw a thin trail leading back to the house. In the laundry room were sheets: Antigone had hung herself. In the kitchen were knives: Nero stabbed himself. She laid the largest one on the dining table. Was there rat poison in the store room? Socrates drank hemlock, Cleopatra shook an asp until it bit her. But other stories said she died by the sword, and history kept evolving until it became myth. There were myths of heroines who turned into trees or stars, who embraced the river or sea and sank beneath it. Her brother had died alone in the bitter air of his workshop.

She turned off the lights and lay down on the cool terracotta floor. Words came to her. He had written them to her the night before he left for England. She had destroyed all his letters from London, but these words she had kept in her heart:

And if we were gods, how would we be?

Would we be cautious or aggressive? Would we hurl our immortal fire against another's immortal lightning? Would we laugh? Would we be bored, as gods?

Would we pity that mortals would never see the same comet twice, or would we envy the urgency of finite actions? Would we care for mortals and fight their wars, or would we forget them altogether?

And if we were unhappy, what would we do? Would our goddess mothers lift us up and say, "Stop sulking, make a mountain, make a species"? And what if our mothers hated us?

How could we suffer, as gods? Would it be when we loved? For who could love us gods as much as we craved, as long as we needed? Who could love us at all, terrifying and lonely as we would be?

If we were immortal, would we not feel immortal love? Would we not be so full of love that we must expire? How else do gods die?

Would our stories at night be of gods who had lived eons before, who had loved, who had suffered, who had passed into night, who haunted us still and whom soon we must join?

When we had passed into night, what would remain?

What prayers would we offer to guide us to night?

And if we were gods, who would answer our prayers?

Anna: Porticoes and Doors

"Dad! Sammy!"

Anna jumped up and down, waving her hand, as they came through the arrivals gate. Sam ran over to her. "*Benvenuto!*" she yelled. He stopped just short of hugging her. He'd grown taller and she could see his white socks beneath the jeans. His face was a nice shade of brown.

"Good trip?" she asked.

"Your hair is so short!" he squealed. "The trip was crazy. We were, like, running late the whole way, to get to the Tube, and then had to run up the escalators and I slipped and..."

"Really? Oh, wow." She was watching Dad approach Mum.

"Hello, Chris."

Dad laughed nervously. He started to lean forwards but Mum didn't notice and bent down to pick up her handbag. Anna ran over and leapt on him.

"Daddy!" She punched his arm and tugged at his hair. She took his hand and grabbed her mother's hand and began leading them to the exit, with Sam a little ahead of them.

"I've been reading and there's so much to do here," she said. "It's the city of porticoes! There's like eighteen churches and the cathedral and this world-famous sculpture of Christ you have to see. There's the university and the opera and the archaeology museum and the best food in Italy. Wait, you guys go on. Sam!" She stepped forward and pulled her arms behind her, so that her parents' hands were now linked, and hurried over to her brother.

"She cut her hair," she heard her dad say.

"Yeah," Mum said.

"Come on!" Anna called as she led them towards the city of porticoes.

They took the bus into town. She guided them to the hotel, a former convent near Via Castiglione. Its vaulted white ceilings were cooling; the reception walls were the blue of a tropical sea. She grabbed the key and led Sam to the room they were sharing. He stood awkwardly by the door, a frown on his face, watching her pack her bumbag – her habit of the past five weeks.

"Have you grown?" she asked. He shrugged. "I can't believe you're here!"

Two invisible Cupids grabbed his mouth and tugged it into a broad smile. He leaned closer – she could see little flecks of acne – and whispered, "We have to plan how to get to Verona."

"Ok," she said and patted his shoulder. The frown returned and she tried to guess what was on his mind. She understood he was upset about their mum, who had either hit him or cursed him, or both (they had each told her a different version). She'd have to help him forget that. She felt confident she could, given her recent successes with Mum.

Mum had flown to Florence a week ago, unusually cheerful. Fearful they would revert to squabbling, Anna had persuaded the ever-patient Su to stay with her for that week. Mum liked Su, mainly – it seemed to Anna – because she was academic. ("Are you sure you don't want to be a doctor, Sumukhi?" "I'm more interested in politics, Doctor Carter." "You should come visit me at the hospital. I'll show you some politics!")

Mum hadn't tried to persuade either Anna or Su to become a doctor in Florence, nor in Pisa, nor indeed had she complained or harangued, apart from light griping over Anna's smoking. ("And how many doctors smoke, Mum?")

No, Mum had been un-mum-ly, had followed rather than led Anna and Su, had listened rather than talked as the girls explained each museum and gallery and church, and after a few attempts to pull Anna aside for some mother and daughter time alone, had given up and joined in their evening banter, giggling, ordering more wine, and supplying explicit stories about the anxieties and medical complaints of teenage boys that put Su and Anna off their dinners, and had Mum declaring that perhaps both girls were right in avoiding her profession.

This girlish woman did not resemble her mother; rather, she reminded Anna of the younger woman whose description she had translated while travelling across Holland and Germany.

With Mum in jovial spirits, it had been easy for Anna to persuade her that Sam and Dad should join them, though Anna had taken no chances and done so over a bottle of wine, with Su beside her, at the end of a particularly long day.

So now Anna's summer hopes had come to their fruition: her parents were together. Her role was to be a happy glue. And Sam must play his part as well.

"Come on, Sammy. It's your first time in Italy. You've got to enjoy it, one city at a time!"

He returned her grin, and she took his hand and led him outside.

The heat in Bologna was beyond temperature: Anna felt it as a weight upon her neck as she led them from their hotel towards the centre of town. "Bloody good, these things," her dad said, pointing at the red and blue porticoes that shielded them from the worst of the sun. She walked behind her parents, frowning at the gap between them. She pretended to study the massive doorways with smaller, people-sized ones built into them. Some were covered in metal spikes that were, she guessed, made of iron. Claudio, she felt, would know.

They passed a pedestrian area that opened into a vast piazza. Dad turned towards two medieval towers. "The *due torri*," he read from his guidebook. "Two towers, Annie?"

"Yes," she mouthed, and sat in the shadow of one of them. Mum sat down beside her but Anna pushed her away. "You're crowding me! Go to Dad!"

"Hello," he said when Mum appeared beside him. "You'll help. Is this Gary-senda? Or Asy-nelly?"

"How am I supposed to know?" she asked, flapping a pizzeria flyer at her face.

"Gary leans more. Which one's that?" "I don't know, Chris!" "Come on!" She went to both towers, looking them up and down. "This one?" "No!" "Then that one!" "No!" Now Anna called out, "That one, Mum! No, that one!" until Mum started laughing in frustration.

"Anyway," Dad said, putting a hand on Mum's shoulder in a gesture that made Anna's stomach flutter, "thirteenth century they are, and in good shape. Just an engineering problem."

"Yeah," Sam said, standing in the shadow of Asinelli. "An en-gin-eering problem."

Anna laughed and got up. "Come on, Sammy, I want to show you a fountain."

She led them towards the Piazza Maggiore. Despite the heat, hundreds sat on steps or by the huge fountain at one end of the piazza.

"What's that?" Sam asked, pointing at the statue in the middle: a giant naked muscular man with a trident.

"Neptune," Chris said, putting an arm on Sam's shoulder. "God of the sea."

"I know THAT." Sam shrugged the arm off and moved towards the fountain. Anna followed, drawn to the smiling nymphs gathered around Neptune. Their legs were immodestly spread, with objects – pillows? fish? – covering what nature would not have. Water danced between the figures and sprayed her skin.

In the distance, she saw her dad standing outside the public library, and led her mum over. He was looking at a plaque, a memorial for the 1980 bombing. "Eighty-four killed," Anna said. She tried to read her parents' expressions but Mum's sunglasses hid her eyes. Dad was frowning with concentration. Sam had moved to the next wall, where rows of photographic portraits glinted in the sunlight. Anna joined him. "These are partisans killed during the War," she told him. He pointed at one of the faces. She saw the name Collina, and steered her parents away.

Her spirits rose further as the day progressed. Her parents did not snap at each other. Her father kissed her mother on the cheek and her mother did not resist or complain. But Anna's breath was shortening; she was tired; she felt dizzy and at times had to stop walking altogether and lean against a wall.

Mum finally announced that they'd go back to the hotel. It was mid-afternoon, and Anna lay down and was asleep instantly. She only woke when Sam was shaking her with a, "Sorry, Annie, but we're late for dinner."

The restaurant's tables were all outside, pristine with white tablecloths, the kitchen hidden in a shop that looked like a pharmacy. They smelled burnt sugar, spiced tomatoes, wine, beef. A scraggly-haired man with grey-speckled beard approached them. He wore a half-unbuttoned shirt.

"Morris? Good, you are forty minutes late, but it is good."

Seated to their left was an Italian couple, the woman a glamorous blonde in a silver dress. To their right was an ancient, solitary man, immaculate in an orange-brown blazer, a glass of red wine in his hand as he advanced through a vast plate of meat and sauce.

Prosecco, water, bread appeared. Anna was enjoying the lack of budget. Sam took a sip of Anna's Prosecco.

"All right," Dad said, moving the glass away.

"Let him have a sip if he wants," Mum said, smiling at Sam who gave her a hard look and said,

"Don't want it anyway."

A tubby man with red-framed glasses ran around giving orders to the waiters, his larynx so rough it sounded mechanical.

Mum winced. "Too many cigarettes." She nodded at Anna.

"Maybe he's a doctor," she answered calmly.

Their waitress was luscious – no other word would do: an amphora of dark wine wrapped in a green dress; Anna wanted to inhabit her body for one day. They chatted happily in Italian and Anna translated for the others, telling them the recommended dishes; she ordered pumpkin ravioli with zucchini and duck in sweet sauce.

After the first course, Mum said, "So what are we going to do for the next six days? We should make a plan."

"Annie," Dad said, "first tell us about your trip."

"Before that," Mum said, voice rising, "we should make a plan."

"We could go to Venice," Anna said. "So, we started in Paris –"

"No, Anna. How will we get to Venice? We need to sort out accommodation. This is the busiest time of year."

"Go on with your story," Dad insisted.

"Let's take the train, I love trains," Anna said. "Can't get enough of them."

"Can we –" Dad began.

"So train," Mum said. "And accommodation?"

"Let's stay in a hotel by the water," Anna said. "Venice has lots of that. And I hope there are trains involved. The one thing I haven't had enough of this summer is trains. Now, can I tell my parents about my holiday, please, pretty please?"

Dad smiled.

Mum sat back, arms folded, and suddenly also smiled. "All right, go on, then, honestly!" Sam coughed. "You're being quiet, sweetie," Mum said.

Anna watched her brother's gentle face darken into a scowl.

"Sore throat," she said hastily. "Hasn't stopped yelling at me from the moment he arrived. Fight, fight, fight. That's all we kids do. Anyway –"

"We could go to Verona," Sam said. "See the Claudio Collina Museum of Myth."

This was a different silence: the entire restaurant seemed to go still. Anna's eyes swung to the table, as if a golden apple had fallen into the middle, rolling this way, now that. Her dad opened his mouth and closed it. Anna wanted to shriek but just then the waitress and maitre d' arrived with their main courses and the apple disappeared.

"Um," Dad said, looking from Sam to Mum.

"So," Anna said, feeling dizzy. "We started in Paris and..." She carried on with a sanitized description of churches and youth hostels and bars. She did not say that she had kissed four boys, and smoked three spliffs, and tried cocaine. She felt ill, then more ill, as if she would throw up, or faint, but she pretended she had their waitress's rounded cheeks and smiled and smiled.

Back in the hotel, she waited until Sam had brushed his teeth and come back into the bedroom before she said, "Sammy, you have to understand something. Mum and Dad are going through a rough patch right now. They're going to be ok. But you've got to be sensitive to that. Talking about Claudio and his stories, and the museum, that's going to make things worse, not better. So please trust me and I promise we'll get to Verona at some point – maybe not this trip – but some day, and please don't make things worse."

She lay down, head pounding. She heard, dimly, Sam talking about Claudio's death, and heard the words *guilt* and *responsibility* and *lies* but she couldn't stay conscious and was soon asleep.

*

Their second day in Italy proved different.

The day seemed more dim, but looking out the window Anna saw no clouds. Her hands too seemed more dim. So did Mum and Dad. They had changed overnight. Before dinner, Dad had stolen Mum's fingers into his hand and she'd not resisted. This morning they were not speaking. Dad hadn't shaved. His head lolled down towards the ground as he stood away from Mum in the reception area, waiting for Sam to come back with a pair of shorts that didn't have a massive stain on them.

"Hi Dad!" Anna said and punched his arm. He grunted a reply. She snuck up behind Mum and gave her a friendly shove towards him.

"Stop it," Mum snapped.

"Just being friendly," Anna said.

"She's just being friendly," Dad said, taking Anna's side.

"It's ok," Anna said, "I'm sorry. Why don't you guys decide what we do today?" But they each were studying different sections of the reception walls and Anna had to suggest they visit the opera house.

The day progressed with stutters of silence and moods. They ate lunch in a restaurant of wicker and wax and glamorous photographs on every wall. "Look at that!" Anna said. "Skiing champions! Strippers!" She pointed at her dish. "This is a funny one – it's called the wolf's head!" Mum sighed. "Hey, Dad, what happened in Bologna in the War?"

"Dunno," he said.

"You don't know something about the War? Do we need to buy you a book about it?"

"There were partisans –" Sam began.

"Yes, thank you," Anna said. They had their three-course lunch and swelled into rounder versions of themselves, sweating tomato sauce and culinary contentment if nothing else. Anna led them on, to churches full of art to stagger their minds and steal their silence away. But each time they surfaced into the bright light, Bologna seemed colder, and her family less present, each hugging their thoughts closer to themselves.

The day was almost over when Sam said, "Annie mentioned an archaeology museum. I want to see it."

"I'm not sure that's interesting," Mum said.

"Not for you, maybe," Dad said. "Come on."

They finally found the archaeology museum and staggered into the shade. In the reception, a man and woman were listening to the Rolling Stones, and seemed puzzled by the arrival of visitors. The entrance led through to a courtyard, where a giggling cherub was being sprayed by an endless jet of water. Anna dipped her fingers in and ran the water down her neck.

The exhibits had no air conditioning. There was a jumble of Etruscan statuettes, Egyptian paintings, Celtic lanterns. *Hordes of hoards*, Anna thought. Sam hurried them through. She followed him past displays of coins from each Roman emperor's reign to a cabinet with ancient jewellery. He stopped by a necklace of dark green stones stamped with images and runes. There were gems. Wax stamps. Statues: Venus's torso, Apollo's, here was the head of Antonius Pio. Anna's breathing was fast and sounded loud to her. She looked for a bench. Dad was talking about the Roman daggers to no one in particular. Mum was reading each inscription. Her parents were nowhere near each other. The air was oppressive. The statues loomed above her. Sam was flitting between the cabinets. She wanted to grab him and yell, *We have to leave this place*! She found a bench and sat down, head between her knees. She felt a hand on the back of her neck.

"Are you all right?" Mum asked. "You need water. Chris..."

"What's the matter?"

"She's needs water."

"Are you all right, Annie?"

"She's fine."

"I'm asking HER."

Anna leaned back and saw her parents either side of her, facing towards each other but too far to touch. She wanted to reach out and move them closer but she worried she'd betray her shaking hands. She put her head down again.

Sam joined them. "I want the museum book," he said.

"We're going," Dad said.

Anna pushed herself up.

Sam turned to Mum. "Buy me the museum book."

"SAM!"

Mum bought him the book.

Finally, back in their rooms, Anna could collapse. When she awoke, Sam was sitting cross-legged on his bed with his book.

"We missed a statue of Vulcan," he said.

"I don't care about those bloody gods, Sam!" She rolled away, trembling.

"It says, In the north of the forum of Rome was a plinth of head height with a statue of the god Vulcan. On the 23rd of August, Romans gathered to burn the live fish and appease this god for the harvest."

"Appease," she said faintly. She closed her eyes again. They just had dinner left; tomorrow they would leave Bologna. The next city would be better.

Ernesto: Museum

It was the day of the solar eclipse and the staff of the museum chattered nervously in the lecture hall. They fell quiet when Ernesto entered and walked to the lectern. He wore a dark blue suit. His back was straight, his stride stiff but confident, the footsteps ringing out in the hall. He cleared his throat.

"You have heard the news. I can't tell you anything new. For sixteen years, the Claudio Collina Museum of Myth has enchanted thousands of locals and tourists. As of today, it is closed."

The emotion grew thick in his voice and he paused. He could hear sobs from various parts of the room. The faces were lined with grief or worry: some of the women had linked hands; the men sat aloof, trying to project calm.

"I see so many friends here. Gina, you've been keeping the museum spotless since my footprints first muddied the corridors." The thin woman, normally so sullen, burst into tears. One of her neighbours put a timid arm around her. "Fabrizio, what will we eat now?" The red-faced canteen chef, still in his uniform, took courage from Ernesto's unusually gentle voice, and called out, "You're all welcome at mine!" There were a few staccato laughs.

"You have all worked with such dedication," Ernesto continued. "You know how much this work is appreciated."

There were sad smiles. Ernesto readied himself to talk about the future but Fabrizio spoke first.

"Where's Signora Collina? Why isn't the president here?" Several of the others called out their agreement.

Ernesto waved at them to be quiet. "Signora Collina agrees with everything I have said. She and her family made our work here possible. I think we can understand, Fabrizio, that the pain we are feeling is nothing like hers."

There was silence as they absorbed this.

"She should still be here," someone said.

"She's not losing a job," another said. Ernesto tried to keep track of who was speaking but it was difficult, the voices came from different parts of the room, and as quickly as one spoke, several others tried to hush them.

Fabrizio stood up and gestured angrily at those around him who were telling him to be calm.

"QUIET! QUIET ALL OF YOU!" Ernesto yelled. The sound of the director's raised voice was so startling that they fell silent. His voice was sharp with anger. "You may think you know what you are fighting about, but none of you have a clue. If you are angry because of your financial situations, then you can stop bickering right now. You will all have work before the autumn is over. I negotiated this with the city yesterday: I said we would close the museum quietly and not make a huge fight to embarrass the mayor, on condition that he ensured you were all employed on an equal or higher salary by first of October. Does anyone object?"

He watched them absorb this. The silence was warm.

"Melissa Collina is the only one who had to sacrifice something in agreeing to this. I worry she cares more about you than you do about her." There were noises of protest, but he pressed on.

"This may not be why you are angry. It may be because you feel such loyalty to this museum that you resent its closure. Well? Does anyone feel this way?" There were noises of assent. "So, then, would everyone please stand up who was involved in the design of this museum, in its conception, who worked hand in hand with the founder to ensure its execution, who abandoned their family in Napoli to come work here, who ran this place with blood and sweat for sixteen years to see it smashed into the dust by the thugs who run this city?"

The silence now was anxious, and Teresa, his secretary, began to speak.

"No, do not be worried for me. I am telling you this because I want you to understand that the one standing here before you has every right to be as angry as you. But I do not want this anger to cripple me. I want my life to continue with the blessed memories this place has left me. If I can think like this, I believe you can too."

Ernesto took a deep breath. He had not yet lied to them, for Melissa had told him to handle the situation as he saw fit. But now he felt he must go beyond the truth: he wanted their memories of Melissa completely untarnished.

"This, too, may not be why you are angry. You have asked, where is Signora Collina? She mourns the death of her father, and the terrible allegations about her brother. This museum has meant as much to her as all of us combined. Yet you ask that she stand here and talk to you about your futures. Perhaps this is not unreasonable. Perhaps it is fair."

Several of those who had protested earlier lowered their heads in embarrassment.

"But let me tell you the truth. Melissa Collina asked to be here today." They began murmuring to each other. "She wanted to speak to you all. But I told her she should not come. I knew the press would chase her here. I did not want a hubbub outside as we tried to conduct ourselves with dignity. Do you understand?"

Gina whirled on Fabrizio. "Shame on you!"

He groaned apologetically.

Ernesto continued over them: "This museum is the legacy of Claudio Collina and his father. Melissa Collina fought like a lioness to keep it open. Should we be angry that she lost her fight? None of you can doubt how she felt about this museum, nor about you. Who was the first with kind words of thanks? With flowers on birthdays, with cakes when we had children? She was our employer but she did much more than pay our wages. So, now, who has any more words of protest? Are we united in this catastrophe, or are we going to fight among ourselves?"

"No," said his secretary, Teresa. "We are as sad for her as we are for ourselves. We wish her all the best." Everyone's heads were nodding. Fabrizio stood up and apologised. Ernesto let the talking swell up again. In the hubbub, no one but Ernesto heard Teresa add, "And we know, *direttore*, how much you care for Signora Collina." His loyal secretary's eyes were shining up at him. He reached down and pressed her hand.

After a minute, he raised his hands again. He spoke of logistics. He would need many of them on hand in the coming days to help with packing and shipping. The statues were moving into storage while their fate was decided. Wages would be paid for the next two months. In answer to a question, he confirmed that their pensions were secure. As for their future jobs, the details were being confirmed with the mayor's office, and each member of staff would have a private conversation with someone from the municipality in the next two weeks. Looking at Gina's fierce expression, he could almost pity whichever of the mayor's cronies found her in their corridors.

The meeting ended after an hour, and the staff packed their belongings and went home. Ernesto said he wanted some of them to return tomorrow, but that there was nothing to do today. He hoped to persuade Melissa to take one last tour of the museum. She should see it as it was. In the past week, he had engaged a photographer to capture images of each room. He had an idea of making a book to commemorate the museum. They had barely begun to discuss the future, for Melissa had refused. Now they had time, but she must first part with what they had achieved.

He called her from his office, but there was no answer at her home, nor on her mobile phone. He paced uncertainly around his office; finally he switched off the light and left. He kept them on in the galleries, thinking, *Let the museum keep its myths one day more.*

Anna: Furies and Train

That evening the Morrises went to a restaurant near Piazza Tribunali. It was the quietest part of Bologna they had yet seen, with narrow streets empty of cars and pedestrians. Anna glanced up and saw shutters closed as for a storm. The air was suffocating: Dad's shirt was transparent with sweat by the time they reached the restaurant. Sam walked behind them, and Anna kept turning to look at him; his eyes were narrow, his fists clenched.

The restaurant was on the corner of two narrow streets. The outdoor area was enclosed behind a wicker wall, a small confining space, so that they could not reach their table without their neighbours standing up.

"This is nice," Mum said.

"Inside's better," Dad said, but they sat down.

They tried to relax in plastic chairs. To their right was a table of teenage American girls. One was yelling a story about the man who tried to sell her a pair of jeans for twice what she would pay at home. Mum raised her eyebrows but was still. Anna rolled her eyes every time the girl said "like" but otherwise mimicked her mother's calm. Dad was breathing heavily, crossed his legs and recrossed them, saying "bloody" several times, and finally beckoned to the waiter, a timid young man whose eyes kept darting to the American table.

"We – move – inside," Dad said, loud enough to cause a temporary silence at the next table.

"No," Mum said, "we're fine."

"Both are great," Anna said, "so let's just decide and then we can enjoy the meal, yeah?"

The waiter handed them menus and stepped back. Dad opened his but kept looking at the Americans. Another girl was now talking about her boyfriend, who apparently did not believe Bologna was a real place. Mum leaned over to Anna and pointed at her menu, asking for a translation of *carciofo*. Anna saw that Sam had not opened his menu.

"There are fans inside," Dad said. "More space. Quieter." Dad nudged Sam and stood up. "Come on."

Anna began to rise, but paused when she saw Mum had not moved.

229

"Eat inside, if you like," Mum said. "Outside is fine for me. Whoever wants to eat inside can eat inside."

"You want me to go inside?"

"No, you want to."

"Or back to London, Jen? Or Leeds?"

"This is NOT the time or place to –"

"So WHEN –"

Sam thumped the table. A glass rolled off and smashed. Anna froze.

"SHUT UP!" Sam yelled. "Shut up shut up! You don't LISTEN and you don't tell the TRUTH. Who gives a shit about your stupid arguments? You're LIARS. And worse, because of what you did to Claudio. You ruined Claudio's life. And you didn't tell ANNA –"

Dad grabbed Sam's hand and tugged. "Needs a walk."

The Americans had shut up.

"You need to talk about CLAUDIO."

"That's none of your business, Sam."

"Why? Cos I'm not a grown-up? Not a surgeon? You can't even keep people ALIVE."

Dad stopped and let go.

"Sam," Anna pleaded, "please! Stop!"

But Sam was yelling, "Like CLAUDIO. Like Claudio who KILLED himself because of you two."

Anna saw her mother drop her head, or thought she saw her, because the street was fading as a fiery breath crossed her face and her vision grew darker. She heard her dad say, "accident," and the squeal of her brother's voice grow more furious.

"NOT an accident. It's all over the papers. He KILLED himself because YOU cheated on him. Venus, his true love. Mars, his best friend. He killed himself because of you. And then, you did something worse. You LIED. Here's Anna. Don't you want to tell her?"

In an instant Anna saw Dad grab Sam's arm, her brother's face contorted in agony, and Dad was dragging him past the wicker wall and around the corner. She heard an alien growl, "Stay here. I'm coming back."

She felt the rush floor tilt with violence as he hurried back towards them. Mum hadn't moved since lowering her forehead onto the table; she seemed asleep but was making quiet moans. The Americans were whispering to each other. The waiter had come out and gone back inside. Anna tried to stroke her mother's back but it felt unnatural and she stopped. Now Dad stood above them, chest heaving, lower lip rolling in and out of his mouth as he chewed in hesitation.

"Where's Sam?" she said.

He waved his hand behind him. "I..." The vowel was unfinished. He grimaced.

She stood up. "I'll go to him. You talk to Mum. Get her water or something."

"Anna!" he called, but she continued onto the street.

Sam wasn't around the corner. Had he returned to the hotel? Too obvious for him. But she had an idea where he might be, and hurried through the quiet streets towards the crowds in the centre. *Oh Sam, Sam...* Her breath was short. Her head pounded with self-recrimination. Why had she not guessed that he must have his own idea of what they were investigating? She managed a faint smile as she remembered the first time she had called him a detective. They'd been in the park; he was showing her clues, pebbles in the ground. Clues to what? *Bad things*, he'd said. Now he had found them, truly bad things: he thought their parents were murderers.

The streets were widening. Anna passed a church glowing orange. A hum of chatter and vague black shapes like petals crowding outside it, the Bolognese enjoying the mild climate after sunset, smoking as they passed the night without fear of this strange idea that struck her, that she was alone in this city unless she found her brother.

How silly of Sam. But that was her fault. She'd let it slip. He'd been so quiet: she should have guessed that his muted reaction meant trouble, not maturity. *Oh Sam, Sam...* Dad had seen Mum's reaction to Claudio's death. What could he think, but that Mum still loved Claudio? *Oh, Daddy...* Anna hid her face as she passed the lights in the Piazza Maggiore. She did not want to be stopped by well-meaning rescuers.

Sam was where she had guessed: leaning over the edge of the low marble wall, looking at the water of the fountain of Neptune. He looked up with a scowl when she called out his name. His soft cheeks were dry; she had imagined him tearful. Angry creases ran up his forehead and into the scraggly hair. He was a semi-grown warrior, dishevelled, unfamiliar. She stopped several paces from him. Her head beat savagely.

"You can't drown yourself in that," she said, her voice sounding to her thin and distant. "It's not deep enough."

He looked at the water and back at her. "I'm going to Verona," he said.

She stepped forward and grabbed one of his shoulders. "Are you a Fury? Is that what you think you are? Sammy, please listen to me. Calm down."

This new, angry Sam gave a sullen flick with his head, as if to say, *Or else what?*

"I'm so proud you're my brother," she said. The old Sam's eyes widened with surprise. He tried to hide a smile. She clutched his shoulder more tightly. "You found all this out, and still you kept quiet. No wonder you went loony. Let's go back to the hotel. You've done your bit. There's no way Mum and Dad can doubt they're guilty. Ok? I feel knackered, been chasing you across the city. Will you help me back to the hotel?"

He shrugged her hand off. "We're going to Verona."

"What? Please, Sammy. Mum and Dad don't need to go there." She felt so tired.

"Not them. You and me. We're going to see Claudio's sister, Melissa."

She laughed. "You can't do this to people, Sammy. This woman, who's just lost her father, god knows how she's feeling. You can't just turn up and say, my parents killed your brother. She'll go cra-a-azy." Sam was frowning, but he half-smiled at her last word, and Anna continued. "She'll cast you in cement and dump you in the museum. Blunderbuss, the god of thickness."

Sam's half-smile vanished. "We're Jennifer's kids. She'll want to meet us." He turned away from the fountain.

"I'm not going, detective."

He started to walk away, calling back, "Fine. I'll go alone."

"How?" But he didn't answer and continued along the massive square, his small figure growing smaller. She heaved herself from the fountain and walked slowly behind him. He was drawing away. "STOP!" He did not slow. "Ok! I'll come with you!" Now he stopped. She walked slowly beside him. Their parents would soon be back and they could deal with this madness.

But she had forgotten how close the hotel was to the piazza. There was no sign of Mum and Dad in the lobby. In their room, she lay down, but Sam quickly finished his packing and headed to the door.

"Wait," she said, "I'm coming. I just need to pack..." He started thrusting her stuff into her rucksack. "No, Sam!" But he was done before she could stop him.

She fixed her eyes on him in the way she knew was frightening, and stared until she knew she had his attention, and said, "Now, look, we are finished, so we'll wait for Mum and Dad, ok, and you can explain to them. Ok?"

Sam hoisted her bag on one shoulder, his on the other, and went to the door.

"Sam!"

She found herself walking down the stairs behind her brother. He got a taxi and jumped in. "No!" she said. But she was in the taxi. Now they were at the train station. "We are not going to Verona, Sam!" But she followed him to the ticket booth and listened as he conducted the transaction in pigeon English. There was one train left to Verona that evening, and it was leaving in twenty minutes. "Annie..." She thought of making a scene: refusing to pay, but then the woman would start to complain, and there were now people behind them in the queue, who would start yelling at her. She was too tired.

"*Senso unico*," she clarified, to save a little off a return ticket, thinking she could still get out of boarding the train.

Sam marched to the correct platform. Where had this monstrous being had come from? Anna pictured him reading the stories and absorbing Claudio's fiery rage. She took small, slow steps.

"COME ON!" he yelled.

Now they sat facing each other in a carriage that was close to empty.

"I'm terrified," Anna said. Sam took a deep, wavering breath. His red-brown cheeks were quivering with emotion. She realised that he was afraid too. "Come on," she said. "You've made your point. Let's get off."

She felt her strength returning. She stood up and Sam did too. Just then the train jolted and they fell back into her seats. It began to move away from the platform. Anna watched the signs for Bologna: slow, slow, less slow, gone. They looked at each other. "What have you done?" Anna asked. Sam giggled nervously. She looked out the window. The train was accelerating. Dim lights, fragments of buildings, gutters and railings, snatches of barbed wire, graffiti. An electronic *ding* and the loudspeaker blared about the stops ahead of them; Verona was fifth on the list.

The train was now at full speed: stasis, but for the hundreds of kilometres an hour they were flying through the countryside.

Sam reached into Anna's rucksack and pulled out her guidebook. She closed her eyes but could not sleep, thoughts churning with the locomotive. She wished she had her mobile. She wished she had her dad. She opened her eyes. Sam had fallen asleep. If only she could abandon him at the next stop! Outside was the darkness of the Italian night. Briefly she saw a pair of lights, as in a home, winking the promise of an unknown family, safe and joyful, but far.

Report of Police Officer Emmanuele Perolesi

I arrived at the Restaurant Fabri near Piazza Tribunali at 20:15 on Tuesday 10 August 1999.

The owner telephoned the police reporting a complaint against a patron.

I was directed by the proprietor towards a large man and smaller woman sitting in a corner of the inside. They were silent.

The proprietor explained that this couple were English. They had been sitting outside with their children. The son began yelling and the father dragged him away. The daughter went running out as the man came back. He led his wife inside.

I asked the proprietor if he was sure this family was not Italian.

He said he was concerned that the man might harm his wife. He also feared the man might refuse to pay the bill and threaten him. (Signor Fabri is 73.)

I approached the couple and spoke in English, which I speak to advanced standard.

"Excuse me," I said, "I am from the Verona police. The owner says you must pay the bill and leave."

"We haven't finished," the large man said. I do not know whether he meant the meal or their conversation. The woman did not look at me. Her face was wet and her eyes were red. She made no sound and was looking at her hands.

I could not restrain myself from speaking forcefully.

"Sir, you are not privileged to finish. The owner is asking you to leave now."

The man pointed at the woman. "My wife is unwell."

"Then please take her to your hotel."

"She needs water and rest. Then we'll go to the hotel. I am a doctor."

I turned to the woman. "*Signora*, would you like assistance?"

She laughed, a very defeated sound. I leaned closer to her and spoke quietly, so that he would not hear.

"Are you in danger? Please nod or shake your head."

She laughed more loudly. "He asked if I'm in danger."

The man scowled in a manner I found frightening. "Not you who's in danger," he said.

Now they began to converse with low voices, and I decided to let them speak, but I stood close enough to intervene if the situation became violent.

*

W: So you will speak to me? Chris? Just tell me. Did you know? Is it true?

M: Is it true?

W: Chris, please.

M: Sam wouldn't make it up.

W: He killed himself. It's our fault.

M: It isn't.

W: But Sam read those stories. They must explain it.

M: I don't know what these stories are.

W: They were in the letter Claudio sent me from Italy.

M: I didn't know he wrote to you.

W: I didn't want to tell you... I don't know what's in them. Sam says he calls us Venus and Mars. It was in Italian. He was angry with us, he said we'd betrayed him. How could he be so full of hate and anger, to write so many pages, and send them, and then do that. Why?

M: We didn't know.

W: I wanted to destroy the letter. This was his reply to mine! I thought he was strong.

M: Why didn't you destroy it?

W: But Anna... I was so confused.

M: I was there.

W: I can't remember what I thought. Maybe I felt they were hers. But I buried the letter. I forgot about it.

M: Hid it where a child could find it.

W: Come on. Ha. I didn't realise you were going to train a detective!

M: Only one reason you kept it. To tell her one day.

W: No. Never.

M: You lied to me for eighteen years.

W: We lied to him.

M: But Sam knows now.

W: No. Not Sam. Him. Claudio. Anna's father.

M: I...

W: Where are the kids?

M: I...

W: Where are they?

M: I don't know. Don't bloody know.

*

The man had begun to weep. I felt that my presence was unnecessary, but I could not depart without reassuring the proprietor.

"The situation is safe," I reported to him respectfully. "They are very unhappy but they talk without violence. I think it is better if you let them finish. They will pay. They are doctors."

"I want them to leave," Fabri said to me. "I don't like to see a man hurt his child."

"I believe they are discussing the end of their eighteen-year marriage," I said.

He looked at them. The man and woman were no longer speaking, nor looking at each other. Fabri sighed. He leaned closer to me. "Should I give them grappa?"

I told him to wait and see how the situation developed.

Report ends.

Anna: Romeo and Nobody

Anna woke first and crept out of their room. She and Sam had checked into a hotel near the station called The Romeo. It looked like a place for murders or trysts, with paper-thin walls and drunken Furies in the room next door. She went to the reception desk and flirted with the young man there until he was happy for her to use their phone. The receptionist at the hotel in Bologna took down her message:

"We are at The Romeo Hotel in Verona. We'll wait for you here."

She considered adding, *Sorry*, but this didn't begin to cover the range of emotions she was feeling, in particular, terror. Her fears should cancel each other out, but they proved cumulative: she feared her parents' anger, and she feared for their marriage. The sum of these anxieties made her legs weak and her breathing short. She knew that something was wrong with her, but whether it was a virus or a condition triggered by the past weeks' anxieties, she still had her duties to fulfil: she was in a foreign town with her half-mad sibling and must stop him from leaving the hotel.

She was sitting by the doorway, musing on how to stall him, when Sam appeared behind her, breathless and furious.

"Where were you? Why didn't you leave a note? You can't disappear like that! Now we're going to the Museum of Myth."

She sat up straight and summoned all her strength to draw up Bad Anna, the one who had tormented and terrified Sam for the last two years at school. "ENOUGH, you dickhead! Who do you think you are? Mum and Dad are coming HERE and YOU can explain why we should all go to this FUCKING museum. But that's it. I'm done."

"Fine," he sniffed, "I don't care. I'll go on my own. I'm doing it for you, anyway."

"What do you mean?" she snapped.

"Forget it." He went out the door.

"For fuck's sake!" She couldn't stop him and she couldn't leave him alone. She was quite willing to forget her past month's affection for her brother and hate him all over again.

Sam was standing on the pedestrian street, frowning into his guidebook, when she came out. He looked up and smiled at her. "Come on, Annie, it'll be fun!" She followed her madcap brother into the city of Verona.

They came to a round piazza dominated by a Roman amphitheatre. "This is the arena," Sam said. "It was built in 50AD." He seemed to have memorised the guidebook. "Come on, Annie!"

"We'd better not get stuck in any Romeo and Juliet shit," Anna said. Sam led her into ever-narrower roads. They turned down another one and there was a graffiti-littered house surrounded by tourists. Anna groaned. "Fucking Juliet."

"Isn't this great?" Sam asked. He was beaming at everything and she wanted to strangle him.

"Let's go back," she said.

"We're going to the Museum of Myth!" he said. He checked the guidebook again and turned left and right and left again. Anna was starting to feel dizzy when they stepped into a large piazza full of booths selling clothes and junk while men with shiny sunglasses and African accents tried to sell Anna more junk. Around the piazza were sculptures – there was a statue of a lion – and painted walls high on the buildings facing them.

"I'm hungry," Anna said and Sam led her into a small store whose counter was groaning with food and bought her a sandwich.

"Just needed to eat!" Sam said, solicitous, leaning close to her. Anna tried to hide her smile but Sam's energy was infecting her. Then she saw the tall tower ahead of them and thought of her parents joking about the towers in Bologna and she dropped her head.

"Annie, you ok?"

"I'm furious with you!"

Sam giggled and stood up. "Now, come on, we're nearly at the river."

She let him lead her down more winding roads. A fat woman in a green dress leaned out of a balcony and smiled down at her. A red Vespa sped past them. Anna smelled fresh baking, sour ammonia, she heard chattering in languages, Italian boys laughing, American girls giggling. Her head was drooping and she let Sam take her hand and lead her to the river. It was wide and grey and slow-moving and she wanted to sit and watch it.

"That's the Basilica of Saint Zeno," Sam said, pointing at a tall spire in the distance. "And there's the Castelvecchio," as he led her across a stone bridge, pointing at a large stone fortress further up the river. Anna remembered how Claudio had described getting drunk by the river, he and his friends daring each other to go swimming. She wondered if he ever had.

Sam pointed up at the hills and a gleaming white building. "The museum," he said, and his voice had a trace of awe. He pointed directly opposite. "And there's the old Roman theatre. And that's the church of Saint, um, Saint..."

"Enough tourist stuff," she snapped. In silence, he led her across the river and began up the hill.

The day was growing hotter.

"Isn't there a bus to this place?" she asked.

"Nearly there," Sam chirped.

The path became cobbled. On both sides were stone walls that blocked the view, but they could see the occasional tops of trees that suggested fields on either side. As the lane widened, the cobbles smoothed and walls fell away, a building came into view. It was made of white stone that blinded them. Its roof was a green dome. They walked through a gate and down a driveway that curved around the front, so that the city was to one side and the museum on the other. Its colonnades faced the red buildings and spires of Verona. Anna looked up and read the huge words above the entrance:

MUSEO DEL MITO CLAUDIO COLLINA

They approached the glass doors. The lights were on inside but they saw a sign that read *CHIUSO / CLOSED*.

"I don't understand," Sam said. "It's a Wednesday, right? The museum is closed only on Mondays." He hurried round the side and came back. "There's no other entrance." As he returned to the front, a man came out through the glass doors and approached them. He wore a blue suit; his face was etched with deep lines beneath silver hair; he wore a pair of steely half-moon spectacles.

"The museum is closed," he said in Italian, his deep voice gravelly with tar.

"We came to see Melissa Collina," Anna said.

"What's he saying?" Sam asked.

"Where do you come from?" the man asked in English.

"London," Sam said. "We came because of Claudio."

The man frowned and the lines on his face grew more hostile. "You come at a very bad time. Melissa Collina is not here and the museum is closed."

Anna turned to Sam and tugged at his shoulder, but he said, "Our mother was the girlfriend of Claudio when he was in England. We have information for Melissa Collina."

The man's frown grew even deeper. "This is the worst time. Why do you come now? Is it the newspapers? Please take your information back to England."

Anna felt dizzy. She raised her hands peacefully. "We just want to speak to Signora Collina. We're not here to cause her harm."

The man hesitated, but something in Anna's voice must have persuaded him, for he pulled out his mobile phone. "Hello, Violetta. I tried calling earlier. Where is Melissa? When did she go? No, I have the number." He hung up and tried another number, letting it ring a long time. "She is not answering," he said finally. "You will have to try her another time. But not here. The museum is closed."

"When will it open?" Anna asked. "My brother really wanted to see it."

The man snorted. "It is closed permanently. The mayor has ordered it shut. Go to the city hall and get the mayor to show you around."

"What did he say?" Sam asked. Anna explained. Sam turned to the man.

"When did the museum close? Is Miss Collina at Lake Garda?" The man bent down to pick up his briefcase. "Did she go alone? When did you last speak to her? Why isn't she answering?"

Anna laughed with embarrassment. "Ok, detective, that's enough, we're going."

"You said the museum was closed," Sam said to the man. "Miss Collina has gone to the lake and isn't answering. Isn't that where Claudio killed himself?"

The man froze. His eyes darted from Sam to Anna, to the city beyond them. He turned and ran round the side of the museum. Sam chased after him. Anna heard a loud metallic noise and an engine roar. "Sam!" she called out. A red car roared past her and down the driveway. She sat on the ground, her back to the marble wall of the museum.

Sam reappeared, panting. "She's in danger!"

Anna snorted. "I think you read too much detective fiction."

"But he'll bring her back here. I'm sure. We should stay here. Or… Maybe he left it unlocked." He tried the entrance. "He did. Come on, Annie! You can't come this far and tell me you're not curious." He disappeared through.

Anna groaned. One day, she vowed, she would have a difficult son, and she would give him to Sam to look after for a summer.

She pushed herself off the ground and entered the Museum of Myth.

Sam: The Showdown

Sam could not believe how close he had come to his goal without Anna guessing his purpose. But he felt anxious: if Melissa Collina was dead, what would he do? He shook his head. He felt sure that the man would come back with Claudio's sister, and then his plan would be fulfilled.

He found a leaflet in Italian in the entrance hall. It was in Italian and when Anna came into the museum lobby he handed it to her. She sat down on a marble bench (she had been woozy and tired the last few days, clearly travelling with friends was an exhausting activity) and translated for him the names of the Myth rooms.

"Birth of the world. Jupiter and Juno, divine monarchs. The realm of the dead, Pluto and Proserpina. The mighty ocean of Neptune. Love, love, love, Venus and Cupid..."

He stared at the giant naked statues of Hercules and Venus as he listened to her. But for Anna's voice, the vast hall was silent and the museum felt creepy. Daylight filtered into the entrance hall; there was a low electric lighting that let him see the wide corridor ahead.

"So where is Vulcan?" he asked.

He advanced down the corridor, his eyes adjusting to the lower lighting. Even dully lit, the marble floors gleamed. The walls were lined with bright coloured illustrations, fragments of pottery, black lines of poetry in Latin or Greek with translations in Italian and English. Sam read one:

So give me a thousand kisses, then a hundred,
another thousand, a second hundred,
yet another thousand, and a hundred...
- Catullus

The room he sought was the second on their left. It was studded with plinths, its walls covered in luminous illustrations of the gods at play and war. There was a sign on the wall in Italian. "What does it mean?" Sam asked.

"It says, um... 'These are the twelve '*Dei Consentes*', the major gods of Rome. They were tied by family and love. Like many families, it was complicated, difficult. But they, um, nurtured the empire, and defended its citizens, and answered their prayers.'" Anna looked around the pastel room, full of statues and gods frolicking and golden fragments dangling from the ceiling. "This is not what I expected," she said.

A large statue of a man holding a vast hammer drew Sam's attention. "Big," he said. His hands touched the muscular calves and white feet. The statue had nothing to do with the stories he had read. He wanted a man with burning eyes and dark hair. He looked across at Anna, her angular face, her dark, narrow eyes.

He led her out. They came next to the room of Venus, where the walls were pink. Sam walked between the Cupids and Venuses, then started heading back out. "Come on!"

Anna shook her head. "I'm going to sit here."

"Ok." He could leave her for a while: Anna couldn't disappear now.

Through the Museum, Sam ran on, plunging into the imagination of the Collinas. Mighty Federico had built the myths that Claudio had once told to Sam's mother. Sam burst into a room that was completely red. Lights crept through, flickering as if from candles, shifting the shadows of the statues and monstrous works around them. A vast snake-like creature stood before Sam, multi-headed and dwarfing a larger-than-life man with a club. A canopy of feathers danced above him. Here was a stable of filth, here an elegant steel tree sweeping up to the ceiling, golden apples lining its filigree branches. In the centre of the room stood a giant man, holding up the ceiling of the museum with all his strength. Sam laughed at Hercules and ran on. He felt he was penetrating even deeper into the mysteries of the man who had loved his mother. This was not a museum: it was the spirit of a man, and the young man he was named after. Vulcan, the fire-wielder and the guardian of the underworld, had imbued Sam with the confidence to shape the world around him, and he paraded through the museum as if he owned it. Soon Melissa Collina would arrive. He would charm her with his sister, and the universe would be as he wanted it. There was nothing Sam Morris could not do.

Anna: Monsters and Gods

Anna studied a statue of Venus. The naked marble was etched with small grooves from the sculptor's tools. The stiff figure had a braid of thick curly hair; this stiffness, and the curly hair, resembled her mother. In Florence and Pisa, she had seen a new version of her mum, whose warmth and slyness Anna could almost see in herself, a tiny, hidden Venus peeping out behind the brown eyes, which Claudio had compared to gems. Perhaps there was a Venus in every girl.

Anna sat on a bench by a chubby Cupid. His eyes were sly, his smile encouraging. She felt dizzy and anxious as she thought of her dad yelling at Sam. On cue, her brother came back in and waved at her. She shook her head; she would rest here. The pink of the room was now less garish and more comforting. She curled up on the bench and closed her eyes.

And Anna slept. She dreamed.

*

It was summer. She was thirteen, Sam was eight. He'd promised to stay near.

"Where are you going?" she yelled, running after him into a patch of trees past the fountain in the park. They called it the forest, where lurked monsters like the Grizzlire, a grizzly-bear vampire. Sam invented the names, Anna acted out his instructions: Louder. Angrier! *Bloodier!* *Grizzlier!*

Sam was scrabbling in the ground when Anna caught up with him. "Do not run off like that," she said. She leant in. "What are you doing?" He showed her the stones he was picking out of the dirt.

"Evidence," he said.

"Evidence for what?"

"Bad people."

"Are you a detective?" He nodded and pointed into the trees.

"I've got to investigate deeper."

She was distracted. A couple of boys were sitting nearby in the sun. One had called out to her. "Don't go far," she said and drew away, walking towards the boys.

"My name is Anna."

"I'm Harry. What's that?"

He was pointing at the stick she had picked up for Sam.

"It's evidence. A game with my little brother."

Harry nodded politely. Then he frowned. "Can you hear that?"

Anna listened. She heard a faint, *Anna! Anna! ANNA!*

She ran through the trees, twigs snapping, face brushing leaves, and broke into a clearing.

Sam was on the ground. Above him was a large hairy man in a helmet accompanied by an enormous black dog. The dog was barking and drooling, the man was red-faced and yelling. Sam was sobbing out her name.

A fire rose within her; she could not channel it; she would do anything to protect her brother. Her voice summoned thunder. "OOOOOOOYYY!" she yelled, sweeping in, savage, leaning forwards, ready to hurl the man and his dog into the sky, screaming, "You get away from my brother or I'll rip your eyes, I'll stuff you, I'll stuff your fat mouth with that dog you fuckoffyoufuckoffyoufuckofffuckoff!" The words battered against them like bullets. The man stumbled back and whirled around and he and his dog fled through the bushes.

Anna crouched and put her head between her knees and sobbed. She felt Sam's hand on her shoulder; he lay across her back. She reached behind and put an arm around his legs.

"Let's go," she said. Her breathing was heavy. The badness was gone but she felt still more afraid. "Let's go before..."

And Anna awoke.

*

She found Sam in the room of Theseus, examining the dense hair on the minotaur.

"Isn't it amazing!" he beamed.

"Do you remember that time in the park, when that man with the dog attacked you?"

Sam shrugged. "Yeah."

"Because –"

"Shh!" Sam hushed her.

She heard the noise of footsteps in the hallway and conversation in Italian, one of the voices was gravelly – the man they had met – the other was higher, feminine, sonorous.

"Come on," Sam said. She shook her head. "It's Melissa, come on!" He dragged her into the corridor. Anna spotted the adults approaching.

The man stopped and waved his hands angrily. "I said it is closed!"

But the woman continued towards them. She was tall and olive-skinned, angular yet shapely. She wore a dark summer dress. Her eyes lingered on each of them. Even in the dimmed light of the corridor, Anna could see that they were lined with dark red veins: she had not slept, or had been crying. Her hair was long and dark, her nose a slender long half-isosceles. She was tall and elegant, elusive in her movements: when she stopped before them, it seemed as if parts of her were still moving.

"Good afternoon," she said in fluent English. "I am Melissa Collina." She enunciated the words carefully, her accent less thick than Ernesto's. "Please tell me what you are doing in here."

"The door was open," Sam said. "We wanted to see the museum named after your brother."

Melissa's lips twitched. "What are your names?" They introduced themselves. "Anna," Melissa repeated. "That is Italian."

"It's from my dad's mum," Anna said. Melissa was staring at her. "So, uh, we heard the museum is closed?"

"Yes," Ernesto said, "as I told you. You should not be here. And we have work to do."

Melissa touched his arm. "You said they are from England?" Sam nodded. "Let us go upstairs. You have seen the museum? Let me show you the view from above. You may be the last people to see it as it was meant to be seen." Her voice grew bitter and for a moment the elegant lady was replaced by someone less controlled. "They are going to put...APARTMENTS here."

Melissa led them to the end of the corridor, through a door marked *PRIVATO* and up a stairwell. Anna passed a black and white photograph of a smiling young man and stopped. Melissa walked back to her. "My uncle," she said. Her hand clutched at her neck, where a necklace of charms hung. Anna looked more closely. She saw a silvery tennis racket, and a small tulip. Her eyes widened. She glanced up and caught the red eyes staring at her.

"Do you know about this?" Melissa said.

"Um..."

"Come," Ernesto said, and gently took Melissa's arm and led her and Anna to a doorway where Sam was waiting.

It reminded Anna of the interview room in Cambridge. There was a fading rug of navy blue and green, and an old wooden desk beside a

247

bookcase. But at the far end, where there might be a fireplace in Cambridge, there was instead a wall of glass overlooking the red buildings of Verona far below them.

Melissa gestured for them to sit. Her fingers played with the necklace as she stared at Anna. "So," Melissa said.

"I found these stories –" Sam began.

"Signora Collina," Anna said, "firstly, we want to offer our condolences for your father's death."

Melissa started to wave her hand impatiently, but then dipped her head and murmured, "Forgive me. I mean to say, thank you."

"We found out only a month ago that your brother existed. Sam found a letter written by Claudio. He had sent it to our mother. He described himself as Vulcan. It was about..." Anna hesitated. Melissa's face had turned white.

"Could you get me some water," she said quietly in Italian. Ernesto left. "Vulcan?" she prompted.

"And Venus," Sam said. "Our mum is Venus and Dad is –"

"Mars," Melissa hissed. "Wait." She pressed her hands to her forehead and did not speak until Ernesto returned with water. He offered it to Melissa but she did not notice. He put it on the desk.

"Wait," Melissa repeated at the sound of the glass. She looked up and seemed to see Anna for the first time. She leaned closer. "But you? Anna? Why do you –"

"Uh, Signora Collina," Sam said. "You didn't know about our mum?" Melissa's lips pursed but she didn't answer. "Because you might find the stories interesting." He pulled a thick wad of papers out of his rucksack. Anna wondered at her brother's determination to share these stories with this strange woman.

Melissa shook her head. "I don't want this. Perhaps I wanted it once, to see what he wrote. But not now. Why did you do this?"

Her voice was sharp, like stabs at Anna's brother, and she watched his brow furrow and mouth droop. "But we brought them for you!"

"No, this is wrong. It is the wrong time. You must leave." Melissa shut her eyes.

"Come on," Anna said, standing up. She wished she had trusted her instinct not to come here.

Ernesto placed a hand on Sam's shoulder and helped him stand up. "Please go."

Sam took a step towards Melissa. "I really think you should read them! They are good." Ernesto pulled at Sam, who spoke more urgently. "That's why I got interested in your brother: because I liked the stories of Vulcan, and I wanted to know who wrote them. So I investigated. The stories don't mention his name. But I interrogated Mum and she told me about Claudio but she didn't say any more. And I worked out he was Claudio Collina, and this was his museum."

"There are stories?" Melissa said.

"Yes! So I really wanted to meet Claudio. But then I learned that he was... gone. So I wanted to meet you. Because Claudio was amazing, he did bridges and engineering, and he wrote these stories, and you really should read them. But I need them back."

There was no noise in the Museum of Myth. Sam was holding out the pages to Melissa. Ernesto and Anna looked from one to the other.

"He wrote..." Melissa said finally. "Claudio wrote all this for your mother? So you know about him?" She sounded wretched. But her hand was extending towards Sam's and he reached further and now she held the pages. She let out a sigh. "His? Claudio? My Claudio?"

She pressed the pages to her face. Her chest was shaking. Anna forced herself to look out the window, staring at the red buildings below, wondering at the emotions of this woman: she had been without her brother for nearly two decades. She tried to imagine losing Sam, suddenly being confronted with memories of him, like this, and she felt dizzy again.

Melissa put the pages down. Her face was wet but she sat straight-backed and spoke composedly. "I am sorry," she said. "This month was hard. Also for Ernesto. I see today, perhaps, cannot be any easier. But – will it be better?" She looked between the children.

"Yes," Sam said uncertainly.

Anna was twisting her foot. She wanted to leave, but felt a strange desire to protect this woman.

Melissa looked at a brass clock on the bookcase. "Did you eat lunch? Will you come to my house?" Sam looked at Anna. She nodded reluctantly.

"Ernesto?" Melissa asked.

"I'll call Violetta," he said.

Anna watched him on the phone; he was looking at Melissa. His face was lined and his mouth tight, but his eyes had grown wider behind the spectacles; the sun was shining through the large window and illuminated him as he spoke.

They went downstairs in silence, Anna walking with difficulty, head pounding.

Down the hill in Ernesto's red car was easier than their climb had been. The Italians sat in the front, silent. Sam's legs were jiggling impatiently. He kept turning to Anna and beaming at her. She felt exhausted. Their parents must now be at the hotel in Verona, she realised, wondering where they were; she must call them.

They drove across a bridge, turning into ever-narrower streets until they reached a large wooden gate that swung open as Ernesto drove in.

"Welcome to my home," Melissa said. She led them into a courtyard. A swimming pool was surrounded by white deckchairs, grinning fat cherubs, bright cherry and orange trees. In front of them, on three sides, were the gleaming cream walls of the house, roofed with red tiles, fluted with false columns and inscribed with Roman numerals, reliefs and friezes.

"Wow," Sam went. Even Anna gave a small "ooh."

Melissa led them into a large hall. A Venus stood here to greet them; she seemed an exact replica of the one in the entrance of the museum. They walked down a corridor lined with fragments of terracotta and ancient figures that led into a wide sitting area, glass-fronted, beyond which was a sight of the pool area. Sam made more noises of delight. At the end of the room was a set of large wooden doors. Melissa led them through to a dining room with bright paintings and a chandelier. An oval glass table held a vase of irises. Melissa gestured for Anna to sit beside her.

A large old woman came in, bearing a tray of bowls with an orange soup that smelled of sweet potato and peppers. Anna said, *"Buona sera,"* and the woman replied in kind, adding, "Is that all, *signora?"*

"Yes, thank you," Melissa said and the woman dipped at the knees and began to turn away. "No. Wait. Violetta, these children – their mother was the girlfriend of Claudio in England."

Violetta cried out. She bent over Anna and Sam and gave each a kiss on the cheek. She wiped her eyes with an apron, then went over to Melissa and kissed her on the hair. With a nod of her head, she left.

"Please, children, start eating." The soup was sweet and soft in Anna's mouth.

"Delicious," Sam said.

"Will you tell me about your parents?" Melissa said.

"They are doctors," Sam said. "They trained at Imperial College. That's where they met Claudio. Mum comes from Cornwall, and Dad comes from Leeds. They are getting divorced."

Ernesto coughed.

"Um, no," Anna said quietly. Her head was roaring.

Melissa spoke calmly. "Such things are hard on the children. But still, they are better than the alternatives. Divorce was illegal in Italy for many years. What kind of doctors are they?"

"Mum's a paediatrician, Dad is a surgeon."

"The best," Anna said quietly.

"I am sure," Melissa said.

"Anna's going to Cambridge University. She was the best in our school at languages. And the best actress."

"Sam is my agent," Anna said. "He gets ten per cent commission."

Melissa smiled. "And I think you will study Italian at university?" Anna nodded. "This is how Claudio wrote the stories to your mother – in Italian? So you translated them?"

Sam pulled her notebook out of his rucksack. "Hey!" Anna said. He must have stolen it from her bag!

"Melissa, you should read these as well," he said. "Anna's translations are really good."

"May I?" Melissa asked. Anna nodded, waving her hand in exhaustion, and Ernesto laughed, thinking she was joking.

"Your mother does not speak Italian, I imagine," Melissa said, taking the notebook and leafing through it. "Why did he send these to her in Italian?"

"He explains that," Sam said.

"My brother never told me about your mother," Melissa said to herself.

Anna hesitated and Sam spoke her thoughts. "The stories sort of talk about that too. They talk about you and your brother. I think he wanted to protect you."

Melissa looked down at the pages Sam had given her as well as Anna's notebook. "I must read them. I must do it now. Will you continue eating, please?" Ernesto got up with her. "No, please stay with my guests. I will only be in the next room, Ernesto."

She walked out slowly, closing the door behind her.

Violetta came in from the kitchen, bearing a tray of plates with veal and vegetables. She waited to see the children of Claudio's girlfriend eat. Anna said, *Delizioso.* Violetta smiled and said, *Brava!*"

"You did not say how you liked the museum," Ernesto said.

"It's amazing," Sam said.

Ernesto patted the table softly. "It was a labour."

"Like Hercules."

Ernesto laughed. "Which room is your favourite?"

"Theseus."

"That is mine, too!"

"I love the fur on the minotaur. And then, when Theseus is by the cliffs..."

Anna pretended to smile and closed her eyes.

Melissa: Atrium

Melissa turned the handle of the glass door and stepped into the atrium, the walls rising above her as she sat down on one of the white deckchairs. She remembered how she and Claudio used to hide under them, fleeing the Furies in the house.

She felt a girlish pleasure as she began to read, happy that her English was as good as her brother's. But this did not last: she read of his distress, his betrayal, a resolution on the day she visited him in the workshop. He described her mood-swings and selfishness. "But I didn't know, Dio," she said. She had dreamed recently of their confrontation before he left for England, when he had said, *Minerva hated Vulcan's girlfriend, and laughed at her, and spilled wine on her at dinner.* That girlfriend's name had been Ariana, a pretty, vacuous girl from Vicenza, whom Melissa had hated. No wonder that Claudio had feared telling her about Venus.

Now he explained the necklace, and she understood. It would once have distressed her to discover that it was not meant for her, but on this day it was only one wonder of many. For he also mentioned his desk and a secret drawer; she must remember to look there later.

His preface came to an end. This necklace, he wrote, *is the last.* He wrote those words on 11 January. It was seven days before he killed himself.

Her hands were trembling as she turned the page and began to read of his banishment. She smiled at how her brother befriended Chris, the children's father, and toured him around the museums showing off the Roman statues. Even then the Museum of Myth remained clear in his thoughts. She realised the story was called Clamshell, and recalled the necklace had a marble clamshell. She took the necklace off and studied it. This hollow piece looked like a helmet, the name of the first story. "So this was what he meant," she said. Claudio had made a necklace whose pieces corresponded to the stories he had written. But then, what were these gold and silver pieces, this tennis racket that was hers?

She read on. Now he went to a ball; he met a girl; he fell in love. She wondered at the passion of her brother, his fluency for love that he had feared to share with her. It was clear that it was love: Claudio loved this woman, Jen. And as the stories progressed, love led him to grow suspicious. The months grew shorter, passion tighter, and suddenly, their mother collapsed.

The next story was called "Racket". In English, Claudio had scribbled that he had written more elsewhere, and Melissa realised this must be the Cosmogony he had mentioned in his letter to Mama. Now the Cosmogony was lost, but these pieces remained – the gold club, the silver lips, her racket ("it must be titanium" she said). So Claudio had made a necklace for Jen which captured not only their extinguished love, but all his memories of family.

She read of his encounter with Mama. How Papa had yelled at him. And smiled sadly when he met her at the gates. She remembered how furious she had been: she had torn his letters to pieces, not even reading them. She hated him for abandoning her in January, and again in October, going back to London.

But he had to go back. He had love waiting for him.

Melissa wondered at her brother's judgment, and no longer felt like a younger sister, rather a woman scrutinising the passions of a twenty-three-year old. What was this love Dio and Jen felt for each other? It lasted mere months, a brief romance. How could it last, when it was obvious that he must return to Italy? She could feel angry at Jen, for promising love and betraying it. But was it so unreasonable for this young Englishwoman to resist leaving her home?

Melissa finished the last story. The necklace was complete. She ran her fingers over the pieces. They caught on one – a little tin boy. Which one of the stories was he?

She had wept enough in the past day, and this moment, holding these stories, thinking of the children eating lunch with Ernesto, was so strange that it was impossible to feel sad.

Her brother had chosen to take his own life. In the light of the morning, her determination to follow him had been weaker. She was distressed, wretched, lost, but alive, when Ernesto found her. His arm gripped her and led her back to his car, as if she might run away. She did not protest; she listened as he explained about the children. She agreed to go with him to the museum.

She heard the laughter of the boy, Sam, and thought of his sister, Anna, who was quieter, more resolute, more strange.

Melissa put Claudio's letter down and found she was still holding the girl's notebook. *A translated work possesses twice the soul*, her mother had once told her. Intrigued, Melissa leafed through the pages.

Anna's versions took Claudio's meaning and added their own emphasis. Of Chris, Claudio had written:

I understood. Chris had a heart hidden by armour. He wanted love, like me, who hid his heart in a clamshell. Now I had a friend.

Anna more than doubled the length of this:

Now I understood: he had a heart. It was gruff and protected by vast fortifications but it beat fiercely inside him. He craved love and hid this from everyone. His heart pulsed beneath the bristling iron of his helmet, the unshaven demeanour and scowling forehead.

Chris wanted to heal because he wanted love. I could see this, for I hid my heart in a clamshell. Now I had a friend.

Claudio's warm curtness had been transformed into a tender, challenging description of her father.

Whereas of Jen, the opposite had happened. Claudio wrote:

You were beauty. You were auburn curls. You were winking gem eyes and the waves rolling through your limbs, the press of Cornish memories that swelled up behind your eyes when you spoke of your father, your home, your dreams and memories; you were the short strong fingers that pressed my thigh, the feet as small as my palms. When I pressed my face against your head I was swallowed by the sea. My hands caught in your joints, my eyes in your shining eyes. You were relentless with curiosity. You are a miracle.

Anna wrote:

You were beauty. You were auburn curls and shining eyes.

And when Jen spoke of her own mother, Anna had added the phrase:

Her mother was a force of nature. Her voice grew muddy. It was hard to explain.

Yes, Anna was stranger – tense and troubled – dark-haired, eyes flashing, hostile and compassionate in the same breath. She loved her father and feared her mother. She had translated Claudio's stories and added her soul.

Another peal of laughter from within. Now Melissa must ask them questions.

She came back into the dining room, surprised to see that an hour had passed since she had left.

"Please give me a moment with Ernesto," she said to the children, and beckoned him into the living room, closing the door carefully.

"I want to be alone with them for a few minutes," she said. He frowned. "I need your help, Ernesto. In my brother's room is a desk. I believe there is a drawer hidden inside it. Could you try to find it, open it, see what is inside?" She laughed. "You know I am no good with my hands." He did not smile. "You don't have to worry about me. I am in here."

She pointed at the dining room. Ernesto folded his arms, and set his face, hard and unyielding. "What do you consider me? Just an employee, someone to use as you will?"

"Of course not. I wouldn't have an employee in my house, meeting these intimate strangers, asking them to look in my brother's –"

He grabbed her hand and she shut up, struck as much by the sudden intensity in his eyes as by this sudden physicality.

"I raced to Garda to find you," he said. "I found you lying on the floor. I thought you had taken drugs, passed out. But you were just asleep. So you said. You were groggy, so I don't know if you lied to me about that."

"Of course I didn't –"

"What were you doing there?"

She sighed. "I wanted to find something out."

He squeezed her hand until it hurt. "You have no one. You have lost the museum, your family. What do you have left? No one in this world cares about you."

She drew herself up, volume rising. "How dare you –"

"No one cares as much as I do."

She fell silent. He released her hand. He spoke slowly, almost painfully, as if gasping for breath. "Please, Melissa. Please just explain to me – why did you go to Garda?"

She turned away from him and walked towards the glass doors. She listened to her breath, to the sound of metal on glass from the dining room, of Ernesto's shifting stance. Then she heard the coo of a turtle dove.

"I was looking for something," she said finally.

"For what, Melissa?"

"A memory." Ernesto walked to one of the chairs behind her. "I hardly saw him after his return from England. He never ate with us, he was working in the factories, or hidden in his bedroom in the evenings, and when I woke each Saturday morning, he had already driven off to Garda.

When I did see him, he was distracted, almost feverish. All this I could remember. But there was something else."

"What?"

"Last night, I remembered it. A shadow darkened my mind. I tried to shake it, to lose it, but it grew, and a thought I had buried rose up, a memory. What did I call it? A shadow. I've kept my old diaries and papers in the house there, away from here, where they could weaken me. I was weak, I was afraid. And I found my diary from 1980. I was so angry with my brother, and so happy when he returned. I wasn't healthy. The shadows grew as I read on, there was a roaring in my ears. And then…"

"Go on."

"I remembered the letter."

He stood close to her, she could hear his deep, slow breaths. "Whose?" he asked.

"I took it, I hid it, I read it, I tore it."

She heard movement in the dining room, as if Sam had come to the door.

"I have to go in," she said.

"What was this letter?" Ernesto asked.

"It was full of lies, a woman trying to drag her love back. It came from England, from her, their mother. It was for Dio. She asked him to come back."

"Melissa –"

"Don't tell me he would have stayed! I know he would have gone. He would have lived. He killed himself because he thought it never came. But it did come, Ernesto, it came to me, and I destroyed it."

"But –"

"Don't you see? He died because he never read it. And now that I know he killed himself, I know that I could have stopped him. I killed him. I killed my brother." Before he could answer, she inhaled sharply, and cried, "And – OH!" and hurried past him and into the dining room.

257

Anna: Brothers and Daughters

"Anna, Anna." Sam was saying her name. When she opened her eyes, she saw Melissa was standing beside her, looking down at the glass table. Her face was pale, shroud-like, a woman who had seen the past revived. In her hands she held the stories of her brother, and Anna's notebook. The pages were trembling.

"These stories," Melissa said. "I wonder, how accurate was Claudio about your parents? As accurate as your translations?"

Anna felt accused. She wanted to explain that it had felt right to translate as she had, but it hurt to speak and she fell silent.

"I understand," Melissa said. "Believe me, I know how my brother told stories. He was always playing with them. Is your mother at all like this Venus in the stories?"

"No," Sam said.

"A little," Anna said quietly.

Melissa smoothed her dress out and sat beside her, resting her fingers on Anna's wrist. They were light and cool, and stayed there as Melissa's melodic voice continued. "Reading his stories brings back memories of my brother as a craftsman. You know, Anna, he was so talented, he did make me jewellery, even when I was little, and I have kept all his presents to me."

Anna realised she still hadn't called their parents. She pushed herself up and tried to interrupt but Melissa continued speaking.

"Please, listen to me. It was me, not my mother or father, nor your parents, who made him come back. You don't know what Claudio was like. He sounds so strong. But he was tender, as fragile as our mother, he hid behind passion. He needed to be here. But what was this great love they felt for each other? They were so young, they had barely finished their childhoods. They said this was love, but surely it was just passion – as Claudio said, she led him into love. No, he was meant to be here." Her hands fingered her necklace. "He wrote about this, didn't he? Look, look, I want to show you."

She pulled it off and handed it to Anna. Gold, silver, titanium, marble – tiny objects dangling on a silvery – no, what did the stories say? A platinum chain. She let the small pieces pass through her hands, one at a time, felt their hardness against the soft flesh at the end of a finger, pricking herself on the racket handle to see she could still feel pain. She felt so dizzy. Sam reached out his hand and with effort she passed the necklace to him. He laid it on the table and immediately began studying each one closely.

"It wasn't for me," Melissa said, "but your mother. I see that now. I think you should take it to her. Where is she?"

"Need to...call her," Anna said.

Melissa looked at the doors. Her eyes widened. She looked at Sam who blushed. "Does she not know you are here? Of course you must call her. Which hotel is it?" She dialled and spoke in quick Italian, then nodded and passed the phone to Anna. The same young man from that morning answered.

"Are my parents there?" Anna asked, heart pounding as she imagined her mum and dad pacing in the hallway.

"*Si*, they are upstairs. I will transfer you."

"No, please tell them we are at –" She looked to Melissa, who gave her the address.

Sam was standing up, waving his hands, but Anna shut her eyes: she'd had enough of his antics. She handed the phone back to Melissa, who ran her fingers through her hair.

"So I will meet your mother? Venus." She took a deep breath. "What will I make of her? And what will she make of me? And what if she knew?"

Anna was content to close her eyes and wait: her parents were coming. She would pull aside her dad and tell him how ill she was feeling. He wouldn't panic.

"Your parents are coming?" Melissa asked.

"Mum and Dad, yes."

"Yes," Melissa said, "yes, of course. But...?" Her voice sounded strange and Anna opened her eyes. Melissa was looking at Sam, who was looking at Anna.

"No," he said.

Both of them were strangely frozen, as if they were underwater. The room felt still, and warm, and Anna felt her breath growing shorter as she looked at her brother and this strange woman who seemed to understand something she did not.

"What are you talking about?" she asked.

"You don't know," Melissa said. "Anna..."

Anna stood up. Her hands were in different places. "What?"

"Annie," Sam said. "I wanted to tell you...but..."

"What?" she said. She turned around. "WHAT?"

"Eighteen years and eleven days ago it was your birthday. That means you were conceived in October 1980." She was moving around the room. "Mum was still with Claudio then."

"So?" she said.

"She wrote to him," Melissa said. "She said that she was pregnant."

"SO?" Anna had stopped moving but was now swaying. Her head hurt. There was another pain, unfamiliar, she could not find where it was.

"They didn't know Claudio was dead," Sam said. "They lied to him. And you. Chris isn't your dad. You are Anna Collina."

"Shut up."

"Your father is Claudio."

"SHUT UP."

"Anna," Melissa said.

"I said shut up! SHUT UP!"

The world turned black. Her chest was exploding.

Shutupshutupshutupshutupshutup

Anna reached for the floor. She fell.

Peter Pan

17 January 1981

My dearest,

I have not heard from you. I wonder why I expected to.

The necklace is complete, and yet I am not ready to send it to you. On Wednesday, I received a letter from England. When I saw that it was not from you, I nearly destroyed it; instead I waited until the necklace was finished. And so, today, I read it.

It came from a man: a man who hides a shy boy within the body of a warrior.

His letter told me that he is my friend. He said that if I choose to be with you, he accepts this – though of course it is neither his choice nor mine. Chris ended his letter as he does every encounter: with a look to the future, with a call to be positive, and with a bad joke.

And I remembered a day last autumn, shortly before he and I stopped speaking altogether. I knew then what was in your heart and his, but I thought that my knowledge was foolish and there was still time to repair your damage. (Ah – see – I am still very bitter.)

We were in the British Museum, where else?

"This tea," I said, "is a wretched drink."

"Came from China," he said. "Like pasta." He gave me a look: your move.

"Marco Polo left the tea and brought the noodles with good reason. He was a traveller like Heracles: only the best prizes for him."

Chris raised his mug and clinked it against mine. Then he frowned. "Who's Heracles? I mean – I know Hercules – same guy?"

"Yes. Hercules was the greatest hero, unconquered, destroyer of villains and monsters. He killed Cacus, the river monster, the son of Vulcan."

"No idea how your Greeks and Romans kept on top of all these different gods and heroes."

"Every system has its rules. Like medicine."

We sipped in silence. Chris likes stories of death and conquest, so I told him about Hercules's labours. There were twelve, I said. His greatest challenge was to fetch Cerberus, the guardian dog of hell. Various gods helped Hercules, including Vulcan, who made castanets to drive away the Stymphalian birds, and greaves to protect Hercules's shins."

"You talk a lot about this Vulcan," Chris said.

"My mother once called me Vulcan. My life is like Vulcan's. There are many strange resemblances."

Chris frowned. "Myths are made up by humans. You'd expect them to mirror life."

"That does not explain why certain things have happened to me. Why my father is like Jupiter, and my mother, who is like Juno, hates me."

Chris shook his head. "If you look for similarities, Claudio, you'll find them. What was the last thing that fitted?"

"Getting banished from Olympus," I said, lying, since I now knew about Mars and Venus.

"Here's what I recommend, as a medical student who knows shit-all about psychology. Find the good things that happened to Vulcan. Fit your life to them."

I drained my cup, thinking how rare were the good events in Vulcan's life. But I said, "That would be nice."

He listed eleven of Hercules's tasks as we passed through the corridors of the museum and came outside. The autumn air is sharp and bites at the nose. "Forgot one," he said, troubled: he hates to make mistakes.

"The hardest of all: Hercules tamed the mighty three-headed dog, Cerberus."

"So after he'd finished all these labours, did he rest?"

"He battled all his life until he died horribly."

Chris put a heavy hand on my shoulder. "Don't you get it? We want nice endings."

(This was how Chris ended his letter to me: *Remember, we want nice endings. Gods forgive me.*)

I removed his hand, but gently. "After that he became a god."

I find myself at an impasse. Your necklace is done, my life is empty, and yet this emptiness seems fertile. My gift to you sprang from unhappiness; that too seems incomplete.

Perhaps Chris is right. We do not want sad necklaces; and if but one more piece could make it glorious…

What good, you may ask, can one piece do among so many?

Well, such is the story of Pandora.

*

262

It was the Saturday after the Ball. We spoke on the phone and arranged to meet in Hyde Park. "On the bridge over the Serpentine, I'll be wearing a red coat," you said.

"I remember what you look like," I said.

"Are you sure," you said, "that you remember anything?"

It was the first Sunday of April. Clouds strayed across the sky so that the sun was hide-and-seeking. April is the month sacred to Venus. Plants open buds to the waxing sun. The cool air slips into the water. Warmth rises. Hearts swell. April is a time to fall in love.

We were walking by the water: swans, kids, bird-shit, rubber balls. "Tell me something," you said, for *Venus loves an utterance full of words*. I suggested Pandora. You made a noise of dismissal: "Everyone knows about her: the box, the ills of the world."

"Do you want to know the real story, or is it easier for you to be ignorant?"

Your face grew tight with shallow breathing. You had swallowed the fire of my heart. "Go on," you said.

Small boats huddled on the water, bobbing with small giggles. We walked north, past blossoming arcadias and green fields draped in tiny pre-flowers, blue and red. There was a game of football, shirts spattered brown. We weaved between trees newly clothed in leaves. We saw a jogger, a palace of Kensington.

And I said: It starts with Prometheus.

"His liver was pecked by an eagle," you said. Your father, you explained to me later, had told you the story once. But you had forgotten the order, and I said,

"Tell me, does sequence not matter in medicine? Shall I continue?"

"Go on," you said.

Prometheus stands before mighty Jupiter with two meals. Oh mighty Jupiter, he says, oh thunderer, ruler of the storms, king of heaven – choose.

On the golden plate he has put white bones and covered them with shining fat to make them look appetising. On the wooden one is hidden the most tender flesh, under an ox paunch so that it looks like mere skin and bones.

One plate is yours, the other goes to mortals. Whichever you choose will be what mortals offer you for all eternity. Jupiter nods at the golden plate. Prometheus hands it to him. The king raises the fat-drenched bones, takes a bite, crunch, crunch, and freezes. He sets the plate down. He is not happy.

("Why does he choose the wrong one?"
"Because gods also make mistakes.")

Very well, Jupiter says, I am a fair king. The mortals get the tasty meat. I hope they enjoy it. They have such short, sporadic lives, it seems fair that they have something nice along the way. But: no fire.

Prometheus protests: How are they supposed to cook the meat?

Jupiter reaches back to the counter and pours himself a glass of nectar. Prometheus holds out his own glass. Jupiter puts the decanter back on the counter. They can cook the meat, Jupiter says, with the heat of their squabbles.

He rises, accompanied by Juno and the other sneering gods. The last one is Vulcan, the crippled smith; fire is his element. He turns to look at Prometheus, is about to speak, when Jupiter thunders out his name and he vanishes in a puff.

(You smiled, with teeth, with tongue, eyes curving like the curls on your head. We were by a bronze statue of a small boy with a pipe. "This is Peter Pan," you said. We continued north. To our right, the water of the Serpentine was growing ever narrower.

"For the next part of the story," I said, "you have to imagine that Prometheus is the kind of titan who carries a stalk of fennel in his pocket."

You close your eyes and frowned in a gesture of imagination. How delicate your face was! I raised up my hands, to measure you with my fingers.

You opened your eyes. "What are you doing?" you asked.

"Measuring your face," I said.

"What for?"

A cloud drew back and sunlight fell on you. *Enough*, I thought. I leaned forward, murmuring, "for this," and kissed you. You made a faint hum and pulled away with a smile.)

Prometheus is distraught. He has failed mankind. But then he looks at the spot Vulcan has just vacated and sees it: fire! The god has given it to him! He carefully gathers it on his hand. In his other hand he holds a fennel stalk, and slips the fire inside it. He makes a small, slow mystical movement ("like this?" "yes") and suddenly is in the land of the mortals.

Humans then were eight foot tall, skins of gold, always smiling, always healthy. But always cold, eating only cold food, for they had no fire. Prometheus appears. What do you have for us today, they ask, for he often comes with gifts.

My friends, he says, this time I have a wonder more marvellous than any other you have seen before. They lean forward, excited, wondering, chattering. He opens his hand and they see...

A stalk of fennel!

You can imagine that the reaction is muted.

But then he turns it vertical, and out slips fire. The women scream. The men pale. A child of incredible boldness approaches and puts his hand close to the flickering flame.

It is warm, cries the child in delight. Warm? *Warm*? Warm! The crowd presses closer, shouting, cheering.

(We reached Speaker's Corner. An agitated crowd milled about us. We stopped to listen to a man yelling about the blood of Christ. He wore a baseball cap that said, "Christ Rules". "Ugh, I hate religion." You turned, nervous, scanning my face, to see what offence you'd caused. I gave you an engineer's smile: you were safe in such opinions, with the son of a classicist and an atheist. I jostled us through the thick crowd and you led me down a shallow hill.)

The fiery march of progress is euphoric and rapid. With thanks, humanity begins to sacrifice to the gods. Burned bones and skin are crushed into the flame and the fragrance rises to Mount Olympus, where Jupiter sits, nose beginning to twitch.

Do you smell burning, he asks the other gods. No one dares to speak, especially not Vulcan. Prometheus, he says, come up here. The command resounds throughout the heavens. Hands to his ears, the titan rushes to Olympus, bowing up the mountain.

I am so sorry, mighty king, he begins.

But.

("Eagle?"

"Yes, eagle. But first – what is this?"

We had reached the south-east corner of the park. Wide arches led to a tangle of roads that resemble the outskirts of Roman Verona. We approached a triumphal arch, classical in design, British in scale. We read that this was the Wellington Arch. On top was a statue of an angel representing peace, descending on the four-horsed chariot of Mars. It was the Quadriga, the feared Roman chariot.

"I don't like war," you said.

"Religion and war," I said. "Soon you will have nothing left to like.")

Prometheus is bound in a cave. It is Vulcan who has to do it, hammering home the iron fetters. He weeps while he does it, bowing to Prometheus, begging his forgiveness.

Jupiter knows the smith is weak-hearted; he has sent brutal enforcers to make sure the work gets done.

It is so hard, Vulcan wails.

The guards sneer at him. How can you pity a traitor to the gods?

The ties of kinship are strangely strong, he says.

But he finishes and leaves.

Now a giant eagle is given instructions: eat the liver of Prometheus. As an immortal, he cannot die: he regrows his liver each night. But immortality spares him no suffering. Each day, Prometheus must live the pain of having his liver eaten. That is the fate of the fire-giver.

("Forever?"

"One day, Hercules will come and kill the eagle and free Prometheus. But that is many eons in the future, after unbearable suffering."

"Still," you said, "he does get out.")

Now for humanity, Jupiter murmurs, I have a different punishment. He pulls Vulcan into his office and seats him opposite. You have it good here, don't you? Jupiter asks.

Vulcan shrugs. He is the caretaker god, the odd-job man. No one invites him to parties, and he has to do what he is told.

Make me a woman, Jupiter orders Vulcan, who raises an eyebrow: Jupiter never lacks for women. SHE ISN'T FOR ME! screams Jupiter. She's for humanity. She must be as beautiful as Venus, as elegant as Minerva, as cunning as Mercury.

I'm not sure, Vulcan begins. I wasn't happy about the whole Prometheus thing...

Jupiter rises and stands above Vulcan. His breath is that of a fiery bull. His eyes sparkle with electric flame.

Vulcan cowers. I mean no disrespect, mighty king.

Jupiter breaks into a smile, like the sun coming out after a month of English clouds. ("Oy!") And if you do this thing, he says, I will give you the hand of Venus.

("He can't do that!" Your eyes were wide with feminist indignation. "Does Vulcan want a woman who doesn't love him?"

"Who says she doesn't?"

"I think," you arranged a loose curl that had fallen over your eyes, "that he should woo her."

I leaned over and kissed you. "I think I agree."

We had walked into Green Park. You pointed at the walls of Buckingham Palace. "You are a princess," I said. You rolled your eyes. I understood this was no romantic Italian girl. I must be practical, be an engineer, build a love from solid parts.

Myths have solid parts.)

Vulcan retires to his workshop. He grabs a ball of that divine clay which only he can work. He presses it firmly in his thick hands. He blows on it, warms it, raises it to fantastic temperatures, cools it, begins to mould it. He strokes the sides until they grow voluptuous. He kneads the front to make it slender, crowning it with delicate orbs. Above it, he slides his fingers back and forth, pressing the clay to produce tiny features that slowly become a face.

("You've thought a lot about this."

"I am an engineer. Vulcan is the god of engineers.")

When the figure is ready, Vulcan summons his colleagues: Minerva to show her deportment; Venus to weave her charms of sensuality; Juno to show her the craft of deceit.

When they have finished, Vulcan stands back and scrutinises the product. Here is a woman so beautiful, so accomplished, he could almost reject Venus for her.

Jupiter nods approval when she is presented, and summons a full council of the gods and points at her. This, my friends, is Pandora, the all-gifter. Now, let us put into this jar every last ill we can conceive, and give them to mankind. Jupiter pats Pandora on the head, and she smiles, not understanding anything. He turns back to the gods. Begin! he cries.

Venus drops in envy.

Minerva stupidity.

("What else?"

"You mean, what other bad things?" You rubbed your cheeks. It was getting colder. "How about...sickness?"

"Good. War."

"Hatred."

"Madness!"

"Anger!"

"Destruction!"

"Death!"

Skipping and yelling down the Mall, hand in hand, we passed nervous policemen.)

When the jar is full, Jupiter sends Pandora to Epimetheus, the brother of Prometheus, the protector of mankind in his brother's absence. Prometheus has told him, whatever you do, beware Greeks bearing gifts. The ancient sources blame Epimetheus for what happens next, calling him dim-witted. But if so, surely it is Prometheus's fault for leaving us in his care? Whose fault: the sibling who stays, or the sibling who abandons?

Just before Pandora goes, she is pulled aside by Vulcan. He is her creator; in a way, her father, and she trusts him like no other. She has lived so briefly, had so little experience. If the world is her oyster, its shell is closed, its contents secret.

Vulcan says, My dear, open your jar once more. But carefully, I have one last gift for mankind. She raises the lid and he thrusts his hands in, fastening something to the inside of the jar. Then he sends her on her way.

("I know what it is," you said.

I smiled and continued.)

Pandora arrives the next day. Epimetheus says, Hullo pretty maiden, lost are we? Epimetheus has a slender moustache that he likes to twirl.

Pandora knows nothing but she has the skills of Venus and Minerva and Juno. She thanks him for the hospitality, lets her dress slip a little, stumbles so he must catch her, says she is hungry, tired, forlorn.

He falls into a glaze of passion. He feeds her beef steak, gives her flowers, shows her his kingdom that is halfway between the heights of the gods and the plains of the mortals. Finally she lets him take her to bed, and now he is hers.

The next morning, she brings down her jar and sets it carelessly on the breakfast table. He twirls his moustache and says, That's a fine piece of craftsmanship. What is inside it?

She shrugs, buttering toast. Nothing much, just the gifts of the gods.

The what? The gifts of *all* the gods? Twirl, twirl. She nods. But that is incredible! What a precious cargo!

She twists her hair in her fingers. Do you want to see what's inside?

Oh yes, yes please, yes.

But won't you let me show you in front of the mortals? So that they can enjoy it too?

Epimetheus is drunk with greed: not just for Pandora, but for his brother's reputation. Prometheus brought fire. Look what Epimetheus has! All the gifts of the gods! What will they sing about him?

He leads Pandora into the great world. The humans, golden-skinned and beaming, gather around them, chanting, cheering, giggling, happy to see them. Is there yet another gift? Why, Epimetheus has brought such a beautiful woman! And what a name she has! All-gifter!

What treats, they ask, lie inside your magic jar?

Do you want me to open it, she asks.

Yes! Open the jar!

Really?

Open the jar! OPEN THE JAR! A thousand thousand voices cry in unison and stamp their feet and beat their drums. Open! The! Jar!

And she opens the jar. Silence fills the world. And everything freezes.

A glutinous, black sludge begins to creep out. It starts so small and yet it does not stop. It crawls across the land. With soft sucking noises, it spreads to the humans' golden figures. It covers toes, hauls itself up their shins and legs, suckles at their genitals, attaches to their torsos, their arms, fills their necks, spreads to their faces, covering eyes and nose and ears and finally mouths – it pours down the mouths of all the humans in the world.

A fading shriek fills the air.

And we have disease and famine and plague and suffering, we have destruction and hatred and anger and madness.

Epimetheus faints. Human skins pall. Their smiles decay. Their bodies stoop and shuffle. They become as we are. With a slow, dusty croak, they say, Pandora, what have you done?

And she, Pandora, daughter of Vulcan, stands alone, holding madness and her jar as she sees the modern world erupt. She will wander the earth for eternity, trapped in her insanity. But for a moment, so brief, she surfaces and remembers herself, and remembers her father's gift.

And she lifts up the jar. There is a tiny flapping noise, as of a trapped bird. She loosens what he attached to the lid. Cautiously, it flutters out.

It is one last gift.

"Hope," you said.

"Love," I said.

You frowned. "I thought it was hope."

"It is love."

Love, that spirals from a park and a city and a country to a continent; from a planet to a galaxy; and beyond, to the universe, that one day may collapse, or one day may evaporate – and still there will be energy – and hope – because there will be love.

You made your hum and gave me a hand.

And somewhere in London, a couple are crossing a bridge.

Verona, one evening

17:19. Collapse of Anna Morris. Melissa Collina calls emergency services.

17:25. Chris and Jennifer Morris arrive at Collina house.

17:28. Ambulance arrives. Paramedic delivers oxygen, nitroglycerin, aspirin, and morphine. Jennifer and Melissa accompany patient.

17:36. Ambulance arrives at university hospital.

17:44. Patient receives ECG. Scans reveal anterior myocardial infarction. Cause uncertain. Status: stable.

17:52. Patient taken to coronary care unit. Melissa and Jennifer, joined by Chris and Sam, wait by bedside.

18:49. Cause of MI suspected to be hypercholesterolaemia.

19:14. Blood pressure begins to fall. Doctor summons cardiologist to examine patient. Dropping oxygen saturations indicate lungs are filling with fluid. Diagnosis: Ruptured papillary muscle. Cardiologist orders immediate mitral valve repair.

19:29. Patient arrives in OR. Anaesthesia begins. Nurses wash patient with antiseptic. Connected to monitoring devices.

19:31. Family arrive in surgery waiting area.

19:35. Surgeon saws open chest. Cuts through membranous sac. Makes slit into left atrium. Connect to heart-lung machine.

19:40. Ernesto Battillo arrives at hospital.

19:52. Surgeon pinpoints papillary muscle with transoesophageal echocardiogram. Identifies major anterolateral rupture. Requests urgent assistance. Torrential regurgitation of blood. Assistant pumps fluids into body but blood pressure keeps dropping.

19:54. Closest surgeon response: 30 mins away. Surgeon to Doctor: "Patient will not live that long."

19:55. Doctor enters corridor.

*

(19:32–19:48)

Melissa knew this place. She had told Anna's mother that Claudio and she had been born here. But this was also the hospital where her father had died, three months ago. Then, she had buried her last living relative, finding small comfort that it was the last such occasion of her life. But now...

She must not think it. Anna was a strange creature, and such creatures deserved study and nurturing, and she was ready to do both. She had lost the museum, but Claudio would have cared nothing for that if he had known he had a daughter.

She kept her eyes focused on the door, but let herself sense the man and woman close to her. In any other circumstance, she would have tried to dislike Jennifer. But this woman, a professional, wracked with the emotions of motherhood, made Melissa yearn to be close to her. From the stories, she had expected a cold-eyed beauty, or a giggling flirt; perhaps Jennifer had been those things in her youth. Now she was a woman, an adult, a human being.

Jennifer sobbed again and Melissa held her. Why was her husband not comforting her?

The door of the ward swung open and they all looked up. The stern face of Ernesto appeared. She had called him and said he should not come, but now that he had she felt a surge of relief.

"What is the condition?" he asked in Italian.

"I don't know."

He looked at the English family and back at her. He reached into his jacket. "I don't know if you want this now. But I found these pages in the desk, where you said. There was a catch at the back. Your brother..." He shook his head, his mouth soft and half-open, wondering.

Melissa took the paper from him. It was same thin paper she had found in her father's study, the same typeface. Her brother's words.

She began to read.

*

(19:32–19:52)

Annananannnannannnannannnannnannnnanaannanna.

Hush. Think. Nothing to be done. Breathe. Wait.

ANNA!!!

Hush. Still. Be quiet. Don't think.

Jen turned to Chris. She opened her mouth but could make no noise. She suddenly remembered a moon and yearned to speak to...

Her daughter. Anna, Anna! It was her fault! For days, Anna had been tired, breathless, dizzy. What was it? Genetic? How had she never once asked that simple question: what had her daughter inherited? *But what should we look for, Doctor Carter*? I don't know! Anything! Anything that might hurt my baby!

This was not her only failure. Melissa had told the doctor that Anna was distressed before she collapsed. Just one look at Sam's face told her what had happened: he had found out the truth about Anna and told his sister, bent on the truth like all those detectives he admired.

"It's not your fault, Sammy," she said. He turned away from her. Why should he listen, when the fault was hers? She had been with Anna for a week. She could have told her in a safe way. But seeing the lie was still protected, she had decided to do nothing.

She glanced at Chris. He was rocking on his seat, eyes on the door into the operating theatre. She remembered a moon, a pane of glass: what was that?

She couldn't shake the image Melissa had described: Anna crying out, *it hurts*, her face contorting with pain, a stumble, a fall. Her dark eyes rolling shut.

As a girl, she had wanted to meet a tall man with bright eyes who would be her escape. But when that man came he had dark eyes. *Come with me, Jennifer.* How he'd said her name, the *n* like the hum in her throat when he kissed her, a long, lip-vibrating *hunnmm*, the noise Anna made when, ice cream on her nose, she'd looked up and said *this is lovely ice cream, Mummmmy, lovely*. But she hadn't called her Mummy for years.

Love should not be ferocious, she'd wanted to hold onto someone gently through life whereas Claudio was a dark-eyed monster swallowing her and driving her to a hot thick-aired land – here! In this very place, where Claudio had died and Anna... Anna...

Hush. Think. She looked again at Chris. *Please won't you comfort me...* She couldn't speak. The moon, the window – spider's webs of frost on the glass... What was it?

This summer. Chris left her, and Anna whimpered down the phone, and the only one she could protect was innocent Sam. Innocent! One day, her son, wide-eyed and timid, said, *tell me about medical school*, and she had no idea what he was asking. She looked at him, clutching Anna's notebook, tears rolling down his cheeks. She gripped his knee. "It's going to be ok, Sammy, I promise." She reached out to hug him and now he let her, and she remembered bath-time with Sam, ducks flying across the water, playing the Storm Game.

– The ducks are going to drown!

– No, Mummy!!!!

– It's ok, Sammy, they're ok.

– Hahaha funny Mummy.

Oh Anna... From the day she was born, she carried her mother's anger and sadness, and it was up to Chris to swaddle her with love, and still, what might Anna have suffered if Jen's emotions came through? She remembered Anna's furious expressions during the week they were alone in Florence, blaming her for Chris's departure. It was true. There were such things as jars full of wretched things, and when you opened them, you got suffering. But still – that cold glass, splinters of white light, a frightening image and yet it only made her feel warm.

She touched her forehead and her fingers came away damp. It was hot. Melissa handed her a glass of water. "Thank you." How gracious this woman was! And yet, did she too know the secret? What must Melissa think of her? And Chris? Oh, he was right: why had she kept those stories? But she couldn't destroy Claudio's letter, just as she couldn't lose his child. *So why put it where a child could find it?* Because what she kept she had to keep tidy. *Oh, Daddy...* Eighteen years had passed and in their bedroom, the lie waited, fermented. Eighteen years. She kept returning to an image of moon, glass, frost, sheets, hand, eyes.

In Bologna, at the dinner table, amid the salt shakers and glasses of wine and Chris's pale face, Anna's giggling smile, and Sam's screaming, *you killed him*, her body had frozen, and she had understood why she felt wretched, what was missing...

But Melissa was speaking? "Oh, Melissa," Jen said, "this is not the time..."

"But I found this, Jennifer, please listen. Claudio's last story ends with love. He died with hope in his heart. I don't know what it means except – Anna will be safe. I believe it. Because Claudio loved you."

That word.

Love.

Wasn't love a myth? She had never told Chris she loved him because she feared to say it, she feared to drive him away as she had Claudio, or she feared that she could not love Chris in the same way, so why lie? Love was a myth, and weren't myths a poison? She had locked away the memories of love, the promise made to her by her father, that she would meet a prince and be happy, and she became this person, Jennifer Carter, a professional, a parent, a spouse – a woman of facts, a woman of concrete.

In that restaurant in Bologna, she had wailed. Chris thought she was crying for Claudio, barking at a policeman because he could not yell at her when she was tearful. But she had sat in the midst of a tempest, trying to work out her head, and understood what was missing. She knew what she had thought at that moment when Sam yelled, *he killed himself.* She had remembered that perfect night when he stroked her flat-again belly, eyes locked on her face, her eyes roaming over the thick rug on the floor and the throw on the bed, the oak doors and the four posts they'd never see again, and every time she returned to him he was watching her, and she never complained. She had forgotten for eighteen years. Yesterday she had remembered. She had wept for forgetting, for the lateness of remembering. But it was not too late. It was not too late. For this vast figure beside her was hers, and she turned to him.

The door opened and the doctor stepped out.

*

(19:32–21:02)

His daughter. Be fine. Complex surgery. But nothing he could do. Useless. His daughter would be fine. She must be.

He didn't trust these bastards.

Who could he call? The embassy. At this hour? Calm down. Professionals. How many Italian doctors did he know? At least ten in the UK alone. Just another bunch of medics. Bastards could fix this. He forced himself to turn towards Jen's tears. Got up. Sat down again. Didn't know what to say.

His daughter would be fine, she would wake, and then... He grabbed the seat of the chair and clenched his fists. She would *know.*

Bologna. Where he'd learned that Jen still thought of Claudio before him. Claudio, Anna's dead dad. Can't compete with a dead man. He was an impostor in his daughter's life.

PLEASE let his daughter live.

He felt Jen stir. Refused to look at her.

A memory came to mind, a story of Dad's that he'd learned on campaign: a man once claimed to have found an oil lamp from Roman times, just another antique. But this one was still lit.

And Claudio's fire burned in his daughter.

That woman, Claudio's sister, was saying something, but he didn't listen. Now Jen was turning to him. Shit. Getting up, approaching him. Shit, he couldn't not hold her, not now. They felt false, his hands on her back. How long would they pretend to be ok after Anna recovered?

Now she mumbled something.

"What?"

She mumbled again.

"Don't say that now."

Three words, repeated, over and over.

He touched her hair. She looked up. She said it again. "Don't." Again.

He put his hand on his face. Armour.

She tugged it away. Repeating.

And the door opened. The doctor stepped through, his face pale.

Jen's words were burning inside of him.

"What's her condition?"

"It is bad. There is mitral regurgitation and the surgeon, he needs assistance. But the nearest surgeon is –"

"How far?"

"Thirty minutes."

Inhale, hold, seconds tick, a tingle in his chest, a rich licking, calm, powerful, breathe out very slowly.

"Chris..."

"Doctor, I specialise in MVR."

"I understand. I did find you on the European register. But you are the girl's father."

Pause. "She's Claudio Collina's daughter."

The doctor looked confused. He stepped closer, till he felt the doctor's nervous breath on his face. He spoke, calm, quiet: "I am here."

Pause.

"This way, *signor*."

So, well, then,

NOOOOOOOOOOOOOOOOOOOOOOOOOOOOW

hands over hands, gel up to the elbows, rinse, repeat, surgical scrubs, "Nurse, how good is your English? One thing: I don't see the face of the patient – you understand?" Into theatre, glance at equipment, heart-lung, tools, assistant, surgeon, nod, anaesthetist, nod. "Explain what is happening." Surgeon walks him through the procedure, starting from the beginning, not knowing exactly who he is, nervous and bureaucratic. "All right. Stop." Turns to anaesthetist. "Status?" Looks at the blood spurting. The image from the TOE. Surgeon is babbling. "Quiet, please." A chill in the air. "Aorta clamp. Micro scissors. Other kind. Thank you. Nurse – fluids. Quicker, everyone." Begin: delicate slip of the steel through the chest of An... the patient, "this here, you can see here" this part of the system has got caught under the "that's it, now we move..." gently "forceps" slowly raise "nurse, swab" and across, pause "oxygen saturations?" *steady*, continue, move this across, "heart rate?" *steady*, now we need "needle" carefully, "can you make the picture clearer" good "thank you, doctor, your equipment is first class," almost done, tricky part, something stuck, "can you see what, can we try another angle," this is why they were having difficulties, "oxygen sats? heart rate?" but why is this not moving,

first feeling of chill in his chest, recalls the operation six weeks ago NO

"we need to sort this out, any ideas?" chill spreads NO

"ideas – please – ideas" spreads NO

"WAIT"

a flickering in the monitor "can you see it?"

like a flame

*

(19:52–23:47)

This was already the worst day of Sam's life before his mother grabbed his father and started a chant of, *I love you, I love you, I love you...*

The last thing he wanted was to feel any kind of emotion about his awful parents who'd hurt Anna and made him hurt her.

Then the door opened and for a crazy moment he thought Vulcan was going to step through and save the day.

But it was the doctor, who looked terrible.

The doctor spoke to Dad and Dad answered; they used hushed, urgent voices. Dad was insisting on something. Why must he make it worse? Let them get on with it, Dad!

Then Dad stepped into the surgery!

"What's happening?" Sam asked Mum. She didn't answer but took his hand and started crying into it. He'd had enough tears for one evening. He pushed her over to Melissa and got up. Down this corridor were a few doors. Were they occupied? This one led into a room with monitor displays...

And one shows the surgery! There's Dad! He's stabbing his finger at the other doctors. They're going to throw him out – why is he so stupid?

Now they're looking at each other. Now at the floor. Now they're nodding? They walk Dad to the body of the patient... It's *Anna*!

Dad is jabbing stuff into Anna. The other doctors and nurses are watching. Dad looks up, gestures to one, to the other. They are running around. His hands are a slow blur. The nurse wipes sweat from his brow, even though the hospital is air-conditioned.

Dad pauses. He is looking around. Why is he not doing anything? He is talking to the others. They are not doing anything. Come on, Dad! What are you doing? He is staring a long time at the monitor.

Suddenly he sits up. He looks up, right at the camera, and nods. Dad turns back to the table. He starts moving, very sure, not slow, not quick, the minutes pass.

He stands back. He nods. The others are nodding. Their faces look relieved. Then Dad is talking sharply and everyone is bowing their heads over Anna again, pulling instruments out one at a time. Dad steps back and nods at the nurse beside him. They finish sewing. Now the ventilator comes out.

Is Anna ok? Please!

The bed is wheeled out of the room as Dad removes his scrubs, hanging his head, looking – tired? Disappointed? What has happened?

And Sam hurried out of the utility room, towards surgery, as his father came out. He was swaying. His large face crinkled and Sam was terrified, his dad looked ready to bellow with loss, but instead he called out,

"Operation a SUCCESS!"

and Sam felt the world spin as his father grabbed him and pressed him to his chest. He smelled of sweat, and a sharp sweet acidity, of surgical spirits, and Sam wanted to inhale and inhale. He was released and staggered back. His mum was there and stepping forward. Dad was half-hugging her, but now she was grabbing him and pressing his head against her chest and they were making noises he did not want to hear his parents making.

He turned to find Melissa standing awkwardly behind him. "Do you want to come to my house?" she asked.

Dad walked past, nodding at Melissa, who grabbed his hand and shook it as he kept walking. Mum was rubbing at her eyes.

"What?" she asked.

"I thought, you and Chris will want to be here with your daughter. I can take Sam. He must sleep."

"That's very kind," Mum said, "but we can manage."

"Please, I insist," Melissa said.

Mum was shaking her head, uncertain, but now Melissa took charge, and Mum nodded and followed Dad. Melissa spoke in Italian to Ernesto and the two of them led Sam out and into Ernesto's car. Sam sat in the back, staring at the seat where Anna had sat hours earlier. But as they drove through the night he gazed out at the strange city of Verona, ancient bricks brightly lit, flashing by. His breaths were short and thrilled. How exciting this was! And Anna was ok!

Melissa led him into the house they had left only a few hours earlier. She held his hand as they climbed a sweeping marble staircase and crossed the corridor. She swung open a door.

"This was Claudio's room," Melissa said, leading him into a clean and bare room. "Since my father's death, Violetta and I have emptied it of almost everything." There was a bed, and a window overlooking the atrium. A shelf held a row of leather albums.

She led Sam to the bed and pulled down one of the albums. "Here, you may enjoy this. You have read so much about him. But this is what he was truly like."

Sam opened the thick leather cover and saw a photo of Claudio standing by an open oven. Inside the cover was written, *23 August 1979*. Claudio wore a ragged grey shirt covered with a thick brown apron. In the next few photos he posed with his rows of tools. He held up hammers and files. Behind him were green and yellow pipes. Sam studied these for a long time. Then he closed the book and climbed out of bed.

He heard voices as he descended the staircase; Melissa must have heard him, for she appeared at the bottom of the stairs.

"Are you all right, Sam?"

He showed her the photo of the pipes. "Melissa, you know that story you mentioned in the hospital? Where did you find it?"

"There was a drawer," she said, her face wavering, like Anna's, between amusement at his detecting and a weary frustration.

"The secret drawer," Sam said. "He mentioned it in his first letter. But what day did he write that?"

"Sam, it is time for sleep."

"But I was thinking. Everyone says Claudio killed himself. But, if he did that, why did he write about love just before?"

279

"Sam," she said gently, "we can't know what goes through someone's mind when..."

"But why did he go to the forge? He wanted to make one more piece for the necklace. Did the story talk about that?"

"Yes," she said.

"Because I thought, your mum had a condition, right? She had a stroke. And Anna was ill now, she had a problem. So maybe it's, like, genetic, and Claudio was sick too. Is that possible?"

"Time for sleep," Melissa said but her voice cracked and he saw that her hands were trembling as he left her and climbed back up the stairs.

He lay down in Claudio's bed and thought of the detective in Raymond Chandler's stories. He always solved the case, but at the end of every story, he was alone, with no family. Like Vulcan.

Whereas his dad had saved Anna's life.

"I don't want to be a detective," Sam murmured, "I want to be a doctor." And he slept.

*

(06:05)
A massive head
floating above
with giant eyes
and fiery heart
no pain
very giggly
and sleepy
safe
"yes, love"
Daddy?
"here, love"
am I
"safe"
Mummy?
"here, darling"
sammy?
"he's sleeping, darling, go to sleep"
sleep
"sleep, love"
...

Verona, one morning

And after the summer storm, the wet soil greets our feet and sinks before us, but only so far before it stops.

Melissa stepped off the grass as the cream pillars rose before her, blinding in the sunlight. Above her was the reassuring sign, *UNIVERSITY HOSPITAL*. She wore dark glasses and a shawl, but hurried through, taking no chances of being spotted. She recalled Gina, the cleaner, whose mother had been here; she would ask Violetta to send another set of flowers.

The housekeeper and her husband were once again in the employment of the Collinas. Melissa had dreaded confronting Violetta again, and was surprised both by the housekeeper's new wardrobe – pale colours, no black – and her reaction: a shrug and a response of, "oh, your father did this all the time, *signora*, threaten to sack us and then change his mind."

Jennifer was waiting outside Anna's private room, wearing the white summer dress Melissa had loaned her; with her tanned face and bare arms, she looked younger and calmer than the anxious mother Melissa had met two weeks earlier.

"Oh, good, you're here," Jennifer said. "You're always so punctual."

"That is my father in me. We all have madness and his was time. The nurses here were terrified."

Jennifer nodded at the closed door. "She is getting stronger. I think we'll be able to leave in a week."

Melissa touched her arm. "You are welcome to stay, as long as you wish."

"One week is plenty. Especially," she sighed, "now that you've persuaded us to go to Venice. I still feel bad..."

"Please, Jennifer," Melissa said. "Anna understands."

"She hardly wants us here anyway." She rubbed her eyes.

Melissa was about to answer when she heard a booming voice from behind.

"Morning, Melissa," and the bulky frame of Chris appeared. "Come for more rehab? Patient likes your treatment. And it gives us a bit of a rest, Venetian style." He winked at Melissa. His eyes too were raw.

"I enjoy coming," she said.

He took her hand and squeezed it with a quiet rumble of "thank you" before leading Jennifer away. Melissa watched their walk, an exhausted shuffle; they had spent too long in the hospital again. Only Sam had struck the right balance, visiting daily but otherwise shadowing Ernesto as the director dismantled the museum's collection.

Melissa entered the small room. The blinds were drawn but the peaceful outline of Anna on the bed meant she was still asleep. A storm of flowers and letters had poured into the ward; amid the undergrowth was a bouquet of roses from a boy called Harry.

Melissa sat down and drew out a notebook. She began to list the pros and cons of the various options she and Ernesto had discussed for the collection, but her thoughts kept drifting to what he would do. He had been offered a job in Napoli, but "I am not sure I want to go there." This was the latest of several declarations that he would stay near her. Melissa could imagine a life in the south, a return to her roots. More importantly, when she pictured herself now, it was no longer standing alone, she saw Ernesto close by. There were no happy endings, but they might journey together. The thought was warm as she sat still and stared at the pages on her lap.

"Cosa fai?"

Melissa looked up at the faint voice. The propped-up head of Anna had rolled towards her.

"I'm writing," Melissa answered.

Anna remained silent, and Melissa began taking notes. She had learned that the girl preferred to introduce their subjects of conversation. The past fortnight had been a frightening time for Anna. She was confused, and angry, and would not speak to her parents. Nor at first, would she speak to Melissa, who had tried to engage the girl, then took to visiting without speaking, at which point Anna had begun talking to her aunt about whatever was on her mind. There was plenty.

"So have they gone yet?" Anna asked in a bored voice.

"Your mother and father are going to Venice tomorrow. They will say goodbye beforehand."

"Not that I care. I won't forgive them. I said to Mum, 'all I want to know is, are you a quote unquote team again.'"

"What did your mother say?"

Anna's angry face melted as she closed her eyes. "She said, 'We're the two worst things to come out of Pandora's jar, and we're yours forever.'" She took several long breaths. Melissa knew from Chris that she must be careful, and not let Anna get too excited. The girl opened her eyes again. "ANYWAY. That's boring. The real question is, what will happen to the Museum of Myth?"

"That is what I am writing here. We have several options. We might sue the city. But I don't want to waste my life caught up in futile litigation. So, we could open a new museum, or let the statues go to another institution. But – I apologise – I was thinking through my own problem."

"What about the statues?" Anna asked. Her voice was croaky. Melissa got up and poured her a glass of water.

"The statues were part of the problem," Melissa answered as she sat down. "We now have to hand them over to the state."

"All of them?"

"Yes, of course. Though... No, we do own some."

"Why not sell them?"

"They belong to a charity, Anna. The money has to go to a charitable cause."

"Could use that money to buy the land of the museum. Turn it into a park or something. Claudio Collina park. I dunno."

Melissa snorted. "Do you think the mayor would let me?" But even as she asked, she realised she would be calling Ernesto about this straight afterwards. And Caspardi. How could anyone object to the land becoming a garden – even a sculpture garden? She studied her niece with an appraising eye.

"What are you going to do when you grow up?" she asked.

"Be a poet," Anna said.

"My mother was a poet," Melissa said. "It is better, these days, for a woman to have a profession that allows her to be independent."

"Sound like my mum," Anna said.

"We all have mothers," Melissa said, "and we are as much a cross to bear for them as they are for us." Anna shrugged, her usual way of ending a conversation. It reminded Melissa of her own father.

The girl pressed a button and the bed began to lower. She yawned and stretched. "I need to go for a walk." But she did not move. "So – Claudio? You didn't know, did you? That he was my dad. You just guessed that night."

"I did not know," Melissa said. "But the difference is not as significant as you believe."

Anna's eyes narrowed. "Not significant? Yeah, no difference to anyone. Just me. Everyone else is better off that he's dead."

Melissa's stare resembled Anna's own, frigid and furious. "Do you really think what you just said is true for ME?" Anna shrugged. Melissa's voice fell to a hiss. "You are lucky to be alive, and I am delighted that you are, but understand this: I would sacrifice you on an altar if it could bring my brother back."

The silence was cold and lasted several minutes. Melissa did not look at her niece, instead staring at the slits of light between the blinds.

"Ok, maybe you understand," Anna said finally, her voice quieter and more appeasing. "But no one else does. Especially not my so-called dad."

Melissa sighed. "Consider, Anna: Chris Morris saved your life. Does he not honour you by letting you call him father? Has he ever let you feel that he is not your father? He has loved you for eighteen years."

"Can we talk about something else," Anna said, looking out the window.

"Would you like to hear more about Claudio?"

"Like, talk about what you want. I can't stop you."

"I have been alone with my loss for many years. When the museum was taken away from me, I despaired, I could not see what life was left to me. But now there is warmth again. I no longer despair, because of you."

Anna turned her head back, and Melissa felt a warmth from her niece.

"Long before you knew anything of my brother, your parents loved him. You know those stories now. There were other stories that he wrote, about my family, which are lost forever. And then there are the stories that I can tell. The stories of my brother. Would you like to hear them?"

"Yes," Anna said quietly.

And Melissa told her: how he had made Melissa bury her troubles in a bag in the garden. How he had hidden with her under the white deck chairs. How they had played by the lake, how he had been Hercules and she Antigone, or Perseus and Andromeda, or warriors fighting each other, or partisans hiding from the Nazis. How he had watched her playing in tennis tournaments, and made her gifts, the first of which was a bronze bracelet which she had kept, she could never bear to lose anything of his. She even told Anna about Ariana.

"His first girlfriend. She was this very pretty empty-headed girl from Vicenza. Her dad was in shipping."

"A sailor girl?" Anna asked with a wink.

"Yes! A sailor girl! An idiot, really, but Claudio doted on her. I was so horrible to her."

"You swore at her?"

"I hid outside their bedroom and whispered, *Ariana, daughter of ships, you will die soon!* Claudio was furious. And I spilled red wine on her and said, *Oh is that what a period looks like?*"

They laughed.

And Melissa told Anna how she came one day in early January '81 to the factory. Claudio was standing on the ramp outside the office, overlooking the machines. He took her into his office to show off his design for a new actuator.

"Did they make it?" Anna asked. She was smiling, though her eyes had started to droop, her walk long forgotten.

"I don't know," Melissa said. "But he was not so angry against the factories as he wrote in that letter. He had ideas. I think he could have been of great help to my father."

"Yeah. But what would you have done if there wasn't a museum?"

Anna closed her eyes and Melissa gave a snort. There was no limit to the love she might feel for Anna, but as with Claudio, a sharp tongue was always lurking.

She thought Anna had fallen asleep, but the girl said, "Can I see that necklace again?"

Melissa put down her notebook and removed the necklace. Anna reached out for it; she was stronger today. "Turn the light up?" she asked. Melissa opened one of the blinds, so that the sunlight would not glare in Anna's face. The girl squinted at the object in her hands.

"It's been bugging me, that I never went through the pieces. He made this – all by himself?" Melissa nodded. "And right after he came back? Jesus. He only had a few weeks, right? He made it in that workshop, the photos you showed me? It's amazing. Look at this one." She held up a small gold club. "What do you think that is?"

"Now I have read the stories you translated, I think I understand these pieces. The gold ones are the history of our father. There is a small medal, which he won in the war. There is a typewriter, the first company he owned. And that one is a golden club, he told us once that his father used to beat them with a club."

"And the golden pistol?"

Melissa sighed. "There was another wife. She shot herself."

"Was that my grandmother?" Anna asked. It was the first time she had spoken of Melissa's family as her own.

"No. But she was pregnant when she died. That is –another story."

"What about these silver ones? This one's a book. Here's a baby. That's your mum, right? She was a poet, and she had babies. And this one is a bottle. Because she liked to drink?"

"Are you finished," Melissa said in a hard voice.

Anna looked across. Her eyes had softened. "I'm sorry, Lissa." It was funny, Melissa reflected, that she had instinctively gone for the name Claudio used to call her.

"Go on, then. The other pieces."

"You know them already," Anna said. But she propped herself further up on the bed and dangled the necklace before her, the pieces tumbling into her lap as she went through them like a rosary, chanting each one out. "This must be your tennis racket. What were they? Titanium pieces. And this, these two towers. Is that... Oh! It must be Bologna! We went there." Anna's eyes grew dim. "That's where it went wrong. But then... It was ok. Or not. And this one – it looks like armour. You said Dio protected you. So did he give you armour? That was how I felt, when I was travelling. Like Vulcan gave me armour." Her voice grew sad. "And these marble ones, they're the ones from London. Dad's helmet. The clamshell. Claudio said he kept his heart in it, I never understood that."

"He had a real clamshell," Melissa said. "The inside was orange, like there was a fire in it." Her voice caught. "I lost that."

Anna wasn't listening, she was continuing to thread the necklace through her fingers. "This is Mum's flower, the tulip. And this is the snake. And the sun that tells all, like Sumukhi says, the visible. But did Mum and Dad cheat on him? I don't know. And this is the marble mask. The end."

"There is one more," Melissa corrected, pointing at the tin figure of a boy. "That, I think, is Peter Pan. He made it the day he died."

Anna had the figure close to her eye. "Yeah you said. Why would he do that?" She had refused to hear the last story, though Melissa had offered to read it to her.

"Sam helped me understand. Your condition, I believe my mother had it as well, high cholesterol. What do you call it?"

"Hypercholesterolaemia," Anna said.

"This high cholesterol can lead to strokes, or heart attacks, if not identified. If Claudio had collapsed while he was working on this tin boy, he might not have switched on the ventilator."

"Or maybe he wanted to die," Anna said.

"Claudio's last story also taught me this: we can choose what the past means. We can choose what happened to him." Anna frowned, shaking her head. "Let me try to explain with an example. What does Collina mean?"

"Um..." Anna's eyes screwed up with thought. "*Colli* means hill. So, little hill?"

"You know that Rome is famous for having seven hills?"

"Yeah. But I don't know the names, so don't test me."

"That is the point. There are more than seven hills in Rome. The Vatican is on a hill, and today, the Roman seven hills include the Vatican. But it was not so in Roman times, that was just another *collina*, not important. So why did the Romans say seven, not eight, or ten?" Anna shook her head. "Because this was the myth the Romans chose – a city founded on seven hills – and that myth became reality." Melissa gestured at the necklace. "I lost my brother. And for many years, I thought it was my fault that he died. But now I see, there is another reality that I can choose to believe: that his death truly was an accident. This is the myth I choose. It is not a happy ending, Claudio and I never believed in those. But it is an ending that offers new beginnings. Such as your life."

Anna was frowning at the necklace, and Melissa could see that her concentration had lapsed. She had not understood, perhaps she never would. She studied the tin boy one last time, then handed the necklace back. Melissa would give the necklace to Anna, but at the right time, when the girl was ready to accept her parents again.

"Annie?" Sam had appeared in the doorway and Melissa beckoned him in. When she looked back, Anna's eyes had opened to slits and were following her brother.

"I will leave you," Melissa said and stood up. She gave Sam a kiss on his head and stepped out. But she noticed the door had not closed properly and when she heard Anna command, "Sit down," she paused by the doorway. She heard the scrape of a chair, and then Anna's voice spoke with the quiet authority of a patient.

"Who are your mum and dad?"

"Why?" Sam asked.

"Answer the question, dumbo."

"Um... Mum and Dad."

"Names. Tell me their names."

"Chris Morris. Jennifer Carter." Pause. "Right?"

"Correct. So what are Claudio and Melissa to you?"

"Step-dad. Foster... Um. I don't know. Nothing?"

"Correct. So why did you do this? Why did you investigate everything to the last degree? Why did you tell me?"

"I don't KNOW, Annie. I just did."

"ANSWER me."

(Melissa leaned closer.)

"I just thought it was going to make me, like, better."

"What do you mean?"

"In your eyes. I'd be the one who helped you find the stories, and then the one who sent them to you, and the one who found out all the stuff. But then, after that, it was about Claudio and Mum and Dad – it was wrong, and I just felt I had a real case and I had to solve it." Tears. "And in the end it didn't make anything better. It just made life more complicated."

(Melissa felt her father lifting her above the ground as she screamed and giggled at Claudio below, ready to catch her; she saw her mother climbing into bed with her and whispering myths to her while Claudio stood in the doorway. She remembered progressing, Claudio's hand in hers, beside the lake, playing out their stories. *Everyone else is better off that he's dead*, Anna had said. If Claudio had received the letter, if he had returned to England, would Sam have existed?)

Anna: "I don't think you can make life more complicated."

Long silence. Scraping of a chair.

"Wait, sit down. No, don't worry, Sammy. It's just I've got a story for you, a new one. It's about Vulcan. It's got a nicer ending."

And she spoke.

*

If you keep your tongue shut up
you'll waste all the gains of love.
London etc., 2012–14

If you enjoyed *If We Were Gods* check out The Odyssey Press's other books.

For weekly updates on our free and discounted eBooks sign up to our newsletter.

Follow us on Twitter and Goodreads.

Acknowledgments

All characters are either fictional or mythical or both.

Vulcanalia was built from many parts over several years.

Those plundered from ancient sources include direct or adapted quotations from Catullus by Cornish (Loeb) and Lee (Oxford); Homer's *Odyssey* by Fagles (Penguin); and Virgil's *Aeneid* by Fairclough (Loeb). Other texts drawn on include Sophocles's *Antigone*, Apollodorus's *Library*, Hesiod's *Theogony*, and Aeschylus's *Prometheus Bound*.

Other quotes come from: Tasker, McClure, Acerini, *Oxford Handbook of Paediatrics*; Chandler, *Lady in the Lake*.

Where I have been accurate about medicine, this is thanks to Tom Kaier, Jonathan Lillie, Isaac Martin, Anshu Sengupta, Sarah Zimmerman, and especially Tamara Karni Cohen. Iman Joy El Shami gave excellent advice on how to make a necklace. Thanks to Ben Jesty for both literary and military advice.

Readers of early drafts were incredibly generous with their time and support, and I am grateful to Rory, Yasi, David, Tamar, Megan, Jacob, Ali, Lucy, Wizzy, and Ed. Thanks also to the North London Writers Group for their insights and comradeship, to Martin Fletcher for editorial advice, and to Nadjia, who not only read multiple drafts but dealt more effectively with an infestation of Roman gods than anyone since Constantine the Great.

To my sisters and parents, who read and listened and supported as always.

And to TSP, who chose to stop on the bridge.

Printed in Great Britain
by Amazon